"Are we trapped?"

Mary Frances Mulrooney sagged into Josh Culhane's arms. Tons of dirt, rock and rotted timbers had crashed into the catacombs behind them, sealing them in the underground maze.

Culhane licked his lips and drank from one of the water bags. The bag was nearly empty.

"These old passages usually have exit tunnels," Culhane said to her. "Ways to get out if the catacombs were used to hide from an enemy.... There's usually a way out."

"The part I don't like," Mulrooney whispered, "is the word 'usually.'"

Culhane put his arm around her shoulders and squeezed as he looked around. He knew just what the inside of a tomb looked like. It looked like this.

THE TAKERS

JERRY AHERN

A GOLD EAGLE BOOK FROM
WORLDWIDE

TORONTO • NEW YORK • LONDON • PARIS
AMSTERDAM • STOCKHOLM • HAMBURG
ATHENS • MILAN • TOKYO • SYDNEY

First edition September 1984

ISBN 0-373-62401-8

Printed in Canada

Acknowledgments

A book that spans so many years, so much of the world and so many fields of expertise requires a great deal of technical detail, and in the face of such detail, the honest writer realizes there is a limit to gleaning information from conventional and even unconventional avenues of research. Time to call on the real experts. Apologies in advance for neglecting anyone—but here is our best attempt at a list: Robert Beaton, U.S. Defense Mapping Agency; Richard Darley, The National Geographic Society; Russ Minshew, WSB-TV Weather, Atlanta, Georgia; Sue D'Auria, Department of Egyptian and Ancient Near Eastern Art, Boston Museum of Fine Arts; Dan Hart, Franklin Sports, Athens, Georgia; Hugh Brock, Brock's Surplus, Atlanta; and Keith Jenner-John, Rand McNally & Company, Chicago. In addition, we would like to extend a most sincere thank-you to Desmond M. Chorley of Agincourt, Ontario, Canada— he dove to great depths in his research. The responsibility for any errors in technical information of course rests with ourselves.

A special thanks is reserved for Jason and Samantha for being so patient with their mother and father during the pursuit of the Gladstone Log.

Jerry and Sharon (S.A.) Ahern
Commerce, Georgia
September 1983

PART ONE
THE GLADSTONE LOG

CHAPTER ONE

The skirt of her gray dress was bunched up over her thighs, her slip nearly as high, and her ankles ached where the ropes dug into them.

She was trying to keep her tongue still, trying to keep it from moving. When it moved it made her start to gag, and then she sucked in her breath hard against the adhesive tape pressed over her mouth and started to cough and choke. She tried to sit perfectly still. This worked for a moment, the gagging reflex stopping. But she had to move, had to wriggle herself away from the corner into which they had put her, because her left hand—her wrists were bound behind her so tight she felt they had to be bleeding—had no sensation at all in the fingers. It was cold. Her flesh felt very cold.

She watched the three men and the woman in front of her. One of the men called out to the woman in a hushed, urgent voice. He called her Sonia. She concentrated her gaze on Sonia. Sonia was black-haired, tall in her medium-heeled boots, and almost painfully thin in her tight-fitting black jump suit. But there was something about the woman, something more than the anger and hatred and the frenzied animal quality that shone from her eyes. Something that she realized men would call beautiful.

The men were pulling books down from the shelves, tearing them apart, while the woman named Sonia was systematically ripping index cards from the catalog. Finished with the last drawer, the woman turned toward the glass case dominating the center of the reference section. It contained a Bible brought to America in 1743 that was at least a hundred years older than that date. Sonia spun like a ballerina on her right foot, her left foot snapping out almost blindingly fast and smashing against the case, the glass shattering. The black-suited figure approached the Bible, lifting it up in her perfectly manicured hands. Glass tinkled as it fell to the floor from the old book, then the woman flipped through the pages.

She watched, trying to scream through the adhesive tape. But the sounds she made were unintelligible and the gagging and coughing started again. She held her breath, lest she vomit and choke, and just watched.

Her captor ripped the center section from the Bible, shook the pages and dropped them carelessly to the glass-littered library carpet. Sonia ripped more of the pages free, shaking them, dropping them, then held the half-destroyed Bible in both hands a moment, raised a knee, braced the spine of the book against her thigh and ripped. Leather tore, and loose pages flew everywhere. And then Sonia dropped the Bible.

"Keep looking," Sonia snarled to the men, then turned to the captive. "We have torn apart your library. Now I think I'll start on you."

The woman advanced on her, glass crunching under her boots, her movements in the black jump suit like the movements of a black leopard.

She heard herself trying to scream again through the adhesive tape. She felt the tears—of her own fear, for the loss of the irreplaceable Bible, for the destruction of the public library she had cared for these many years—welling up in her eyes. She could hardly see for the blur they caused. Sonia was crouched in front of her now, and Sonia's left hand, the nails as perfect as they had been when putting on the adhesive strip, reached out to her face. She felt a scream start, then die in her as the tape was torn from her skin. She stared in terror at the knife in the woman's right hand, her eyes crossing as its point pressed against the tip of her nose. She sobbed, from the pain where her skin was laid raw by the tape, and from fear of the woman with the knife.

"I'm...I'm not...I'm not this...this Ethyl Chillingsworth. You have to—"

The knife pressed against the tip of her nose, and she could feel it puncture the skin. She sucked in her breath to scream but didn't.

"I don't care if you call yourself Evelyn Collingwood. You are Ethyl Chillingsworth. Ethyl—Ethyl Chillingsworth. I want it."

"I'm not Evelyn—I mean, Ethyl Chillingsworth...."

Sonia smiled, her voice soft. There was almost a musical quality to it. "Oh, yes you are, Ethyl. Evelyn Collingwood never existed until 1953. She never had a Social Security card, never had a driver's license...."

"I'm Evelyn—" she started to scream, but then the knife blade—long, what they always called wicked-looking in books—swept down across her cheek, and the pain made her want to scream even more. But she knew that if she did, the knife blade would move again.

"That's not a very bad cut, Ethyl—not at all. Now—I want you to give it to me."

She sobbed, her head hanging down, her chin against her chest, her eyes riveted to the tracing of bright red blood across the gray fabric of her clothes. "What...what do—"

The almost singing voice began again. "You know what I want, Ethyl." The voice rose and fell, up and down, like notes on some invisible scale. "I want it now. Because soon I'll cut that ugly dress off your ugly old body. Then—just to make sure you know what I want—I'll write it in your blood across your breasts. Do you still have breasts? They haven't shriveled up...?"

She slowly raised her head, staring at the woman with the knife, wanting to curse at her.

Sonia continued to croon. "I want what you know I want, Ethyl—Ethyl Chillingsworth. I really can't blame you for changing a name like that, especially when there was no hope anyone would marry you and change it for you."

She stared at the woman named Sonia, and hated for the first time in years.

The song went on and Sonia's hand stretched out and hooked the point of the long blade into her left nostril, raising her head, forcing her head back against her neck, making her start to choke, her breath coming in short gasps. "I want the Gladstone Log."

"The—the—" She coughed, and blood spurted from her nose as she looked across its bridge at her torturer.

"Gladstone Log," the woman with the knife cooed. "The Gladstone Log, Ethyl. And I want it—"

"Sonia!" said one of the men, the voice a harsh whisper like the sound of a file drawn fast across a stone. "Somebody's comin'!"

Sonia moved the point of the blade. It was against her throat now. She could feel it. Sonia hissed at her to be quiet, then the pressure of the knife was gone. The woman's hands moved quickly, and another piece of adhesive tape was slapped so hard across her mouth that she felt the hand ram against her teeth. She sucked in her breath, gagging, sagging back as the black-clad figure stood up, moving out of her line of sight.

Her eyes didn't follow Sonia and her long knife; they rested, wide open, on the bloodstains on her dress. She shut her eyes and turned her head away so as not to see the blood. Then she opened them and could see Sonia and the three men; the men held guns with long things on the front ends. She had seen these bratwurst-shaped black objects in spy movies. Silencers.

The woman held no gun, just the knife.

Sonia and the three men were edging back along the library shelves. She told herself that if she could no longer see them, they could no longer see her.

She could taste the sticky adhesive as her tongue brushed forward in her mouth.

She blinked her eyes as tears filled them again.

She heard a very faint whistling. Someone was whistling. Michael, the night security guard. She joked with him when she worked late—he always worked late, of course—that he was the only person who worked for the library who was older than she was. Now Sonia and the three men were waiting to kill him.

She let her body slump to her left, the impact hard against her left arm as she hit the carpet. The floor was concrete beneath. She moved her legs, pushing herself forward, moving like a snake or a worm. She realized Sonia and the three men had reduced her to that, to crawling like a legless animal, a mute creature—one that bled and ached and was afraid, that sweated and cried. She swallowed hard, the exertion making her start to gag again. But she pushed herself forward along the carpet toward the back of the charge desk. She shoved herself ahead with her feet, her left shoulder slipping as she sprawled onto her back. She breathed hard, and closed her eyes against the blood on her dress, against the pain. They would really hurt her now. Sonia would enjoy using her knife. She had disobeyed; she had not stayed in the corner where they'd put her.

She rolled onto her stomach, her jaw hitting hard against the floor. More tears welled up in her eyes. She moved her legs, and as she wriggled forward, she forced herself to move her fingers despite the pain and numbness in her hands. She would need her hands.

Lonnie Sidler had broken the good shears when the United Parcel Service man had come that morning with a box of books. Lonnie had used the shears instead of the razor-blade knife to open the box. She had told Lonnie he'd have to pay for new shears and was sorry now that she had said that. But she wasn't sorry she had taken the shears and thrown them into the wastepaper basket beside her feet when she'd stood at her desk scolding Lonnie. That morning she had stood on her own two feet as a human being was meant to, not crawl on her belly as she did now.

She could see the wastepaper basket. Had Lonnie emptied it? She tried to remember. Did he empty it before he left work? The can was near her now; she could have reached it in one step. Instead, she inched toward it using her chin against the carpet to propel herself forward.

She sagged down, resting her head, leaning on the left side of her face. The carpet fibers stung the wound made by Sonia's knife. She inched forward one more time, her head next to the wastepaper basket. She raised her head and shook it against the waste can, which moved but didn't fall. She had to edge farther forward. She knocked her head against it again and again, her hair falling across her eyes. Suddenly her head wouldn't move; something pulled at her left ear. She tried to lift her head from the carpet, but the pain in her left earlobe was almost blinding.

She realized her pierced earring had snagged on a loop in the carpet nap.

She closed her eyes against the pain to come, and snapped her head up and forward. Her left earlobe ripped, but her screams were silent. Tears streamed down her cheeks.

She was free of the earring and could move her head once more. She felt a wetness near her ear—her own blood—but she had no time to look. She shook her head against the waste can, more hair falling across her face, and finally it tipped over.

She drew her face back as a cockroach crawled out

of the wastepaper basket. She watched it. It moved along the carpet more slowly than she thought a roach could ever move. Roaches in her library? She'd have to talk to the maintenance people. The roach stopped as though looking at her. What if it crawled onto her, into her hair?

Her shoulders shook as she shivered.

But the roach moved on.

She dragged herself forward with her chin against the carpet, pulling herself beside the trash can. Her chin rubbed against the part of the carpet where the roach had been. She shivered again.

She rolled onto her right side, her fingers stiff and painful but able to move. She felt paper, a rubber band, a cigarette butt. Lonnie had been smoking in the library again. She felt a metal tab from a soda can. She smelled something, something spoiled, sour. She felt wetness where her hands touched against her dress near her rear end, felt the wetness on her hands. It was spoiled milk; she had put the nearly empty half-pint container in there that morning.

Then she felt the broken shears.

One blade had been broken halfway down its length. Holding the shears, afraid to drop them, she started to saw and felt the blade against her skin, knowing it was cutting the rope as well.

What if she cut a vein? She knew she was bleeding at her wrists; she could feel that. They had used rope made of woven plastic to tie her wrists, the kind used for waterskiing. As she tugged her wrists apart, she felt something snap. One cord of the rope, she realized. She kept the shears sawing, her fingers aching as she fought not to drop them. She tugged again at her bonds and felt another snap. Then she dropped the shears, and the noise they made sounded incredibly loud. She lay there, holding her breath, waiting for Sonia and the knife—waiting for Sonia to punish her for leaving her corner, for disobeying, for trying to get free. Tears welled in her eyes once more.

But all she heard was the sound of old Michael whistling. The tune was one she recognized. It began, "I hate to see that evenin' sun go down...." She sniffed against her tears. A night watchman might well hate to see the sun go down in the evening.

But she heard no returning footsteps.

No Sonia. No knife. No punishment.

She moved her fingers across the carpet surface, finding the shears, picking them up, her fingers hurting again as soon as she held them. She started to saw. There might only be one more strand, or there might be another loop. She tugged with her wrists and felt something loosen. But still her wrists were bound.

She tried to bite her lower lip, the tears still in her eyes, her hair all but obscuring her vision as she struggled with the shears. Her head was bent forward, her chin touching the blood on the front of her dress.

She kept sawing. She tugged her wrists—a snap. Still they couldn't move. She kept sawing. Another snap, the pain in her fingers numbing them to the point that she could barely hold the shears any longer.

She tugged hard again. There was another snap, and she fell to her left with the force of it as her wrists were finally free.

It hurt her shoulders to move her arms forward, and she didn't dare sit up. Somehow Sonia would know.

She moved her body and freed her right arm.

She stared at her wrists. They were swollen and purple, the impressions of the cords of the rope visible in her flesh, the skin all chafed. And there were large cuts where the shears had sliced her arm instead of the rope.

She so wanted—she so needed—to remove the adhesive from her mouth. But she knew the pain would make her scream.

She could hear the library doors opening. Michael, the watchman.

She picked up the shears and cut the rope binding her feet together. Her hands were shaking so badly she cut her ankles and stockings, but at last she was free.

She dropped the shears and lay stock-still, curled up on the carpet. Listening.

No Sonia.

For some reason, the three men with their ugly guns didn't frighten her. But Sonia and her knife filled her with terror.

She rolled onto her belly and slowly got up onto her hands and knees. She doubted her legs would have held her up.

She crawled forward toward the bulletin board to the left of the desk.

She was getting used to the adhesive tape over her mouth; it didn't gag her anymore. Breathing hard, she continued to crawl toward the wall.

Something stabbed through her stocking into her right knee. It was a staple someone had dropped. She plucked it out, crawling on. She stopped beside the wall, reaching up to the base of the bulletin board. She would have to stand.

She pulled up one knee, then moved the leg forward to get her foot under her, pushing herself up, sagging against the bulletin board and the wall as she got her other foot under her.

Her ankles hurt and she felt slightly dizzy.

She stood there, her head swimming.

She reached under the bulletin board with the fingertips of her right hand. She saw that one of her nails was broken. Sonia's manicure, she'd noticed, had been perfect.

She could feel the envelope taped against the wall behind the bulletin board.

She tugged at it carefully, afraid the bulletin board

might drop. It was only screwed into the wall in two places at the top. She tugged again, and the envelope came free, the tape making a ripping sound.

Again she froze. Sonia must have heard that. Sonia was coming with the knife, coming to punish her, coming. . . . She held her breath.

Sonia wasn't coming.

Michael whistled a new song—louder, meaning he was nearer—but she didn't know this one.

In the semidarkness she could read the address label on the envelope: M.F. Mulrooney, and a P.O. box number.

She pressed her back to the wall near the bulletin board. She could see Michael's light. If she ripped off the adhesive tape, she could scream to warn him. He carried his old gun, the gun he'd carried when he'd been a state policeman. But there were three men with guns against him—and Sonia with her knife.

His flashlight beam hit the pile of books in the middle of the floor. It swept across the destroyed contents of the card catalog, across the broken glass of the case that had housed the Bible, then across the old book's torn pages and ripped binding.

"Hey," she heard his firm old voice saying.

If she did nothing, he'd have no chance at all. She found the edge of the adhesive tape, ripped it off and screamed, "Michael—they've got guns!"

Clutching the envelope, she started to run toward Michael's light.

"Hey—what the hell—" It was Michael's voice.

She had to make the double glass doors of the library that led into the civic center corridor. She passed Michael as she ran for them.

There was a sound like someone coughing, then another and another. "Holy—" Michael grunted, then a gun sounded loudly.

"Shit—the old fart hit me!"

Another gunshot, then the coughing sounds, again and again. The glass of the door on her left shattered as she threw herself against the door handles, pushing them outward. She half fell into the corridor and looked behind her only once. Michael lay by the pile of books, his head resting on the torn pages of the Bible, his lit flashlight rolling slowly across the floor.

Its beam caught the glint of the steel of Sonia's knife.

"Help me—somebody help!" she screamed as she ran down the corridor.

She knew the front doors of the civic center would be locked, but there were panic-bar locks on the side doors leading onto the wide, flat steps of the old part of the building.

She ran for these, hearing shouts behind her. "She's got the Log—it's gotta be in that envelope! Get her!"

She heard the coughing sound, and the glass in the probate court office door shattered beside her.

She ran, pushing her hair back from her face, lost her balance and stumbled slightly, almost falling against the doors. The panic bars crunched down, and the doors opened outward. She lurched across the concrete pavement to the steps and ran down the broad, low steps that were wet from the misty rain hanging in the air.

She felt her legs giving way and fell to her knees, catching herself with her hands on the handrail. She stood up and kicked off her shoes.

Behind her, the doors were opening again. She ran across the sidewalk toward the town square; a policeman might be there. She slipped in a puddle of oil as she ran into the street, but she kept running.

She heard the coughing sound, then a whining noise, and the headlight of a parked car shattered.

She kept running.

"Stop her, goddammit!" It was Sonia's voice, but Sonia was not singing now.

She looked over her shoulder and saw Sonia, her knife out of sight, and one of the men, his right hand under his windbreaker. They were running after her.

She started across the street, headlights coming toward her. She stopped, looking back. Sonia and the man in the windbreaker were still running. The car was a block away. She waved her arms in the air at it, screaming, "Help me! Help—"

She threw herself to the pavement. The car, skidding as it swerved, passed her.

Tears filled her eyes again. She picked herself up and lurched forward, running.

Another car approached, its brights on. This one slowed.

"Thank God," she breathed.

The car skidded to a halt less than ten feet from her, and the front doors opened, a man getting out from the passenger's side. He was holding his left arm, his light-colored jacket stained dark red as he stepped into the light. The other man, on the driver's side, held a gun with a silencer.

She started running. "Shoot her in the ass, dammit!" It was the same voice that had complained of being wounded by the watchman. "Just shoot her!" Coughing sounds followed her as she reached the end of the street and started past the restaurant—it was closed—and into the square.

The mailbox. She ran toward it. She had put postage on the envelope when she'd addressed it.

The mailbox. She fell against it. She pulled open the chute drawer and put the envelope inside. The envelope was too big; the chute wouldn't close.

"There she is!" She heard the voice of the man Michael had shot.

"She's mailing the damned thing!" It was Sonia's voice.

She folded the envelope at the edges against the

cardboard she'd put inside to stiffen it and protect the contents.

She shoved it back into the chute drawer, reaching down, her fingers stretching. The envelope finally dropped through and fell inside.

She let the chute drawer on the mailbox slam, then she ran.

The coughing noises were still behind her. A chunk of pavement flew up and hit against her right leg. She screamed, breathing hard, her chest burning from the strain of running.

Eight streets opened into the square, and she picked one of the two nearest her and ran down it, seeing a recessed doorway. She sank to her knees in the doorway of a pawnshop.

She held her breath, only hearing her heart beat as she looked down at her bloodstained dress. Finally she exhaled. Still on her knees, as if she were praying, she peered around the edge of the doorway. She could see the mailbox, see Sonia beside it, see Sonia launching one kick after another at the blue box. She heard Sonia shriek, "Why the fuck is this the only thing the government builds right?" Sonia was reaching down inside it, then her hand and right arm reappeared, and Sonia kicked at the mailbox again. It wasn't a karate-type kick this time, but a kick like a small child throwing a tantrum. "That Chillingsworth bitch just mailed the Gladstone Log to somebody!"

And she watched as Sonia pointed in her direction and started to run across the square toward her.

She pushed herself to her feet, slipping in her wet, torn stockings, and she ran again.

ABNER BRYCE FELT THE JEEP settling on its springs as he stepped out into the square. He reached down to his right side for the long brass chain attached to his belt, looking up at the black sky—no stars tonight—and feeling the heavy mist on his face. He shook his head, then stared at the blue mailbox.

"Destruction of government property," he murmured to himself, standing there and getting wet because Phillip Cahill had taken the raincoat out of the Jeep the other night and he—Bryce—hadn't noticed it when he'd taken the Jeep out to make the last collection of the day.

He shrugged, then looked again at the mailbox. There were dents all over the front of it.

"Kids," he snapped, dropping to a crouch in front of the box, his gray canvas sack already heavy. He found the right key and opened the mailbox. He started to scoop up the contents, snarled, "Damn those kids," and stared for a second at the paper cups and hamburger wrappers. He crumpled them, setting them on the sidewalk near him, then scooped out the mail. A letter from Mrs. Billy Leigh Teasdale to her son in Montgomery. Anastasia Frederickson answering her Book-of-the-Month Club late, as she always did. Cleve Jessup sending away to one of those latex novelty mail-order places for something or other. A large package from Evelyn Collingwood, the librarian—there was no return address, but he knew her handwriting. He weighed the fat envelope in his left hand—enough postage, he decided. The envelope was gnarled and bent; she must have had a hard time getting it down the chute.

He stuffed all the mail inside the canvas sack with U.S. Mail stenciled on it and closed the front of the box.

He stood up, stiff from being wet.

He started back toward the Jeep, then stopped. "Shit," he murmured. He turned around and walked back toward the mailbox. He picked up the crumpled paper cups and hamburger wrappers from the sidewalk. He looked around the square for the litter basket and walked over to it, his left foot going into a puddle. "Damn kids," he muttered again, dropping the garbage into the litter basket.

He walked back to the Jeep and threw the canvas bag in the empty space behind the seat. He started the engine, flicked off his emergency flashers and drove over the curb of the square, the Jeep bouncing as he turned into the street.

Abner Bryce yawned. He would have to file a report about the damaged mailbox.

"THAT OLD BASTARD," Marv Cooksey snarled, thinking about his left arm and the old night watchman who'd shot him. The bleeding had practically stopped, and he was pretty confident nothing had been broken and that the bullet had gone through—he'd been shot before while working for Sonia and her father—but it hurt when he cranked the Ford's wheel hard left and against the curb of the square.

He reached across his body with his right hand, working the door handle, and stepped out. It was raining more heavily now. He eyed the mailbox to which he had returned as instructed.

"Goddamn keys," he mumbled. He reached back through the open door of the LTD and got the keys out of the ignition. He slammed the door this time. No sense getting my butt wet when I get back in, he thought.

He found the round key, stopped behind the car and looked across the trunk lid with contempt at the mailbox. The blue mailbox.

"Shit," he snapped, stabbing the key into the trunk lock, turning it right, the trunk popping open. He pushed it up all the way.

There wasn't much light. He had to find the crowbar by feel.

He finally found it snagged in the jumper cables. He

shook it loose, hitting his head on the trunk lid as he raised himself to full height. He slammed the trunk closed so hard the entire car shook, and he started to lift the crowbar to pound it against the trunk lid but stopped just before metal hit metal.

"To hell with it," he said, shaking his head and eyeing the mailbox again. He started toward it; it would take his vengeance.

He stopped in front of it. He snapped the crowbar out in his right hand, and the mailbox almost rang with the sound. "I'll get you, sucker," he told it, starting to edge the end of the crowbar between the front panel and the body of the box.

CHAPTER TWO

Jeff Culhane leaned forward to see through the rented Ford's misted windshield and bumped his head against the glass. "Dammit," he muttered. Halfway into the deserted intersection, he was finally able to read the street sign in the rainy darkness. He stomped on the Ford's brakes, the car skidding a little, then threw the car into reverse and backed up, cutting the wheel hard left as he did, and hit the brakes again. He moved the gear selector into drive, double pedaling and accelerating as he cut the wheel hard right, then slightly left, then full right, making the right turn he should have made going into the intersection.

He could see the civic center ahead; the library would be there. He'd tried Evelyn Collingwood's house. No one was home, but the place had obviously been searched, searched professionally and with deliberate destructiveness.

He slowed the Ford at the curb.

The guy who had the rented car waiting for him also had the gun waiting for him.

Culhane opened the glove compartment and took it out. A boringly standard Smith & Wesson Model 19.357 snubby, loaded with .38 Special 158-grain lead hollowpoint plus Ps.

He shrugged, thinking about his brother for a second, and smiled. Josh Culhane wouldn't be caught dead with a factory-standard gun. Jeff Culhane laughed; he hoped *he* wouldn't be caught dead with one, either.

He started to get out of the car, then reached back into the glove compartment for the box of ammunition. He opened it and poured half the contents out of the Styrofoam carrier into the right side pocket of his jacket, the other half into the left. The blued Model 19 he shoved into the waistband of his trousers approximately between his navel and his left hipbone.

Culhane stepped into the rain.

The doors into the civic center were open above the low steps. He hurried around the front of the Ford, running up the steps three at a time, nearly slipping on the rain-slick stone. Culhane dropped to a crouch beside the doors. There had to be a reason why the panic-bar-locked double doors were open. Culhane drew the revolver from his waistband, balling his right fist around the wooden grip plates so hard he could feel the checkering digging into the flesh of his palm. His left hand felt the throat of the old man at his feet, the body half in the doorway and keeping the doors open. The lack of pulse confirmed what he'd already known: the old man was dead.

Culhane reached into his pants pocket, found his lighter and flicked it, moving the flame over the body. He could count five bullet holes and saw shards of glass embedded in the gray fabric of the uniform shirt.

"You were brave, old-timer," Culhane told the open eyes. With his left thumb, he gently closed the lids.

He stood up, stepping over the body into the dark corridor beyond the doors, the cigarette lighter closed and put away, the Smith & Wesson hugged tight against his body, muzzle pointed forward into the darkness.

His hands were sweating, and whatever he'd eaten on the plane—he couldn't remember what—was rolling in his stomach.

Culhane stopped in the middle of the corridor to let his eyes become accustomed to the dim light. Then he started walking toward a sliver of light visible beyond the bend in the corridor. Glass doors. They opened. Licking his lips, he stepped through the doorway. The beam of light was more than a sliver now. In the grayness from the high windows over the bookshelves he could see behind the beam: a flashlight.

He walked toward it, his eyes moving from side to side. He bent over and picked up a Kel-Lite police flashlight. Glass crunched under his feet as he stood up. The old man had been shot in the library, either his fall or whoever shot him breaking the glass of some cabinet. The old man had dragged himself across the floor of the library and along the corridor, had reached the doors—and died.

Culhane shone the light across the library floor and saw the remains of a glass case.

A book—an old one. He walked toward it, crunching more glass under his shoes, and bent over, picking up a section of the book still attached to part of a leather binding.

"Only a Bible," he murmured gently setting the piece of the old book down. Still crouched, he held the flashlight in his left hand and swept its beam across the floor.

A revolver. He walked over to it, stuffing his own revolver into his belt, picking up the one from the floor. A Model 10 Military & Police Smith. The pearl grip panel on the left side of the grip frame was cracked. He thumbed forward the cylinder release catch; the revolver's six rounds had been fired, the primers in all six indented.

He closed the cylinder and returned the revolver to the floor, first wiping it clean of his fingerprints with the side of his coat as he held the flashlight awkwardly under his left armpit.

He drew his own revolver again, still inspecting the library. Almost every book had been taken down from the shelves, many of the books ripped apart. The card catalog drawers had been emptied.

Culhane walked toward the charge desk.

In the light he could see pieces of nylon cord, a broken pair of shears, and a bloodstained piece of white adhesive tape.

He looked at the tape more closely and noticed what looked like dark pink lip gloss.

"Evelyn Collingwood," Culhane murmured.

He looked up, dropping the tape to the floor. On the wall behind the charge desk was a bulletin board. There was something funny about it, all the little notices tacked there somehow disturbed.

He approached the bulletin board. He reached under it and felt something sticky.

He jammed the still-lit flashlight into his side trouser pocket, his gun into his belt. He pulled the bulletin board at an angle from the wall, took the flashlight into his left hand and shone it between the bulletin board and the wall.

Four pieces of masking tape formed the corners of a rectangle.

"An envelope," he whispered.

He let the bulletin board flop back against the wall with a dull thud, the papers tacked to it rustling.

He shut off the flashlight, closed his eyes, then opened them.

She had the Log in an envelope! He shone the light back across the floor to the pieces of nylon cord and the smeared white adhesive tape. They came in, tied her up, ripped the library apart. The old guy came in. She crawled over here, cut herself loose. Then she grabbed the Log—she's gonna mail it!

Culhane started to run, jumping over the glass and the old revolver in the middle of the floor, past the piles of torn cards and mutilated books and through the double glass doors. He noticed that one of them was shattered. Shot out?

He raced along the corridor to the panic-bar-locked doors, jumped over the old watchman and took the steps two at a time, stopping only when the flashlight he shone ahead of him caught something next to a handrail.

A woman's shoe. He picked it up, threw it down. A second shoe—the heel broken.

He flashed the light into the street and saw a footprint in a smudge of oil—maybe it was a footprint.

"That way," he rasped, running around the front of the Ford, throwing himself in behind the wheel, gunning the engine to life, tossing the flashlight onto the seat beside him, still lit.

He cut the wheel hard left, accelerating into a U-turn away from the curb. He miscalculated, and the right front wheel rammed into the curb, up and over it, then down.

On impulse he took the first right, thinking that if he were a woman running, alone, afraid, chased, rather than attempt a full-out run, he'd try to dodge his pursuers. And Evelyn Collingwood—Ethyl Chillingsworth—had to have been fleeing.

Culhane took the first right hard, corrected the wheel and saw a large square ahead of him. Ethyl Chillingsworth had been twenty-three years old in 1943; she was now in her sixties. Maybe physically fit, maybe doddering—he didn't know.

Culhane stomped on the brakes and cut the engine. The wiper blades stopped dead halfway across the streaked windshield. He pulled the keys to avoid the door buzzer's noise and stepped out into the rain.

He glanced down across the seat. The old watchman's flashlight was still on.

He reached into his waistband and grabbed the revolver with his right hand.

A man was hacking at a mailbox with a crowbar, then the crowbar was thrown down to the concrete beside the blue box with a loud clanging sound, bouncing on the ground. The man leveled a kick at the box. Culhane noticed that the man's left arm was held stiffly, and he thought of the six fired cartridge cases in the pearl-handled revolver. "Good for you, old man," he whispered to the night and the rain.

The man who'd used the crowbar was walking back to his car now, apparently oblivious to Culhane's Ford. The man started to get into the car, and Culhane raised the Smith & Wesson in a two-handed hold, aiming toward the man's head through the still-open door, the distance perhaps fifty yards.

But he didn't fire. The car's engine gunned to life, and the car reversed quickly, jumping the curb and heading across the square toward the mailbox.

"Holy..." Culhane began, the sound of metal crunching against metal loud in the night, the mailbox sailing skyward as the car skidded and stopped.

Culhane started running toward the mailbox shouting, "Freeze—federal officer!"

The man in the car got out and wheeled, something visible in his right hand. Culhane's left biceps was suddenly burning hot, his body punched back and to the left, his legs flying out from under him.

He fell onto the arm, cursing, when another shot from the man beside the car caused a chunk of pavement to explode beside Culhane's face.

Culhane's left arm—alternately numb then throbbing like a toothache—was useless. His right arm punched toward the man with the silenced pistol, his fist clenched tight, the first finger drawing through the trigger double action, the stubby-barreled revolver loud, making his ears ring as the sound reverberated off the buildings on both sides of the street. He double-actioned the revolver again, the gun bucking against the web of his hand.

The man beside the car turned around toward the vehicle. Culhane's pistol—now clear in silhouette from the reflected glare of the headlights on the puddles dotting the square—discharged once, then again, sparks flying as the projectiles hit the hardness of the concrete and ricocheted. Culhane started to fire a third time, but the man beside the car fell forward, his head smacking against the car's roof, and the body bounced back and sprawled on the concrete.

The revolver in his right hand, his left hand not working, Culhane pushed himself up to his knees. His hand was wet and his clothes were soaked. He'd fallen into a puddle of rainwater. He got his right knee up, then his left, stumbling forward but keeping his balance.

He was walking—not well, he told himself, but getting one foot in front of the other.

He had halved the distance to the man and, more important, to the mailbox. Its front was twisted open. Culhane kept walking.

He stopped beside the body, kicking the pistol away just in case the man wasn't dead. He couldn't bend well enough to pick it up. He looked at his arm. The sleeve of his jacket was dark with his own blood. "Fuckin' wonderful." He glanced down at the pistol the dead man had used: a Walther PP. A .22, he guessed, and apparently no slide lock. High-performance ammunition was out of the question or he would have heard the sound as the projectile cracked the sound barrier. He looked at his arm again; whatever ammunition had been used, it was effective. He walked on to the mailbox and stopped beside it. It was clearly empty.

If the man who'd shot him had been so determined to break it open, the man couldn't have known it was empty.

Either Ethyl or Evelyn—or whatever she really called herself—still had it, or it was in the custody of the U.S. Postal Service.

Nobody'll ever get hold of it that way—it'll just keep floating around because it doesn't have a Zip Code or something. Culhane laughed out loud.

But when he laughed, his arm hurt more.

The only way to find out what had happened to the Gladstone Log was to find Ethyl Chillingsworth.

He looked around the square, trying to judge where the woman might have gone after mailing the Log. Arbitrarily, he picked a street.

Jeff Culhane started back for his car, clenching his teeth against his pain.

CHAPTER THREE

"The bitch is up there." Sonia pointed across the construction site to the high girders above. "Looks like ten stories—probably a skyscraper for this shit town." She looked at the two men flanking her. "Well? What are you waiting for?" And she started to run, hearing the two men running after her.

She'd read all the information on Ethyl Chillingsworth, all the information on Evelyn Collingwood. Ethyl had been a track star in high school in the thirties. Evelyn jogged every morning and swam three times a week at the YMCA pool in the town twenty miles away. Sixty-three years old—she was tough for an old lady, Sonia thought. But it wouldn't do her any good.

Sonia stopped running at the base of the construction elevator; a metal ladder paralleled the shaft. She shouted, "Ethyl, it won't do you any good to run. We know you mailed the Gladstone Log, Ethyl. We know you're up there. We're getting the Log back, Ethyl— out of the mailbox. Now we only want one thing—*I* want it, Ethyl, you withered bitch! I'm going to kill you, like my father almost did in 1943—remember, Ethyl? But I like a knife—you won't like my knife. If you come down, we'll just shoot you quick, Ethyl. But if you make me climb all the way up there. . . ."

She stopped shouting, listening.

There was a sound of movement above her, something like metal clanging against metal. "Watch out Joe, Don—the old broad's tough. Might have a hammer or something and bash your brains in." She laughed as she started up the ladder. They didn't have brains. . . .

She had second-guessed Evelyn Collingwood but had hedged her bet. She'd left Joe at the lowest floor near the elevator and the ladder, the only ways down. With Don behind her, she climbed the rest of the way to the top. She broke a nail on one of the ladder rungs; Evelyn would pay for that.

As she stood on the platform she heard the sound of automobile tires below her, wet rubber against wet pavement, screeching.

"Go back down!" she rasped, turning to Don beside her, watching his square face in the light of a dim bare bulb hanging beside the ladder. "Get Joe down to the ground. If that's a cop, have Joe kill him. I don't need interference—or witnesses. Get your ass down there! Then get back up here!'' She saw little comprehension in his eyes, but he started down the ladder. He was good with a gun and could fight acceptably. He followed orders. She realized she had no right to expect him to be good-looking or brilliant.

She turned away from the ladder and started across the wooden platform toward the track for the crane. If Ethyl was up here, Sonia figured, she would have set out across the track to the far side.

"Ethyl," she called out in a loud whisper. "Ethyl? I broke a nail. Do you know what a good manicure costs? I mean, a really good manicure? The last time I broke a nail was when a horse threw me. Do you know what I did to that horse, Ethyl? I cut the tendons behind its front legs so it couldn't stand up. Every time it tried, it just fell down to its knees and rolled over in the dirt. It couldn't get to water, couldn't get to its grain. It took the horse four days to die. I used to go out to the stable and watch it. Do you wonder what I'm going to do to you, Ethyl? Maybe I can do to you what I did to the horse, and then cut off your tongue, Ethyl—cut it out of your mouth so you can't scream, can't even beg me to stop hurting you. Don't come out—I'll find you!'' Sonia started across the catwalk, bare bulbs every fifteen or eighteen feet along its length, sniffing for the fear that waited along its length in one of the patches of darkness. . . .

Sonia was halfway along the stretch of catwalk when she heard Don's voice calling behind her. "Miss Steiglitz. . . I—'' And there was a gasp from the darkness ahead of her.

"Shut up, Don!'' Sonia listened. The sound had been from Ethyl.

"But Miss Steiglitz—'' Don ventured.

"What is it?'' she snapped. She'd placed the gasp. It

came from a girder extending from the catwalk three feet ahead of her.

"I sent Joe down like you said and he—"

There was a gunshot, loud and unsilenced, from almost directly below. Then two more gunshots, then two more. Sonia Steiglitz held her breath, listening for more sounds of gunfire; the shots could have been .38s or .357s—police weaponry. There was another shot, then another and another and another. There was a long pause and two more shots.

She didn't take her eyes from the darkness at the end of the girder. "Don, stay here. If that cop gets past Joe, kill him—and I mean kill him. Blow his head off." And she started to walk the few steps to the girder.

She reached into the shoulder bag she carried and pulled out the knife from the sewn-in sheath. It was custom-made, the pear-shaped blade nine inches in length, the lower edge double hollow ground, the upper edge with serrations like sawteeth across it, ending in a broad ricasso on both edges just ahead of the double quillon brass guard.

Her right hand squeezed the phallus shape of the handle. She started ahead, cooing to Ethyl. "It surprised you, didn't it? I thought you knew that my name was Steiglitz. My father's alive—my father's well, Ethyl. But you know that. I saw all the clippings when we searched your house for the Gladstone Log. I'm his child—all the way. My mother was beautiful—not like you. You wanted him, didn't you? Wanted him so bad that you trusted him. Fool! All he wanted was the Log—never you. We used to laugh about this homely woman he knew when he was in the OSS, this WAC. And how she couldn't keep her hands off him."

Sonia squinted her eyes against one of the bare bulbs that suddenly went on. She could see Ethyl Chillingsworth, knees bleeding, stockings ripped. Sonia's eyes adjusted to the light. She could see Ethyl Chillingsworth's hand still near the bulb, see the face filled with hatred and fear, see tears streaming down dirt-stained old-lady cheeks wrinkled and ruddy with exertion.

"Liar!"

Sonia Steiglitz laughed.

"Liar—lying bitch!"

Sonia laughed again.

"I hate you!"

Sonia's laugh was cut off by gunfire. Six shots, loud, unsilenced, fired in rapid succession from beneath her; it would be the policeman.

"And I hate you," Sonia whispered. "My father searched for you. My mother would drink while my father was out at night looking for you and the damned Gladstone Log. Some nights she'd beat me because she couldn't love him. I hate you, Ethyl. So even if I hadn't broken my nail, even if you hadn't tried to mail the Log, I would have carved your heart out. My father's obsession tore mine out a long time ago. I'm twenty-six years old. I stopped playing with dolls twenty years ago. I taught myself to hurt things and feel nothing—all so I could be with him when he looked for you, be with him—*be with him*, just like you wanted to be. It was never my mother—I don't know if he loved her. It was always finding you, killing you after he got the Log. The Log—always finding the Gladstone Log...the power...the power he wanted. I hate you." She started toward Ethyl Chillingsworth with the knife, the sawtooth edge up to gut her.

"I trusted him—your father," Ethyl Chillingsworth shrieked. "He tried to cheat me, tried to kill me. He lied when he said he loved me!" Then she turned her back. Sonia lunged for it, but the back was gone. Ethyl was gone.

A loud scream.

There were many more bare bulbs at the base of the construction site—to discourage vandalism, Sonia deduced. In the glare she could see Ethyl Chillingsworth, see her old body, her dress up to her skinny hips, something metallic thrusting up through her body below the abdomen, like a huge penis stabbing through her.

Dead.

Sonia Steiglitz spat down toward her.

There was more gunfire. The police-type revolver again. Sonia turned away from staring at the prettiness of Ethyl's impalement and hurried through the darkness. She moved swiftly along the length of the ladder, down toward the sounds of the gunfire, toward the figures she could see below her. Joe's body was sprawled at the base of the ladder; Don was hiding behind an automobile. A man, his left arm stained dark, crouched near the ladder, near Joe's body, a revolver belching tongues of fire held in his right hand. She stopped her descent; she could see him, but he didn't see her. Perfect.

Even though she saw him crouching, she guessed he was tall. The shoulders were broad under the coat. Brown hair reflected gold and red in the bare bulb light cast over his head from above. Clean-shaven as he turned his face for an instant, the features were strong, the chin prominent.

She couldn't tell the color of his eyes.

She perched on the ladder twenty feet above him. With all the gunfire, with Ethyl's screaming, there would be more police soon. At least she assumed this man with the handsome face and the wounded left arm was a policeman.

She had replaced the knife in her shoulder bag, disappointed.

She reached into the bag again and removed a Walther PPK/S .380. She'd put wooden grips on it to make it prettier. Her left thumb worked the slide-mounted safety up and off. She aimed straight below her, firing.

The man who might be a policeman lurched away from the ladder, falling to the dirt, firing up at her. She tucked back against the ladder for protection.

Don was up, running almost directly below her. The policeman or whoever he was rolled in the dirt, raising his gun, firing it once, then once again. Don went down, rolling once, arms splayed from his sides. He didn't move again.

She fired downward at the policeman, seeing the bullet kick up dirt near his head.

He raised his revolver; there was a click, another click, and another.

He was up on his knees, then to his feet, running.

She fired after him. He stumbled, lurched forward, but he kept running. He made the car—a Ford—and was inside it when she fired again, hearing the bullet ricochet off the roof.

The car was in motion. She fired at the windshield, seeing the glass spiderweb, seeing the car beneath her flick-turn, U-turn and head away from her. She fired after it, not seeing if her bullet had impacted. The car was heading toward the chain-link fence. She fired again. The rear window was hit, but the car burst through the fence into the night.

"Fuck you!" she called after it, then shrieked, *"Fuck you!"*

CHAPTER FOUR

Josh Culhane leaned back from the typewriter, searching the littered desk to his left, finding the half-empty pack of unfiltered Pall Malls. He picked it up, shook out a cigarette and looked at the page in the machine. He found the gray Bic lighter and rolled the striking wheel under his right thumb. Cupping the lighter—unnecessarily, really, for there was no wind in his office except occasionally from the air conditioner, and that wasn't on—he poked the brand-name end of the cigarette into the flame. Adventure heroes always lit that part of the cigarette first, so you burned away the name and someone following you couldn't tell you'd been where you'd been just because you smoked a certain brand of cigarettes. He wasn't an adventure hero, he thought and smiled, but he wrote about one. Just as good—almost.

Culhane inhaled the smoke deep into his lungs, reading aloud as he exhaled, " 'Sean Dodge kept his way through the tree line—' " He picked up a blue-capped pen, changed *kept* to *crept*, then continued to read. " 'The stainless Detonics Scoremaster .45 was held in his right fist as if in a vise. He swallowed hard. Colby was out there, and Colby had a sun gun.' " He picked up the pen again, changed *sun gun* to *sub gun* and kept reading. " 'And a musette bag full of grenades. Dodge's .45 had a half-empty magazine, and all the spares were empty. If Colby won it all, if Colby and his sub gun and his grenades won it, the hole thing—' " He picked up the pen again and added a *w* to *hole*.

He leaned back, stubbing out the cigarette.

He lit another Pall Mall, and the telephone rang.

Josh Culhane started to reach for it, glancing at the luminous black face of the Rolex Sea Dweller he wore. He always thought of it as luminous because he labeled it that way in his series. Sean Dodge wore one just like it.

And it was luminous. It was also 11:43, give or take.

Maybe it was his agent, Jerry, though it was only 8:43 in Los Angeles. "Josh, your publisher just called me—wants to know where the hell the last six chapters are. They weren't with the manuscript. Josh, where the hell *are* they?'' But Jerry never talked like that; he was pretty even-tempered.

Culhane took off his glasses and picked up the phone. The final six chapters were waiting for the last ten pages of the fight scene between Sean Dodge and Colby, the assassin. "Yeah? I mean, Josh Culhane." He shook his head. He was tired. He never answered a telephone just saying "Yeah." He thought it was boorish.

He recognized the voice when he heard the first word. The voice was a duplicate of his, just like the face, the build, the hair color, the brown eyes, everything about him except a mole on his chest. It was his identical twin brother, Jeff.

"Josh—that you?"

He scowled into the phone's receiver. "Who the hell do you think it is? I sound just like you, don't I?"

"Listen, kid, gotta talk fast—"

Josh Culhane hated it when Jeff Culhane called him kid. It wasn't his fault he had been born one minute and thirty-eight seconds after his "older" brother.

"What is it, Jeff—I got work to do."

"I'm in big trouble, kid. I need ya."

"Bullshit."

"Listen, I've been shot three times, Josh—no shit."

Culhane laughed into the receiver, lighting another cigarette. "Bullshit, Jeff. If you've been shot, call the cops or the FBI or the CIA. Call the CIA, Jeff."

His brother was in the CIA.

"Shut up, will ya? This is an open line."

"Most lines are open lines, Jeff. Look, I got back from Egypt three days ago. I got terminal jet lag, and I got ten pages or so to go before I get Sean Dodge's latest out of the machine."

"Get yourself a word processor," Jeff said, then coughed.

"Wouldn't go with my rough tough macho image—you know, the unfiltered cigarettes, the manual typewriter, the .45."

"Yeah—get yourself a porkpie hat and a slinky secretary. But this is no shit, Josh. I got myself shot in the left arm."

"I don't care if you say you got shot in the left ball. Stop by for a drink—tomorrow. And stop wasting taxpayers' money on crank phone calls."

"Dammit, Josh! You're the only one I can turn to."

"You've been readin' too many of my books."

"That crap? Hell—comic books are better. But I can't call the Company—there's nobody now I can trust." Jeff coughed again, and Josh Culhane pulled his ear away from the receiver for an instant. "The only one. Can't trust my business associates."

Josh Culhane felt the corners of his mouth turn down. "Come on."

"Hey, no shit, kid, I'm hurt bad, got somebody on my tail. Croaked three of 'em, but the dame picked up some more recruits—picked up my tail about thirty minutes ago. I lost 'em—no telling for how long, Josh."

"Aww, come on—for Christ's sake, Jeff!"

"Ever hear of the Gladstone Log?"

"Yeah, it's a happy piece of petrified wood. Of course I never heard of some Gladstone Log."

"They want it. And they want me 'cause I know too much."

"Aww, geez, Jeff."

"Look, kid, I'm callin' it all in—all the favors, all the years, Josh."

"Favors? Like the time in high school you took my biology test and flunked it for me? Like—"

"Listen, I mean it, kid. You're my brother."

"What do you want?" Josh Culhane asked him flatly.

"You know the way up to Helen from your place on the lake?"

"Yeah, I know the way."

"Okay. There's a service station across from a bank that looks like a funeral parlor. I'll meet ya there."

"Hey, that's forty-five minutes from here, man."

"Bring a gun or two for yourself, Josh—some of that fancy crap you like—and bring me a box or two of .38s, plus Ps."

"What—government on an austerity kick?"

"Shut up and do as I ask, huh? Come on—for mom, okay?"

Josh Culhane sneered. "Don't give me 'for mom,' Jeff."

"Look, life-and-death time, kid." A cough. "Drivin' a white rented Ford LTD."

The line clicked dead.

Josh Culhane stared at the receiver for an instant, then slammed it down. Another practical joke in a long line of practical jokes, almost three and a half decades of practical jokes. He picked up his coffee. It was cold.

He picked up his cigarette. The tip had fallen off and it was out.

"Damn!"

He stood up, pushing the ancient Underwood away on the gray metal typing table, the pages on the left side falling to the floor, the whites and the yellow carbons getting mixed up. "Dammit!"

He looked at the telephone.

He bent over to pick up his pages. Only ten or so more to go, and the book, number seventeen in a series featuring Sean Dodge called The Takers, would be done.

"Aww, hell!" He grabbed the cigarette pack and the lighter and walked to his office door, through the doorway and across the cedar A-frame's living room to the open staircase. He took the stairs three at a time.

"Stupid!" he shouted. "Letting your brother con you again. Stupid! You damned stupid...."

He turned into his bedroom. He kicked off his rubber thongs, opened the right-hand sliding door of the closet and faced a rack of dresses, blouses, slacks and a dozen pairs of women's shoes and boots. "Mulrooney—" he slid the door shut with a vengeance "—hasn't lived with me for five months and twelve days and she still leaves her stuff here." He opened the left-hand door.

He reached down to the bottom of the closet, found a pair of brown Tony Llama cowboy boots, dropped into a squat on the floor and pulled them on.

He stood up, then pulled his jeans down over the boot tops, looking from side to side, angry.

He reached into the top drawer of his dresser. It wasn't there.

He walked back to the closet.

It wasn't on the top shelf. "Office," he told himself.

He looked on the hook in the closet and found the black shoulder holster—a Cattle Baron Leather Black Marauder—and carried it in his left hand, hitting the light switch out with his right as he left the bedroom.

He descended the stairs two at a time, and stomped back into his office. The Detonics Scoremaster was on the mantelpiece of the office fireplace. He took it down, dropping the Cattle Baron shoulder rig on the chair nearest him.

He tossed the magazine onto the chair, jacking back the slide. The chamber was empty.

He let the slide run forward, picking up the magazine, counting the seven rounds there through the witness holes, whacking the spine of the magazine into the palm of his hand, and jamming it into the Scoremaster's butt. He jacked back the slide again, running it forward, upping the ambidextrous safety.

"Holster." He looked around, remembering where

he'd put it. He slipped the .45 into the holster and
started to sling it across his shoulders as he killed the
office light and walked out. "Safe," he told himself.
He walked across the great room to the large closet.
He opened the door and started working the combination to the safe inside. "Why'd I get a dumb-ass
brother with a rotten sense of humor? Huh? Why
me?" And he looked up at the ceiling.

There was no answer he could discern.

He finished dialing the combination, wrenched the
handle and swung the safe door open.

Josh Culhane and his brother had grown up liking
guns and shooting. Jeff had been in Army Intelligence
during Vietnam, switched to the Green Berets and
joined the CIA after the war. Josh gave a child a pony
ride when he was a teenager, had fallen, and had dislocated his shoulder. He'd dislocated his shoulder
several times after that and was disqualified from
military service.

Josh Culhane reached into the safe and found two
boxes of Federal .38 Special 158-grain lead hollowpoint plus Ps. He assumed his brother was carrying a
Model 19.

He set the boxes down outside the safe on the floor.

He reached into a bin, pulling out the Milt Sparks
Six-Pack with six Detonics Scoremaster magazines in
it—all empty—and two boxes of .45 ACP, 185-grain
jacketed hollowpoints. "Damned foolishness," he
murmured.

He set these down beside the .38s, then took the two
Detonics 8-round spare magazines—they stuck out a
little at the bottom of the Scoremaster—and dropped
them into the side pockets of his jeans. These magazines were loaded.

He closed the safe, picked up the magazines and ammo and walked across the living room to the coffee
table. He set them down, rolled down his sleeves,

secured the shoulder rig to his belt and took a fresh pack of cigarettes from the coffee table. He picked up the things, walked to the hall closet and got his brown leather bomber jacket.

"Wallet, keys, money." He walked back into his office, found the light switch, got his wallet, his keys and his money clip, then killed the light and walked to the front door. He navigated the opening, switched off the lights, closed the door, then walked around to the driveway. He hadn't garaged the Firebird.

He found the keys, juggling the ammo and magazines, and opened the white Trans Am's driver's side door.

He slid behind the wheel and threw the ammo and spare magazines into the passenger seat beside him.

He rammed the key into the ignition. He knew where to drive to. He was tired. His brother was playing another lousy practical joke. He'd punch him out. But what if he was really shot?

Josh Culhane threw the transmission into gear and laid rubber out of the A-frame's driveway.

It would be slow going—not much over fifty—until he was away from the lake.

But then he could open it up.

A gas station across from a bank that looked like a funeral home not far from Helen, Georgia, could be reached a lot more quickly at eighty.

CHAPTER FIVE

He thanked God it was his left leg the woman had hit. He'd caught sight of her in the instant he'd tried firing up at her; it was a stupid, amateur reaction, not counting his shots. He smiled at himself despite the pain as he cranked the Ford's steering wheel gently right into the curve along the mountain road. All the training, all the simulations, nothing prepared you for the real thing even when you'd experienced the real thing—combat—more often than you wanted to remember.

In Vietnam he'd been wounded twice and nearly captured by the V.C. once, but he'd pulled it out of the fire.

Jeff Culhane nodded to himself. I'll pull this one out, too. His brother would come with some ammo, with that fast sports car of his, with one of his fancy guns to back him up. He smiled, thinking of his kid brother. He tried remembering just how much difference there was between himself and his twin, cranking the wheel left out of the curve and accelerating down the straightaway. Thinking about his brother kept him from thinking about the pain in his left leg, the pain in his left arm, about the burning gouge across the top of his right shoulder. But at least his right arm moved.

Jeff Culhane wondered what it would be like to fight beside his brother in a real fight. They'd fought plenty in the old days, he remembered—sometimes each other, sometimes together against another bunch of kids. They always won.

Josh was into tae kwon do these days, he remembered, and his brother was good at it, too. He was a good shooter, not in competition, but a good combat shooter. They had gotten together eight months earlier—or was it nine, maybe ten—and spent a few days at the cabin; they'd done a lot of shooting.

He laughed out loud, thinking about his kid brother. He was one of the most successful men's action-adventure writers in the English language. Aside from the sports car, the guns, the big cedar A-frame on the lake, Josh spent practically every dime he earned on traveling around the world, living out his adventures. Hadn't Josh said he was just back from

Egypt? Jeff laughed. He'd heard about Josh and his "research."

He decided that he'd talk to his kid brother, try to straighten him out. Running around the world chasing after danger just to fill up his damned books was crazy.

But the kid had done some neat stuff.

There was one of those yellow signs with the squiggly line showing a succession of curves. He slowed the Ford as he started into it. Lights in the mirror—fast-moving lights.

"Aww, shit," he snarled, stomping on the accelerator a little more despite the curve.

He lost the lights, cranking the wheel hard left, then hard right, hearing his tires screeching as he took the curve too fast. But he held it. Josh wasn't the only one who could drive a car fast. The rain was starting more heavily now....

He wondered about the Log. To whom had Ethyl Chillingsworth mailed it? Had she jumped from the top of the construction site, or had she been pushed by the woman who'd shot at him?

He'd only caught a glimpse of the woman; she was beautiful. It had to be Sonia Steiglitz.

He shook his head, exhaling hard against the pain, wheeling out of a curve and into a straightaway. He glanced up at the rearview mirror—the lights again, brights, coming up fast. They grew larger as he watched them.

"Wonderful," he muttered. All he had left for the Model 19 was two rounds besides the six already in the cylinder.

The headlights were growing larger. It had to be Steiglitz's and Sonia's organization—it had to be.

He studied the shadowy roadside. He was maybe ten minutes from the gas station across from the bank building in the middle of nowhere. They'd been raised in Illinois, but Josh had moved to Georgia many years ago. Jeff had spent so much time with him since then that he knew north Georgia almost as well as he knew the south side of Chicago where they were born.

Ten minutes.

The car was coming up fast, and Jeff Culhane accelerated to evade it. If he could stay ahead until Josh showed, with two cars they could get the pursuit car into a box.

He tried moving his left arm, but a flood of pain washed over him, making him suddenly cold. He shook his head to clear it, breathing in shallow gasps, trying again to move his arm.

He got the arm up high enough to hold the bottom of the steering wheel.

He reached down to the CB radio. He'd insisted it be installed in the rental car when he'd had the resident agent in Atlanta set it up for him. He flicked it on. Maybe Josh was close enough to hear him. He switched to Channel 19. "Breaker breaker for Kid Brother, this is Jeff. Come back." Only static. "Breaker breaker for Kid Brother, this is Jeff. Come back, dammit!" Only static, and the pursuit car was closing in.

His right hand still free, he picked up the Model 19 from the seat beside him, not bothering to check the cylinder. He knew how many it held.

He raised the revolver across his chest toward the window, which was almost closed.

He nodded to himself, setting down the revolver, switching his right hand all the way across his body and twisting slightly in the driver's seat so he could reach the window handle. The top of his right shoulder suddenly burned horribly. . . .

He cranked the window halfway down and that was good enough.

The pursuit car was closer now, less than a hundred

yards behind him, the high beams blinding him when
he glanced into the rearview mirror.

Culhane grabbed his revolver again. The pursuit car
would come up alongside.

His right fist balled on the 19's grips.

The pursuit car's lights flooded the passenger compartment now. He squinted against the reflection on
the interior of his windshield, hearing a low whistling
sound as air was pushed through the spiderweb crack-
ing in the upper left portion of the glass where the
woman had shot at him.

In the upper right portion of the rear window, there
was a similar bullet hole.

The pursuit car was nearly alongside him, but he
had to be sure. Maybe it was just a crazy fast driver;
maybe it wasn't Sonia Steiglitz. He cut the wheel hard
right, then hard left, accelerating. Then something
that sounded like a cannon—a sawed-off shotgun, he
guessed—blew away the glass behind him in the passenger window. Culhane felt the glass spray across his
shoulders and the bare back of his neck beneath his
hairline and above his open collar.

He rammed the Model 19 out the window, firing
once as the car evened with him again, hearing something like a curse on the wind of the slipstream. Maybe
he'd hit someone.

The pursuit car dropped back.

Culhane felt a grin spread across his face.

Flooring the accelerator, he set the revolver on the
seat beside him. He picked up the CB microphone.

"Breaker breaker for Kid Brother. The pizza's hit-
tin' the fan, Josh, help me. Come back."

Static.

CHAPTER SIX

Less than a mile to the gas station now, Josh Culhane told himself.

He switched on the CB radio. He always kept it on Channel 19 unless he was driving in convoy with someone, and then they'd pick a little-used frequency, like Channel 14 or 10.

Static.

A voice. "Breaker breaker for Kid Brother. Where the hell are you, Josh? I've got a pursuit vehicle on my tail. They've got a sawed-off shotgun that's blowing out my windows! Come back!"

Josh Culhane picked up the microphone, looked at it and took a deep breath. "Shove the Kid Brother handle—and cut out the practical jokes. Some cop'll hear you and think somebody's really shooting at you. Come back."

"Josh, hurry it up—this is no joke! For God's sake!"

Josh Culhane clicked his push-to-talk button several times to interrupt his brother.

"Look, man, I'm here, all right? You can cut the joke now—you suckered me."

His brother was doing the same thing with his talk button. Josh Culhane let his up.

"You have to take over. They're gonna get me—my gun's empty. Can't reload and drive—maybe I can— but don't trust anyone...." Josh Culhane smiled at that. Don't trust the eternal practical joker, Jeff. "Ethyl Chillingsworth—she's dead in Ventnor, Georgia—called herself Evelyn Collingwood. Real name was Chillingsworth. Worked in the library in Ventnor. She had the Gladstone Log."

Josh Culhane murmured to himself. "Gladstone Log, my ass."

"Ethyl mailed it to someone tonight just before she died. Watch out for anyone named Steiglitz, kid—especially a dame named Sonia. Find the Gladstone Log somehow, Josh—and watch out for Steiglitz—" There was a loud, roaring sound, and Josh Culhane saw a white Ford on the opposite side of the road just past the gas station, a flash of flame dying from the window of a car flanking it on the driver's side.

The white car—his brother's car?—was starting off the edge of the road, almost in slow motion. Josh Culhane hit his brakes, down-shifting fast, letting the car skid into the oncoming lane to take a straight line across the bow of the curve and toward the white car. He snatched at the cocked and locked Scoremaster in the shoulder rig under his jacket.

The voice of his brother crackled on the CB radio: "Josh, I love ya, kid—"

Static. The white car shot over the edge of the road, gone from sight, the car beside it veering into the right-hand lane.

Static. A fireball burst up from beyond the edge of the road, black and yellow and orange against the black sky, the colors distorted through the rain washing across Josh Culhane's windshield, through the tears washing across his eyes.

The static died.

Josh Culhane threw open the driver's side door of the Trans Am, half falling out, the Detonics Scoremaster in his right fist, the car that had flanked his brother's car even with him now.

His right thumb wiped down the safety. He saw a woman's face in the car and what looked like a sawed-off shotgun being raised. "Bitch!" He screamed the word through his tears, firing the .45 once, then again and again and again, hearing glass shattering from the car, seeing a long tongue of flame in the darkness beyond the rim of his headlights, hearing a roar, feeling chunks of pavement pelting at his legs and feet. He fired the .45 again and again, the slide locked open. The car cut through the gas station lot across from the funny-looking bank, then was gone around the curve.

He started to run, working the slide stop down on the pistol, ramming it inside his blue jeans, reaching the edge of the road. The car below him was washed in flames. He started down the embankment, not seeing clearly, the tears in his eyes mixing with the rain pouring down.

A figure like a burning scarecrow was coming from the car, the sticks that were arms and the torches that were hands waving horribly.

Then an animal scream.

Josh Culhane hurled himself down the embankment, rolling, catching his clothes in the thorns, tackling the flaming stick man with his own body, slapping out the flames that caught at his jeans, scooping up handfuls of dirt, smothering the flames with the dirt and with his own body. "Jeff—Jeff!"

The screaming stopped.

He smothered the flames with his jacket, though he had no memory of ripping the jacket from his shoulders.

The face was blackened, puffed, almost inhuman, with a crack for a mouth. He bent his own face to the distorted face and voice of his brother.

"Gotta...gotta get...the Gladstone Log," and then something that sounded like a laugh. "Kid... kid—"

The head that he cradled in his hands, his skin sticking to the burned flesh, sagged back.

Josh Culhane, on his knees, his hands blistered, his eyes streaming tears, the rain now a torrent from the total blackness of the sky, cradled his brother Jeff in his arms. He swallowed hard, talk hurting him, making him choke. "Kid...."

CHAPTER SEVEN

"This is really dumb." Her hands reached out along the front of her skirt, peeling back the wet fabric from her thighs.

She threw up her hands and arose from the raised flat tombstone she'd been sitting on.

She looked down at the slab, then fished inside her massive shoulder bag to find her lighter and cigarettes. She lit a Salem, the cigarette already wet. She bent her head to shield the cigarette from the rain, but her hair only streamed water down across her face, making the cigarette wetter. She stubbed it out, then dropped into a crouch beside the headstone, her skirt dragging in the mud.

Cupping her hands around the lighter—Josh Culhane had hooked her on the Bic disposables—she tried to use the flame to read the words on the tombstone she'd been sitting on.

It read Beecher—nothing else. "Sounds like you had an interesting life," she told the grave.

She stood up, looking to her right. Cletus Ball was bending over a grave about twenty yards from her, moving his tape recorder over the earthen mound—it was a fresh grave—and then finally setting it down. He looked up. In the glow of his flashlight, she could see his face. "Miss Mulrooney, could you bring the second tape recorder from the car, please?"

"The second tape recorder from the car? The car that's all the way back there?" She pointed to the edge of the cemetery about a hundred yards distant.

"Yes, please, if you could, Miss Mulrooney."

"The second tape recorder," she said again. "Sure, why not." And to herself as she started across the cemetery, the rain drowning her, "Why not—lovely night for a walk through a cemetery, anyway." Her clothes were soaked, and she tugged at her skirt so she could walk better. "Dumb, very dumb, M.F.—graveside recordings of the dead speaking from beyond the grave—very dumb, dumb, M.F."

She kept walking, tripping on a headstone and falling into the mud. "Ohh, this is just wonderful. Geez!"

"Miss Mulrooney, are you all right?"

She picked herself up, shook some of the excess mud from her clothes and wiped her hand across her face. She didn't worry about smudging her makeup. It had washed away an hour ago. She looked back across the graveyard. "Yes, I'm just fine, Mr. Ball—just tripped."

"The—ahh. . . ."

"The second tape recorder. I know—I'll get it, Mr. Ball." She stepped into a hole filled with muddy water, the hole deep enough and the water high enough to slosh inside her right boot. Now her right foot squished as she walked. "Terrific, M.F. Way to go, beautiful."

She stopped beside the car and could see the tape recorder on the front seat, but the door was locked.

Cletus Ball presumably had the key, since they'd driven to the cemetery in his car. She closed her eyes and leaned her head against the roof of the car for a moment. Then she turned around, blinking her eyes against the torrents of rain and tried to keep her voice even. "It's locked, Mr. Ball. The car is locked."

She could see his flashlight, not his face. She heard his voice—high-pitched for a man's. "I have the key right here, Miss Mulrooney. Should I—"

"No, you just go right on recording from that grave over there, Mr. Ball. I'll come and get the key. Coming!" She forced a smile. The smile left her as now her left boot filled with water as she stepped into a deep puddle at the cemetery road's edge. . . .

She stood beside him, her clothes so heavy she wasn't certain she could move. The heels of her boots had sunk into the mud; she thought she'd be trapped there beside Cletus Ball forever.

The rain was even heavier now.

"This is a good night for this kind of work, Miss Mulrooney," Ball said, looking up at her across the beam of his flashlight. The light from below made his skinny, bony face seem almost ghoulish.

He moved the flashlight to look at his watch. "Almost time for the dead to speak to us, Miss Mulrooney."

She licked her lips. They felt cracked, but more lipstick would have washed off in ten seconds, considering the force of the rain. "That's good, Mr. Ball," she told him.

She wasn't wearing a watch; she hated wearing watches. Where was Culhane and his Rolex diver's watch when she really needed him?

"Not around," she said aloud.

"What was that, Miss Mulrooney?"

"Nothing—nothing, Mr. Ball." She opened her purse and found her lighter and cigarettes. At least the pack wasn't too wet. She took out a cigarette, hesitated before lighting it, then pulled her brown leather coat up over her head to shield her face against the rain. "Do you think the dead would mind if I smoked?"

Ball stared at her. The rain was a curtain between them. "I don't think the dead would mind, Miss Mulrooney."

She nodded to him, lighting the Salem. "Glad to hear that," she said.

SONIA WATCHED HER FATHER. He was sixty—yet tall, straight, muscular with his shirt off. Today he wore a shirt and an open gray cardigan, his hands stuffed into the hip pockets of his black slacks as he stared away from her and out the window across the patio and toward the rolling pastureland. There was still shadow visible, the night barely gone. The sound of water dripping from the leaves of the trees outside came through the open study doors, but the rain had stopped and the sky—what Sonia could see of it from the leather padded armchair in which she was curled up—looked blue.

He turned around, saying nothing. She watched his gray eyes, a deeper gray than the silver of the thick hair on his head.

He stopped and took his hands from his pockets. Her eyes followed him, then her body turned around to present itself straight on to him as he came from behind the chair and leaned toward her, his hands—firm, large, bony fingered—resting casually on the arms of the chair.

"You fucked up, Sonia. I'm gravely disappointed." His voice was even, low, almost musical. He sounded like an operatic baritone.

"I—"

"What?"

"Father...I—"

"You tried? Has trying ever been good enough, Sonia? Haven't I taught you that trying means nothing unless the end result is total success? Haven't I taught you that, Sonia?"

"Yes, but—"

"But what, Sonia?" He stood and looked away from her, staring at the rows of bookshelves lining the wall behind his desk that held the classics as well as reference works in science, mathematics and linguistics.

"Well?" His voice was chill.

She curled up tighter in the chair. "I'm sorry, father...I...."

He turned to face her. "I should beat you with my

belt the way I did when you misbehaved as a child. You've ruined everything—everything!''

"I'm...don't—"

"Why? Tell me why not!" He stared at her. She watched his belt through the open front of his sweater.

"I...I did what—"

"What I said? Hardly." He turned away from her again and sat behind the massive, ornately carved desk. He splayed his fingers across the green blotter. "You were to bring Ethyl Chillingsworth to me, and bring the Gladstone Log to me. You caused Ethyl Chillingsworth to die. The policeman you followed and thought you killed after you picked up more men? He wasn't a policeman. He was Jeffrey Culhane, a case officer with the Company. You lost the Gladstone Log to the United States Postal Service. How else would you term it, Sonia, but that you fucked up— and badly. Irreparably, if it weren't for my contacts, my abilities. What will you do when someday I'm dead? Cringe in your chair? Go out and butcher your horse because he caused you to break a fingernail? What? Tell me!''

She pushed herself up from the chair and moved around to the side of his desk, dropping to her knees at his feet. She rested her forehead against his right knee and cried. "I'm sorry...please...I'm sorry...."

He said nothing.

She sniffed back her tears and raised her head, her hands folded in her lap as she knelt beside him.

"Please, father?"

He pushed his swivel chair back from the desk, rising and looking down at her.

"Will tears repair the damage that your violence and stupidity have caused? I hardly think so,'' he told her coldly, moving still farther away from her. She stayed on her knees, not wanting to rise, her hands still folded in her lap, her eyes cast down again so she couldn't see him. But she listened to his voice. "I cannot allow my anger to cloud judgment at this time. We'll determine your punishment at a later date, Sonia. I have waited more than forty years for the Log. I can wait a little longer."

She finally looked up, finally able to hold back her tears.

She stood, but stayed beside his desk.

"Possibilities," he said, walking toward the open study doors, not looking at her. "Possibilities—yes. First, a process of elimination, Sonia—elementary logic. She would not have mailed the Gladstone Log to the CIA or to any other government agency. As you indicated and as I had already strongly suspected, she had followed my career. Though she knew I was forced to resign from the Company, she would surely have suspected that I have strong contacts within the CIA, FBI and NSA...."

"Yes, father," Sonia said.

"Yes, she followed my career since London. I criticize you," he said, turning away from her, "but if I had killed her in 1943, taken the Log from her, this would all have been settled. The world would be vastly different than it is." For the first time that day, since her return at four that morning, he smiled. "She came to me with six pages of Latin—copied in her own hand—and couldn't read a word of it. I know I've told you this story a hundred times, but I translated those six pages. Her great-uncle, Henry Chillingsworth, had written them. And I realized what that stupid woman possessed and that even if I'd translated it for her, she wouldn't have understood it—not a damned word of it." He laughed.

"Possibilities," he said again. "She might have sent it to herself at a postal drop box under a name other than Evelyn Collingwood."

"My men are checking into that," Sonia said quickly, her voice low. If he heard her, there was no way she could tell.

"She might have mailed it to one of the large newspapers, or perhaps one of the really good small ones," he continued. "Perhaps a scientific institution. I have a great deal of work ahead of me on the telephone, favors to reclaim. The port areas will need to be monitored—likely spots where a large expedition might be mounted, assuming whoever translates it has sufficient knowledge to understand its importance. And San Rafael—it must be watched from today on, until there is a resolution to this."

He built a cathedral of his fingers against his forehead as he looked past her. She could see that his eyes weren't seeing her. "It is very likely, yes, that the first concrete lead will surface there if we are unable to intercept it. Before the time and expense of the expedition, San Rafael will be searched. For all her stupidity, Ethyl had a certain instinct for survival; she would have sent the Log to someone with the knowledge to use it. And today isn't 1943, of course—science moves rapidly. Even if the authenticity of the Log were doubted by its recipient, still—" he was thinking out loud, she realized "—the recipient would have to verify San Rafael at the very least. That is the key—the island."

Her father, Jeremiah Steiglitz, moved his hands from his forehead, a smile settling on his face. The look of pleasure was quickly displaced by a frown as he saw her.

"Clean yourself up. Put on a dress—anything besides those awful black jump suits you like. My daughter can't look like something the cat dragged in. Your hair—just look at yourself in a mirror." He walked past her, through the open double doors, and disappeared into the hallway.

She stood up, walked across the room to the mirror

and obeyed her father: she looked at herself. Her blue eyes were clear, the whites red-tinged. She was with him again.

CHAPTER EIGHT

"Rats," she snarled, the right front wheel bumping hard against the curb as she nosedived into the parking space in Athens, Georgia. She hauled the yellow Mustang's transmission into reverse, her clothes sticking to her again. She pulled her skirt away from her legs; it was still sodden. She looked over her shoulder, backing the Mustang, stepping on the brake, the car bouncing, stopping. She pulled up on the console-mounted emergency brake, leaving the stick in neutral, then cut the ignition.

She glanced into the sideview mirror. There was a break in the early-morning traffic and she took it, almost jumping out of the car, slamming the door, running around the front of the Mustang and then easing her pace as she started to the curb.

She stopped beside the parking meter and looked at it distrustfully. She started to open her shoulder bag, then looked up and down the street for a meter attendant or a cop. A girl, a college-student type, was staring at her.

M.F. Mulrooney looked down at herself. Her boots were wet and mud stained, and she was sure they were filthy all the way to their tops, which she couldn't see because of her skirt. That was mud stained, too, the once gray-green color now splotched with brown and dark in places where it was still wet.

She brushed at the matching green top; it was saturated.

She ran her hand through her hair. She'd combed it

out in the car, but it was still soaking wet. She picked up a dark brown strand and looked at it. It felt like overcooked spaghetti. She let go of her hair and looked at the curious student. "Bitch," she whispered, then she walked away from the parking meter. She'd be in and out in a hurry.

She took the steps two at a time, running, going through the metal-framed door and into the lobby. A sign, yellow with black print, read, Caution—Wet Floors. She felt herself smile. Might as well be wet—at least nobody'll notice my footprints. She walked along to the side, where the post-office boxes were, digging in her purse for her keys, feeling the ring, finding the wafer-thin post-office-box key, inserting it into the lock and opening the box.

A card with Hallmark embossed on the flap of the envelope. Typed, the name on the address read, Miss Mary Frances Mulrooney; it was from her mother. She stuffed the card into her purse. A check—she smiled and ripped it open—from her publisher via her agent, minus the ten percent. She glanced at the note: "Dear M.F., I am pleased to enclose...." She skipped the rest, looked at the amount he was pleased to enclose and compared it to his check. She dropped the envelope and the note into her purse, putting the check into the pocket of her skirt. Then bills—she filed these in the purse. Fan mail was filed there, as well.

A big envelope—no return address. She looked at the postmark: Ventnor, Georgia. "Big letter bomb," she muttered and tried stuffing it into her purse; it would fit only partway. She noticed the postmark date—the previous night.

She closed the post-office box, holding on to her keys, knowing she'd never find them in her purse with all the junk in it, then exited the post-office building and started down the steps—one at a time this time—and stopped.

A woman police officer or meter maid—most likely the latter since the woman didn't wear a gun—was standing beside the Mustang. Mulrooney started to run toward her. "Hey...hey, lady...." She stopped running as the woman turned around to face her.

The meter maid ripped a ticket from a black leather citation book and smiled. "Merry Christmas," she chirped, then walked down to the next hapless vehicle.

Mulrooney looked at the ticket and looked at the meter maid. "And Happy New Year to you, lady."

She stuffed the ticket into her purse along with the letters and the card from her mother and the mangled manila envelope from Ventnor, Georgia.

She crossed in front of the Mustang, waited for a break in the traffic, and made it to the door. She opened it and slipped behind the wheel, trying to unwind her wet clothes from her legs. She reached into the pocket of her skirt and found the check. "Bank," she murmured. There was a pen in her purse, but she knew she'd never find it. It would be bad enough finding her checkbook to get a deposit slip.

She leaned across the center console, noticed the meter maid watching her. "Go ahead and give me another ticket," she muttered, and opened the glove compartment. Parking tickets—more than she could count with no sleep and no breakfast and no shower. The revolver Culhane had given her and taught her how to shoot. A pen. She left the tickets and the Smith & Wesson .38 and took the pen.

She looked at the tickets again.

She reached back into the glove compartment, took out the tickets in fistfuls and stuffed them into her purse. Once she cashed the check she'd be flush again, anyway. She took the gun and stuffed that into her purse, too. She had put it into the glove compartment the previous night in case Cletus Ball had more than dead bodies on his mind. He hadn't, which was good since she'd forgotten to take it along when they switched to his car with all the recording equipment inside it.

The meter maid was starting toward her.

Mulrooney flashed her best, toothiest smile and started the Mustang. There was a break in traffic, and she hit the gas and took it.

CHAPTER NINE

"This is the Ultra Two, one of our very best caskets. A bit higher in price than some of the others, but not when one considers the peace of mind it affords. Of course the satin pillow, the interior panel lining and the overlay are completely removable in the Ultra Two, and since the condition of . . . the deceased . . . since his condition is such that the casket will be closed, there can certainly be a substantial saving there." The plump-faced, rosy-cheeked man in the black suit and black tie took a solar-powered calculator from his breast pocket and started pushing buttons.

Josh Culhane touched his bandaged left hand to the closed lower lid panel of the Ultra Two. "Give my brother the best you have—coffin, vault—all of it. Just as if it were going to be open. Because I'll open it before we put him in the ground. And if it isn't perfect. . . ." Culhane let the sentence hang. He started to walk away, hearing his heels click across the Congoleum floor, shouting without looking back, "You got my number. Call me when you have everything figured out." When he stepped outside into the parking lot, he stood there, letting the doors of the funeral home bang closed behind him, and inhaled the morning air.

He flexed his left hand, and it hurt a little. The doctor at the emergency room in Cornelia had told him that the bandages should stay on for at least a week. His other hand just had the hair singed off the tops of the fingers; it'd grow back.

The cops had given him back his gun. He had a concealed carry permit for it in Georgia, anyway. They'd all been sympathetic about the death of his brother.

He looked at the burn marks on his leather jacket. He had another one just like it, but newer, and this one could probably be cleaned.

Culhane looked across the lot at his car. The white Trans Am hadn't even been scratched, but it was mud splattered and needed a wash.

He rolled back the cuff of the bomber jacket. The Rolex read morning. "Ohh," he groaned. He found his Pall Malls, lit one and started across the parking lot. There was a small restaurant on the opposite side of the street. Looking at food would either make him throw up or get hungry, and he needed some coffee. He played bumper pool with the morning traffic and reached the opposite curb, then checked out the restaurant, which seemed okay.

He'd already talked with the doctors and with the police. Soon it would be his brother's employer—the CIA. He had a feeling the CIA had already heard somehow, had already talked with the local and state police, because there wasn't a single question asked him about the spare ammunition and spare magazines on the front passenger seat of the Trans Am. He'd since put the stuff in the trunk, after reloading the spent magazine from his pistol.

He entered the restaurant.

Along with the gun, he also carried the two Detonics 8-round magazines. His dead brother's playmates had been a rough bunch.

He found a table that was empty but decided against it, going up to the counter instead.

It was a small place with some truckers, a few women who looked like factory workers or office help. Whatever they were, they didn't look eager to finish their half-empty cups of coffee.

A television set—a small black and white—flickered behind the counter.

One of the local news-type midmorning talk shows.

He sat down at the counter and smiled at the chubby waitress who handed him the menu. "Too late for breakfast?"

"Never too late for breakfast 'round here, mister," the woman smiled back.

"Good. Steak and eggs and hash browns—make the eggs sunny-side up and barely cook 'em."

"Don't have no steak until three or four this afternoon. Got hamburger, though—ground round. Started out same as the steak."

"Fine," he said, nodding. "Hamburger and eggs."

"Don't want no bun, do ya?"

"No. Gimme some toast. And plenty of coffee."

The woman finished writing the order on her pad and ran a rag over the counter, then turned away for a second and came back with a glass of water.

The coffee came, then the toast and the eggs and the hamburger and the potatoes. He decided he wouldn't get sick—not yet anyway—and started to eat, watching the talk show to keep from thinking about his brother being autopsied somewhere.

He heard a voice—a familiar one—and looked up from his coffee. "Aww, shit," he said out loud. The voice was M.F. Mulrooney's; she was the talk-show guest. "Hey, lady," Culhane called to the waitress. "Miss?"

"Hey, with breakfast you forgot orange juice," she said, coming over.

"Fine, gimme some orange juice and some more coffee. And find another station, huh?"

"Can't."

"Why?"

"Don't have no outside antenna. Can't get no other stations."

"Wonderful," he muttered, trying to ignore Mulrooney. She'd lived with him for nearly a year. He continued to eat, trying not to listen, but he kept hearing her. He looked up as the interviewer finished a long question; there was a tight shot on Mulrooney's face. He could tell the program had been recorded; she never looked that good this early.

"And I call it *Occult Murmurs*."

"Occult Murmurs," the blond-haired interviewer, her hair piled high on her head, repeated with a well-practiced expression of interest.

"Yes, *Occult Murmurs*," Mulrooney said again.

"Geez, they got the title by now," Culhane snapped at the television.

Mulrooney was talking. "It's pretty much what the title of the book implies—murmurings of the occult."

"Murmurings?" the interviewer asked.

Mulrooney pushed her dark brown hair back from the sides of her face. She did that because she knew it made her look innocent, ingenuous. "For years there have been reports of otherworldly communications—messages from the dead—through spirit mediums, through mysterious voices in old houses, even mysterious murmurings in wooded areas and other places like that where some violent death may have taken place."

"Stuff it," Culhane muttered.

"But *Occult Murmurs* deals with only the documentable kinds of these reports. I've built my reputation as a writer on honest research."

Culhane started to choke on a piece of toast, scalding his throat on his coffee when he tried to wash it down.

"That's why I only selected certain types of occult

murmurs. Like graveside recordings. There is hard, physical evidence that humanlike voices can be picked up very faintly on specially tuned ultrasensitive tape-recording devices. The dead do speak.'' She smiled, lighting a cigarette.

"Damn menthol cigarettes," Culhane hissed.

"I'd like to talk to you about one of your earlier books—one that really fascinates me," the interviewer said, leaning toward Mulrooney and touching her knee. Culhane laughed. If a male interviewer tried that, Mulrooney would have cracked him in the head. "The one about Atlantis."

"You mean—"

"Here comes the title plug," Culhane snarled at his eggs.

"*Legend Beneath the Waves*, isn't it?" the interviewer supplied.

"Yes, *Legend Beneath the Waves*."

"Sounds like a dirty novel about women sailors," Culhane thought out loud. He noticed the waitress staring at him, but he ignored the woman and watched Mulrooney instead.

Mulrooney was talking. "The mystery of Atlantis has intrigued men and women for thousands of years, ever since Plato first mentioned it. It became an obsession for some, a hobby for others, but it is perhaps the most intriguing enigma of history. If Atlantis did exist, then an entire continent was destroyed and is only remembered in the human racial subconscious as a 'legend beneath the waves.' ''

Culhane groaned.

The waitress brought his orange juice. Culhane gulped part of it down and noticed the woman was staring at him. "What's the matter—ground glass in the orange juice and you're waiting for me to croak?"

"Nope. That lady on television—that's M.F. Mulrooney. I read all her books. What's got you so all-fired put out, mister?''

Culhane sneered at his orange juice. He didn't know if the burly cook visible through the opening into the kitchen was the waitress's husband, so he didn't sneer at the waitress. "I used to live with Mary Frances Mulrooney. No offense, lady, but that stuff she writes is a pile of crap.''

"I think she writes damn good, mister. You ever try writin' a book?''

The waitress walked away and Culhane, shaking his head, returned his attention to his eggs, rubbery by now, nearly rubbery to start with. Mulrooney was defending her research techniques to the interviewer. He decided maybe he would throw up after all. "Research is careful research. Careless research is no research at all. Take the concept of Atlantis. How many people who scoff at the idea that Atlantis ever existed—except in Plato's mind or in the minds of some Egyptian priests—even know that in the 1860s the prime minister of England, Gladstone, attempted to have Parliament launch a naval expedition just to search for it?''

"Gladstone?" Culhane set down his fork. "The Gladstone Log...holy shit.'' He jumped up and threw a ten-dollar bill on the counter. He ran for the door, then turned back toward the unhearing Mulrooney. "I love ya, Fanny!'' he shouted, to the surprise of the other customers, and blew a kiss toward the TV screen.

Three men were standing on the sidewalk outside. The three-piece suits, the sunglasses—they had Feds written all over them. Right down to the ID case, black leatherette with fake gold trim around the edges.

The card in the ID case read, United States Central Intelligence Agency and it had a neat little picture of an eagle in the middle.

"Joshua David Culhane?" the man with the ID case asked.

He figured they had to be legit to know his middle name.

CHAPTER TEN

She felt better. She'd done her exercises, drunk four cups of herbal tea instead of coffee, showered and washed her hair. Tucking her bathrobe around her ankles, she sat down on the floor beside the coffee table and emptied her purse.

She took her lighter and the fresh pack of cigarettes she'd put on the coffee table and pulled out a Salem, lighting it, inhaling, setting down the lighter and re-adjusting the towel wrapped around her wet hair. Using a metal nail file from her purse, she opened the card from her mother. It was for Mulrooney's birthday, but the birthday had been two months earlier.

"Thanks, mom," she said and set the card down. She sipped at another cup of Celestial Seasonings Almond Sunset tea. Her mother could never remember birthdays. One year she'd missed Christmas by a week because she'd stayed indoors all the time and forgotten it was December.

Mulrooney looked at the pile of parking tickets and shrugged. "What the hell." She crawled two steps to the television set and flicked it on, letting it warm up for a few seconds, then ran through the channels until she saw herself staring out from the screen. It was the interview she'd done about *Occult Murmurs* that had ended with her discussing her book on Atlantis. The interview was nearly over, but she left it on and slunk back beside the coffee table. She found her checkbook and started writing checks for the parking tickets. "What a lousy interview," she said aloud.

And then the show was over. She glanced at the television after the commercial break. It was the same woman interviewer. "Our next guest is Eunice Clink. Eunice's exciting new book—it's made it to the *New York Times* bestseller list this week—is called *Fun With Vegetables*. Let's give her a warm welcome!"

"Yecch," Mulrooney said, leaning forward and shutting off the TV.

She finished the last of the parking tickets and the last of her tea and decided the other bills could wait. She began to sort through the letters from her readers: a woman claimed to have seen a flying saucer when she was hanging her laundry in the backyard; a man claimed to have been abducted by a group of female aliens and forced to have sex with them constantly for two days; miscellaneous kudos for her research, her writing style and questions about her next book. She always liked those. She answered all reader mail. She guessed it stemmed from the days when she'd only been free-lance writing for magazines and newspapers and barely made enough to keep alive. Readers were the important ones—not the publishers. If the readers wanted you. . . .

She got to her knees, then to her feet, catching up the hem of her robe so she didn't trip, and went to the kitchen, carrying her teacup. She put on more hot water for tea. She should go to bed and sleep, she told herself, but she was too hyper to sleep.

She had to sift through her notes for *Occult Murmurs* while all the stuff from the graveside recording session was fresh in her mind. Cletus Ball had promised to make more recordings from fresh gravesites for her. He was going to check police reports and pick some especially violent deaths; the violently murdered dead usually had the most to say. She shivered. It was scary stuff.

She wondered what *she'd* say from the grave.

The teapot whistled, and Mulrooney shut off the burner and poured the boiling water over the tea bag, letting it steep a little.

She needed her cigarettes. Perched on the edge of the couch, she lit a Salem and saw the envelope—the big one from Ventnor, Georgia. She set down her lighter and picked up the envelope, weighing it in her hand.

She slipped her nail file under the edge of the envelope flap, struggled against the tape, finally ripping through and opening it.

Mulrooney spilled the contents of the envelope onto the coffee table on top of the parking tickets. From the large envelope fell two pieces of cardboard stiffener and another large envelope.

Her forehead furrowing, she opened the second envelope, making a mental note to save the cardboard. The right thickness of envelope-sized cardboard to protect photos was hard to get.

She emptied the second envelope's contents onto the table.

An old, leather-bound book. She opened it.

Latin—great. Almost flunked that back in high school. A third envelope—letter sized—slipped from the old book to the floor.

She set down the book, reached between her pink-slippered feet and picked up the brown envelope. She used the nail file again and opened the envelope to find a handwritten letter in a woman's writing. The letters were carefully formed, spidery-looking. There was a signature at the bottom—"Ethyl Chillingsworth"— but no return address at the top.

I don't know an Ethyl, Mulrooney thought.

She began to read: "Dear Miss Mulrooney—I can't say I'm a fan of your type of books."

"Thanks a lot, lady," Mulrooney told the letter.

"But in my profession—I'm a librarian—I encounter a great many of them." Mulrooney hated public libraries even though she used them; they took away from book sales. "I must say, however, that your books seem to be the best researched of all. It is for this reason that I send the enclosed journal and tell you about an evil man named Jeremiah Steiglitz."

Steiglitz, Mulrooney mused, her mind working the name. Director of Covert Operations for the CIA until the mid-1970s—some kind of scandal involving assassinations. She kept reading.

Just before he tried to kill me more than forty years ago, and just after he read the first six pages or so of this old book, in Latin, he gave it a name, which has stuck in my mind all these years. Steiglitz called it The Gladstone Log. It was the logbook of the H.M.S. *Madagascar* on its journey to seek the Lost Continent of Atlantis at the request of then British Prime Minister William Gladstone. My great-uncle, Henry Chillingsworth, was the *Madagascar*'s cabin boy; his uncle was the ship's captain. This logbook had been handed down to me. It is now yours, for if you are reading this I have already died or am the prisoner of Jeremiah Steiglitz, in which case I shall soon pray to be dead. I have never read the enclosed material. What my great-uncle told me of it when I was a little girl only served to frighten me. Jeremiah Steiglitz, when he was an agent in London with the Office of Strategic Services, the predecessor of the CIA, read the first few pages and thought the contents important enough to kill for, important enough to pursue me for forty years, to force me to assume another name, to hunt down members of my family and murder them. God bless you, Miss Mulrooney, and do not try to find me. It would be useless now.

Mulrooney stared at the letter. She realized her hands were shaking.

She picked up the book—the Gladstone Log—and bit her lower lip. She stood up, pulling the towel off her wet hair and dropping it on the couch. Her right hand holding the book, her left running through her hair, she searched the bookshelves as she entered the dining room that she used as her office.

"Latin dictionary, Latin dictionary," she murmured, scanning the shelves for it.

CHAPTER ELEVEN

His lips were too dry to whistle properly, so he drummed the opening rhythms of the "William Tell Overture" with his fingertips on the white linen room-service tablecloth. The room-service waiter was pouring coffee from a metal pot, but Josh Culhane's eyes were looking past the waiter, past the center of the suite's living room toward the solitary man silhouetted against the tan drapes over the glass sliding door leading to what Culhane presumed was a balcony.

The waiter walked away, Culhane glancing after him as he paused at the doorway for one of the three penguins in the CIA-issue suits to give him a tip, then let himself out.

Culhane went back to staring at the man by the drapes, only seeing his dark silhouette because of the light.

"Have some coffee, Mr. Culhane," the figure at the window said, the voice deep, authoritative. "It isn't drugged—no need for it."

Culhane shrugged and raised his coffee cup. "Here's looking at ya."

"You know that your brother worked for us—for what we euphemistically call the Company?"

Culhane took another sip of the coffee, put down the cup and found his cigarettes. He lit one. The cigarettes and the lighter were the only things left in his pockets besides his handkerchief.

"We know that your brother must have called you before he died," the man with the deep voice continued. "He called you so you'd be there on the road to meet him. And he made a special request that the rental car we supplied him with have a CB radio. And your car has a CB radio. There was ample opportunity—more than ample—for him to detail all or part of his activities to you."

"Jeff and I had an agreement," Culhane said in the direction of the figure at the sliding glass door. "I didn't ask, he didn't tell."

"What did he tell you, Mr. Culhane?"

"What's your name?" Culhane returned.

The man turned around, Culhane still unable to see features or a face because the light was behind the man. "What if I said Jeremiah Steiglitz?"

Culhane sipped his coffee some more.

The man laughed. "You're as cool as your brother Jeff was, Culhane. He must have told you the name Steiglitz somewhere along the line. That was a pretty well-known name ten years ago. But you didn't bat an eye. I know Jeff told you something."

Culhane started to move, but he felt hands on each shoulder keeping him down. A squarish object sailed across the room, landing at his feet. The pressure of the hands holding him down at his shoulders was gone, and Culhane leaned over to pick up the object the man from the glass door had thrown.

It was an ID case—leather, expensive looking. Culhane opened it. The same cute picture of the eagle, the same organization, but the name wasn't Jeremiah Steiglitz. It read, Calvin Partridge.

Culhane looked up at the man whose face he hadn't

seen. He was walking from the glass door now, the light catching his features—dark hair, brown eyes, the eyes laughing. A chin that looked as if it had been carved either out of granite or out of Marine Corps boot camp. Culhane guessed the latter. Calvin Partridge laughed. "You should be happy I'm not Jeremiah Steiglitz, or you'd be dead by now, just like your brother."

Culhane didn't tell Partridge that he didn't think so.

CHAPTER TWELVE

"Dammit!" She stood up and looked at the cuckoo clock. She'd forgotten to adjust the weights and wind it before she'd left the house the previous night, and it had stopped.

Mulrooney threw down the Latin dictionary and looked at the yellow legal pad. Words—a meaningless jumble of words. Two years of Latin in high school and she couldn't remember the declensions.

She looked under the television at the Panasonic VCR, which had a digital clock. "Fine time to sit around in your bathrobe, M.F.," she said aloud and started for her bedroom. She could always contact the university; they had to have someone who could translate Latin for her. Or Berlitz—they could do anything with languages. But it would take too long. With any outside source, maybe twenty pages a day would be top speed.

She pulled off her robe and, naked except for her slippers, walked through the bedroom into her bathroom. She picked up her hairbrush and dryer and started to work on her hair, thinking to herself all the while.

When she was done with her hair she walked back

into the bedroom. The Log was probably an expensive practical joke, anyway. None of the words she'd more or less translated connected to make any sense.

She started rummaging through a dresser drawer, found a pair of panties and stepped into them. She was looking for a bra when she found a picture frame, the kind with the fold-down, felt-covered cardboard easel. She knew what was inside as she picked it up, turned it over and stepped back until she felt the edge of the bed against her calves. She sat on the bed and looked at the photograph in the frame. It showed her wearing a pair of washed-out blue jeans and an old shirt; her hair was in a ponytail. She was holding on to the reins of a horse. The man beside her was holding the reins of another horse. Brown hair, brown eyes, clean-shaven, tall, he wore blue jeans, boots, and a cowboy shirt with pearl snaps instead of buttons.

She remembered he was about six feet tall and that his arms were strong.

She smiled at the photograph. "*Josh* can read Latin! All right!"

She jumped up, stood the picture on the dresser and went back to hunt for a bra.

CHAPTER THIRTEEN

Partridge seemed taller when you walked beside him, Culhane observed as they strolled in the crowded shopping center that formed the mall of the hotel where Partridge held the suite of rooms. Two of the three penguins in the CIA suits walked some distance behind them, the third man off doing something that no one had bothered to explain.

A black kid with ice skates over his shoulder walked past them. A woman carrying a slice of pizza in one hand and dragging a child with the other cut in front of them. Piped-in music from the skating rink was so loud you couldn't help but hear it even on the second level and at nearly the most distant point from the indoor ice rink.

"I like moving around in crowded places when I'm talking business, Mr. Culhane, but you should know all about sophisticated electronic eavesdropping stuff from your writing."

"Yeah," Culhane nodded. They had given him back his wallet, his money clip, his keys, the Detonics Scoremaster and the two spare magazines. But he still felt uneasy.

"I'm sorry about your brother," Partridge said. "I was his boss for the last two years and his friend for the last nine or ten. Rough way to have your brother die. Mine died in Korea, but I wasn't there."

Culhane looked at Calvin Partridge, muttered "Yeah" again, and kept walking.

"Why do you write the books?"

"Why do you work for—" a man in a three-piece suit walked past them "—who you work for?"

"Patriotism, fighting the slimy tentacles of Communism—stuff like that. And it pays the bills. Now it's your turn."

"Pays the bills and I like to write. I always figured good books didn't have to be devoid of excitement, and exciting books didn't have to be devoid of good characterization, setting, things like that. I guess the idea caught on. A lot of people buy my books."

"You know, your brother turned me on to your series, The Takers. I've read 'em all. Number sixteen out yet?"

"No, but I'm just finishing seventeen. The bad guy works for the CIA—you'll love it."

"Then Jeff did tell you about Steiglitz."

"I don't know what you're talking about," Culhane said, his voice a monotone.

"How long does it take to write a book?"

"Maybe four weeks of actual writing time. But a lot more in research."

"Jeff told me, you spend most of your time and most of your money wacking around in jungles and climbing mountains and shit like that."

"If Sean Dodge does it in a book, I've usually done it first."

"How about dames? You do as much nighttime work as Sean Dodge?"

"What's that old line about gentlemen not discussing things like that?"

"Just like Dodge would have said it. I'm enjoying this, Mr. Culhane. But I wish it were under more pleasant circumstances. Must be dangerous, what you do—the research part, I mean."

"It was so safe for Jeff being in the CIA?"

"I understand you've dodged a few slugs yourself. You know what it's like."

"No, I don't. I never died by burning to death. I don't know what it's like," Culhane said, stopping and looking at Partridge. "Was he fighting Communists, terrorists, Nazis—any of the standard bad guys? Or just some crazies? Whoever it was, it was a hit, pure and simple. It wasn't anything he was carrying, nothing like that. They just drove up beside him, shotgunned him through the window or the windshield and ran him off the road. Maybe it was your guys."

"He told you, then. I knew he did. About the Gladstone Log."

"The what?"

"You can lie and tell me you don't know, but you do. And you're right; he didn't trust contacting the . . . the firm through the usual channels. He never should have had the local resident rent him the car. Maybe that made it too easy to pick him up—I don't know. But last night in Ventnor, Georgia, some old woman librarian by the name of Evelyn Collingwood had her house broken into and searched. We found Jeff's fingerprints there, but it wasn't Jeff who did the searching. We found no other fingerprints. Then her library got torn apart and we've got evidence somebody had her bound and gagged there. Found a dead night watchman at the library with all the bullets fired out of his revolver. But the bloodstains on the floor weren't the same type as your brother's or the Collingwood woman's or the watchman's. Tests show it was probably a man's. That's all we know. Then the woman turns up dead in a construction site a couple of blocks away, impaled on some piece of equipment. Looks like she tried flying without wings. More bloodstains—some of them could have been your brother's. And a mailbox ripped to hell. More bloodstains around that. No bodies. Somebody came along and cleaned up, at least sent a meat wagon. They left poor old Evelyn, though. We think that's how your brother got shot up. The people who searched the Collingwood house and the library were the ones following Jeff, the ones who killed him. All adds up to Steiglitz—everything does.''

"So why didn't Jeff trust the Company?" Culhane lit another cigarette as they walked, circling the ice rink below them.

"Steiglitz—you know the story. Got in trouble in the sixties, was made to resign from the CIA in the early seventies. He still has connections—plenty of 'em. The innocent kind—the kind you can use best. You know—hey, guy, you owe me a favor; what's the current status on whatchamacallit?—that kind of stuff. That's why Jeff called you instead of us—Steiglitz. Jeremiah Steiglitz.''

"There was a woman in the car.''

Partridge stopped walking and grabbed Culhane's left forearm. "Did you see her face well enough—''

"All I can tell is that it was a woman, or it was a guy with a skinny face and long hair behind that shotgun."

"It was Sonia Steiglitz—Steiglitz's daughter."

"But can't you arrest them? Or have the FBI do it or just—"

"Just what?" Partridge laughed. "Kill him? Kill her? He's got enough dirt on...on...well, got enough dirt to fill up the headlines for months, maybe years. He's protected himself. Unless we get him cold—nothing."

"A powerful man," Culhane said unnecessarily, starting to walk again. Partridge was nearly through with his ice cream cone.

"Yeah, you know the story?"

"Not all of it," Culhane told him honestly.

"Well, Jeremiah Steiglitz is like this—genius-level IQ, hell on wheels with foreign languages, had a Ph.D. in physics by the time he was nineteen. Because of the language ability most of all, he was able to get into OSS—youngest field agent they ever had. He could go into any country and convince 'em he was a native, he was that good. Still is, I guess." Partridge shrugged. "And he served brilliantly—got a chestful of medals awarded to him after we took Berlin. He stayed in OSS, worked in some kind of research group after OSS was broken up, then joined the CIA when it got started under Truman. Did great—became chief of a special branch of Covert Operations during the sixties. I used to work for him." Partridge laughed. "He got into hot water over some unauthorized projects."

"Assassinations," Culhane supplied.

"Well, yeah—that and some other things. You'd be surprised. You think you've got an imagination with your books and everything—that guy was something else. And after it all cooled down, he tried it again. Finally he had to leave. One hell of a career man, let me tell ya...."

Culhane stopped; Partridge stopped. They looked at each other. "You sound like you almost—"

"Admire him? Yeah," Partridge admitted. "Sometimes he was brilliant, but he also used all of us for his own purposes and U.S. policy be damned. Sure, sometimes that was all right—U.S. policy was fucked up. But it wasn't like that. It was like he had personal axes to grind, and he'd use Covert Operations to do it. Your brother worked for Steiglitz just before he was forced to resign. Nobody knows the extent of his contacts. Come on, I'll buy you an early lunch."

"I thought you liked to move while you talk."

"What I'm gonna tell you now, well, if you didn't already know it and listened, you'd think I was probably crazy. And if you did, so what? Besides, the Marine Corps doesn't only make men, it makes sore feet. Come on." Partridge gulped the rest of his cone, crunching it loudly as he started back toward the hotel.

Culhane had been in the restaurant before. The prices were too high, and the food wasn't all that great. But it was dark, quiet, and Partridge was paying. They'd driven over with the two remaining penguins, who now were at another table on the far side of the place.

Partridge sipped at a glass of white wine. "All I can drink. I used to really put it away—thought everybody had diarrhea in the morning, ya know? Anyway, now I go light."

Culhane picked up his glass—Smirnoff 100 vodka and grapefruit juice, a Salty Dog minus the salt. "If Jeff didn't trust talking to the CIA, even considering his longstanding friendship with you—" Culhane paused "—then why the hell should *I* trust the CIA?"

"Or me," Partridge concluded. "Very simple. What you tell me goes no further than myself and the deputy director, period. I'd say just me, but what happens if I die of a heart attack or something? You're left out in the cold, that's what. Always make a backup system—just like Sean Dodge does in your books. If you work with us, well, maybe we got a chance, maybe even you've got a chance of staying alive. If you don't, well, maybe you can get a retroactive family rate at the mortuary, huh? You'll wind up dead going against Steiglitz. And you got no choice but to go against him, 'cause he'll come after you. You're a loose end.''

"What—Steiglitz a traitor?"

"A traitor? Jeremiah Steiglitz? Wash your mouth out with soap, son. Hell, no. He's as anti-Commie as they come. Hates the Russians almost like it's something personal. During World War II he had an assignment working with a Russian agent—think it was the Cheka in those days—"

Culhane interrupted. "It was the Cheka, then the Gosudarstrenov Politicheskoe Upravlenie, and then it became the KGB, at the outbreak of World War Two. Its name changed a few more times, but eventually it ended up as the Committee for State Security—the KGB again."

"Yeah, well, anyway, Steiglitz arranged things so he could kill the Russian afterward."

"Sounds like a hell of a nice guy, Steiglitz does."

"Hey, I wouldn't do it, even if it was a Commie I got stuck working with. But that was Jeremiah Steiglitz. He's no traitor. Scratch that. This thing has nothin' to do with espionage. It's the Gladstone Log. What did Jeff tell you about it?"

"Nothing,'' Culhane said noncommittally.

"Nothing, my ass—but I'll tell you about it. You've heard of Gladstone—William Ewart Gladstone, prime minister of Great Britain from the late 1860s on and off until the mid-1890s. How about Ethyl Chillingsworth?"

Culhane said nothing; he didn't move a muscle. The waitress arrived with the main course, and Culhane moved his drink aside while she set down the plate with the steak he hadn't been able to get that morning. Partridge was eating prime rib. She asked if they wanted coffee. Culhane asked for Nescafé Decaffeinated, Partridge ordered another glass of wine. When she left, Partridge continued. "Ethyl is the real name—Ethyl Chillingsworth—of the dead woman, Evelyn Collingwood. At least Jeff thought that, and since she is dead, he was probably right about it. Especially if Steiglitz had his daughter kill her or cause her death. But anyway, Ethyl Chillingsworth was the grand-niece of Henry Chillingsworth."

"I've never heard of Henry Chillingsworth," Culhane said truthfully.

"No reason you should have. He was twelve or fourteen at the time, and he vanished along with about forty-two other men after leaving Nassau in the Bahamas for the return trip to England aboard the H.M.S. *Madagascar* on July 9, 1885."

"What's all this got—"

"That's what this whole thing is all about. See, Henry Chillingsworth apparently didn't die along with all the others aboard the *Madagascar*. And Ethyl Chillingsworth inherited what might be the logbook of the *Madagascar*."

"The Gladstone Log," Culhane said slowly.

"Exactly," Partridge said through a mouthful of food and wine. "I did some homework on it." He wiped his hands on his napkin, poured some more wine down his throat and reached into his inside left breast pocket, producing a small notebook. He started flipping through the pages, Culhane watching intently. "Okay, a guy named Ignatius Donnelly—remember the name. Born in Philadelphia in 1831. Passed the bar at age twenty-two. Became what they call an Atlantologist. Wrote a book called *Atlantis, the Antediluvian World*, among others. Wrote thirteen theses about Atlantis. Today not much of it holds any water." Partridge laughed. "You know—water—a sunken continent—" But Culhane didn't laugh. "Anyway, this Donnelly guy hit the lecture circuit. William Gladstone would have been in his second period in the prime minister's job when Donnelly's book was published in 1882. And Gladstone, like a lot of other people, got hooked on the idea. Gladstone got himself so hooked that he decided England should find Atlantis once and for all. He went to Parliament and asked for funds to launch an expedition. They put the kibosh on the idea—that's all historical record."

"But apparently," Culhane said, finishing his food and lighting a cigarette, "that didn't deter Gladstone."

"Well, see, everybody thought it had. But your brother dug up something that seems to indicate a group of private investors put up the dough—some guys just as hot for this Atlantis deal as Gladstone. They sort of rented the expedition, so to speak. Ethyl comes along in 1943 with this logbook of the *Madagascar*, and she's a WAC working in London where Steiglitz is based for the OSS. She meets Steiglitz— always a good-looking guy—and he was just about her age, though I think he was born thirty-five. Anyway, she goes gaga over him. That much is on record, too— OSS operatives who spent as much time behind enemy lines as Steiglitz did were kept pretty close tabs on in case they tried turning into doubles and working for the Axis. She gave him the first few pages of the Log to translate—it's in Latin, we figure. He translated it and tried to kill her to get the rest of it. But there was an air raid, and in the end she got away from him. We learned that later; we thought he'd killed her. Steiglitz figured nobody knew about the murder attempt, but he was wrong. It was assumed that he tried to kill Ethyl for sex-related reasons, and since he was too important to lose, the OSS let it go—covered up the assault. Steiglitz went on, no other bad reports, got all those medals and kept right on being great in the CIA. But that woman who died in Ventner, Georgia, last night had Ethyl's fingerprints. So—''

''So how do you know all this? And why didn't Steiglitz cover it up later when he was in the CIA?''

''Ohh, he did,'' Partridge said and smiled. ''He did, but he couldn't cover up the stuff the British Secret Intelligence Service and Naval Intelligence had. I'm sure he tried, though.'' Partridge downed the contents of his coffee cup in one long gulp. ''Your brother was digging through some stuff in London and he discovered the dope on Ethyl Chillingsworth. Well, he remembered some things I'd told him about the days I worked for Steiglitz and from the short time he had worked for Steiglitz. Jeff was always a good researcher, and he came up with—''

''What killed him,'' Culhane said flatly.

Partridge exhaled loudly, nodding his head, licking his lips. ''Yeah, that's what he did all right. And he found this in the British archives.'' Partridge tapped his breast pocket. ''He had it sent to me in the diplomatic pouch. God knows how he got permission to copy it, or if he did, or how he got it through all the State Department channels without one of Steiglitz's old buddies finding it.'' Partridge reached into the pocket and produced an envelope. ''Here—keep this, read it, give it back to me later. It's a copy of a partially burned manuscript page photographed in Steiglitz's room in 1943 on the night he tried to murder Ethyl.''

Culhane couldn't help it. He laughed. ''All this crap over finding Atlantis? So stupid.''

''Hey, wait a minute. I'm ahead of you, I think. Most modern researchers agree that if anything sparked old Plato, and those Egyptian priests who told it to somebody who told it to Plato, Atlantis was really the island of Thera in the Mediterranean and some kind of tidal wave—''

"A tsunami," Culhane said.

"Yeah, whatever it was—"

"No," Culhane corrected, feeling he must be sounding like M.F. Mulrooney at this point. "There was a volcanic eruption on Thera—one of tremendous magnitude—and the end result was a tidal wave. Some researchers think the sudden upheaval in the level of the Mediterranean might have caused a sudden drop in the level of the Red Sea at just the time Moses was leading the Israelites across to escape the pharaoh's armies."

"Yeah," Partridge said. "I saw the movie—man, Heston and Brynner were great! Don't make movies like that anymore."

Culhane nodded. "A fine movie. Anyway, Thera was all but wiped out by the eruption, which sunk most of it."

"Right. So if there ever was an Atlantis, it should be in the Mediterranean, right?"

"Right," Culhane agreed.

"Trouble was, the *Madagascar* didn't go anywhere near the Mediterranean. The expedition was moving on some kind of information—private information. Information we have no knowledge about, at least not now. It was all top secret."

"But you said Parliament killed the idea of the expedition."

"They did, so Gladstone either went to private investors or was approached by some, like I said. On the hush-hush, they leased the use of the H.M.S. *Madagascar* and two other ships, got Henry Chillingsworth's uncle to captain the thing—got him on detached duty from the Royal Navy or the Admiralty or whatever they call it. Got up a crew of old Royal Navy personnel and merchant seamen. We know the *Madagascar* and the other two ships sailed due west from England to one of the islands just off the coast of Georgia. We're not sure which one. From there they went to Nassau, where some private dispatches were sent. They left the Bahamas, heading south, and were gone five months. Only the *Madagascar* returned. It took on supplies in Nassau—just the usual stuff, we think. And Captain Chillingsworth was given a dispatch, we guess, based on the earlier information he had sent back five months before. We know Chillingsworth made a big stink about leaving his nephew behind—the cabin boy, Henry. Word was, no dice: every crew member was to report back to London for debriefing. Captain Chillingsworth reportedly feared a mutiny aboard the *Madagascar*. Still no dice. The *Madagascar* left Nassau on July 9 and was never seen again. There was a violent storm the night after it left—and it wasn't the hurricane season. And yeah, it was passing through the Bermuda Triangle, but that's a lot of crap.''

Culhane said nothing.

"It was eventually presumed the *Madagascar* went down with all hands. But since Ethyl had the Log from her great-uncle, either Henry and maybe some others survived the wreck, or Captain Chillingsworth did what I would have done and said to hell with orders and left the kid in Nassau on the sly. No one knew.''

Culhane still held the envelope in his hands, not opening it. "You had this—why the hell didn't anybody do anything in the forties, or even right after the war?''

"Once you look at that manuscript fragment, you'll see why. Sounds like whoever wrote it was bonkers. And nobody in the OSS, U.S. Naval Intelligence, British SIS, or British Naval Intelligence had any access to the files on the *Madagascar*, or any knowledge of Henry Chillingsworth or his uncle, the captain of the *Madagascar*. There was nothing to connect it to until Jeff started digging.''

Culhane stubbed out his cigarette. "And just what the hell—" his voice was trembling and he didn't know why "—and just what the hell did my brother find out?"

Partridge waved the waitress over. "You got ice cream?"

"Yes, sir." The woman smiled. She was pretty enough, Culhane noticed absently. "Chocolate, vanilla and butter pecan."

"Gimme three scoops of chocolate." Partridge looked at Culhane. "Want some ice cream? Good ice cream here."

Culhane shook his head. "No, thanks."

"Would you like more coffee, sir, or care for another drink?"

"No," Culhane said. "Thanks." He smiled back at the waitress.

"And I'll get you some more coffee to have with your ice cream, sir," she said to Partridge.

Partridge grinned.

The waitress left.

"What the hell did my brother find?" Culhane pressed.

Partridge looked after the waitress, then turned his eyes to Culhane's. "For the past forty years, Steiglitz has been pursuing Ethyl Chillingsworth. He finally caught up with her the other night. Presumably to get the Log. He had feelers out for her everywhere with all the friendly intelligence communities, other federal agencies, some of the large urban police departments—for her and for anyone related to her. And Jeff checked into that part."

"What part?"

"The relations. She had a father and mother."

"We all did."

"Hers got killed in 1953. A fire consumed their whole house—started in their bedroom under their bed. That was right after Steiglitz got back from Europe. In 1961, Ethyl's younger brother, who'd been living under an assumed name in New York, was the victim of a fatal mugging. In 1968, Ethyl's kid sister was the victim of a rapist murderer in Iowa. The sister was married, but before that she had lived under an assumed name. And then, of course, Ethyl herself puts the clincher on it. For years, no record of Ethyl Chillingsworth. Never turned up after that night in 1943 when Steiglitz tried to kill her. But Jeff sorted that out, too. It was some kind of reference, maybe a tip—I don't know what—but it somehow led him to the name Evelyn Collingwood. And sure enough, the dame was wearin' Ethyl's fingerprints. Your brother discovered the granddaddy of all conspiracies—all over some damn Gladstone Log.''

When the waitress came back, Josh Culhane changed his mind and ordered another Salty Dog minus the salt.

CHAPTER FOURTEEN

She punched the touch-tone buttons again and listened as the connection was made. There was no answer at the house on Lake Lanier. She let it ring twenty-four times, then hung up.

Mulrooney turned her attention back to the television set and to the VCR's digital clock. The news would be on soon.

She picked up the telephone again, dialing a different number than Culhane's, squirming her blue-jeaned legs under her into a squat on the couch. The number rang twice before the switchboard operator answered.

"Give me Jeffers at the City Desk."

The phone clicked, clicked again, then there was more ringing. After five rings, it was picked up. "City Desk, Jeffers."

"Bill—M.F. How're ya doin'?"

"Fine, sweetheart, and you?" the whiskey voice cracked back through the receiver.

"Fine, Billy. Hey, did anything interesting happen in Ventner last night or around—"

He cut her off. "You want a list? Home of the local librarian broken into and ransacked. The library ransacked—maybe eight thousand bucks in books destroyed, plus an old Bible insured for a thousand dollars. Security guard at the Civic Center where the library was, was murdered after he'd emptied his gun into somebody. No other bodies though. Then they find the librarian's body in a construction site. She impaled herself on something after she did a swan dive—looks like from the top floor or so."

Mulrooney lit a cigarette and rearranged her legs under her so she was kneeling. "Anything else exciting happen last night? Sounds like you guys were busy."

"Two fires in Atlanta, good sized, one of them maybe arson. Up in Elberton, the GBI busted a bunch of guys in a hearse loaded with cocaine on the way in from the coast. Chemical spill in a little town near Savannah—no injuries, just a lot of scared people. And a kind of funny-looking automobile accident near Helen and Cornelia. I can read it off the wire for you if you want—any of this stuff."

Her guts started to churn. She didn't know why. "Tell me about the auto accident. What's funny about it?"

"Looks like maybe somebody got deliberately run off the road. Holes in what's left of the car could have been bullet holes. The cops put a lid on the thing real quick. The driver's name was—hey, maybe he's related to your old boyfriend the paperback writer."

"Culhane?"

"Yeah, name was Jeff Culhane. Worked for—what the hell was it—some West Virginia-based computer-software outfit. Don't remember the name."

Mulrooney stared into the telephone receiver, inhaling on her cigarette. "Thanks for the info, Billy. Give you a tip if you don't say who gave it to you."

"I got a pencil. Shoot, sweetheart," the whiskey voice came back.

"Jeff Culhane was an ex-Green Beret, and he worked for the Central Intelligence Agency. Be good, Billy," she said and hung up.

She inhaled on the Salem again, then tried Josh Culhane's house on Lake Lanier once more. This time she let the phone ring thirty times.

She stood up.

There was a mirror on the far side of the room, and she looked at herself, at the old shirt half out of the faded Levi's, the house slippers, her unmadeup face. She looked at the coffee table, at the Latin dictionary, the yellow legal pad and the old leather-bound book. The Gladstone Log.

"Can't let him see me like this," she told the mirror. She strode her long legs into the bedroom.

CHAPTER FIFTEEN

They were on their way back to the funeral home, where his car, the white Trans Am, was still parked unless it had been towed away by now. Culhane sat beside Partridge in the back seat of the Lincoln Town Car and opened the envelope. The copy was a Xerox or a Xerox of photographs, but it was legible when he held it at the right angle to the light coming through the venetian blind that covered the rear window of the Lincoln.

"We think it's a kind of introduction to the actual log of the H.M.S. *Madagascar*, written by Henry Chillingsworth himself," Partridge said. "And this is Steiglitz's translation into English, very literal no doubt."

Culhane said nothing and began to read. The first few lines were missing.

And so when my uncle, Captain Miles Ridgeway Chillingsworth, my father's youngest brother and always my hero from when first I was given to meet him, presented me with my father's approval that I go to sea with him on a scientific expedition to search for the Lost Continent of Atlantis of which I had read in my study of Plato in the Greek, I was smitten with joy.

"I think you're right about the translation," Culhane remarked, then read on.

And when I assumed my duties as cabin boy aboard Her Majesty's Ship Madagascar, I was thrice fortunate indeed to win early the friendship of the First Mate, Mister Fife, his friendship greatly easing some of the arduous tasks that lay before me in the pursuance of my duty, and his friendship—Sweet Jesus, his dear soul—accounting my survival to write these words. Mister Fife, I learned soon, was not only aboard as an excellent First Mate, but as our guide once we reached the island off the Georgia coastal waters, for only he survived of those who had first found the map, which was to eventually lead to such devilish terror. It was he, too, who had first seen the demon skull that was to be our undoing during the strong winds that seemed to arise from the bowels of the ocean itself to claim the mutineers. I cannot write these words without recalling that brave visage of my Uncle Miles when he charged Fife with somehow saving me as we were bound and made to watch as our mutinous crew prepared to perpetrate the unthinkable. My dear uncle was raised up, his bootless feet kicking high and wide like a rider unhorsed, his face purpling, the demon skull bound into his hands and his hands bound in front of his bloodied coat, and as his neck snapped with a crack like thunder I screamed—damn their souls to Satan! The demon skull in his hands shattered against his own dear face.

Mister Fife and I were able to break free. There was a longboat at hand and we took to this, I helping as best my young arms could to lower it into the boiling ocean waters. There were curses and shouts of rage and epithets of foul deeds to befall us, but Mister Fife heaved to his oars and I held the tiller fast against the rocking of the waves. For the longest while the storm raged and lightning crackled. The Madagascar heaved up as if lifted by some demonic hand, and the hull cracked in two and there was fire on the water. Soon the Madagascar vanished under the waves, and all their mutinous souls and the cruelly abused body of my uncle, Captain Miles Ridgeway Chillingsworth, were gone from this world. It was thence how I came to the island of San Rafael, Mister Fife with his dying breaths hauling me on his strong back out of the surf there and onto the sand after our boat was washed under the waves as well. He died there in my young and trembling arms, my hands white with the fear of it all, the kind monks about me who afterward raised me as their foundling child. It was the expedition that brought this all to pass, and its story must be set down here that I may cleanse myself of—

The rest was charred and illegible.

"This doesn't make sense. Steiglitz would have known they couldn't have found Atlantis. And what the hell is this 'demon skull' he talks about?"

"I don't know," Partridge answered cheerfully.

"That Mr. Fife sounds like—"

"A brave man," Partridge finished.

"Yeah. Why did you give me this?"

"Steiglitz will know Jeff had to have learned something. He probably figures that any way you cut it, you're gonna wind up on San Rafael."

"Where's San Rafael?"

"In your favorite spot, the Bermuda Triangle. But you probably don't worry about stuff like—"

"What's this other island—and this map? The place where they found the skull?" Culhane interrupted.

"We don't know. We're trying to figure that one out, too, and I don't think Steiglitz knows, either. Otherwise, why bother with wanting the Gladstone Log?"

"But based on what's here. . . ." Culhane said slowly. "Geez—there's no way Steiglitz would spend forty years. . . . This Henry Chillingsworth could have been a nut himself, could have been a would-be science-fiction writer or something."

"Yeah," Partridge nodded. "Maybe it tied in with something he'd already heard about, maybe something he picked up on while he was in OSS. God knows. But you've gotta find out, Mr. Culhane. Like in the Westerns, to avenge your brother. And to stay alive yourself. It's the only way you will."

"You're out of your tree. If Steiglitz expects me there, he'll—"

"Yeah, well, you're a resourceful guy. Otherwise he'll track you down. But if he figures you know something maybe he doesn't know, he'll want to keep you alive until he finds out what it is."

Culhane lit another cigarette, the car slowing, the funeral-home parking lot in view. His car was still there. "Why didn't that work with Jeff?"

"Got a point there," Partridge said. "Maybe he'll just try to kill you outright. But I'm betting he won't. Going to San Rafael will keep you alive—at least long enough to get there and do some looking around. And we can't do a thing to stop Steiglitz until we know why he wants the Gladstone Log. He may already have it. But maybe not. Maybe you can get it. Try it and maybe it'll work, Mr. Culhane. And maybe we'll know what the *Madagascar* found a hundred years ago."

"Atlantis?" Culhane laughed. "Demon skulls and mysterious maps? What a pile of crap!"

"I don't know what they found, but it was important enough to Steiglitz for him to spend forty years on one chase, to kill probably a lot more people than we imagine. Will you go to San Rafael for us—and for yourself?"

The Lincoln stopped. Culhane closed his eyes, then slowly opened them to stare at the building where his brother's body would soon be lying after the autopsy.

"Yes. After the funeral I'll go to San Rafael. I don't know what it is I'm supposed to look for."

"It won't be as hard as you think—at least at first. There's nothing there now but an abandoned monastery—oh, and some kind of radio-transmitting station, but it's very small and away from the monastery. Nothing else—no town or harbor or anything." Partridge leaned forward to one of his two cronies in the front seat, the man on the passenger side. "Fred, check out Mr. Culhane's car to see that it doesn't have any explosive surprises."

Then he turned to Culhane. "Welcome aboard."

Culhane looked at Partridge. "Bullshit." And he stepped out of the car, handing back the translation pages.

"I'll keep in touch."

Culhane turned away from the Lincoln and tracked after Fred the penguin toward the Trans Am.

CHAPTER SIXTEEN

It was late in the afternoon. His brother was being buried at eleven the next day; he'd stopped at the funeral home to check before getting into his car. There were still ten pages to do in Takers number seventeen. He hadn't slept in almost thirty-six hours.

He pulled into his driveway but couldn't get all the way in; a car blocked his way. A dead brother, an undoubtedly angry editor, a trip to an island in the middle of nowhere to find information about some comic-book adventure and now Mulrooney's yellow Mustang.

Culhane realized he was smiling. He was almost glad to see her.

He let himself out of the Trans Am and started across the driveway, up the stepped walkway to the porch and across the porch to the front door. In case it wasn't only Mulrooney, he pulled the Detonics Scoremaster from the shoulder holster under his burned and stained bomber jacket, his left hand hurting a little where it had been burned.

He started to insert his key, but the door opened under his hand.

"Hi!"

Culhane realized he had the .45 pointed at Mulrooney's abdomen. "You forgot I drove a yellow Mustang," she said with a smile.

"No," he told her. "As a matter of fact, I hadn't."

"Good." She smiled again, her green eyes sparkling.

"I thought I might have some other company, that's all," he explained and looked down at the .45, suddenly feeling very awkward, suddenly feeling very frightened that he'd almost killed her. He'd automatically thumbed down the safety as he leveled the pistol.

"I heard about your brother. I'm so sorry, Josh. I, uh. . . ." She was dressed up, he realized: high heels, a blue dress with white dots and a white sailor collar with blue dots, a white tie at the front of the V-shaped neckline. Her overall image was softness, and he wanted to hold her. He didn't. "Do you have any idea who. . . ."

He didn't want to lie to her; they had never done that. "Some theories, maybe. . . ."

"I let myself in with my key. Discovered I still had it."

"I'm surprised you could find it." He eyed the maroon leather shoulder bag on the hall table. He stepped in through the doorway.

"Well, even if I didn't have it—" she smiled again "—you always said I was the best amateur lock picker around."

"Yeah." He nodded. "I did." And he walked past her a little, setting the Detonics on the table beside her purse, starting to skin out of his leather jacket.

"What happened to you?" he heard her say, not looking at her, feeling her hand against the left side of his neck and his left ear.

"My brother was, uh, he was on—" Culhane turned around toward her, licking his dry lips, watching her eyes "—on fire and—"

"Your hand."

"It's fine. His car went over the, uh, the embankment, and it caught fire. Big fallacy in movies and books like I write—cars don't always explode and catch on fire when they do a nosedive, you know, but, uh, but his did and he was on fire and I knocked him down to the ground and tried putting the fire out and—"

Culhane closed his eyes and felt her arms folding around him. He lowered his head and felt the softness of her hair against his forehead. "I'm home—for as long as you need me," he heard her whisper. He couldn't say anything. His throat was tight. But he held her close against him. . . .

The "being honest with each other" thing again. He sat on the kitchen stool beside the counter with a cup of coffee she'd made him, the coffee laced with brandy. She sat on the stool opposite him, the counter between them. "Why'd you come? Not to offer condolences—I mean, I'm glad you came, but—"

"A thing I'm working on. I need your help. I was going to come anyway, before I heard about Jeff, but then it just seemed. . . well, I came. But I meant what I told you back in the hall before we closed the door."

"I know you did," he said, looking at her. He let out his breath in a long, almost whistling sound and lit a Pall Mall. He lit a Salem at the same time and passed it over to her.

She nodded, murmured her thanks and inhaled.

Culhane watched her. "We were always fighting."

"Yeah, we sure were," she said, exhaling. "I don't see that stopping, do you?"

"No," he answered abruptly, his mind starting on another train of thought, then coming back.

"Wanna live together for a while until we have another big one? I've been thinking about you on and off a lot. No kidding." She laughed a little.

"Yeah. . . well. . . yeah—"

"You don't want to. Gotcha, Josh," she said, and started to stand up.

Culhane reached across to her nearest shoulder and pushed her down. "It's not that. There's something I have to do after they bury Jeff tomorrow."

"Ever notice that? It's always 'they bury.' Never 'I bury' or 'we bury,' it's always 'they bury.' "

"Yeah," he said. "Look, Fanny...." He was the only person who called her that, and he didn't think she liked it, but she never said anything about it. The one thing they never fought over.

"Something to do with Jeff, right? Got some macho crap to do because they murdered your brother? You see, I know about the bullet holes in the car and everything."

He looked away from her, studying the glowing tip of his cigarette, and looked back at her face, into her eyes. "Then you know why you can't stay here."

"Hey—" She reached inside her purse on the counter beside her, rummaged through its contents, came up with the little stainless Model 60 Smith he'd given her, holding it between thumb and forefinger by the grip panels and friction. "I'm ready for anything."

"Yeah. And I liked that quick draw, too, babe."

"Check this out," she said, setting the gun down, the muzzle toward him, and plowing through her purse again. Culhane turned the revolver around so the barrel pointed toward the end of the counter and not at either of them. "Here." She handed him a water-stained, ripped-open manila envelope. "Look at the postmark and the date."

He read the postmark and he read the date.

He didn't say anything.

"You're the only person I can trust with this. I don't know what it is. It might be nothing—some crackpot's idea of a joke—but maybe it's the biggest thing that ever happened to me—at least besides...but it might."

"Who'd you get it from, Fanny?"

"A woman—Ethyl something. You know me, I'm bad with names," she said, stubbing out her cigarette. And she reached into the purse, pulling out an old-looking leather-bound book. "She called it the Gladstone Log."

He touched it, not opening it.

"It's in Latin. You're good with languages. I took Latin in high school and almost flunked the second year. I need it translated, Josh."

Culhane sighed. He looked at the Rolex. Maybe he could stay awake long enough. "Make a pot of coffee, then keep me company while I take a shower. We can talk. It'll wake me up enough to start to translate the thing."

"I brought my Latin dictionary. It's in the car."

"Terrific, Fanny," Culhane groaned, and started unbuttoning his shirt.

MULROONEY HAD REBANDAGED HIS LEFT HAND, using the tube of ointment the emergency-room doctor had prescribed that Culhane had picked up on the way to the house after leaving the funeral home. She had read him the letter from Ethyl Chillingsworth. But Culhane hadn't told her about Partridge yet, or the additional information Partridge had given him regarding Steiglitz.

He sat on the parquet floor, his shoes off, his legs stretched out under the coffee table, his toes almost able to touch the edge of the bearskin rug. He'd shot the big brown bear on Kodiak Island with his .44 magnum revolver almost a year ago when the animal, aroused—"horny," the guide had called it—had charged them.

On the table beside him was a blue-and-white floral pattern soup cup, an eight-inch-square amber glass ashtray already containing more than a half-dozen butts, his own Cassell's Latin dictionary, a pocket-size Collins Latin Gem dictionary and volumes one and two of an interlinear translation of Ovid's *Metamorphoses* just in case a truly esoteric construction had to be dug for.

More quickly than he'd thought he could, he had

translated the first few pages of the book, duplicating Steiglitz's work, which was excellent. Chillingsworth was vastly more proficient in Latin than Culhane would have imagined; it was almost as if he worked with the language day in and day out. A monk's life, or at least the company of monks to a boy already schooled in Classical Greek, was the only way to achieve such intimacy with the language, he conjectured.

But the use of the Latin had a classical rather than an ecclesiastical flavor to it, Culhane determined as he worked.

He was several pages beyond Steiglitz's work and, he conjectured, beyond what Steiglitz had ever seen.

Culhane looked behind him on the couch. Mulrooney was lying there, her eyes open but tired looking, her legs tucked up under her dress. A weary smile crossed her lips as she noticed him watching her. "Can't I help? I mean, more than pouring coffee and emptying the ashtray?"

Culhane glanced at the Rolex; it was after eleven. He didn't even want to think of how many hours he'd been up. He stubbed out a half-smoked Pall Mall.

"Okay, Fanny, I'll whip some Latin on you." He picked up the book and read from the page he'd just worked on.

" 'The picture writing on the walls there in this weird, tomblike temple was beyond ordinary belief and the poor powers of my description. Creatures neither human nor animal, both, yet neither at once, adorned bizarre inscriptions made of smaller, letterlike symbols. These were a bafflement to us all. And still more of the strange illustrations were everywhere. Bizarre ships, which somehow seemed to be represented among many of the constellations of the stars in Heaven that

Mister Fife had so kindly taught me at night aboard the Madagascar. One scene, which so much perplexed us all, was of these inhuman figures seated like men inside one of these strange ships, more of the poorly drawn constellations about them, as though the ship sailed like the moon and the clouds among the very stars.' ''

He looked up halfway down the page. She was asleep. Culhane set to more translating.

MULROONEY OPENED HER EYES, her shoulders and legs stiff. Her neck ached, too. She was in Culhane's arms beside him on the floor. Culhane's head rested on the head of the Kodiak grizzly he'd shot, and her head was on Culhane's right shoulder.

She sat up, a little cold as she did so, leaving his warmth.

She folded her arms across her chest, hugging herself and briskly rubbing her upper arms. Then she reached down with both hands as she tucked her knees up nearly to her chin to pull her skirt down from where it had twisted and bunched at her hips. She covered her legs with it.

Her mouth was dry and tasted of too many cigarettes.

Mulrooney could have looked at the read-out on Culhane's VCR, but instead she leaned back and across him, raising his left arm to get the time from the watch on his wrist as she had always done when they had lived together, slept together.

It was nearly eight-fifteen. She could let Culhane sleep for a while longer. His brother's funeral wasn't until eleven, and he wouldn't need to be at the funeral home until a little after ten.

She yawned and stood up, her feet cold as she stepped off the fur and onto the parquet floor.

"Brrr," she murmured, walking on tiptoes across the room to the closet just above the three stairs leading down into the living room. She opened the closet door. Culhane's other leather bomber jacket was hung up there, and she took it down from the hanger and pulled it across her shoulders, hugging it to her.

She closed the door and started down the stairs and back across the room toward the kitchen. He'd need coffee when she woke him, and she needed some now.

She started the teakettle, deciding to make a cup at a time. The coffeepot was still dirty from the previous evening, and Mulrooney was in no mood to wash dishes; she rarely was, she reflected. She searched the refrigerator, then opened the freezer compartment above and took out a can of frozen orange juice and set it on the counter.

She walked back into the living room and picked up the coffee cups. On the coffee table were Culhane's wire-rimmed glasses he was so vain about wearing and the yellow legal pad she'd brought in with her dictionary, its pages now filled with handwriting. She picked up the pad, glanced once at Culhane—he was sleeping like a little boy, peaceful looking, she thought—and returned to the kitchen.

She made one cup of Nescafé and started to read the translation, reading what she assumed were the first few pages of the Log, about how Henry Chillingsworth was asked to be cabin boy of the *Madagascar* by his uncle, Captain Miles Ridgeway Chillingsworth, about his friendship with the first mate, a man named Fife. She stopped reading and pondered the idea of the map and the demon skull. Had they actually found a map to Atlantis and the remains of one of its inhabitants? She shook her head; Thera in the Mediterranean almost certainly was Atlantis. Had they found perhaps some other lost civilization? Was that why the record of the discovery was in Latin, in order to confine the knowledge to scholars rather than those more obviously ignorant or mercenary?

"Orange juice," she said out loud, remembering the can still on the counter. She set down the pages and rinsed a brown pitcher, then squeezed the can until the still-frozen juice slipped into the pitcher.

As she poured in the first can of water and took a plastic spoon to break up the chunks of concentrate, she tried to think what would have made relatively sophisticated men of one hundred years ago label remains as a "demon skull." Maybe it had horns, she thought.

She finished making the juice, then poured some milk into her coffee. She sipped the warm drink and decided to watch Culhane sleep. It was better than reading his notes.

THEY HAD BOTH NEEDED A SHOWER ANYWAY, and Culhane had convinced her—not having had to try very hard at all—that water conservation was important. She had scrubbed his back and other parts, and she was in his arms, the warm water bathing his face more than he liked as he bent to kiss her left shoulder.

"So poor Ethyl didn't have the Log after all," Mulrooney panted in his left ear.

"No—poor Ethyl," Culhane told her, kissing her neck, getting a mouthful of water, feeling her fingers against his crotch.

"What's this? My God, it's growing!"

"The water does it—hydroponics."

"Or hydro*penics*."

"Hmm," he mumbled, kissing her behind her left ear, getting more water in his face. "No, all she had— you taste good, you know that?"

"I never tasted myself."

Culhane drew her closer to him, almost an impossibility. "All Ethyl had was the personal memoir of

Henry Chillingsworth. All it does is recount some things about the trip—some really bizarre stuff. You'll have to read the rest of it."

"What kind of bizarre stuff?"

"The constellations appearing misshapen in wall drawings, nonhuman creatures depicted in ships flying through the stars—things like that. He never gave any real details, though—at least not as far as I've gotten. I got the impression—ouch! Watch the nails, huh?"

"Sorry," she said. He didn't think she was really sorry at all.

"But I got the impression—that's better—the impression that he was afraid to give details, afraid somebody'd use his memoir as a means of finding whatever the hell the *Madagascar* found. Maybe I'll know more when I get a chance to finish it. He talks a lot about the night the *Madagascar* went down and reaching San Rafael Island."

"Where you said you're going. I'm coming, too."

"I'm not letting you get yourself killed."

"Even if we ever got married, I would never let you tell me what to do. It's a free country and I've got a passport." She moved her hands from where they were.

"Fanny—"

"The water's turning cold."

"No, it isn't. I don't want you getting killed. This Steiglitz Ethyl talked about—I think his people killed Jeff and will probably be after me once I hit San Rafael."

"Great—but I'll be there anyway."

"All right," he agreed. "All right—but you do what I say once we get there, okay?"

Her hands came back to do what they had been doing—only better. He assumed she agreed, but Culhane reflected that he had, on some previous occasions, made dumb assumptions.

"So, what else did he talk about?" Mulrooney murmured.

"Well, ohh...don't stop that—he...ahh—he talked about—yeah—how he joined the monks and stayed with them there on San Rafael until he was in his fifties—that's about 1920 or so. The monastery was being closed down, and the monks that were still alive were going back to Spain. But he went to America, found his younger brother's family somehow and went to live with them. I guess he'd kept in touch with his brother over the years by letter. He doesn't explain it, or he hasn't yet."

"So this is a washout. Oh, I don't mean this—" and Culhane felt her hands leave him, then come back "— I mean the whole diary or whatever it is."

"No, it's just the opposite. Miles Chillingsworth, the captain, gave Henry the Log when it looked like the mutineers would take over the *Madagascar*. He figured maybe somehow the boy would survive and so would the record, I guess. And Henry pinpoints where he actually hid the Log, assuming it hasn't rotted away or dried to dust in a hundred years."

"When do we leave?"

"I have to make reservations—I hope tonight, or maybe even late this afternoon."

"I've got enough clothes here if you'll lend me a suitcase."

"Yeah, I'll lend you a suitcase."

"Come here," she whispered, and he felt her hands at work again.

They stood there in the shower, her back against the side of the stall, Mulrooney standing on her toes, Culhane holding her up that way, tight against her, the water not yet running cold. They moved together, but they weren't dancing.

CHAPTER SEVENTEEN

Josh Culhane, his throat tight, Fanny Mulrooney holding his left hand so hard that it hurt, heard the small organ's shrill playing. He murmured under his breath, his throat tightening more, "Amazing grace, how sweet the sound, that saved a wretch like me. I once was lost, but now I'm found, was blind but now I see." And suddenly, very suddenly, he couldn't see the casket. The casket and the flowers around it washed away as he closed his eyes, Mulrooney's hands moving up the length of his left arm, holding it tightly, her nails digging into his arm through the fabric of his dark blue three-piece suit, the only dark suit he owned. The Presbyterian minister was still speaking, saying that Jeffrey Alan Culhane had been loved by his friends and family—Josh Culhane was his only surviving family—and respected by his co-workers.

Culhane, tears still in his eyes, looked away from the minister and the coffin of his brother to the faces of the mourners. Was one of the faces Jeremiah Steiglitz? Was one of the women Sonia Steiglitz? He could see Partridge and the three penguins, this time in CIA-issue black suits with dark ties. He had told Mulrooney about the meeting with Partridge, about the whole thing with Steiglitz and the CIA, hoping to make her realize she shouldn't come with him to 26°15' north latitude, 74°30' west longitude—San Rafael Island in the Caribbean, smack in the Bermuda Triangle. But Culhane should have known better, he realized; the more he had told Mary Frances Mulrooney, the more it had intrigued her.

As they'd driven to the funeral home—she had taken them in her Mustang—she'd rambled on about Atlantis, supercivilizations of the past, all the funny things that happen in the Bermuda Triangle, demon skulls, ancient maps.

And after the funeral was concluded, they would return to the house to pack, then fly to Nassau, from there moving out into the Caribbean to San Rafael and the Gladstone Log. After the funeral. . . .

Swallowing hard, his throat aching, his eyes burning, he stared at the gray coffin.

"Ashes to ashes, dust to dust. . . ." Culhane had heard the words often. His mother and father—*their* mother and father. Friends. He had used the words in his books.

Other words, these whispered to him as he felt her breath on his face—"I love you, Josh"—and he watched later as the dirt he threw down from his right hand onto the coffin lid caught in the wind and some of it blew away.

FLOWERS, REAL ONES—poinsettias, purple bougainvillea, and others he couldn't identify—grew in manicured gardens of scarlet poinciana trees near the hotel entrance. The bellman ferried their luggage ahead of them, Mulrooney literally wide-eyed as Culhane watched her. "You stay in places like this all the time when you go boppin' around the world, Josh?"

Culhane shrugged and lit a cigarette, the bellman holding the door as they passed through into the lobby. The song "You Go to My Head" filtered in from a piano bar off to their right as they started across the lobby's maroon-and-gold carpets. Culhane looked at Mulrooney again, thinking the song's words were somehow never more right. "I've always found an expensive hotel isn't really much more expensive than a cheap one, all things considered. And relax—it's on me."

"Damn right it is. Women's lib is terrific except for the going dutch part," she said.

They registered, Mulrooney more wide-eyed still as they entered the small suite Culhane had reserved. "I'm going to go home and burn my apartment," she told him, setting her giant purse—more gigantic than the purses she usually carried—on the floral print bedspread. The bellman hung the two garment bags—one with Culhane's shirts and two summer-weight suits and the other with Mulrooney's dresses, skirts, slacks, and blouses—in the walk-in closet.

"Would the gentleman and madame prefer the air conditioning or to have the doors to the balcony opened? The height of this floor is such that insects would be of no concern."

"The balcony doors open, please. That'd be perfect," Culhane answered for them. Mulrooney, still in her black dress and pearls, sat on the edge of the bed and kicked off her high heels, crossing her long legs and rubbing the sole of her foot.

She was tugging off her earrings as Culhane tipped the bellman and chained the door after him. Culhane could see her reflection in a mirror in the sitting room as he turned away from the door. "Want a drink?" he sang out.

"No, I want more than one, but one'll do me for now," she called back.

Culhane slipped out of his shoes and walked in stocking feet across the sitting room to the small bar. It was white, like the louvered closet doors, the wood trim and molding of the room and the balcony furniture, making the green background of the sitting room's floral-print wallpaper seem even greener.

He reached up and pulled his dark blue silk crocheted tie to half mast and opened his collar button and vest. He remembered that Mulrooney liked rum drinks. He found some Myers's dark and opened the quart bottle, deciding that tonight they'd drink it straight, as he didn't feel like calling downstairs for

Coca-Cola or some other mixer. He grabbed two bourbon glasses. As he filled first one bourbon glass and then the other, he remembered that as a boy he'd always called these "Doc Holliday" glasses, seeing them for the first time when Kirk Douglas had portrayed the fast shooting, hard-drinking, consumptive dentist in one of the many film retellings of the O.K. Corral gunfight of October 26, 1881.

"Come and get it," Culhane called out.

"Wait a minute. I'm changing into something sexy for you."

"Great," he said, leaving her drink on the bar, gulping down part of the rum. It made a warm feeling in his throat and in the pit of his stomach. He refilled his glass and walked toward the white wicker easy chairs and white wicker sofa surrounding the glass coffee table.

He sat in one of the easy chairs, the cushions soft and comfortable after the airliner seats and the bouncy cab ride. He leaned his head back, stretched his legs out, and closed his eyes.

It had been a unique day, one he would never forget, he thought. He'd gotten back together with Fanny Mulrooney, something he had wanted since they'd agreed to part, despite his allergic reaction to her TV persona. He'd buried his brother—his twin—and a part of him was gone forever. And he had decided that however trite the idea, getting the man who'd gotten his brother was growing to proportions amounting to obsession.

His eyes were still closed when he heard her slippers slapping against the soles of her feet. "Well—so open your eyes and tell me I'm beautiful."

He opened his eyes. He saw her green eyes, her hair down and slightly past her shoulders, wavy ever since she'd gotten a permanent a year ago.

She wore a white nightgown that hung from her

shoulders on thin straps, the top of the gown lace trimmed, its whiteness stark against the honey of her bare shoulders and arms. A shoestring-thin white tie pulled the gown in around her waist and was knotted in a bow at the small of her back. She twirled once for him to look at her.

"You're beautiful—okay?"

"Thanks a whole lot."

Culhane stood up, taking her into his arms, drawing her close to him. "You're beautiful, Fanny." And he caught the hair in his fingers, pulling her head back, her eyes steady as he looked at her face, his face moving closer to hers, her lips parting slightly and he kissed her, his arms folding her more closely against him, feeling her hands move along his back. . . .

CULHANE BENT HIS HEAD, his lips touching the nipple of first her right breast, then her left, then he shifted his weight from her body, rolling onto his back, only the moonlight through the balcony doors of the bedroom giving the bed, Fanny Mulrooney beside him and even his own body recognizable shapes in the darkness.

His arm snaked around her and she rolled toward him, his hand stroking her neck, feeling her hair. And he could feel her breath against his chest when she whispered to him in the darkness, "If you ever say I said this, I'll deny it, but I never. . . well, since we, ahh. . . well. I just didn't."

"Shh," he told her, tilting her chin up so when he bent his face toward her, his lips could brush hers.

She whispered again in the darkness after a moment, "And don't tell me about you—'cause either way, I don't want to know, Josh."

"Shh," he told her, and kissed her again.

CHAPTER EIGHTEEN

At the hotel desk, they had been told the names of some of the more reputable charter-boat operators working out of Nassau Harbor and how to find them. As the cab took them dockside, Culhane had explained to Mulrooney that what they were looking for was a large sport-fishing boat, forty feet or better, something that could cruise comfortably at about twenty knots. If they could find such a craft for an overnight charter, perhaps for two nights, they could reach San Rafael in ten or eleven hours, lay over the first night offshore and explore the old monastery in daylight.

They walked along the marina now, smaller boats docked everywhere, their owners or sometimes small children hawking each as the best of the charter runners who knew the best places to fish for the best trophies. They kept walking, Mulrooney wearing a blue floral print sundress and white sandals, a huge blue canvas tote bag hanging from her left shoulder, Culhane watching the wind catch her hair.

They stopped. Culhane stabbed his hands into the side pockets of his white tennis shorts and rocked on his heels as he stared at the name on the stern of the big white boat: *Cherokee*.

"Like the Indians?" Mulrooney asked him.

"Like Cherokee Sound, more likely. It's off Great Abaco Island—north and a little east of here. We'll pass it on the way out to San Rafael." He stood by the sport fisherman's stern, seeing a face appear on deck and start toward the fighting chair. He always felt stupid shouting "Ahoy," so he called out, "Hey—aboard the *Cherokee*!"

The face—black, like most faces in the Bahamas—looked up, noncommittal. "Yeah?"

"I'm looking for Junius Grey."

"Wait a minute," the man called back, turning away from Culhane and Mulrooney and leaning against the gin pole rising vertically behind the fighting chair. "Hey, Jun—some folks heah to see ya, mon!"

The clerk at the hotel desk had described Junius Grey, captain of the *Cherokee*, as a big man, and if Culhane could get him, the best man in the harbor for taking on something besides fishing. And Junius Grey—at least Culhane assumed it was he—was indeed big. He was immense vertically—at least six feet five, maybe better than that—and laterally; his shoulders looked as though he wore football pads. But he wasn't. He was naked from the waist up and little more than naked from the waist down, his bikini-style swim trunks barely covering anything. His dark body glistened with sweat, making the muscles that were so prominent in his arms and legs seem to ripple all the more. Five-pound ham-sized hands held a greasy-looking rag, and he wiped his hands on the rag now as he came aft along the narrow portside deck, reaching out his left hand to the nearest vertical for the bridge ladder, then swinging down to the cockpit deck. He was missing the little finger of his left hand.

"I am Junius Grey," the man announced, white teeth suddenly dominating the lower portion of his face as he smiled broadly. His black hair—short, tightly curled, and wet with sweat—gleamed in the sunlight as the wind picked up, blowing across the marina.

"My name is Culhane, and this is Miss Mulrooney. We were told at our hotel that if I could hire you, you were the best man in the harbor for what I needed, where I wanted to go," Culhane told the man. Cupping his hands around the lighter's flame in the wind, Culhane lit a cigarette, then dropped lighter and cigarettes into his shorts pocket.

"It depends muchly on what you need, Mr.... Culhane, it was?"

"Culhane."

"And of course where you want to go."

"Want to talk about it?"

The big man shrugged, making his muscles ripple under the sun. "Yes, sure I want to talk about it." He turned to the first man they'd seen, skinny by comparison and more than a full head shorter, still leaning against the gin pole. "Ebenezer, help the gentleman and his lady aboard, and we will talk."

Culhane started climbing over the transom, reaching up for Mulrooney. The man called Ebenezer took her blue purse from her, then Mulrooney's full-skirted sundress ballooned up in a sudden gust of wind as she stepped over onto the gunwale. It gave Culhane a view he'd seen before and made Ebenezer smile; she wore no slip and no stockings, only light blue panties.

But then she was down on the deck beside him, her clothing under control, Junius Grey saying, "Why don't we go below to the salon. We can talk better there." Culhane only nodded, letting Mulrooney follow after Grey, he starting down after her.

Culhane stepped through the doorway into the salon and let the door swing to behind him, watching as Grey moved, stooped over, across to the far side by the small bar forward. There looked to be a head up there, and there was a gleaming stainless steel galley in the center. Grey suddenly seemed shorter, and Culhane realized the man was now sitting on a stool behind the bar. Grey opened a bottle of Coors beer.

"May I offer you and the lady some refreshment, Mr. Culhane?"

"How do you get Coors down here?" Culhane asked, feeling himself smiling. The portholes on the sides of the salon were open, a breeze ruffling the short brown café curtains framing them.

"With considerable difficulty, Mr. Culhane, considerable difficulty. Would you like some?"

"If you've got Michelob, I'd rather, but Coors would be fine."

"Michelob I have. And for the lady?" Grey asked, Culhane following his stare as Mulrooney sat on the settee. Culhane figured it opened into a bed.

"The lady'll have a beer," Mulrooney answered for herself. "Michelob or Coors—whatever you're pushing is fine."

Culhane walked over to the bar, took a bottle of Michelob for Mulrooney, moved over to the settee and handed it to her along with an inverted cone-shaped glass. He declined a glass for himself, taking a swallow of the Michelob from the bottle instead. He looked over at Mulrooney, who sat perched on the edge of the settee, her massive purse beside her, her skirt almost touching her ankles. She was lighting a cigarette.

Culhane looked at Junius Grey, who was watching him intently. "So, Mr. Culhane, Miss Mulrooney, where are you bound?"

Culhane found an ashtray, got rid of the ashes from his Pall Mall and sculpted a tip for the cigarette against the glass, then looked across the bar at Grey.

"To 26°15' north latitude, 74°30' west longitude."

"San Rafael Island. But the fishing isn't that good out there, Mr. Culhane."

"Doesn't bother me," Culhane told the man.

"I didn't think that it did, really. And the beach—for the young lady, the beach is really very poor for soaking up the sun."

"And that doesn't bother me," Mulrooney added from across the salon, exhaling a cloud of cigarette smoke as she spoke.

"No fishing, no sun on the beach. I only smuggle Coors beer and that's for myself alone, so I can't help you to smuggle drugs or other contraband. I am at a loss as to why you would wish to go to San Rafael Island."

"No mystery, really," Culhane lied. "I'm a writer. I write adventure novels. Miss Mulrooney is a writer, as well. We heard about the old monastery out there and wanted to check it out. I'm planning to set a novel I'm working on—part of it at least—in a place like San Rafael. Figured I'd be able to handle that section of the book better if I went there. Anyway, it'd give us a little while away from Nassau."

"If the seas are right, and the wind is right, and I keep her to maximum cruising speed, I can bring the *Cherokee* off San Rafael in maybe eleven hours, give or take a little."

"When would you be able to get under way if we agree on terms?" Culhane asked him.

"Not until late this afternoon, which would mean we wouldn't slip in until well after midnight. It's either that or leave first thing tomorrow morning. I run two four-hundred-horsepower diesels for the *Cherokee*, and the starboard clutch has been giving me some trouble." Grey smiled, wiping his hands on the rag again, then taking another pull of the Coors. "That's what I was doing when Ebenezer called me aft—cleaning a clutch plate up there on the foredeck."

Culhane looked at Mulrooney. Her eyes said something, but he wasn't sure what.

"We'd be out two nights then," Culhane told Grey, "if we leave this afternoon. And Miss Mulrooney and I can explore San Rafael tomorrow during daylight."

"Two nights—and a round trip of maybe twenty-four hours' running time for the *Cherokee*. I'll supply the booze—I can buy it cheaper," Grey added, scribbling with a pencil on a blue note pad.

He ripped off the top sheet, wrote something on the next sheet, drew a circle around it and pushed the pad around one hundred eighty degrees, shoving it across the bar to Culhane.

It was the price. "That's American dollars I quoted in," Grey said.

Culhane studied it, then reached for the pencil. "May I?"

"Sure," Grey said, his eyes laughing.

Culhane drew an X through the price, cut two hundred fifty dollars from it and wrote that figure down, circled it, then passed the pad and pencil back to Grey.

"Hmm—you've hired boats before?"

Culhane lit another cigarette and nodded.

"I will split the difference with you, and if the running time lasts longer than twenty-four hours because of high seas or rough winds, I won't even think about adding on for my time and diesel."

Culhane extended his right hand across the bar. Grey took it. "Agreed," Culhane told him.

"Be here at the docks by maybe two-thirty. You and the lady—unless you had something different in mind— can share the forward stateroom. I use the aft stateroom, and either Ebenezer or I are on watch day and night."

"Sounds good to me," Mulrooney said, Culhane glancing over to her.

"Any kind of food you or the lady can't eat—I mean, either of you Jewish and don't eat pork—like that?"

"With names like Culhane and Mulrooney?" Culhane looked at her as she said it, and he laughed.

CULHANE STOOD IN THE FLYING BRIDGE to the right of Grey in the helmseat, Grey throttling up the starboard engine a little, a cool wind with a fine salt spray flowing across the windshield as they skated near the shallows surrounding Eleuthera Island along the Northeast Providence Channel. "Can you stick her to the channel, Mr. Culhane? Take the wheel for me."

Culhane, shouting over the noise of the engines and the noise of the waves breaking across the starboard bow, told him, "Yeah, I think I can manage."

Grey nodded, then turned toward Mulrooney. Wearing a strapless one-piece bathing suit that defied gravity, she was stretched across the companion benchseat reading galley proofs for one of her books. "Would you or the lady care for a drink? I have Scotch, vodka, Canadian blended whiskey, bourbon, beer and of course, rum."

"What kind of rum?" It was Mulrooney.

"Myers's dark."

"Straight in a bourbon glass would be fine," she called back and returned to her reading. Culhane looked away from her to the control console as Grey got up, then he slid into the helmseat.

"And you, Mr. Culhane?"

"The same is fine," Culhane called back, Grey already walking away.

"The same it is. And watch the port throttle: she's a little speedier than she might be, so you don't have to goose her that much." As Grey passed Mulrooney, he said to her, "Sorry for the choice of vocabulary, miss."

She looked up, slid her round-lensed sunglasses down along the bridge of her nose for an instant and smiled, pushing her glasses back. Grey disappeared down the ladder into the cockpit.

Culhane stared ahead through his sunglasses toward the island off to starboard. He felt Mulrooney's hands on his bare shoulders. "Like I told you on the way back to the hotel, Josh, like I told you over lunch, like I told you on the way back to the docks, I don't trust this guy."

Culhane only nodded, saying nothing.

"Too accommodating, too—"

"Yeah," Culhane agreed. "But I look at it this way:

until we reach San Rafael and start prowling around that old monastery, nobody's gonna touch us. If Steiglitz figures we've got an idea where to find the Gladstone Log, he'll let us stay alive long enough to get it into our hands. That's when he lowers the boom. Just keeping a nautical flavor to my speech here," and he laughed.

He felt her nails bite into his shoulders. "Couldn't bring a gun, huh?"

"Not into the Bahamas. It's not easy, the way it is in movies and books. Permission's impossible, and smuggling is dicey unless you've got the right connections. Anyway, I'm sure Captain Grey has at least one."

"That's what I'm worried about," Mulrooney said, and Culhane felt the nails dig into his bare flesh again.

CHAPTER NINETEEN

Mulrooney opened her eyes; she'd heard something. She'd been hearing things all night—the sounds of the *Cherokee* underway, the sounds of footsteps in the companionway between the salon and the cockpit, footsteps she assumed belonged to Junius Grey or to the skinny man called Ebenezer....

Her nightgown was wrapped around her legs, and she eased up her rear end, tugging at the gown so she could move. She leaned across Culhane, who was sleeping on her left, picked up his left arm and studied his Rolex. It was almost 3:00 A.M. Maybe the sound had something to do with the *Cherokee*'s slowing down because they were nearing San Rafael.

She pushed the sheet down and swung her legs over the side of the double bed. She hadn't brought a robe, nor had she brought slippers. She stepped into the rubber thongs she'd worn earlier in the day and grabbed Culhane's dark blue knit shirt. She pulled the shirt on over her head, and it reached past her hips as she smoothed it down.

Culhane had brought his flashlight, the kind policemen carried: big, holding three large D batteries. It was heavy; Mulrooney could see why policemen sometimes used them as nightsticks. She took it off the small bedside table and started for the stateroom door three short steps away. She put her hand on the latch, not yet working the switch on Culhane's flashlight. There was an uneasy feeling in the pit of her stomach. She knew Culhane had his big pocketknife inside his shoe on the side of the bed, but she could always hit somebody on the head with the flashlight.

She opened the door, stepped out into the companionway and pulled the door closed behind her. It didn't lock because there was no key, and Captain Junius Grey had explained that the key was lost somewhere.

She held her breath, her shoulder blades and the cheeks of her behind flat against the companionway wall. She walked past the head, reminding herself to get up early so she could get a shower before they went ashore on San Rafael. She walked past Grey's little bar, smelling the odor of stale beer where used bottles were in a plastic wastebasket in the corner. She kept walking, the vessel swaying under her feet as she reached her left hand to the overhead to help steady her, her right hand holding the flashlight—still unlit— and holding up the hem of her long nightgown.

Why was the vessel swaying? For an instant she wished she wrote adventure novels as Culhane did; you learned about boats and the things they did by writing stuff like that.

The creaking sounds were louder now.

She kept walking aft.

There was a sliver of light coming out through the

darkness between the door and the doorframe of the aft cabin.

Suddenly she thought, why am I sneaking around? She was a passenger paying a good price—Culhane had told her how much—to travel on the *Cherokee*. She was restless and just going for a walk. She walked ahead with longer steps, surer steps. If he saw her, Grey would simply say, "Good evening, Miss Mulrooney," or something like that.

But she stopped beside his door; she heard voices. One voice was Grey's heavy baritone, but the other voice didn't sound like Ebenezer's. "And if Ebenezer's belowdecks, then who the hell is driving the boat?" she asked herself under her breath. Maybe it didn't need someone up top if they were stopped. They had to be at San Rafael. Maybe you could see from the cockpit. When she'd glanced out the stateroom portholes while pulling on Culhane's shirt, she'd seen nothing but blackness, but maybe the *Cherokee* had turned around and was facing out to sea, and the aft section faced the island of San Rafael.

She started past Grey's stateroom.

The door opened.

A white face with a long purplish scar running down the left cheek glared at her. She raised the flashlight to use it like a club and opened her mouth wide to scream, sucking in her breath.

Grey was next to the other man, a handgun in his big right fist.

"Scream and I blow the top of your pretty little head off, Miss Mulrooney."

Her mouth was still open, but she didn't scream, and the next instant, the white man with the scar had his hand clamped over her mouth. She couldn't scream if she tried.

They pulled her inside the stateroom, then closed the door quietly.

"Don't want to awaken Mr. Culhane—no need to just yet," Grey told her.

The white man's hand was still over her mouth. His other hand pulled up the bottom of her nightgown, and she reached out to scratch at his eyes with her fingernails but saw Grey's gun. It was aimed at her face. "I really will shoot you, Miss Mulrooney, if need be," he said to her, then pushed the white man's hand away from her thighs.

She sat on the bunk, her nightgown up to her crotch, not daring to move, the white man's hand still covering her mouth. Her nose hurt where his hand was against it. Grey was talking to him. "If you want to sample the merchandise, do it after we kill Culhane. He's a big enough man to put up a little resistance. And anyway, this one'll fight you," he said, and he touched his hand with the gun in it to her cheek. "You want a cabin torn up, do it on your own vessel, Gastman."

"Mm—mmm—mm—" The man's hand was locked so tightly over her mouth, it was all she could do to make strangled grunts.

"Don't tell me—you want to know what's going on." Grey smiled, his teeth showing wide.

"Mm—hmm—mm."

"I'll tell you," he said. He stuffed his automatic into his belt and picked up a pillow from the bed. She watched him as he stripped the pillowcase from it. "Pretty simple, actually, Miss Mulrooney." He set the pillowcase down and pulled a red-and-white bandanna handkerchief from his pocket. "We're going to kidnap you and kill Mr. Culhane." Before she could react, the white man's hand was gone from her mouth and the red-and-white bandanna was going between her teeth, her head pushed forward and down almost to her knees as she felt Grey's hands tying it too tightly behind her neck, felt some of her hair pulled into the knot. "The *Cherokee* is a fine old vessel—I'm sure you'd agree. Don't build them like this anymore." Her head was pushed back up, her hands pulled behind her. She felt the white man tying them with something. "One reason they don't build them like this anymore is that they're too costly to repair. Your friend Mr. Culhane wondered about my beer before. Well, I smuggle it into Nassau, but just for myself. I lived in Colorado in your United States for four years and really grew to like it. But the other things I smuggle are a little more important than beer—like rifles to pro-Castro terrorists in the Caribbean, explosives, things like that. And I smuggle drugs from Colombia with this nice gentleman, Mr. Gastman. He's what you'd call a pirate."

Her wrists were tied behind her as Grey knelt at her feet, binding her bare ankles with cord. "I've skimmed one or two of your books, Miss Mulrooney—I'd love to say I found them fascinating, but unfortunately I didn't. But what more appropriate place for the famous M.F. Mulrooney to disappear than in the infamous Bermuda Triangle, hey?" When he was through tying her ankles—she couldn't twist them against the rope even a little—he stood up, then pulled down her nightgown so it covered her legs. "Wouldn't want you to catch cold." And he took his gun from his belt and held it again in his fist. She wondered what he had planned for the pillowcase and knew she wouldn't like it. "But you see, in the Bermuda Triangle—devils and the occult and flying saucers aside—there are still pirates, such as Mr. Gastman here. Pirates will attack this vessel and kill everyone aboard her except me. I'll be found cast adrift but somehow surviving, so I can collect my insurance money. Even poor Ebenezer will have been murdered." Grey looked past her to the white man crouched beside her whose breath she could feel on her cheek. "Has he been murdered yet?"

"Naw—just hit him up side the head, Grey—less'n he's got a delicate head or such."

Grey turned his eyes back to Mulrooney, smiling again. "But what really happens is vastly more profitable. I'll be cast adrift, suffer from exposure perhaps, but I've been toughening my skin to the sun the last few weeks looking for a likely prospect to come along. That's the reason I was on deck in my swimming trunks earlier, when you and Mr. Culhane first came to me. The sun can be a killer—really. A fair person like yourself, Miss Mulrooney—it can wreak devastation. But in any event, the *Cherokee* won't really be scuttled. She'll be repainted, the serials on the engine blocks altered, things like that, and she'll be sold into the drug trade running from South America up to Florida. All valuables will be taken off, but the insurance company won't know that. My liability insurance will cover any claims from either your estate or that of Mr. Culhane. And Mr. Gastman and I shall make a handsome profit indeed on you."

Mulrooney felt her eyes widen.

"Now I know you're a journalist, Miss Mulrooney. Surely between flying saucer photographs and Bigfoot legends you must have heard of white slavery. Catchy name, actually," he mused, stroking his chocolate-brown skin. "Mr. Gastman has connections in South America, from where you can be shipped into Southeast Asia and sold for a very handsome price. Some fascination for fair-skinned women in brothels, I suspect."

She brought both feet up, aiming her toes at Grey's crotch.

But he sidestepped, and she felt Gastman's hands at her back, shoving her off the edge of the bunk.

Her rear end hit the floor hard and she lost her breath.

"But relax for now. Your trip to South America and

then to Southeast Asia—'' he smiled, shoving the pistol into his belt and picking up the pillowcase ''—will be a pleasant one. They use heroin to keep you calm, then to addict you so you behave well in the brothel. And now we—'' Grey glanced at his watch as he lifted the pillowcase ''—must go and murder Mr. Culhane.'' He swiftly brought the pillowcase down and covered her head with it. She could still see diffused light as she felt him tying it around her neck; her face was sweating already.

''But a good little girl will get to Southeast Asia with a lot fewer bruises and welts than a bad one, so while you wait for us, why don't you think about ways to be pleasing to your new masters.''

She heard footsteps, heard a click and then the diffused light was gone. She was in total darkness when she heard the door close.

She was alone.

Then she felt the hand moving up along her legs, under her nightgown, felt it grab hard at her crotch and heard the laughter. Gastman.

His voice was near her ear. ''You be good to me, girlie, and I'll be better to you,'' he whispered, his hand hurting her, but then it moved away. Her breath was coming in short gasps from the pain and from the fear. She heard footsteps again, heard the door close again, heard a lock being worked.

She leaned her head back against the edge of the bunk, suffocating inside the pillowcase, frightened, her eyes welling up with tears. But already she was trying to work on the knots at her wrists. Gastman had tied these, and he hadn't struck her as being anywhere near as competent as Grey. And if she didn't get her hands free, Culhane would be dead and she would wish she were.

''THE MIND NEVER SLEEPS.'' It was something Culhane had Sean Dodge use as a pet expression in The Takers, something Culhane had learned on the Lateriquique River in Paraguay when he and his guide had been stalked for six days by bandits, and the only way to stay alive was to let the body rest but never the mind.

The expression his guide—a hunter, a fighter—had used was an expression Culhane had taken to heart, to his soul. Ordinary sounds were cataloged automatically and dismissed. As he rolled over and felt the still-warm indentations in the mattress where Mulrooney had been, he assumed he'd heard her get up and dismissed it. She'd gone to the head; she usually did that sometime during the night when they had made love.

His eyes were wide open. There had been another sound, an unusual sound. He rolled over onto his stomach and reached into his shoe. The Bali-Song knife, his only weapon, was hidden there. The sound that had awakened him was a key in a lock. But there was no key for this stateroom, Junius Grey had said. And Grey had even told him there was no key for the aft stateroom Grey shared with the skinny man, Ebenezer.

So why should a key be turning in a lock when there were no keys?

The Bali-Song was a knife said to have originated in the Philippines, but the design was quite possibly brought there by an American sailor. Rather than the blade opening out of the handle between the slabs, the handle was made in halves, the halves splitting to bare the blade. Culhane's Bali-Song was handmade of the finest stainless steel, the handle halves skeletonized and held together by a flip lock similar in principle to the locking mechanism of the band clasp for his Rolex Sea Dweller. His right thumb flipped the lock up and open, the thumb slipping down to the left side of the rear handle half. His hand opened, letting the forward handle half and the blade fall open, then he closed both handle halves together in his fingers, the Weehawk pattern blade locked in his clenched right fist.

His left palm flat against the mattress, he pushed himself up and off the bed, naked, backing against the doorway, pulling the king-size pillows from the bunk into the bunk's center. He glanced toward the door. Footsteps.

He reached out across the bed with the knife in his right hand, shagging the point of the single-edged blade into the sheet and lifting it up, then dropping it down across the pillows so it looked as though a body still lay in the bed.

He was worried about Mulrooney.

His navy blue shorts were on the chair next to the bedside table, but he noticed his shirt was gone. Mulrooney's panties were on the floor; she hadn't left them there when she had undressed. Her bra—taken off along with the panties when she'd changed into her swimsuit—was still there. The swimsuit was there as well.

He felt the corners of his mouth tensing, his palms sweating as he moved the knife in his hand for an instant to flip the lock closed. Danger was somehow always easier to face in the pages of his books than in real life. He moved his knife back into position, a rapier hold.

He heard something and looked down at the door handle.

It was turning.

Culhane drew himself up behind the door as it started to open.

It was like something out of a movie. A pistol—mechanically he recognized it as a Walther P-38—was being stabbed through the darkness of the space between the door and the frame. From where he stood he could only see the gun and the hand that wielded it.

The pistol discharged once, then once again, the sharp crack of the 9mm parabellum rounds deafening in the confined space. Culhane's right hand with the

Bali-Song flashing out, down, back. The pistol discharging again, then falling from the hand. Culhane's left shoulder lurching against the door, hammering it shut against the anonymous gunman. A scream of pain as the gunman's left hand clasped the right wrist, Culhane snapping the door open again, his left hand punching out into the darkness, finding a face, wet lips and a shirtfront as his hand dropped, wrenching the body toward him. His right hand ramming forward, low, under the elbows of the gunman with no gun, his right wrist feeling the shock as the knife stopped dead against bone, the blade rammed up to the handle halves, a groaning sound as the man crumpled toward him, Culhane leaving the knife in as he guided the man to the floor.

In the pale starlight that lit the stateroom, Culhane could see the face—a white man, the eyes open and staring. The sphincters had relaxed in death, and the smell of human excrement and urine began to fill the room.

Culhane searched the man's pockets: two spare magazines for the Walther—from the weight of them, seemingly fully loaded; what felt like a slick-scaled, multibladed pocketknife—maybe the Swiss Army type; a small leather sack. He opened the sack and could feel a plastic lining with his fingers. In the sack—from the smell of it—was marijuana. "Wonderful," he whispered to the dead man. "See? I told you I'd help you kick the habit." He replaced the sack and threw the knife under the bed.

The gun was in his right hand and he shifted it to his left as he picked up his Bali-Song knife again, cleaning the blade on the dead man's shirt. He set the gun down, closed the knife with one hand, locking the handle halves, then set it down on the bed beside the gun and the two spare magazines. He stepped into his navy blue shorts, picked up the knife and dropped it into a

pocket next to his cigarettes and lighter. It was a big
knife, and Culhane thought it made him look like he
had an erection coming out of his left thigh. He picked
up the Walther; he realized he'd worked the safety
lever on and then off again to lower the hammer without even being conscious of it. He put the two spare
magazines in his other front pocket and stepped out
into the salon. He could hear sounds on the deck
above now, as if the shots had somehow signaled a
party to begin. He heard Grey's voice shouting,
"Careful with that fighting chair when you're loading
her aboard the *Temptress*—the damned thing cost
good money!"

Strange time to be moving furniture, Culhane
thought. And then he moved ahead across the salon's
almost palpable darkness, his bare feet taking each
step as soundlessly as he could, the Walther P-38 tight
against his body in his right fist, ready. He had to find
Mulrooney.

He passed the open galley, liberating a handful of
popcorn as he did. He was hungry, and since he
couldn't smoke, the popcorn was the next best thing.

It wasn't bad popcorn.

He stopped beside the door to the aft cabin, heard
footsteps in the cockpit and drew back into the shadows. "Turn on some fuckin' lights, Grey—Stowbridge
already shot that Culhane asshole, anyway."

Grey's voice. "All right. Then we get the girl. Go
through Culhane's things and then hers for anything
of value."

"You can trust me, Junius." The voice had a
curious blend of southern U.S. and New York City ac-
cents.

"Trust you my ass, Gastman. All I believe is that
you want fifty percent of the insurance money, and
that's more than this boat'll bring in the drug trade.
The man's watch is a good one, means good money on

the black market. The woman had two cameras and a camera bag full of lenses. Those looked like real pearls she was wearing when she came aboard. I trust you the same as you trust me. And when you sell the woman, be damned certain I get half the money.''

Culhane's mouth was dry. He lied to himself that it was the popcorn. He knew better.

"All right then—let's get to that Culhane fella's corpse before old Stowbridge picks him clean. He's been in there two or three minutes since we heard them shots.''

"And get the woman on the way up. She'll keep.''

Culhane tucked back farther into the shadows as Grey and the second man walked past him, the captain ducking his huge frame as he walked forward.

Culhane realized Mulrooney was in Grey's stateroom. Maybe drugged, maybe unconscious, but damaged goods brought poorer prices; more likely just tied up or clapped in a storage locker. Somehow he felt better knowing she was salable; it meant she was alive and in one piece.

There was only one way to do it, something he rarely had the characters in his books do and something he'd never done: shoot both men in the back, fast. There were—he hoped—five shots remaining in the Walther. Perhaps six if the man had used a full magazine plus one in the chamber.

Grey would be the one to take first. He was the biggest, the strongest and the smartest from what he'd heard of the conversation.

In an instant it would be too late.

He tried rationalizing a way out of double murder; there wouldn't be time to get Mulrooney once they found out his body wasn't in the stateroom. And then would be more men on top. Most likely both Grey and the other man— what was the name, Gastman?—had guns. Culhane could use them.

He stepped from the shadows, raising the muzzle of the Walther P-38, setting the barely visible front sight on the outline of Grey's back. He squeezed the trigger twice as fast as he could do it evenly, the sound of the 9mms in the confined space making his ears ring again. Grey's bulk slammed forward, and the second man spun around, starting to shout, "What the—"

Culhane pumped the trigger three times, the body taking each slug and moving with it, dancing, spinning, falling.

Culhane was running forward now, working the base-of-the-butt magazine catch release and dropping the empty magazine, jamming a fresh one into the butt of the pistol. The Walther still had a round in the chamber. Culhane felt the muscles in his neck tightening. Grey was still moving. He squeezed the trigger anyway, the shot aimed at Grey's head. He could have hit, he could have missed.

But there was no more movement.

Culhane reached down with the pistol, ready to fire again, then rolled over the white man. He pried the gun from his fist—a Government Model .45, unmistakable even in the darkness. A quick search turned up three spare magazines, one in the pocket and two on the belt.

Grey had carried a Luger. "Yecch," Culhane sneered. Two spare magazines.

Both pistols in his waistband and the spare magazines in his pockets, he started forward, expecting at any second that men would pour down the companionway from the cockpit.

None was coming.

Grey's stateroom. Culhane tried the door; it was locked. It had been the locking of the stateroom door that had awakened him.

If all the previous gunshots hadn't gotten anyone to come below, he thought—

But if Mulrooney were near the door. . . .

He took a half step back, then snapped his bare left foot against the door and the doorjamb as he wheeled, balancing on his right. A double tae kwon do kick and the door sprang inward.

Culhane stepped through, the Walther in his right fist. Mulrooney was on her knees, a pillowcase on the floor beside her, her mouth gagged, her hands free, the fingers splayed like a cat ready to claw.

Culhane dropped to his knees beside her. "So you're the one who stole my shirt, huh," he said as he undid the gag in her mouth.

"I heard those shots—I was working as fast as I could to get untied—"

"You did okay, kid," Culhane told her. "Come on."

"My ankles."

Culhane eased toward the edge of the bed across the floor, snatched the Bali-Song, handed her the Walther. "Don't put your finger in the trigger guard unless you want it to go bang." He hacked the cord binding her ankles and helped her up. She was cold, her flesh covered with goose bumps as he held her arm.

"Did they, ahh—"

"No," she answered shakily, leaning her head against his shoulder. "But the white man, the one with Grey—his name was Gastman—he came back and he . . . well, he would—"

"He's dead. So's Grey. There must be more of them topside, but I can't see why they didn't come below."

Culhane stepped into the companionway. The Walther, back in his right fist now, was pointed up toward the cockpit. There was no sound of footsteps overhead, no sound at all but the creaking of the boat in the water.

"I heard them talking about killing Ebenezer. He wasn't in on this," Mulrooney whispered into his left ear.

"Was he dead yet?"

"No. Gastman said he didn't think he'd killed him. He'd just hit him on the head. They were going to clean out the boat, then sell me."

Culhane folded his arm around her. "I know, and I wouldn't have let 'em, Fanny." She leaned up in the darkness and kissed him quickly on the mouth. "What was that for?"

"In case we get killed."

"Thanks for the encouragement, baby," Culhane murmured. He worked the safety catch on the Walther, lowering the hammer, then worked it back up to where all Mulrooney would need was a long double-action trigger pull to fire the first shot. "Take this. Just pull the trigger—safety's already taken care of." He handed her the one remaining spare magazine for the Walther. "And take this—loads up the butt."

"Like an editor I once knew," Mulrooney said and laughed.

Culhane ignored her. "The magazine release is at the base of the butt—just pull it back to dump the empty. Come on." Culhane started into the companionway, taking the Government Model .45, working back the slide enough so he could feel with his index finger through the ejection port that there was a round chambered. He thumbed back the hammer to full cock, trying the safety. It worked, but he put the safety off as he started up the three steps to the cockpit. He glanced back at Mulrooney, the Walther in her right hand, the white nightgown under his blue shirt bunched up in her left hand and up to her knees as she followed him.

Culhane stopped in the companionway hatch. A boat was about a hundred yards astern and to starboard, lights visible on the deck, the boat more or less identical to the *Cherokee* but slightly bigger in overall proportions.

Culhane started to reach out to the cockpit freezer. It was gone. The fighting chair was gone. "Wait here a minute." Culhane started to go up the ladder to the flying bridge but stopped. He saw a body in the bait well. He leaned down to it. Ebenezer.

"They said they didn't kill him," Culhane heard Mulrooney murmur.

"They didn't, but he drowned," Culhane whispered, his left thumb closing the man's eyes as he shifted the body out of the water.

"Bastards," Mulrooney murmured.

"Yeah. Now stay here a second." Culhane started up the ladder, the .45 in his right fist. He kept his body below the level of the safety rail as he slipped from the ladder and past the companion benchseat and across the deck toward the control console.

The control console was intact, as he'd hoped it would be, the keys in the switch.

He started back but changed his mind, edging toward the starboard rail by the ladder up to the tuna tower platform, peering into the night toward the lighted sport fisherman one hundred yards off. Keeping low, he started back to the ladder, then down to the cockpit, dropping beside Mulrooney. He pushed her back into the companionway.

"Pull off that nightgown—white out here in the darkness is like wearing a neon sign."

"You just wanna see my bare rear end."

But she was already pulling her arms out of the sleeves of his knit shirt, and in the next instant, crouched in the companionway beside him, she slid the straps of her nightgown down her arms, the nightgown dropping to the companionway steps around her feet. Her arms came back out through the sleeves, and she tugged down at the knit shirt. "I look so much less conspicuous naked from the waist down. Thanks a lot."

"You just be quiet and listen. Get up to that flying bridge—you were standing behind me while I was running the control console to get up through Northeast Providence Channel—and get ready to fake it as soon as I'm back on board."

"What the hell are you gonna do?" she whispered.

"I don't know yet—it isn't like writing a book." He stepped down into the salon, rifling the drawers in the counter. "I'm going over there to the other boat—screw up their controls or something so they can't chase us. They look faster somehow." He found what he was looking for: a large Ziploc sandwich bag.

"But what are you going to do?" she insisted.

"Play it by ear. I'll let you know as soon as I figure it out myself." Culhane returned to the companionway and took the Luger from his waistband, worked the toggle action and popped a round out of the chamber. "Already was loaded. Use this after the Walther runs out—that's the one on the steps next to your nightgown." He handed her the Luger, then the two spare magazines.

"You're gonna get yourself killed," she said as he started to move away.

"That's right, build up my confidence," he told her.

She grabbed his face with both hands, kissing him hard on the mouth. "You get killed, I'll never forgive you!"

Culhane nodded, stuffed the cocked and locked .45 and two spare magazines into the bag, closed it, then handed Mulrooney his cigarettes. "Yeah—me neither." He was at the starboard gunwale and rolled himself over the side into the water.

CHAPTER TWENTY

The Rolex read nearly 4:00 A.M. as Culhane reached his hand out of the water for the sheer line, then edged his way forward along the starboard side of the boat, which was vastly larger and most likely much faster than the *Cherokee*. He moved ahead, hoping the plastic-bagged .45 in his right fist would still work— hell, he hoped it worked, period, since he had never fired the gun. He was careful not to scrape the pistol along the side, lest he make some noise to alert whoever was on board.

He could hear voices from the cockpit and from the flying bridge far above—laughter, some cursing, drunken shouts. He knew now why no one had heard the shots or, if the shots had been heard, had bothered. This crew was too drunk to care.

There was an anchor chain running out through a hole in the hull on the starboard side and Culhane clung to it, water dripping from his hair into his eyes. He rubbed the water away and cleared his vision. He remembered there were sharks in these waters—and tried to forget.

The pockets on his shorts were deep, and he stuffed the bag with the .45 and two spare magazines into his right pocket, hooking the tang in the lining and holding a good thought the pistol wouldn't slip out. But he needed both hands to climb the anchor chain, and the pocket was safer than his beltless waistband.

He started climbing up the chain, something else that was easier for Sean Dodge to do in books.

Somehow the laughter and loud shouting—though the difference in distance was minor—sounded very much closer. Culhane stopped at the rub rail around the foredeck gunwale and looked from side to side, then up. Men were on the flying bridge, laughing and talking. Something shot through the air past his head, and Culhane instinctively ducked back. He heard a splash and looked into the water. One of the starboard running lights caught it: a beer bottle.

"Litterbugs," Culhane murmured, then swung up on the anchor chain, reached for the gunwale and rolled over the side and down onto the foredeck.

There, in the shadows, Culhane drew the plastic bag from his deep side pocket; the shorts were made to hold tennis balls but did all right as an improvised holster. He opened the plastic bag, taking the .45 out, thumbing down the safety, creeping aft, going flat on the deck, listening. He heard three voices from the flying bridge, but there could have been more men.

There was a dinghy with an outboard motor attached in tow at the stern. Culhane figured it was the way Gastman and Stowbridge—the one who had tried to kill him in the stateroom—had come aboard the *Cherokee*. Then whoever brought them returned with the launch.

He filed away the location of the dinghy, his only practical means of escape after he did what he had to do. But what exactly that was, he wasn't certain. If he burst up over the windshield.... Something in the pattern of the talk changed, and he heard a voice more sober sounding than the rest. "Gastman's been over there too long. Maybe that Grey is up to somethin'."

"Hell, you wouldn't trust your own mother," a drunken voice shouted.

"I'm takin' the launch to have a look over on the *Cherokee*. I need somebody with me."

There goes the dinghy, Culhane thought, but also two of the opposition.

"All right, I'll go with ya," a third voice, very drunk, chimed in.

"Then let's go," the sober voice shouted.

Culhane heard the sounds of footsteps on the flying bridge above him, then the sounds of footfalls on the ladder rungs leading down into the cockpit.

He bided his time.

"Aww, shit—hit my shin—"

"Just shut up and get in the boat," the first voice called out.

He heard more footfalls, then the starter rope being pulled, the motor sputtering, the starter rope being pulled again. "Wish they'd perfect these suckers," the first voice growled. Again the sound of the starter rope being pulled, a sputter, then a loud, rhythmic chugging. The chugging increased in intensity, then Culhane listened as its sound gradually diminished. The dinghy was gone.

Culhane was up, reaching past the main salon window, reaching and getting a handhold on the windshield, his hands pulling him up, his legs and torso vaulting it.

He skidded on his rear end across the console and down toward the helmseat. Two men were there, and one of them started to rise.

The .45 was in Culhane's right fist, and he backhanded it across the nearer man's face, the right cheek splitting, blood spurting, Culhane wheeling right. The second man came from the companion bench. Culhane's left foot snaked out and up, a double tae kwon do kick with the sole of his foot landing dead center on the man's chest.

The man fell back, skidding off the companion bench to the deck surface. Culhane regained his balance on both feet, dropping to one knee beside the man as he crashed the .45 down across the top of the second man's skull.

The head slumped, the eyes closed.

Culhane bent over the first man, who was down for the count; it would take him a long time to bleed to death—if ever.

Quickly he frisked the men, finding one pistol between them: another .45, this a Colt Combat Commander with the satin nickel finish. He checked the pistol's condition of readiness and upped the hammer, keeping it cocked and locked. Two spare magazines were in the man's pockets. He took them. A long-bladed Fairbairn-Sykes pattern commando knife was on the belt of the second man. Culhane took it and tossed it over the side.

"Hey—what the hell's goin' on up there?" came a shout from the cockpit below and aft.

Culhane looked up, hearing footfalls on the ladder.

The .45 he'd taken from the dead man on the *Cherokee* was in his right fist, the .45 from the man he'd just laid out was in his left; both safeties were down.

A man stood on the ladder, a revolver in his right hand.

"What the fuck—"

The revolver whipped down and forward to fire, but Culhane was faster, shooting first with the .45 in his right hand, then with the .45 in his left. The figure on the ladder rocked back and was airborne for an instant.

Culhane was up on his feet and to the head of the ladder. A pistol rose in the hand of one of the three men in the cockpit. Culhane fired the .45 in his right hand once, then again, and the man's body rocked twice, sprawling back, the upper half stretched out over the stern gunwale.

The .45 in Culhane's left fist barked once, then once more at a man raising an assault rifle to fire. The body snapped back, the gun spitting a long burst of muzzle-flashing automatic fire into the night sky. It was an M-16.

A pistol in the third man's hands barked once, then again, the companion bench beside Culhane's left thigh ripping. Culhane fired both .45s simultaneously, and the remaining man went down to his knees, his torso jerking back, his body finally falling to the deck with legs bent grotesquely.

Culhane practically slid down the ladder into the cockpit. He upped the safeties on both .45s, rammed them into his waistband and grabbed the M-16.

He had the assault rifle in his hands when he heard shouts coming from the dinghy. He didn't take time to listen, swinging the M-16 on line with the dinghy just at the waterline, firing a 3-round burst, then another and another. Then he moved the M-16 left, toward the outboard motor, let go another 3-round burst, and a small fire started in the outboard.

He lowered the rifle, edging back beside the starboard gunwale. He shouted, "Throw your weapons into the water and stay with the boat. Otherwise I'll shoot you like fish in a barrel."

Culhane watched the two men across the M-16's sights. The rifle was fitted with a 30-round magazine, so he should have enough ammo left to keep his promise if he had to.

First one man, then the other, both standing in the now badly listing dinghy, tossed a handgun into the water.

Culhane decided he could release the anchor chain, get this boat alongside the *Cherokee* and still keep tabs on the two men in the quickly filling dinghy.

As he started along the side deck going forward, he breathed easier. There could still be men hiding aboard, but if they didn't bother him, he wouldn't bother them.

He found the pin locking the anchor chain. It was well oiled, and he easily released the chain from where it was secured, running it over the side.

Now it would be back to the *Cherokee* and Mary Frances Mulrooney.

"Let's see Sean Dodge top this," he said to the night sky.

Mulrooney rose up on her toes, waving back to Culhane as he eased the more massive pirate boat alongside the *Cherokee*. "I was impressed," she shouted over to him from the *Cherokee*'s flying bridge.

"Yeah, so was I," he called back.

She laughed. She'd been worried sick, worried he'd get himself killed. Writing books on the occult wasn't exactly as safe as staying home in bed, but she reckoned it beat by a mile trying to outdo your own fictional adventure hero.

"What are you gonna do with the two guys in the sinking rowboat?" she called out.

"Leave 'em there while I disable the controls enough so they can't follow us. Keep half an eye on 'em. If they do anything, fire a shot and I'll take care of them with the rifle."

"Right," she called back, turning her attention to starboard, watching the two men clinging to the upturned hull of the dinghy.

Her own cigarettes were still below, but she had Culhane's and it wouldn't be the first time she'd smoked one. She tapped the filterless cigarette against the control console's dashboard to keep the loose tobacco from getting on her lips, then lit the Pall Mall with Culhane's Bic. Mulrooney inhaled the smoke deep into her lungs, examined the pistols Culhane had given her to use if needed, then looked out across the stern at the two men.

"Almost kidnapped by pirates at the end of the twentieth century—Geez." She chuckled to herself. It was hard to imagine, harder to believe. But it had happened.

She made a mental note to sit down and reread Sabatini's *Captain Blood* when all this business with the Gladstone Log, with this man named Steiglitz—when all of it was over.

She could no longer see Josh aboard the other vessel. She assumed he was doing more sabotage below the flying bridge.

There was still a little left of the Pall Mall, and she inhaled hard before stubbing it out in the ashtray near the control console. She wondered what time it was. It was still dark, but she guessed it was close to five. Mulrooney massaged her wrists, rubbed raw in her efforts to get out of the ropes the white man with the scar had bound her with. She'd cajole Culhane into rubbing hand cream on her wrists. She smiled at the thought.

And Captain Junius Grey, despite her reservations about the man, had seemed so, so..."Nice," she said aloud.

"What's nice, Miss Mulrooney?" a rich baritone asked.

She whirled around, reaching for the nearest of the two pistols, but Grey, the left side of his face dripping blood, his left eye closed, his massive shoulders hunched forward, lunged for her. She screamed, "Josh! Josh!"

She felt the blow across her face, saw Grey's hand move in slow motion, felt her head snap back and her legs go out from under her. *"Josh!"*

Grey was standing over her. She didn't really remember falling, but her vision was blurry. He held both pistols in his hands. "Now, Miss Mulrooney, get to the control panel and start the engines. I'll tell you what to do. There's a long way to go before I'll have to kill you, so be a good little girl."

She spat at him. His bare left foot stabbed out toward her, hammering her down as it hit against her chest.

"Or I'll kill you now, miss."

She edged back along the deck on her bare behind, putting her hands under her, getting awkwardly to her feet, using her hands to pull down the knit shirt and try to cover her crotch.

"I wouldn't rape you, Miss Mulrooney—I haven't the energy," Grey said with a strangled laugh.

She stepped to the controls. Where the hell was Culhane, she asked herself. "You monitor those engine-oil-pressure gauges once she's started—and the tachs, too."

"Aye-aye," she snarled, not looking back at him.

THE CHEROKEE HAD NEVER DROPPED ANCHOR, drifting on the calm seas. When Culhane heard the noise of the *Cherokee*'s engines firing, he knew something had gone very wrong.

He'd been searching for more ammo for the nearly spent M-16. He'd found none. Reaching the cockpit, he'd looked first far astern; the two men from the dinghy still clung to it.

Then he had heard the engine and looked to the flying bridge of the *Cherokee*, which was already pulling away. Mulrooney was at the helm, and the massive black man behind her, two handguns visible in his fists, was Junius Grey.

Culhane, throwing the guns he couldn't carry into the sea, but both .45s still with him, broke into a dead run along the pirate vessel's portside deck, reaching the foredeck as the *Cherokee*'s prow came around port and the stern started turning away.

Culhane's hands reached out, and he jumped for it.

He clung by his fingertips to the *Cherokee*'s gunwale, feeling one of the .45s slip from his waistband and sink away. The wake of the *Cherokee* tossed his body right and left, tearing at him to make him let go as the twin screws beneath the waterline churned faster and faster, the *Cherokee* making speed.

Culhane tried moving his left hand to get a better grip and found a line half over the gunwale. He grabbed at it, the grip of his right hand going.

The boat picked up speed, and the wake was greater,

tossing him from side to side, hammering at him, the line tight in his left fist, the right hand's grip gone. But the line was giving way, and Culhane's left hand, still holding it, slipped from the transom's gunwale and slid down into the water. He grabbed at the line with his right hand, the line still playing out, the *Cherokee* outdistancing him as he rose and fell in its wake.

He held the line—and the slack was suddenly gone. The line went taut, and his arms felt as though they would be wrenched from their sockets. Pain pounded in his chronically bad right shoulder. The line was attached to something aboard the *Cherokee*—Culhane didn't know what—but as the boat raced ahead, it was dragging him along.

He was pulled under, his eyes open in the dark waters, his head breaking the surface again, the foam of the wake seeming almost to glow around him, his mouth gulping air before the water sucked him downward. And the second .45 was gone.

CHAPTER TWENTY-ONE

Mulrooney's nipples felt stiff and cold. She was more afraid than she had ever been in her life. And when she heard Grey's voice behind her, felt what had to be one of the pistols jabbing into her back, she wanted to throw up.

"Your Mr. Culhane—I think he reads too many of his own adventure novels. He tried jumping to the cockpit of the *Cherokee* from the late Captain Gastman's vessel. But he didn't make it."

Her heart sank.

She rammed the starboard throttle full ahead, the deck lurching under her, and threw herself to her right against the flying bridge's safety rail.

"Bastard!" she screamed, jumping up and hurling herself at Grey, hammering her fists against his face and chest, smashing her right knee again and again against his crotch.

She felt his hand knotting into her hair, wrenching her back, and pulling her down to her knees as he practically fell on her. He leaned over her, one of the pistols pointed at her face. "Now is the time for you to die, Miss Mulrooney, and there's no one to save you. You will just simply die."

She could see it, hear it and almost feel it as his massive right thumb cocked the pistol's hammer back. His left hand drew her head back still farther, the fingers twisted in her hair.

She reached her hands up to claw his eyes out.

A voice. "Hold it, Captain Grey!"

Grey's eyes flickered. Mulrooney punched her right fist into Grey's already bleeding left eye. The man screamed.

And then Grey was gone, Mulrooney feeling a handful of her hair being wrenched out by the roots. She sprawled back against the far starboard edge of the companion benchseat.

Grey was on his knees, and Culhane was on his knees as well. Both men were face to face, their noses almost touching, Culhane's right fist locked around Grey's right wrist, Grey still holding the pistol. There was a shot, the pistol licking a tongue of orange flame into the night sky.

Mulrooney edged back. She tried pushing herself to her feet but lost her balance and almost fell over the safety rail. The *Cherokee* was moving in a wide, bouncing circle in the water, cutting across its own wake, lurching up and down and from side to side. Salt spray pelted her face, and the wind blew her hair in front of her eyes. She pushed it back so she could see, trying to keep her balance, and tried to get to the other gun.

She saw it on the deck just between Culhane and Grey.

The pistol Grey held discharged again, a bullet ripping into the benchseat near her left hand. She screamed and drew her hand back.

Culhane sprawled backward, Grey lurching over him, Culhane's right fist still on Grey's wrist. The giant's left fist hammered out again and again, despite or maybe because of Culhane's body slumping under him.

"Oh, shit!" Mulrooney screamed.

But then Culhane's legs moved, and Grey sailed over him, landing against the benchseat almost directly beside her. She screamed again in spite of herself.

Culhane was up, throwing himself against Grey, the pistol discharging into the back of the helmseat. She saw a blur of motion as Culhane lurched away from Grey, his left foot snapping into Grey's face, Grey rolling away across the deck. Grey was raising the pistol to fire.

"Josh—look out!" Mulrooney cried, feeling stupid for not doing something else, something better than that.

The pistol fired as Culhane threw himself down on Grey, Mulrooney seeing the pistol's flash in the night. Culhane, his brown hair black with wetness, the hair on his chest plastered to him in streaks, was straddling Grey now, his knee grinding down against Grey's arm. Culhane's fists lashed out, crossing Grey's jaw again and again, Grey's head snapping from side to side, Culhane still hitting him. Then suddenly Culhane fell back, both hands clutching at his crotch as he rolled to the portside of the flying bridge's deck.

Grey was up on his knees, and Culhane started for him.

Mulrooney dived to the deck, her hands grabbing the pistol. Her finger found the trigger and pressed it as she stabbed the pistol outward, the boat lurching under her as she fell forward, the pistol bucking hard in her hands.

Grey was still moving as she rolled onto her back. His right foot kicked at her face, but she rolled away from it.

Culhane was up on his feet now, his left fist hammering into the center of Grey's face, then his right fist, then his left, then his right, then his left into Grey's abdomen, doubling the huge man over. Culhane's right knee smashed up into Grey's face, and Grey sprawled back across the deck.

The gun. Grey still had the gun.

Culhane's hands ripped the Luger from Mulrooney's.

Two shots, then two more. Mulrooney couldn't tell from which pistol, from which man.

Culhane sank down to his knees beside her, doubling forward.

Grey was motionless.

"You killed him!" Mulrooney shrieked, moving on her knees toward Grey.

But she stopped, feeling Culhane's touch on her bare calf. And then she saw Grey's eyes as a wash of spray flew across his face; the eyelids didn't flicker.

"You're... you're... beautiful...."

Mulrooney looked over her shoulder at Culhane, his head bent as though he were talking to the deck beneath them. But then he looked up, their eyes meeting.

"Beautiful when you're angry, Fanny," he rasped, sinking against her as she opened her arms to him.

Mulrooney helped Culhane get the bodies locked away into the aft cabin, then operated the boat's control console while he called the Coast Guard with an anonymous tip about a disabled pirate vessel. She cleaned the cuts on his knuckles and watched the controls again while he quickly showered and changed.

After all that, she very calmly told him, "I'm going below to the head to throw up in peace. Please don't worry about me if I'm gone for a time," and then she left the flying bridge.

Smoking a Pall Mall, watching the pink sunrise, Culhane steered them toward San Rafael, expecting to sight land at any moment. He decided he would contact Partridge and take the *Cherokee* into Miami or Fort Lauderdale rather than back to Nassau. It would be easier for Partridge and the CIA to explain a few bodies to U.S. police than to foreign police.

Scrounging ammunition from the Luger—a gun he had never much cared for—he discovered he had a full magazine plus one in the chamber for the Walther P-38 and two loaded spares plus a half-dozen loose rounds in the left front pocket of his Levi's.

He heard footsteps on the flying bridge deck behind him, turned around and saw Mulrooney. She wore very short blue denim shorts, a top that looked like a pink T-shirt with a low neckline, and her brown hair—still wet from the shower—was up in a ponytail. He looked at her feet; she had on running shoes with the funny kind of socks that don't come up on the ankles at all but have a little pompom at the back. These little balls of fuzz were the same shade of pink as the top she wore. "How're you doin', Fanny?"

"I've done better." She smiled, cupped her hands around her lighter, lit a Salem, then perched on the right armrest of the helmseat, leaning against him. "It looks a lot different up here, seeing daylight again."

Culhane smiled, too, looking at her, then he stared back at the line of the sunrise, roughly the way they were headed. "Yeah, it sure does."

"Do you actually know how to steer one of these things so we hit San Rafael Island instead of Europe?"

"More like Africa at this latitude," Culhane answered, "but...yeah, I think so. From the charts, it

looks like there's a bay on the far side of the island—
the Africa side—"

"Gotcha," she said, her left arm moving around his
shoulders, Culhane feeling it rest there.

"But I figure we can lay out on the near side of the
island. It's about the same distance either way up into
the mountains and to the monastery. If Steiglitz is
looking for us to come by commercial charter—and
he probably is—he'd more than likely expect us to
come from the far side where the ship could put in
close."

"I didn't think this thing drew that much water."

"It doesn't. I was checking the specs."

"The instruction booklet?" she teased.

"Yeah," he admitted with a grin. "Draws about
two feet ten inches with a full load of 425 gallons of
diesel, 128 gallons of fresh water and five persons
aboard. So we're drawing a little less than that. Fuel's
down a bit, so's the water, and maybe the dead men
below don't weigh as much as live ones."

"Thanks for reminding me, Josh," she told him.

"Relax, lady. The charts show a lot of coral on the
near side of the island, and I don't want to risk gutting
the hull taking her in. The *Cherokee*'s maybe safer out
offshore anyway. There's a rubber raft we can use."

"We could always swim for it."

"We might have to on the way back—we'll see. I
figure it should take us maybe three hours to reach the
monastery. There's a swamp we need to skirt and then
some climbing into the rocks. But not much. Don't
worry."

"Who's worried?" And she laughed, but the laugh
sounded less than genuine to Culhane.

MULROONEY HAD CHANGED INTO LEVI'S on Culhane's
advice. She'd stuffed a change of clothes and shoes for
each of them in her massive blue canvas bag along with

Culhane's flashlight and some sandwiches she'd made in the ship's galley.

Crisscrossed on his shoulders as he walked, swinging under his arms, Culhane had two bota skins of fresh water. The spare magazines and his cigarettes were in the dark blue cowboy shirt's pockets to keep them above the waterline. He clutched the Walther P-38 in his right hand, held high as they moved ahead through the swamp. The green, slime-coated water broke in tiny waves around his knees as he picked his way forward, watching the surface for snakes.

They had beached their inflatable boat at precisely 7:47, the *Cherokee*'s anchor down five hundred yards offshore. They had drawn the boat up into the rocks beyond the narrow stretch of yellow sand and hidden it under palm fronds Culhane had hacked down with the Bali-Song knife. The jungle, birds screeching as Culhane and Mulrooney moved beneath their treetop perches, had lasted less than a mile before the level of the ground dropped drastically and muddy puddles had given way to loose sandy clay and then finally to the swamp itself.

And the going had been slow since they'd entered the swamp. Cypresslike trees rose straight as urban utility poles; moss and occasional snakes hung from the thin branches. But the trees and the moss—Culhane supposed even the snakes—made shade, and since the sun was brutal, the inky green shadows were welcome.

By moving ahead carefully rather than quickly, Culhane could pick his footing, and so far the water had gotten no higher than his waist.

"This is beautiful—scary—but it's beautiful here," he heard Mulrooney pant from behind him.

"Yeah, but before you put your feet down, remind yourself about the scary part," Culhane said as he swatted at a huge black insect that buzzed by his nose.

Ahead, across the overgrown waters of the swamp, he could see an empty stretch. There were almost no trees in the part of the swamp into which they were walking, and the hot sun glared down as a flock of birds off to their right took flight noisily.

"Could be deeper here—maybe that's why there are so few trees. We might have to swim for it."

"Wonderful," Mulrooney called back.

Culhane lit a cigarette and blew the smoke onto his arms to keep the mosquitoes away from the parts exposed by his rolled-up sleeves. "And if we do have to swim for it," he added, "don't swallow the water. You get things like meningitis and polio from swamp water."

"Gee, keep talking. It makes me feel so good," he heard her say.

In the "clearing," the swamp started deepening dramatically. At one point Culhane took a step, slipped and nearly lost his balance before catching himself. He was now standing in water up to the bottom of his rib cage. He shouted to Mulrooney, "Stay back, Fanny— gotta find another way!" He edged back, trying to retrace his steps, and finally reached the higher ground behind him. He looked back to Mulrooney.

"You know, Josh, I'm getting awful tired of this."

He just looked at her. He nodded, breathing hard. "We'll circle around to the right here—unless you want to swim for it."

Mulrooney said nothing but began circling to the right. . . .

Culhane pulled his left hand out of the water and read the Rolex. They had been in the swamp for nearly two hours, and there was no end in sight. They were following what seemed to be a river course, or something like it, not cutting straight across the swamp as they had been, but sticking along the bank in the reeds of the shallows. Suddenly Culhane froze. A snake—a cottonmouth moccasin, he thought, judging from its size and brown coloring with darker brown stripes—appeared in the reeds and darted past him into the deeper part of the swampy river bottom after opening its mouth at him in a show of defiance. Mulrooney bumped into him from behind, leaning against him, Culhane feeling her weight on his back.

"How much longer, old buddy?"

"I don't know, kid. Maybe another hour or two, maybe a lot less. The water's too deep to keep to a straight course. We've gotta follow this river or whatever it is even though it probably zigzags enough to double or triple the distance from the coastline into the rocks."

"Wonderful. Any more encouraging news? Tell me about how we have to walk out through the swamp the same way we walked in."

Culhane turned and wrapped his arms around her. She sagged more heavily against him. "Maybe we'll have to, maybe not. But from all I could figure, this seemed like the best way into the monastery without someone finding us."

"I know."

"Here, have some water." Culhane lifted one of the bota skins, wiped off the leather around the mouthpiece, opened it and handed it to Mulrooney. She squirted some of the water into her mouth like a kid with a water pistol taking target practice. "Wish it were wine, huh?"

"Yeah," she said, handing him the skin. Culhane nodded, shooting some of the water—it was warm but clean tasting—into his mouth.

"Want any more?" he asked her.

She nodded, taking the bota and shooting some more water into her mouth. "I can carry it—"

"No," he interrupted. "I'll do it. These things get heavy."

"I can carry one."

"No," he said and took the bag from her, closing it tightly so none of the brackish swamp water could get in. Then he started ahead, Mulrooney behind him again. The Walther was in his belt now, the water low enough so that it came only to his midthigh.

Mulrooney was talking again; she talked a lot when she was nervous or tired. Culhane sensed that she was both. "Nothing a girl likes better than a good old-fashioned swamp-water douche," she was saying.

"No kidding?"

"Oh, yeah—would I kid a kidder, Josh?"

"Naw," he told her, keeping it up. "Naw."

"Listen, you ever marry me, I think we oughta come back here for our honeymoon."

"I don't think so," Culhane said and laughed. "The marrying part—well, I guess we're both wacko enough that someday maybe we will—but the honeymoon part here—no way. I checked the AAA guide for the swamp, and there's no Hilton—not even a Holiday Inn."

"Aww, gee, I didn't know that," she said in mock disappointment. *"Culhane!"*

She almost never called him by his last name.

He turned quickly, grabbing her as she started sinking down and forward, taking two steps out into the river, feeling himself starting to sink as well.

"You aren't gonna like this, Fanny," he shouted, trying to haul his feet out of it, trying to pull her with him. "This is quicksand!"

Culhane slumped his body forward, reaching out to an exposed root of one of the cypress-type trees, both hands going out to it in a push-up position, still keeping his chest above the waterline. "Hold on to my legs!" he shouted to her, feeling her hands grabbing at him.

"It's pulling me under, Josh!"

"Try not to thrash around. Stay still—as still as you

can,'' Culhane gasped, his fingers knotted into the root, trying to pull himself and Mulrooney out of the morass. ''Just don't let go of me—don't let go—''

''I'm trying not to! Oh, Josh!''

He glanced back at her. The quicksand was up to her waist now, moving like a slow whirlpool around her, the goo depressed in a circle around her body.

''Hang in there, Fanny!'' Culhane's fingers, his hands, his arms ached. His shoulders were still sore from clinging to the line in the wake of the *Cherokee* earlier that morning. ''Just hang in there, kid!''

He threw his weight forward, his chest crashing down against the tree root, his hand groping to a vine running down from the trunk of the tree. A smile crossed his lips as he grasped the vine. Then he tugged at it. ''Aww, shit!'' The vine crashed down, a tree branch tumbling down with it, hitting him on the head.

''Josh! I'm sinking! Josh, come on!''

Culhane reached out again, this time for the tree trunk itself, wedging his body against the tree root, tugging himself forward, but there was nothing to grab hold of.

His right hand was against the tree trunk as his left slipped down to his pocket for the Bali-Song knife. The slime was creeping around him, his legs being drawn into it as Mulrooney held on, Mulrooney being dragged deeper and deeper. He glanced back at her. The muck was up to the level of her breasts now.

''Josh!''

He didn't answer.

''Josh!''

His left hand had the Bali-Song, the smooth stainless steel slippery to the touch, his fingers finding the holes in the handle halves, holding on tightly as he brought his hand up and out of the mire.

He opened the Bali-Song slowly so he wouldn't drop it. The lock was open. The forward handle half dropped, then the blade. He moved his fingers, nearly losing it, but managed to close the handle halves into the open position.

He edged his left hand forward, his eyes scanning the mud around him looking for something solid. Farther up along the tree root he noticed a bulging knot.

He guessed he'd have one chance. Looking back, he saw Mulrooney mired in the quicksand to a point midway between her breasts and her chin.

"Josh!"

"Hang on, dammit!" His left hand swung up, his arm forming a pendulum, his fist balled tight on the handle halves, his fingers gouging into the small holes in the handle so the knife wouldn't slip from his slimy fingers.

The pendulum of his arm rose, then hammered down. "Do it!" he shouted as his hand stabbed the knife for the tree root's knot.

The knife bit deep.

Culhane's head sank forward and he exhaled.

His left hand still on the knife, he dragged himself forward, Mulrooney's weight on his legs making his muscles burn, making them feel as if they would tear apart. His right hand had full contact with the tree trunk now. He thrust himself forward again, the knife his only means of locomotion, his only handhold.

He sagged forward, his right arm half around the trunk, his right hand finding a notch in the bark's surface.

Both of Culhane's hands could pull him forward now. His breath was coming in short gasps. He pulled. He sagged forward, gulping air, pulling again, feeling Mulrooney's nails digging into his flesh through the Levi's covering his legs. He pulled.

Culhane fell forward again, pushing against the knife now to get himself nearer the tree trunk.

He sagged down, both hands on the tree trunk.

Culhane looked behind him. Mulrooney was submerged nearly up to her chin, but she was closer to the edge of the quicksand pool than she had been, and her hands still held on to his legs.

On his chest, craning his neck to look at her over his right shoulder, Culhane said, "Now, you're gonna have to let go of my legs for a second so I can get my legs out and—"

"No!"

"You have to, Fanny! If I get my legs out, I can use this vine and pull you out!"

"No!"

"Do it! For once in your life do what I say! Now shut up! I love you, dammit! I don't wanna come back here every year and throw flowers on a quicksand pool! Do what I say!"

"All right," she panted.

"When I say let go, just move your hands away and stay very still." He licked his dry lips. *"Now!"*

He felt her hands leave his legs. His own hands on the tree trunk, he heaved himself forward against it, his right foot free of the mire.

Culhane tugged his left leg free, rolling onto his back.

Mulrooney was sinking, her head cocked back to keep her chin above the water. Her eyes were wide in terror.

There was no time for the vine. He reached to his waist, opening the Federal Cartridge Trophy buckle holding his belt closed. He tore the belt from his trouser loops, his right fist locking on the belt's tongue like a vise.

"Catch the belt buckle and hold on!"

Her right hand above the level of the quicksand, Culhane snapped the belt out across to it, not daring to overreach lest he fall into the ooze and they both die.

She missed the belt buckle, and Culhane dragged it back.

He whipped it out again, nearly striking her in the face. "Sorry, Fanny."

He was breathing hard, his face dripping, the salty sweat stinging his eyes.

He swung the belt out again. Mulrooney's chin was now touching the quicksand. "It's pulling me down!" she screamed.

The buckle settled on the surface of the mire, inches from her right hand.

"Fanny! Grab for the buckle!"

"I can't—"

"Yes, you can! You some sissy who's gonna die or old rough-and-tough M.F. Mulrooney?"

"I can't!"

"You know what the newspaper guys around Atlanta always used to say the M.F. stood for? Not Mary Frances but Mother Fu—"

"Damn those assholes!"

"Reach for the buckle, Fanny!"

She reached for it, missing, and the buckle started to sink. She reached for it again. "I got it!"

"Hold on! I don't care what else you do—just hold on!"

Both of Culhane's hands were on the tongue of the now slippery leather. If he lost it, he lost her. "Try to keep your face up—here goes!"

He threw himself back against the tree trunk, using his full weight to pull her.

He crashed down, looking along the length of his body. Mulrooney's breasts were out of the muck, her hands clawing for the tree root.

Culhane was up, thrashing through the shallow water and mud, reaching down to her, his hands locking on her wrists. He pulled. He dragged her out and to her knees in the mud beside the tree root.

Somehow the big blue purse was still under her left arm.

He sagged down to the mud, edging up on the tree root, Mulrooney on her hands and knees looking at him. "Those clowns," she panted. "Those clowns on the papers—they really said that about the M.F.?"

Culhane laughed. "Yeah, but if I were you I'd thank 'em." And Mulrooney, leaning her head against his knee, her hair full of the slime from the quicksand pool, began gently, giddily to laugh.

THERE WAS A ROCKY WATERFALL with worn, slick stones leading out from the stream's bank to the cascade, and Culhane and Mulrooney—holding hands to steady each other, still fully dressed, the stench of the swamp on them—walked out across the stones and stood under it. Mulrooney began shivering, the water surprisingly cold considering the heat of the swamp below them. Culhane helped her to strip off the pink T-shirt and her bra, then supported her as she skinned out of her Levi's. She'd left her shoes and socks by the edge of the waterfall. Culhane undressed, having left the Bali-Song, the pistol, the spare magazines and his shoes beside Mulrooney's massive blue bag beyond the reach of the waterfall's spray.

The clothes were beyond help, but Mulrooney's plastic-lined canvas bag had held together, and a change of clothes for each of them was inside it.

And so they washed each other, Culhane taking her into his arms and holding her tight against him, feeling too tired to do what his body was telling him it wanted to do, watching Mulrooney's face as she pushed away from him a little and smiled.

There was no soap, but the pressure of the falling water was so great that they were able to rub themselves clean. They stayed under the water for a long time, trying to let the water work to soothe them. Culhane's right shoulder ached badly. Mulrooney had been so weary during that final hour's walk out of the swamp and up into the rocks that he almost had to carry her.

After a while, abandoning their old clothes, they walked from beneath the waterfall and sat naked on the edge of the swiftly running stream at its base, listening to the roar of the water, silent between themselves.

Mulrooney finally spoke. "You saved my life back there. That makes two or three times today you did that."

"Yeah, well, it seemed like a good idea at the time—each time." He fished inside her purse for his cigarettes and lighter.

"Let me smoke one of yours?" she asked.

Culhane lit two with one flame, inhaling on them both, then handed one to her.

"We've still got Steiglitz and company to look forward to, haven't we?"

"Yeah," he said and nodded, exhaling, watching the smoke as it formed a cloud, then suddenly dissipated as the breeze passing across the stream caught it. "Yeah, we still have Steiglitz."

"Will the gun work?"

Culhane shrugged his bare shoulders. Mulrooney moved closer to him, and he put his arm around her.

The gun—the P-38—was on the rocks beside them. He had washed the gun clean of mud before they had washed themselves. He had wiped the cartridges clean after stripping them from the magazines, then set them on a rock far enough back from the water to keep them out of the spray. Six cartridges had been in Mulrooney's purse. Once the magazines were dry, he'd load them so they came up first in the pistol. At least he knew those six would work.

They sat there, the breeze drying their bodies, Mulrooney huddled beside him, knees up to her chin, his arm around her bare back and shoulders, his fingers resting on her breast. He was very tired. . . .

MULROONEY, WEARING HER BLUE DENIM SHORTS and a blue-and-white striped T-shirt, walked beside Culhane, sandals having replaced the running shoes. Culhane carried the two spare magazines for the pistol in the left pocket of his khaki shorts. The Bali-Song—which he had cleaned thoroughly—sat in the right pocket along with his cigarettes and lighter. The belt buckle was in Mulrooney's purse. He had thrown away the belt.

It was hard climbing up along the rocks, but already the monastery was in view in the distance on what he'd been told was the island's highest promontory. It was simply called Holy Rock.

At noon, according to Culhane's watch and the position of the sun, they stopped, and Mulrooney unwrapped the sandwiches she had made. The bread tasted damp, but both of them ate as though they were starving, Mulrooney eating one and a half sandwiches, giving the other half of her second sandwich to Culhane. He took it, not knowing if she was no longer hungry or just being nice; he suspected the latter. And then they resumed their climb, Culhane scrambling up ahead of a barefoot Mulrooney; she had packed away her sandals because they gave no footing on the rocks.

They kept moving, and the monastery loomed larger above them, now visible in greater detail. They could make out gray stone and what looked from the distance to be wooden posts.

"I wonder if we'll find it," Mulrooney said. "I wonder if it's still there."

"We shouldn't have any trouble," Culhane said.

"If Steiglitz knew about San Rafael Island, why didn't he just tear the monastery apart to find the Log?"

"What if Henry Chillingsworth had hidden it by that waterfall, or wrapped it in oilskins and put it inside a chest and covered the whole thing with wax and dropped it in the swamp?" Culhane replied. "No—if they've been keeping tabs on us, they must know by now that we're going to the monastery. And even if it is buried outside the monastery, they'll wait," Culhane insisted. "They'll wait until we actually have the Gladstone Log—then they'll close in on us."

"Just where the hell did he put it?" she said, panting, stopping beside him as he stopped. They had reached the crest of a ridge, the monastery about a half mile distant along a natural, not too steeply ramped smooth stone path.

Culhane slipped his arm around her waist.

"Well, I hate to ruin the suspense for you, but he hid it under the altar stone—the kind of place a kid would pick. He hid it the first week he was with the monks on the island here. And he never went back to look for it."

"Just under a stone?"

"I think I know what he did. Don't worry."

"You mean he doesn't say?"

"Relax," Culhane said. "Call it a sixth sense—like ESP or something, drawing me to it."

"Bullshit," she said and laughed.

Culhane marched along the pathway of rock, toward the monastery and toward the Gladstone Log.

PART TWO
ISLAND OF PERIL

CHAPTER TWENTY-TWO

She resented her father's presence. His simply being here insinuated her incompetence. She made the walk up into the rocks take her anger, moving ahead of her father and the others, shifting the weight of the M-16 on her shoulder, listening to the indistinguishable murmurings of her father and the other men behind her.

His men liked him, obeyed him more willingly than her men obeyed her. But they did obey her out of fear.

She finally stopped, sitting on a flat outcropping, taking the M-16 off her shoulder and leaning it against the rock, careful not to bang the scope mounted over the receiver carrying handle. She watched her father.

Jeremiah Steiglitz moved with better grace, greater strength and more energy than any of the men with him, all of them in their twenties and thirties. He carried no rifle, no submachine gun. Only a .45 strapped to his right hip in a military-style flap holster.

Nothing more.

His expression almost a smile.

Sonia had been to San Rafael with him before, gone through the ancient monastery from end to end, side to side, top to bottom, helped him dig beneath the fruit trees that the monks had once kept, had walked the monastery grounds with metal detectors. She'd found an old cross from a rosary once and wanted to keep it as a souvenir, but he had made her throw it away.

Another time they had found an old iron box. Inside the box was a bottle, the cork rotted; the bottle had the lingering smell of rum to it. Some monk burying his conscience bottle, her father had said.

And they had kept on.

But they had never found the Gladstone Log.

There was a forty- or so foot sport fisherman on the far side of the island. Josh Culhane and M.F. Mulrooney would have come upon it, Steiglitz figured. They had watched the boat from the rocks near where they had landed the helicopter that had brought them to the island, but saw no sign of any crew aboard.

Sonia laughed. Perhaps Culhane and his slut had thought to bring the crew with them through the swamp and up into the rocks where the monastery was. "Safety in numbers," she said aloud, and then she laughed.

She looked up. Her father had outdistanced the other men and stood before her.

"A private joke, Sonia?"

"I was thinking—perhaps they brought others with them, expecting us to wait for them to uncover the Log."

"An academic matter, my dear," he said and smiled. "In another half hour, the depth charge I had planted on the hull of the *Cherokee* before they left Nassau will detonate. And, of course, no one but ourselves will ever leave the monastery alive. As I said, an academic point. Come." He started ahead.

Sonia got to her feet, picked up her rifle and followed after him. She would always do that, she knew.

CHAPTER TWENTY-THREE

It was built like a fortress. Rocks cemented together like bricks formed the falling walls surrounding it as Culhane, the Walther P-38 in his right fist, Mulrooney beside him, passed to the side of a half-collapsed archway and then beyond the wall.

A length of the wall on the near side of the island survived, extending along the farthest border of the natural stone pathway and disappearing as the ground curved down from the height of the rocks and back toward the sea.

"Ambitious builders," Culhane said to Mulrooney, stopping just beyond the arch. The monastery seemed to have comprised several buildings. Ruined walls of brick-sized rocks were everywhere, and half-rotted timbers still stood in spots, reminders of once-standing structures.

"Didn't you say something about a hurricane that hit the island in the early thirties?" Mulrooney remarked.

"Yeah—can't remember the year. But the monks were lucky the Church had closed them down." The path of some strong force of nature could still be read along the monastery grounds—a path of fallen buildings and ripped-up flagstones that had once really been paths. Stone paths that, Culhane imagined, had led the monks to their daily chores or perhaps to prayer.

One central building dominated the grounds, its north wall all but destroyed, its south wall still standing as did—miraculously seemed the right adjective, Culhane thought—a portion of the flat roof that had once covered it.

Culhane started walking toward it.

Mulrooney was moving beside him, her voice a hushed whisper as she asked, "That's the altar?"

"And the altar stone," he murmured.

To the right side, to the south, were small rooms, perhaps used by monks or perhaps—during troubled times—used as resting places for those seeking asylum on Church ground. Altarlike structures made of smaller stones piled together were positioned on the far wall of each of the cubicles.

"Beds?"

"Yeah, probably," Culhane answered.

"Boy, what a mattress salesman with a good delivery system could have done here."

Culhane didn't answer her, his eyes shifting from the small, occasionally windowless cubicles to the altar—a stone table made of hewn slabs of rock—dominating the front of the church. There had been wooden pews on either side of a central aisle, the wood now all but rotted away, only the blocks of stone that had supported them still standing in a recognizable pattern.

He started walking toward the altar, noting a rotted horizontal timber—the only reminder of what had once been, he supposed, an altar rail for the taking of Communion by the monks.

Culhane mounted three stone steps, Mulrooney beside him, her hand in his, and they stood before the altar stone. "I always hoped you'd get me to the altar, but I never imagined it'd be like this," Mulrooney said.

Culhane looked at her, smiled, then started toward the altar itself.

To their left was a crude stone pedestal looking something like the base for a birdbath.

"What was that for?" Mulrooney murmured.

"Baptismal font, probably," he answered.

At the base of the stone altar, forming its broad front, figures had been crudely carved in low relief, but it was clearly a representation of Christ carrying His cross, other figures surrounding Him. This dominated the left side. In the center was a more accomplished carving of a crucifix. And to the right was another of the more crudely carved designs: Christ ascending to Heaven on a cloud, the figures beneath presumably His disciples.

"This place gives me the creeps," Mulrooney whispered.

Culhane ignored her, staring at the altar, walking from side to side, then walking completely around it.

"What are you looking for?"

Culhane dropped into a crouch at the front of the altar again, touching its base with his fingertips, feeling across its length where he could reach. "This base—beneath the altar itself—is the altar stone. That's like the foundation for the altar."

"I knew that," she said.

He looked up at her and smiled. "I knew you knew that, but I don't see any way of moving it—aside from blowing it up or getting ten strong men in here with crowbars."

"You mean—"

"I don't know what I mean yet. But if a twelve- or fourteen-year-old boy was able to get the altar stone out of the way enough to hide something beneath it, then we should be able to do the same without all that muscle."

"You mean some secret panel or something—to make the altar move?"

"Yeah, well, assuming there is one and we find it. Then we have to assume it still works after maybe a century of disuse, and a hurricane that ripped down half the church."

"I love it when you're brimming over with youthful optimism."

He winked at her, rising, feeling the altar with his fingertips.

"You're looking for the secret panel, right?" she asked him.

"Right—but I don't really know if I'll recognize it when I find it. I've been on some archaeological digs over the years. There aren't as many secret panels in these old places as you see in the movies."

"I was doing this series of articles for a women's magazine on haunted houses once," she told him, dropping to her knees before the altar, feeling the altar stone, "and a lot of these old houses really do have secret panels—sometimes in case of trouble, sometimes to hide things, and a lot of times just because the owners were eccentric enough to want secret doorways."

"You ever find any ghosts?" he asked.

"Cold spots, but never any strange apparitions or anything. And a lot of weird stories that seemed pretty genuine when you considered the sources."

"No kidding," he answered absently.

She was quiet for a moment as Culhane explored the upper surface of the altar. "Yecch—what's this?"

Culhane looked down to where she knelt beside the altar stone.

"Rat droppings, most likely."

She looked up at him, then got to her feet in the most fluidly graceful move he'd ever seen her make and stepped back two steps. "Ohh...yeah, that's what I thought it was."

Culhane went back to examining the altar.

Mulrooney was talking. "Sometimes in those old houses, you'd be looking for a secret panel because you knew where the door was or where the passage ran, but you couldn't find the—"

There was the audible sound of her sucking in her breath, a grating sound, and then a low rumble as Culhane looked up, feeling the stone beneath his feet—the lip of the altar stone—moving.

He looked at Mulrooney. She was staring at the stem of the baptismal font. She had been leaning against it while she was talking. Then their eyes met. "Pretty smart of me, huh?" she said, her eyes sparkling.

Culhane nodded, looking from her eyes to the hole beneath him where the altar stone had slid away.

Stone steps led downward into blackness.

"So that's beneath the altar stone...."

"It's probably a crypt for burying the dead."

Mulrooney's nervous cough echoed around them in the old stone church at the center of the monastery.

HER HANDS WERE AGAINST HER THIGHS, her fingers splayed as she followed Culhane down the stone steps, followed the beam of his flashlight as it led beneath the altar.

She could hear scratching sounds in the darkness, and her bare arms and legs suddenly felt cold. "What's that noise—those little scratchy noises?"

"Rats—maybe bats. Watch the floor. Could be kind of slimy underfoot."

"And I hadda wear sandals. . . ."

He didn't answer her. She moved her hand, extending it out into the darkness until it contacted his shoulder under the knit shirt he wore. It felt better holding on to him. She kept walking down the steps, not taking her eyes off the beam of his flashlight, once seeing something scurry out of the light across the steps ahead.

"What the hell was that?"

"A rat, I guess. Relax," he told her.

"You get a rat coming up to bite your big toe, he's got a running shoe to go through. With me, all the little sucker's got is nail polish."

"Hope it's chip-proof."

She dug her nails into his shoulder until she heard him murmur "Ouch, Fanny," and she eased the pressure a little but not much.

He stopped moving and she didn't, crashing into him. "Why'd you stop?"

"Ran out of steps."

Mulrooney looked at the flashlight beam and watched as it played across a floor. Parts of the floor seemed alive with dark, moving spots. "Just roaches," she heard Culhane whisper.

"I almost had a landlord once who told me the same thing," she answered, still watching the beam of the flashlight.

The flashlight stopped. She felt her jaw drop. A stone coffin, the lid half off, a skeleton's hand reaching out the side. She figured the hell with it—it was scream or faint, and the floor was too horrible to fall on. She screamed.

"Relax."

"I hate that word!"

"All right, don't relax," Culhane muttered, shining the flashlight over the coffin. It wasn't stone but of hewn wood covered with mud. Part of the mud had cracked away.

Culhane shone the flashlight beyond the coffin into the chamber. Rats scurried over other coffins.

"You know what you're looking for?" she asked him.

"Yeah. When Chillingsworth talked about hiding the Log under the altar stone, he mentioned this monk—one of the monks had been especially kind to him when he was first found—dying suddenly of some illness where his chest seemed to tighten."

"Heart attack. I know the feeling."

"Yeah, but if you were a kid hiding something, who would you hide it with? Who would you trust?"

"A friend," he heard her answer through the darkness, her hand in his.

"And which one of these coffins would you open up? One full of rotted flesh and bones—strangers—or maybe one that had a relatively fresh body in it?"

"Neither—if I had a choice—but I see what you mean."

"The names of the monks are on little plaques on the coffin lids."

"So we gotta read all the names until—"

"Brother Diego—that's the coffin we want."

"Brother Diego—right," he heard her repeat.

He stopped beside a coffin, and a rat scurried across the lid. He felt her squeeze his hand. The dust was too thick for him to read the name, and he set the flashlight on the coffin lid so he didn't have to let go of her hand, then brushed the dirt away.

The name there was Felippe.

"Next coffin," he told her.

She didn't say anything. Culhane figured she was either getting used to it or was too frightened to keep talking.

"Watch it," he said as he stepped across a swarm of cockroaches.

"Ick," he heard her whisper from the darkness. "I think one just ran across my foot."

"Probably a foot fetishist. Relax."

"I really hate that word, Josh."

He stopped beside the next coffin.

Again he set down the light to dust the nameplate. He read the name out loud. "Diego."

He shone the light toward Mulrooney. "You hold this. I'll pry open the lid."

"With what?"

"My fingers, I hope."

"I'll hold the light."

He handed the flashlight to her. "Shine it over here—around the edge."

A rat ran across the lid, almost brushing his hand. He would have said something, but he didn't want to frighten Mulrooney. His fingers felt along the mating point of the coffin lid to the coffin box, a paper-thin gap.

There was his knife, but despite the Bali-Song's strength, it might break if used as a lever. "Shine that light around the floor. Look for something I can use like a crowbar."

"Only if I don't have to pick it up."

There was darkness on the lid of the mud-encrusted timber coffin as Culhane tried prying at it with his fingers. Tiny red dots—eyes of rats—were visible at the outer edges of the flashlight beam as he glanced behind him. And then Mulrooney was saying, "I hate to use this—and I even picked it up," and she handed him a simple metal cross. "It was on one of the other coffins, just resting on top."

Culhane took it from her. "Shine the light over here," he said. "Where the lid meets the box."

The cross seemed to be made of iron. Holding the shorter end above the crossbar, he edged the longer end between the coffin lid and the box, chipping with it at the wood of the lid. Some of the wood fell away, and white, antlike creatures crawled over it.

"What are those? Termites?" Mulrooney asked.

Culhane didn't speak. He was working on enlarging a chink in the coffin lid. He pried away a six- or seven-inch-long section and wedged the cross under the lid.

"Sure it isn't sacrilegious to use a cross?"

"It's in a good cause, anyway." Culhane kept prying, hearing a creaking sound, feeling the lid starting to give. He rammed the cross forward between the lid and the box of the coffin itself, using the cross in his right hand as a lever, his left hand going under the lid and pushing up. Mulrooney was beside him, also pushing. "Watch out!" Culhane pushed her back, stepping away, the coffin lid sliding from the box portion, Mulrooney's flashlight beam catching it as the coffin lid skidded off the near side and the bottom, coming to rest inches from their feet.

The sounds of the rats were loud now, the rodents disturbed by the movement of the coffin lid. Mulrooney's flashlight beam swept up from the floor and settled on the upper interior of the coffin, on empty eye sockets, on dessicated flesh clinging in patches to the yellowed, shiny bone.

He felt Mulrooney's hand squeeze his arm.

Culhane set down the cross and took the flashlight from her, sweeping the flashlight beam down the length of the coffin. Tattered dark fabric clung to the limbs—a monk's habit. What perhaps had been a blanket lay in tatters beneath the bones.

By the feet was a roughly square package. Culhane moved along the length of the coffin and reached inside, trying not to touch the bones as he picked up the package. Leather thongs—rotted, falling apart as he touched them—bound the package. The package itself was wrapped in what Culhane assumed were oiled skins shaved of hair.

Carefully, with Mulrooney beside him—he could hear her breathing—he unfolded the skins. He set the skin that covered the package at the feet of Brother Diego. Another skin. He unwrapped this as well, but more carefully than the first. It was less cracked than the first, less old looking, though of equal age, he was sure.

A third skin lay beneath.

Culhane unfolded this with the greatest care, baring a leather book, similar in shape and appearance to the memoir of Henry Chillingsworth, but woodburned into the leather of the cover were three initials and a word: H.M.S. *Madagascar.*

Mulrooney said it. "The Gladstone Log."

And then a voice from the steps they had left behind them in the darkness. A woman's voice. "This is Sonia Steiglitz. Come up the steps with your hands raised and the Gladstone Log in view."

A flashlight flicked on with an audible click, the high-intensity beam bathing the coffin, Culhane and Mulrooney in its light. Culhane's right fist held the Walther P-38. He double-actioned a shot toward the light, and the light went out.

He shoved Mulrooney down beside the coffin, covering her flashlight beam with the Gladstone Log as the darkness from the head of the catacombs erupted in tongues of flame, bullets thudding into the coffin, ricocheting off the walls, whining past their heads.

CHAPTER TWENTY-FOUR

He held her head down, Mulrooney talking but Culhane not listening to her, the gunfire making his ears ring, so that listening to human speech was impossible anyway.

"Keep down!" he shouted.

More gunfire echoed and re-echoed in the burial vault, chips of the coffin's rotted wood spraying everywhere around them. A submachine gun, Culhane guessed.

Another flashlight illuminated the interior of the crypt. Culhane, instead of poking the Walther around the side of the coffin and firing at the light, glanced up and saw wooden beams across the vaulted ceiling, making a triangular shape there, then wedging a large support beam against the flat rock.

There was more gunfire, and this time Culhane stabbed the Walther's muzzle around the side of the coffin, firing the P-38 twice just to remind Sonia Steiglitz and whomever she had with her that he and Mulrooney were still alive.

The light still bathed the chamber.

The gunfire stopped.

A man's voice, deep, resonant and self-confident, filled the chamber. "Mr. Culhane, please don't shoot for a moment. This is Jeremiah Steiglitz."

"Holy shit," Mulrooney murmured.

"Shh," Culhane rasped, then he turned off his flashlight. He could see the old cross they had used as a crowbar an arm's length away, at the meeting of light and shadow where the powerful beam from the head of the catacombs was blocked by the end of the coffin.

"What do you want?" Culhane shouted back unnecessarily.

"Are you both all right?" Steiglitz called out.

"No thanks to you, you son of a bitch!" Mulrooney answered.

"Ahh—the intrepid and ever genteel Miss Mulrooney. It is you, yes?"

Culhane answered for her. "What do you want?"

"Impatient, aren't we," Steiglitz's voice called from behind the screen of light. "But then I, too, would be, in your position. You see, you have something that I have spent two-thirds of my life trying to possess."

"Tough shit," Culhane called back.

"Yes, quite. But nevertheless, you have the Gladstone Log, do you not?"

"You mean the thing I can burn the pages out of with my cigarette lighter? Yeah, we've got it."

"Ahh—such bravado—I like that. Your brother had a great deal of bravado, Mr. Culhane—your late brother. I want the Log."

Silence.

"Don't give it to him," Mulrooney hissed in Culhane's left ear.

"I'm not going to," he whispered back. "Why do you want this thing?" he then shouted to Steiglitz. He was stalling for time, watching the beam of light. It moved slightly to his right. He set the Walther on the edge of the coffin and reached for the cross. He grabbed it.

"I suppose telling you won't matter. The Log should contain directions to what an archaeologist would consider the most spectacular find in history, to what a scientist would consider the key to knowledge undreamed of, at once ancient and of the future. But more for me—I am a simple man. Power is what I seek. And what you or Miss Mulrooney hold is the key to power, the greatest power that ever held sway on the face of this earth."

Mulrooney shouted to him. "Atlantis? If the Atlanteans had such power, why the heck did all of them die off when their island was inundated? Why didn't they just fly away or something?''

Steiglitz roared with laughter. "Neither of you suspects—and that is wonderful, because then no one else suspects. But suffice it to say, you have the Log and I do not." Culhane handed the gun to Mulrooney, took the flashlight from her and put a finger to her lips. He started edging behind her, handing her the Log as well.

"What's your deal?'' Culhane shouted to Steiglitz.

"A one-time offer—never to be repeated,'' Steiglitz came back. "In exchange for a speedy handing over of the Gladstone Log, I will allow you both to live as my prisoners until I have brought the information contained in the Log to its inevitable conclusion and I possess the power I have sought for forty years. After that, you'll be free to go, as it would be impossible then for any efforts to succeed against me."

"Bullshit,'' Mulrooney's voice shouted from the darkness beside the coffin. Culhane was beside the vertical support timber just between the coffin and the light source.

"Shut up, Fanny,'' Culhane shouted to her. Then he called to Steiglitz, "How do I know you're on the level?''

He had the iron cross wedged between the support and the stone of the wall. He gave it a test pry. The timber moved perhaps a quarter inch, dust filtering down and making a barely audible noise as it rained down around him, Culhane feeling it on his arms and legs and face.

"How do you know I'm on the level? What a picturesque expression. Yes, no doubt you are a writer, Mr. Culhane. Well, as a matter of fact, I'll give you my word. It is my only and best assurance. What is your answer?''

"What kind of power are you talking about?'' In

the half-light of the washed-out edge of the flashlight's glow, Culhane could see the iron cross and the wooden beam. If he drove the cross in hard against the wall. . . .

"What kind of power? Does it intrigue you? Well, it is vast power, undreamed-of power, the power any man would willingly risk death for in order to achieve. It is that power. What is your answer?"

"Well," Culhane called back, holding the flashlight like a club, its butt ready to swing, the lens in his fists, "it's a tough decision. Wouldn't wanna give me a minute or two, huh?"

"Now—your answer."

"Go to hell," Mulrooney shouted.

Culhane, as he swung the flashlight toward the base of the wedged cross, shouted, "Sounds like a great idea to me!"

The flashlight's aircraft aluminum base hammered against the wedge, the timber slipping, moving, the beam of light from the top of the stairs sweeping toward it, the chatter of submachine gun fire ripping into the wall beside Culhane's head, the support collapsing, dust flying, raining down, small rocks and dirt pelting him as he ran for the coffin. He grabbed Mulrooney's shoulder and shouted, "Run like hell, Fanny!"

He started to run, turning the flashlight in his hand, hearing the crashing sounds behind him, hearing the sounds of timber splitting, rocks and dirt falling. The Kel-Lite still worked despite the punishment he'd given it, the beam showing the ground as they ran, Mulrooney shouting loud beside him, "What the hell did you do, Josh?"

"A cave-in—" Culhane looked behind him. The beam of light from the head of the catacombs was obscured. He flashed his own flashlight that way and saw that the wooden beams were still falling—like dominoes in a run—after them. He reached out in the darkness, grabbing Mulrooney's arm, half dragging, half shoving her to get her to run faster. "Run—run for it!"

The sound of the rupturing timbers was like a roar behind them, the dust and dirt forming a cloud so thick the flashlight beam couldn't penetrate it.

Holding Mulrooney's arm in a death grip so he wouldn't lose her, Culhane threw himself ahead, blindly running, slamming against a wall, coughing, not seeing through the dust, then pushing Mulrooney ahead of him to the left, gut instinct telling him that if the catacombs took a bend it was that way. He ran, not letting go of her, stumbling, lurching, getting his footing. In a passage to their right, the dust was less thick—the flashlight penetrated—and Culhane could see a dead end in front. He dragged Mulrooney toward it, half wheeling as he thrust her ahead, the flashlight's beam catching the devastation behind them, timbers still crashing down. Mulrooney in front of him, Culhane jumped through into the passage, sagging against the bare rock wall there as the catacombs behind them closed in tons of dirt, rocks and rotted timbers.

Mulrooney sagged into his arms. "Are we trapped?"

Culhane swallowed, breathing hard, coughing from the dust. "Maybe—maybe not. Don't know. But Steiglitz—Steiglitz—wants the Log. He'll dig after us."

"That could take days. . . ."

Culhane licked his lips. He took one of the water bags and opened it, offering it to Mulrooney. She drank from it, coughing, then Culhane took it from her hands and drank. The bag was nearly empty.

"These old passages usually had exit tunnels," Culhane told her, resting his hands against his thighs, doubling over to catch his breath. "Ways to get out if the catacombs were used to hide from an enemy—like that. There's usually a way out."

"The part I don't like," Mulrooney whispered, "is the word 'usually.' "

He put his arm around her shoulders and squeezed.

CHAPTER TWENTY-FIVE

"If there were catacombs, there should be an escape tunnel out of them," Jeremiah Steiglitz announced. "We must find this escape tunnel before Mr. Culhane and Miss Mulrooney find it—"

"*If* they survived the cave-in," Sonia said.

Her father glared at her, saying nothing. "I'm sorry I spoke," she told him.

He didn't nod, didn't blink, but turned his eyes away. "If they did not survive, we'll return here with laborers, dig them out and find the Log—"

"But witnesses—" She hadn't caught herself in time, interrupting him again.

But he spoke to her, and she noted the other men watching him, too. "We will kill the laborers afterward, of course, much as the Egyptian Pharaonic architects would order the deaths at the hands of the priests of those who sealed the royal tombs, the priests made tongueless afterward so they too could not reveal the secret."

All her life, her father had sounded to her as though he rehearsed what he said—the syntax, the grammar, the imagery.

"Our man in the boat on the near side of the island—contact him, Sonia, that he may observe the shoreline there. I recall Jennings had binoculars with him. Have him scan the rocks for our two friends." Steiglitz turned away from her, looking to the others. "The course of the catacombs was reminiscent to me of catacombs I once saw in northern Italy during the

war—on a much smaller scale, of course." Steiglitz
unfolded a knife from his trouser pocket and used a
slender, primary blade to scratch the stones near the
altar stone itself. Sonia stood behind him now as he
crouched, looking across his broad back and straight
shoulders.

"The pattern seemed to run thusly," he explained.
"It would indicate to me that the course of the catacombs runs in a southwesterly direction. That should
mean an escape passage, if it were dug, would have
gone at approximately a right angle to the main tunnel—or due northwest more or less, or to the southeast."

He looked up to the men surrounding him. "Harkin, Radner—split up, use the church here as your
base, and take your compasses and work azimuths in
those directions. Follow them out, then signal on the
radio if you find something. Wait a moment until I've
ended the briefing." He looked back to the tunnel
diagram.

"But a more likely event is that a natural cave or
chink in the rock of the mountain was found, and the
tunnel was dug beyond the reach of the cave to end
under the altar. I believe in this hypothesis more
strongly—you'll all have noted that the catacombs
were offset to the rear of the altar stone by the steps.
These monks were undoubtedly learned men, and it
would appear that mathematical calculations were
devised to angle their digging to reach under the altar.
But such calculations are frequently imprecise—like
the tunnels dug by Allied prisoners during the war to
escape German prisoner-of-war camps. These monks
used the rather overly long steps to get a smooth angle
up to the altar. If that is the case, on a far narrower
line from northwest to southeast in those rocks, almost
directly behind and below us—" he gestured behind
the altar "—there should be the entrance to this cave.

Doubtless hidden, and doubtless even further obscured by the monks, it should take Miss Mulrooney and Mr. Culhane considerable time to work their way to this if indeed they survived the cave-in. And it should be difficult for us to find it, as well. But we must." He looked up at his men around him. "So, necessity dictates speed and keen eyes, gentlemen. Let's be off. Harkin and Radner, you have your jobs." He stood. "Sonia, contact Jennings, then join me." He looked to the remaining men. "The three of you will come with me."

Sonia took up her radio from the ground beside her M-16. There was a certain thrill to following one of her father's plans—the thrill of genius.

"Jennings, this is Sonia. Where the hell are you?" she snapped into the radio.

THERE WERE NO SOUNDS OF DIGGING from behind them. In the light of the flashlight beam as they moved along the natural rock-walled side tunnel into which they had fled, Culhane could see Mulrooney's fear- filled green eyes. He had the pistol in the waistband of his shorts, the flashlight in his right hand, and he held Mulrooney's right hand in his left. Culhane was worried, but he didn't tell her that. Sometimes underground tunnels like this were dug from natural cave entrances back, leading to the structure that they served. And after all the excess rock and dirt had been carted away and the tunnel completed, the outside entrance was sealed. Forever.

It was getting harder to breathe. He couldn't be certain if it was a lack of oxygen or just the heat from the tunnel itself, from being in a confined space. He stopped walking, took his Bic lighter from his pocket, and let go of Fanny Mulrooney's hand.

"What is it?" Her voice sounded subdued, tired.

"If we're near the tunnel exit, there might be a crack

somewhere up ahead large enough to let in an air current.'' He watched the lighter flame; it was rock steady, unwavering.

"We're not near it," she told him.

"We're not near it," he echoed. Culhane pocketed the lighter and took her hand again, and they started ahead.

Culhane had been periodically checking his watch. They had collapsed the catacombs behind them more than an hour ago. It was nearly three-fifteen.

They walked on, Culhane noticing the tunnel ceiling lowering, ducking his head a little, not mentioning this to Mulrooney until it was unavoidable. By three-thirty, the tunnel ceiling was sufficiently low that Mulrooney, too, needed to duck. "This is a good sign, I think," he told her. "We should be nearing the end of the tunnel."

She said nothing. Culhane watched her eyes again in the flashlight's beam. The light was still strong, but it wouldn't last forever, no matter how good the flashlight itself was, no matter how strong the batteries were.

Ducking their heads, they quickened their pace. They walked until it was nearly four. The tunnel was too low now to walk in at all unless they completely doubled over.

He looked at her in the light of the flashlight. "We're gonna have to crawl the rest of the way, Fanny."

"All right," she said dispiritedly.

"I'm going to shut off the light—just in case the tunnel goes on longer than we anticipate—so we have light when we need it."

The beam was aimed at the ground, and a rat scurried under the light. Mulrooney pressed against Culhane, shivering. At least the cockroaches were no longer in evidence, and as Culhane tracked the rat for a split second he saw a substance that looked like something he had once seen in a cave in Mexico: bat droppings.

He looked at Mulrooney. "Now I don't want you to let go of me. I'm going first." She was staring at the ground. He knew she'd seen the rat. "I think I just saw bat droppings on the floor—"

"Bats?"

"Fruit bats—I'm sure that's what they are—just fruit bats. This time of day they'll cling to the ceiling of the cave and—"

"We'll be crawling under them."

"Their droppings will be on the floor—it'll be like crawling through sticky mud. Just tell yourself that's what it is. Mud. Don't touch your hands to your mouth or your eyes."

She shook visibly.

"And don't let go of me. If we keep the light off, we shouldn't disturb them. But it's a good sign—the bats. That means there's a way in and out of the tunnel. Will you be all right?"

She nodded almost imperceptibly.

"I'm going to shut off the light. Hold my hand." He worked the switch of the flashlight. There was nothing for their eyes to become accustomed to; there was no light except the glow from the face of his Rolex. The single triangle, the dots, the bar for the minute hand and the dot on the hour and second hands were like stars in a night sky.

"Now, hold on to my shoulder while I get down on my knees, then drop to your knees and slide your hand down along my leg until you have my ankle. Don't let go of my ankle. No matter what you do, don't let go of it."

"All right, Josh," he heard her whisper in the darkness. "We're never getting out of here—with the Log, with our lives . . . ."

"Sure we are," he said, but he didn't really believe it.

Mulrooney had slid the Log under her shirt inside the waistband of her shorts earlier, and Culhane presumed she still carried it there now.

He dropped to his knees, his bare flesh feeling the wetness of what would be bat droppings. He felt Mulrooney doing the same, heard her rasp, "What's—"

"Bat droppings. Remember—it's just sticky mud."

"Sticky mud," she repeated.

"Now move your hand down and hold my ankle and—"

She screamed.

"What is it?"

"I think... I think it was a... ohh, shit, Josh—it was a rat—something furry ran across my right hand, Josh...."

"Shhh—it'll be all right. We'll be out in the sunshine soon. I'll use that word again—relax."

"Relax," he heard her repeat, then felt her hand move down along his left thigh, along his left calf, grasping his left ankle.

"All right," she whispered.

"Let's get started," he told the darkness.

Culhane began to crawl ahead, the small rocks in the dirt and bat guano of the cave floor sticking to the palm of his left hand, the knuckles of his right—he held the shut-off flashlight in that hand—and to his knees.

He hadn't told her that bats were very flexible creatures and could insinuate themselves between two objects a quarter of an inch apart. A crack through which he and Mulrooney could never move.

There might be no way out at all.

SHE WAS BREATHING HARD ENOUGH TO HYPERVENTILATE and tried telling herself to stop doing that. She could feel the stuff on her hands, all over her knees and calves, under her toenails and fingernails, on the palms of her hands.

She could feel it dribble down her neck, on her bare arms, hear the high-pitched squeals, the fluttering of wings, feel—

"Jesus, Josh—there's one in my *hair*!" She screamed the last word, feeling the thing, feeling it tangled there. She let go of his ankle, wanting to reach up to her hair to get the thing out, to get it away from her, but she was afraid to touch it. *"Josh!"*

She felt something slap at her, heard more of the high-pitched squealing sounds, felt something leathery brush her left cheek. She screamed.

"It's all right—I got it out of your hair." Culhane's voice came to her in the darkness.

She was crying, sobbing as she hadn't sobbed since she was a little girl. His arms, slimy but comforting, were wrapped around her. Her face was against his chest. "Can't you turn on the light? Please?" she begged.

"It'd only get them flying—then they'd be all over you," she heard him tell her.

She shivered despite the suffocating heat of the tunnel. "I can't stand it, Josh. Those...those...." She couldn't say the word, her throat tight with crying, her eyes smarting with the salt of her tears. "I don't want to die here!"

"Shh," she heard him say, feeling his breath against her face, smelling his sweat and her own mingled with the suffocating stench of the bats. "If anybody can do it, we can—right?"

She nodded, not saying anything, not knowing if she really believed him but wanting to believe him.

"Right?" he persisted.

"I—I guess." She nodded in the darkness.

"Then hold on. The faster we get started, the faster we'll be out of here."

She held his ankle tightly, bending forward, putting her other hand into the bat droppings, hearing the squeaking sounds again. She held his ankle as she crawled after him.

She tried telling herself stories, remembering things from her childhood. She tried to remember what her first pair of earrings had looked like. She made a mental picture of the long dress she'd worn to her senior prom in high school. Then she tried imagining what the Gladstone Log really talked about. What was the power Steiglitz had raved about possessing?

The tunnel ceiling was lower now, a curse but a blessing, too, because the bats were no longer overhead, and the muck under her hands and her bare legs was less thick. Had Culhane taken a wrong turn? She didn't want to think so. She went back to the mental picture of her prom dress; it had been white. She kept crawling, bending lower now because she was bumping her head into the ceiling of the tunnel, feeling it closing in on her on both sides.

Culhane stopped ahead of her. She felt him turning around, his hands finding her hands in the darkness. "It's getting too narrow—for me at least. Another few yards and my shoulders won't get through. This mustn't be the main tunnel. We must have missed it— maybe when we ran from the cave-in—I don't know."

"What are you—"

"I'm saying that just because it's too narrow for me to get through doesn't mean you can't. I think you can make it. The tapering of the walls seems less drastic— maybe it levels off. You can take the gun, get to the end of the tunnel, and get out. Maybe come back for me—"

"I won't leave you! I'll die with you first! I won't even go ahead of you. You can't force me to leave you!"

"Look, I love you—I don't want you to—"

She reached up her hands in the darkness, encircling his neck. "That's why I won't leave you. We came in together." Her lips were beside his left ear. "We'll leave together or we won't leave at all, Josh—or we won't leave at all." She pulled her face away, moving her hand down to his knee. "I'm ready to crawl after you again. What are we waiting for?"

"All right," she heard him say to her in the darkness. "All right, Fanny."

He was no longer crawling—wriggling was more like it—and she was following him on her elbows and on her belly, trying to hold on to his ankle, the overhead room such that her shoulder blades scraped against the top of the tunnel. Culhane stopped at times to twist his body—she could feel it—when the dimensions of the tunnel were just too narrow.

She crawled after him, on her belly now, flat—there was no room left even to push herself along on her elbows—clawing her way through after him, her left hand touching the heel of his shoe.

It was their only contact.

She had given up hope of anything sweeter than dying folded in his arms.

HIS SHOULDERS WERE BLEEDING from scraping against the rough stone walls. "Stop," he told her, feeling her head rest against his ankle. She said nothing. Shifting his weight, he tried moving his arm back to get the lighter in his pocket, but he couldn't move his arm. The cave walls around him, the ceiling above him— everything was too close; there was no room at all anymore. He figured he could go perhaps another six feet before he would be wedged so badly he could only crawl backward.

"Fanny," he panted, not knowing if his shortness of breath was from exhaustion or lack of oxygen. His eyes burned and his throat was tight and he had a headache. "Fanny, reach up and try to get my lighter out of my pocket—my right side pocket."

"All right," he heard her rasp.

He felt her hand moving along his bare leg, felt the pressure of her head or perhaps her shoulder against his right foot. He tried edging his leg forward to give her less distance to reach.

He felt her hand near his pocket, then felt her hand inside it.

"I can't—no—wait—I got—I got it!" He felt her hand move. "Want me to light it?"

"No, it's so narrow here that even if there is an opening, we'll never know; I'd block the air. I'll try to get my right hand back by my right side, by my waist. Can you reach up that far?"

"I—I think so," he heard her whisper, then he heard her cough.

"You all right?"

"That's a dumb question. Of course I'm not all right."

He felt her hand moving along his upper thigh, along his right hip, his own right hand reaching back, his arm folded at the elbow, his right hand squeezed between his torso and the wall.

He could feel the tips of her nails.

Then the lighter.

He had it in the tips of his fingers.

He dropped it.

"Shit. I—"

"I got it," he heard her pant. "Hold on—keep your hand there." He could feel her nails again, then he felt the lighter. He had it wedged between his second and third fingers. Slowly, slowly, he drew his hand forward along his side, raising his right shoulder, scraping against the rock, getting the hand in front of his head, turning the lighter in his fingertips to work the striking wheel.

The lighter flicked on. The flame wavered. He had exhaled. He held his breath. The flame wavered again, toward him.

He held his breath, watching the flame. It bent toward him.

"It's bending toward me!"

"What?"

"The flame, Fanny—the flame is bending toward me—"

"There's—"

"An opening—close to us!" He sank his head against the dirt, wondering if they could reach it. He closed the flame, wriggling ahead, pulling his shoulders in tight. "Come on—keep behind me—come on!"

An inch gone. He could barely move his legs enough to push himself forward. His hands clawed ahead, the lighter in his right, the flashlight in his left. Turning on the light was senseless; if there was air ahead, an opening, there would be light. And he wanted to see it.

Another inch—maybe a little more.

His shoulders were jammed. He felt his flesh chafe against the rock, his shirt long since torn away at the shoulders.

Another inch.

And another.

He closed his eyes, refocusing. A tiny something. A lighter shadow. He crawled, dragging himself.

Another inch. It was no longer a shadow.

"I see something—I really see something!"

He dragged himself, Mulrooney laughing behind him. It was only a narrow crack, but he pulled himself toward it anyway, the floor beneath him suddenly angling downward steeply. "Watch it, Fanny!" he called as he slid, but there was more room at the sides of his shoulders now, more room above him. He continued sliding through dirt for a few seconds.

He skidded and stopped.

The crack of light was perhaps an inch and a half wide.

He wanted to cry, but there was Fanny. He had to keep trying. Maybe they could go back another way.

"Is it the opening—is it . . . ?" And she shrieked as she began sliding, Culhane feeling her body crash against him in the darkness.

"You okay?"

"My wrist . . . hurts a little. It's—ohh, Josh—my God. . . ." He felt her head go against his chest. "It's too little—it's—"

"Here," he whispered, holding her. He turned on the flashlight. "Let's give ourselves a little light. We'll feel—"

"Josh!"

He could see her face, dirt streaked and tearstained. Her hair fell around it, tangled and sticky as he brushed it from her face with the back of his right hand.

"Josh!"

"It'll—"

"No—look!" She wrested the flashlight from his hand and moved it nearer the crack.

There was dirt there, and small rocks.

Culhane shifted his position, his back aching, his shoulders raw. He was on his knees, stooped over beside the crack. In his left front pocket he found the Bali-Song knife and opened it. Mulrooney was already clawing at the dirt and rocks with her hands. He shoved the Bali-Song's blade under the edge of the rock nearest to the crack of light and air. He pried, but it didn't move. He dug around it with his fingertips.

Mulrooney was digging at it with her nails.

"Get your hands away—watch out," he said, and he rammed the knife blade into the dirt under the slab of rock and pried again, Mulrooney's fingers under it.

He could feel the rock moving and got his left hand under it. Then he let go of the knife and got his right under the rock.

The rock shifted against his leg, and he drew his leg back.

The light was gone from the crack, and the sound of dirt filtering down made his heart sink for an instant.

Then he found the knife, and aimed the flashlight's beam on their digging. And he and Mulrooney, with his hands, the knife blade, her hands and her nails, began digging.

He stabbed at the dirt. Stabbed at it.

He threw his weight behind the knife and stabbed at it.

He was falling, losing the knife, his hands splaying out in front of him, dirt filling his mouth and nose, his eyes closing against it.

Coolness on his skin, on the sweat, made him suddenly cold.

Mulrooney was screaming like a cheerleader at a homecoming game.

Culhane opened his eyes. She was kissing his face.

He could see her. He could see her face in the light of the setting sun as he lay in a heap of dirt and rocks, the sky above him.

"Thank you," he whispered as he looked up at the blue sky. "Thank you very much, Sir."

CHAPTER TWENTY-SIX

He had thrown away his shirt, and Mulrooney wished she could do the same. Streaked with bat dung along her legs and arms, she sat crouched beside him. His headache was dissipating now, but his back and legs—all of him ached. His shoulders were tender to the touch as Mulrooney tried to clean them with water from the one remaining bota—they had drunk all the water from the first bag—and her handkerchief.

Through all the crawling in the cave, she had kept the blue canvas purse on her shoulder.

She was cleaning her face with the wet handkerchief, and he watched her as she finished.

He started to laugh as she took her lipstick from the bag and started to apply it. "You gotta be kiddin'!"

"Well—"

He looked at her, shaking his head.

"If we found our way out," she was saying, smoothing the lipstick with the tip of her right index finger, looking at herself in a compact mirror, "then Steiglitz should be able to find us. He's a smart man, I figure."

"Yeah," Culhane said and nodded wearily, "a smart man."

"Just think how good it'll feel being able to walk standing up straight instead of crawling."

Culhane nodded again and tried to get up. His legs worked, but he wouldn't bet on them in a race.

But he was standing.

He reached out and helped Mulrooney to stand. She sagged against him.

They were on a flat spit of grassy ground on what seemed to be nearly the very top of the island. Almost nothing of the rock was visible behind and above them, and they were surrounded by air. The small cave mouth through which they had eventually crawled was about twenty yards behind them and some five feet lower than the spit of ground.

"Let's reconnoiter," he told her, taking her hand in his and starting toward the farthest reach of the promontory.

They walked ahead, stopping a yard from the very edge of the rock and dirt peninsula. The ocean was below them, gold shimmering off it as the sun to their right caught the shallow swells. He could recognize the beach area several hundred feet below them. But on the water where the *Cherokee* had been anchored there was nothing but what appeared to be floating pieces of rubble.

"They got the *Cherokee*," Mulrooney said, her voice hushed.

Culhane only nodded. There was a smaller boat there in the water, a fast, trim-looking boat like a ski boat. It couldn't have made the trip from Nassau or from Florida; it would have to have been brought there by a larger craft, or perhaps by air.

Culhane shoved Mulrooney to the ground beside him. He saw the glint of sunlight and then the glint was gone. "There's a man in that small boat. He has binoculars or maybe a telescopic sight on a rifle. I can't be sure. But something caught the sun for a second."

"From Steiglitz?" he heard her ask.

"Yeah. It would have to be."

"Maybe we can get down there—maybe somehow steal that boat."

Culhane just looked at her. "You're gettin' into this rough-and-tough stuff, aren't you?"

"You got a better idea?" In her eyes was a smile, the first he'd seen since they'd entered the catacombs and endured the crawl through the escape tunnel.

He laughed. "No, I don't have a better idea. But I've got a way we might try just that. Come on. We've got a good hike down the mountain, and I think Steiglitz's men probably have us boxed in up here, anyway."

Running in a crouch, Mulrooney beside him, he started back from the edge of the rock peninsula. He still had the gun, and he'd loaded a fresh magazine into it.

MULROONEY DIDN'T EVEN KNOW if there was enough light for Steiglitz's man in the boat to see her clearly.

She stepped out from behind the rocks, not knowing

what she should actually call out. "Hey, sailor" sounded stupid. She felt stupid. She'd taken off her shorts and top, and all she wore were her panties and bra, which didn't even match, the bra white and the panties baby blue.

And what if the man in the boat shot her when he saw her?

She started walking across the sand, hoping the man would notice her and she wouldn't have to shout to him across the water to get his attention.

The climb down from the rocks had been hard, but climbing down meant they didn't have to cross the swamp again, saving hours of travel. Night travel through the swamp would have been incredibly dangerous, she thought. Reaching the base of the rocks, they swam when necessary—the water had at least cleaned the bat droppings from her hair and body—and walked across the rocky strips of beach when possible.

And now she was alone. She had counted by thousands to sixty thousand ten times to give Culhane the ten minutes he'd said he would need.

Nearly naked, barefoot, she stood in the surf now, hands on her hips, trying to look provocative. The man in the ski boat hadn't noticed her yet.

She shrugged her shoulders, looked away from the man for an instant, then turned toward him across the water, hands still on her hips, standing on her toes in the sand, her breasts thrust forward. "Hey—hey! Help already! I surrender!"

The man in the ski boat moved, and her heart jumped to her throat. He was swinging a rifle toward her, one of those ugly-looking rifles that looked like something from a space movie. Culhane called them assault rifles.

"Hold it right there, lady!" the man's voice shouted back at her across the two hundred yards of water.

"I surrender. I already said that," she screamed back.

Now it was up to Culhane.

For some reason, Culhane realized, he was smiling. Maybe it was the chance to strike back at Steiglitz. The Bali-Song locked open, the handle clenched tight in his teeth, he raised his hands out of the sea, reached for the ski boat's starboard gunwale and grasped it. The man in the ski boat held the M-16 trained on the surf where Mulrooney stood.

Culhane heaved himself up and rolled over the gunwale. Steiglitz's man swung the M-16's muzzle around, and Culhane rolled under it into the man's midsection, hammering him back. The impact against the man made Culhane's raw and bleeding shoulders scream with pain, and the M-16 discharged skyward. Culhane's left fist pounded into the center of the man's chest, then Culhane's right went for his midsection, aiming for the solar plexus but missing it.

The assault rifle fired again, a burst of perhaps a half-dozen shots. Culhane was too busy to count.

His right hand reached up, and he gripped the Bali-Song. He snatched it from his teeth and rammed it, catching its blade tip in the center of the man's abdomen, ripping up. There was a scream, the rifle discharged again, then the body slumped back.

Dripping water, Culhane fell across the body, making sure the knife had completed its job. They weren't playing a game. It was life or death.

He jerked the Bali-Song free of the dead man, wiping the blade clean on the man's clothes.

He glanced to the ski boat's control panel. The key was where it should be. He started to search the man's pockets and found two spare magazines for some single-column 9mm pistol, but no pistol. A cheap pocketknife. No identification.

Culhane rolled the body over the gunwale and into the water with a loud splash.

He glanced up to Mulrooney on the beach. She looked pretty in a leggy, grown-up-little-girl way, standing there in her bra and panties, the surf around her feet, her hands on her hips.

He shot her a wave to let her know he was all right.

Quickly, he started to search the ski boat, and under the driver's seat he found three spare magazines for the M-16. "All right!" he breathed. There was a pistol as well, a well-worn Smith & Wesson Model 39.

He dumped the magazine, checked the chamber—loaded—and replaced the magazine, leaving on the pistol's safety.

He dumped the partially spent magazine for the M-16 and replaced it with a full, 30-round stick, leaving the magazines, the pistol and the pistol magazines he'd taken from the dead man on the console between the front seats.

Setting the M-16 on safety, he leaned it between the seats as he slipped behind the controls. He closed the Bali-Song and fired the ski boat's engine. It rumbled like a '57 Chevy needing a muffler. He glanced around the boat; no anchor was dropped.

He gunned the engine, taking the craft into a wide port arc and back toward the surf, waving to Mulrooney to run down into the surf and be picked up. She waved back, disappeared up the beach for a moment as he closed in, then reappeared carrying a bundle of clothes and gear and the Walther pistol. She ran into the surf, her purse over her shoulder, and Culhane slowed the ski boat as Mulrooney waded out. Culhane reached across the front passenger seat, took the bundles of clothes and gear from her, then reached for her hands and helped her as she came over the gunwales and settled in beside him.

"I was worried," she said breathlessly.

"Yeah, so was I," he admitted with a grin.

"How far can this thing take us?"

"Not far enough," he replied. There was a hand-held radio—a sophisticated walkie-talkie—and a voice was coming over it.

"Jennings, this is Sonia. My father and I are aboard the helicopter. Has the woman told you about Culhane yet? Over."

Culhane started to press the Talk button, but Mulrooney closed her hands over his. On her bare thighs was the Gladstone Log wrapped in a plastic sandwich bag. He looked at her eyes. "Let me—please." She was smiling wickedly.

Culhane laughed, handing her the radio.

"You push this button?" She gestured to the Talk button.

"Yeah, you push that button, Fanny."

She was still smiling. She pushed the button. "Sonia? This is the woman. M.F. Mulrooney? Remember? Well, Josh Culhane is right beside me. Your man is dead. And you can take your father, your gunmen and your helicopter and just ram 'em right up your—"

Culhane put his hand over her mouth. "A lady wouldn't say that," he told her.

He moved his hand away from her mouth. She smiled at him. "This is Mulrooney again. Go to hell!"

She handed back the radio set.

Culhane gunned the ski boat. The gas gauge read nearly full, and there were two gas cans in the rear of the boat. It wouldn't get them that far, but it was better than nothing.

CHAPTER TWENTY-SEVEN

"Ahoy in the ski boat—surrender now!"

Culhane glanced over his shoulder. The helicopter was closing in, the voice on the bullhorn blaring. "Ahoy in the ski boat—you haven't got a chance! Heave to!"

"Here—let me take the controls," Mulrooney shouted over the throb of the engine and the roar of the waves as the bow knifed through the water. "Take that rifle and blow those suckers out of the sky. Now's your chance!"

Culhane just looked at her for a minute. "What?"

"Blow 'em out of the sky—like this!" Mulrooney picked up the rifle, visibly studying the left side of the receiver.

"What the hell are you doing?"

"Like this!" she insisted.

She shouldered the M-16 and pulled the trigger.

Hot brass pelted Culhane's face and neck and hammered against the windshield, the rifle rising with the recoil, Mulrooney shrieking, Culhane reaching out from the ski boat's controls, grabbing the rifle. "Stop that, dammit!" Culhane shouted, and he tore the rifle away from her. He guessed she'd blown nearly the entire magazine.

He held the rifle in his right hand, Mulrooney looking at him. "Well, like that—you know—you shoot a lot. I see 'em shoot down helicopters all the time in the movies. That one spy movie we saw—you told me he was using a little .22 rifle. Well, hell, you should be able to—"

Assault-rifle fire ripped across the ski boat's forward hull, the windshield spiderwebbing. Culhane dropped the rifle and forced Mulrooney's head down as he cut the ski boat's wheel hard left, then hard right, bouncing as they took a wave head on and rolled over it. The helicopter was skimming close to the water now, and more assault-rifle fire made loud thudding sounds in the water and pinging sounds as it ripped into the hull.

"You hadda go and shoot at those assholes—"

There was more assault-rifle fire, and Culhane tried to steer the ski boat out of it.

"Pick up that little radio, press the Talk button and hold it in front of my mouth—now!"

Mulrooney picked up the radio and almost hit Culhane in the teeth with it as she held it up to his lips. Culhane rasped into it, "Mayday! Mayday! U.S. Coast Guard or other authorities monitoring this frequency— Mayday! Being attacked by armed helicopter—Mayday—for God's sake, Mayday!" Assault-rifle fire came again, then the lighter pinging of submachine-gun fire, hammering into the hull and shattering more of the windshield.

Culhane looked at Mulrooney. "Get over here and slide under me as I push myself up—works just like a car only not as responsive. Get to the controls and I'll shoot at those bastards!"

Mulrooney started shifting over as Culhane raised himself in the driver's seat, holding the control wheel as he edged over into the passenger seat. When Mulrooney's hands were on the wheel, Culhane shouted, "You got it—zigzag if you have to!"

He took the assault rifle, buttoned out the nearly empty magazine, and rammed a fresh one into the magazine well.

He twisted his body in the seat, trying to keep the rifle from moving as the ski boat bounced and rocked and shuddered under him, trying to line up the front and rear sights on the chopper. It was a Bell and looked like one of the 222 Series machines. In Takers number fifteen Sean Dodge had used one to rescue a beautiful girl from the piranha-infested waters of the Amazon. Culhane had studied helicopter designs until he saw them in his dreams.

The twin turbines would be mounted above the passenger compartment, beneath and to the rear of the twin-blade rotor.

He settled the sights on the machine and fired a 3-round burst. The helicopter pulled up, then dropped back.

"Yay! You hit the bastards!"

Culhane looked at Mulrooney, saying nothing. Then, as the helicopter started another pass, he yelled, "Keep drivin' the boat, Fanny!" He picked up the radio set. "Mayday to anyone monitoring this—" The chopper was coming fast, assault rifles firing from both sides of the machine through the windows. He put down the radio, firing again, this time at the Plexiglas panels themselves and the riflemen behind them. The helicopter dropped back as the chopper's starboard front passenger window shattered.

He picked up the radio again. "Mayday off San Rafael Island heading due west! Helicopter with armed criminals attacking our ski boat! Mayday! Mayday—come back!"

Nothing.

Then Sonia's voice: "Give up now, Culhane—or I'll skin you and the girl alive!"

"Shove it, Sonia," he snarled into the sky, firing the M-16 as the helicopter started another pass.

The bullhorn was blaring again: "Surrender or we'll blow you out of the water! Heave to!"

Culhane fired the M-16, a long, ragged burst raking up along the portside window near where the pilot would be. The helicopter skimmed low to the water, hovering and getting out of range, assault-rifle fire coming from it. Then the helicopter was up again, high, and diving toward them.

"Cut the wheel starboard!"

"That's to the right?"

Culhane didn't wait for her. He reached out and wrenched the wheel toward him, gunfire hammering into the surface of the water on both sides of them.

He shoved the M-16 up, firing again and missing completely.

He picked up the radio. "Mayday, dammit—Mayday!"

He threw down the radio and raised the assault rifle, firing as the helicopter made a low pass, submachine guns and assault rifles blazing. "The windshield!" Mulrooney shouted, and Culhane, hearing the sound of it shattering behind him, threw himself across her body to protect her, the boat bouncing, rocking, assault-rifle and submachine-gun fire all around them, ripping at the seats, shattering the control panel as he reached out for the wheel.

The boat rocked once and stopped, rising and falling with the swells. Culhane looked up; Mulrooney's green eyes were wide with terror. The ski boat was dead in the water.

A voice boomed down from the helicopter's bullhorn, Steiglitz's voice: "You will lay down your weapons and raise your hands over your heads."

A voice squawked from the radio beside Culhane's left thigh: "This is the U.S. Coast Guard. We received your Mayday. Fire a starburst flare to home us in. Over."

The helicopter rose quickly, apparently on full power now, and headed south.

Mulrooney, pressed against Culhane as he shielded her body, said, "Do we have a starburst flare?"

"DROP YOUR WEAPONS!"

Culhane looked at Mulrooney, Mulrooney's eyes on his. "That's the same thing the other guys told us to do," she said.

Culhane set down the M-16, then made a big show of raising and setting down the Walther P-38. "They probably think we're drug smugglers."

"Ohh, good—drug smugglers. That's wonderful."

"Do not throw anything overboard!"

Culhane looked up at the deck of the cutter. He guessed its size as a 350-footer. "Yeah," he told Mulrooney without looking at her, "they think we're drug smugglers."

It was hard standing in the ski boat because of the swells the Coast Guard cutter's prow was making, but it was worth it. . . .

"YEAH—HEY, I READ THE TAKERS. That Sean Dodge—one hell of a guy. My kid reads 'em, too," the captain of the *Brunswick* told Culhane, shaking his hand. "And Miss Mulrooney, I read your book on the Bermuda Triangle. Scared the pants off me—ha— well. Fancy meeting you two out here."

Culhane leaned back in the seat across from the captain, the desk separating them. Mulrooney sat to his left, wrapped in a gray rescue blanket. "A gentleman named Partridge," the captain continued, "arranged things so a cutter'd be in the general area around San Rafael—something about two Americans, a man and a woman who might need assistance. Never said it would be you two. Wow, is this exciting!"

Another man, one of the crew, came in carrying a tray with three mugs of coffee on it. "Thanks, Hansen," the captain nodded, and the corpsman left.

"Well, who the heck were those guys in the helicopter?"

Culhane didn't answer at first. Mulrooney said, "Must have been working with Captain Grey and those pirates we told you about."

"Too bad you folks didn't get a registration number on the helicopter—"

"We were busy shooting back at them," Culhane interrupted, lighting a Pall Mall.

"Gimme a light," Mulrooney said, taking one of his cigarettes. She leaned toward him, the blanket falling from her shoulders, but she quickly rewrapped herself. He fired the cigarette for her.

"Just how did you get that M-16 and the other weapons?" the captain asked.

Culhane wasn't about to admit to killing the previous owner. "The P-38? The Walther? It came from the pirates during the fight. And I was fighting with the guy who was running the ski boat, and he went over the side. The rifle was there and so was the Smith & Wesson auto."

"Must have known Grey was supposed to take you both to San Rafael and followed you there. Hmm—this Partridge. I was just told to follow his orders. What agency is he with—DEA?" And the captain smiled a knowing smile.

Culhane gave him a wink. "Well, I think he'd better tell you that."

The captain nodded, standing. "All this cloak-and-dagger stuff—didn't know you did this stuff for real, Mr. Culhane."

"Call me Josh." Culhane grinned at him.

"Gonna have to reread some of your books, Josh, and get a few pointers—ha!"

"I wouldn't do anything that drastic, Captain," Mulrooney said.

PART THREE
SECRETS BENEATH THE ICE

Partridge had come for them by helicopter. Culhane laughed as he remembered the look of girlish excitement in Mulrooney's eyes as, wearing borrowed jeans and a work shirt expropriated from the ship's stores, she was lifted in a sling to the waiting chopper hovering above the *Brunswick*'s afterdeck.

They sat now in the beachfront lounge of Partridge's Miami Beach hotel, Partridge buying the drinks, Culhane trying to figure out why. Mulrooney wore her own clothes, as did Culhane; their luggage had been retrieved from Nassau, the CIA picking up the tab. She wore a dark pink sundress with a crocheted shawl of cream-colored yarn around her shoulders. As Culhane watched her, he thought she was beautiful.

Partridge spoke as soon as the waitress had put down their drinks and left. "I'm proud of you both. You really showed Steiglitz what for. Got the Gladstone Log—a job well done."

Culhane thought Mulrooney was choking on her drink as she set it down, raising her index finger. He watched as she noticeably swallowed hard. "Hey, wait a minute. The job isn't finished yet. We've gotta know why Steiglitz wanted the Log and where the hell the *Madagascar* actually went."

"I assumed," Partridge began, "that you and Mr. Culhane—"

"Read the Log?" Culhane finished for him.

"Yes."

"I did. I let Fanny sit with the captain of the *Brunswick* and keep him interested, waiting for her to lose her blanket. I read part of it then. When you and your guys didn't take it from us after we boarded the chopper over the *Brunswick*, I read part last night and part of it while Fanny and I were getting changed tonight. I've read enough of it to know that we still don't know it all—but there's more I want to read. It's not the kind of thing Evelyn Wood would start you out with for a speed-reading course.''

"It's not just a standard ship's log?" Partridge asked.

"No, it's more like a narrative, as if Henry Chillingsworth's uncle, the captain, was very conscious of the fact that somebody would be reading this and it wouldn't just get tossed into some dusty file in the Admiralty.''

"There's a prologue—kind of," Mulrooney added. "I read parts of it on the *Brunswick*, and more of it while Josh was shaving. Miles Chillingsworth—'' She stopped, looking at Culhane across the rim of her glass as she sipped at a rum and Coke. Culhane nodded to her, silently trying to convey the thought "good girl" and hoping she could read his mind. He didn't fully trust Partridge, but sharing the information in the Log was unavoidable.

"Miles Chillingsworth," Mulrooney began again, "was the first officer on a Royal Navy vessel that was running interference for Confederate blockade runners during the Civil War along the Georgia coast. Miles was on a ship that was part of a larger fleet—a half-dozen ships or so. There was a bad storm. It was the late summer of 1864—would have been hurricane season. The fleet got broken up; two of the British ships were disabled, and one of the British ships went down. Five of the blockade runners were lost. Well, this Mr. Fife that Henry Chillingsworth mentions—the man who saved him and was the first mate of the *Madagascar*—'' She stopped, lit a Salem for herself and exhaled a cloud of gray smoke. "Mr. Fife," she went on, "was then just an ordinary seaman.''

Culhane picked up the story. "He'd been on the British ship that had gone down, and he survived. Seems like he was quite a survivor. He and three other men took refuge on what sounds like Cumberland Island—"

"You mean right up the coast here?" Partridge asked, his voice excited.

"But that's not Atlantis," Mulrooney replied. "What they did find there—what Fife found, because he was the only one who eventually survived—was what led the *Madagascar* on the chase twenty years later."

"I don't understand," Partridge declared.

Culhane gestured to Mulrooney to continue. "You see, according to what Miles Chillingsworth said in the *Madagascar*'s logbook, Fife and the others weren't really out of trouble when they reached the island. The seas were high and there wasn't a safe place to wait out the storm. They worked their way inland."

"The way Miles Chillingsworth talks," Culhane interjected, "it almost has to be Cumberland Island."

"I agree," Mulrooney said. "They went inland and found some rocks, and eventually found a little cave. This is where it gets good. There was a carving on the wall of the cave, some kind of a map. Fife and the others thought some pirate had carved the map there. But part of the map was covered up, and while they were digging to uncover the bottom of the map, they uncovered what they called the demon skull—"

"Like Henry Chillingsworth talked about during the mutiny?" Partridge interrupted.

"Yeah," Culhane said.

"And I guess Miles Chillingsworth had the demon skull in front of him when he made the Log entry," Mulrooney said, "because he described it in perfect detail. From the crown of the skull to the tip of the jaw, it measured just a little less than twelve inches."

"Is that peculiar?" Partridge asked.

"I've got a reasonably large head—big hat size—" Culhane began.

"You're tellin' me you've got a fat head," Mulrooney said.

Culhane grinned at her but kept talking. "My skull would measure maybe nine and a half or ten inches measured like that."

"And this skull," Mulrooney went on, "was just a little less than fourteen inches wide—"

"Mine'd be about nine or nine and a half that way," Culhane interjected.

"So," Partridge said, sipping at his wine, staring down at the small table between them. "Some kind of big-headed prehistoric man?"

"No, because they found horns," Mulrooney said.

"A Viking!" Partridge exclaimed.

"No," Culhane told him. "The horns weren't part of a helmet. They were part of the skull—like bull horns or steer horns."

"A human skull with horns? A devil?"

Culhane looked at Mulrooney. Mulrooney stubbed out her cigarette, turned around in her chair, looked down at her lap, then over at Partridge. "An alien. It has to be."

"Doesn't have to be an alien," Culhane contradicted. "Could be—"

"A lost race? A genetic freak?"

Culhane looked at her and shrugged. "I don't know."

"And we won't know until we go to where the *Madagascar* went," she said, looking at her hands. "In 1884, when Gladstone knew that Parliament wouldn't sponsor a search for Atlantis, he wasn't just influenced by Ignatius Donnelly and his writings. He was also influenced by Miles Chillingsworth. Once back home, Chillingsworth and Fife got to be pretty friendly. You see," Mulrooney explained, "after the storm, Fife was eventually the only survivor. When they dug to find the bottom of the map and found the skull, the other two men Fife was with ran out into the storm, leaving the shelter of the cave and the fire. They both died from exposure. Their bodies were never recovered. Fife toughed it out, reburied the skull and waited until the storm subsided. He was considered a hero for a while when he returned to England. He told Miles Chillingsworth all about what they'd found, and Miles Chillingsworth somehow got Gladstone's ear and told him about the map and the nonhuman skull. Gladstone felt it had to be a survivor of Atlantis, and the map had to be one showing where Atlantis had been."

"Is it?"

Mulrooney shrugged. "How would I know? But Gladstone thought it was. And when Parliament nixed the money, a group of private investors leased three ships from the Royal Navy and appointed Miles Chillingsworth—he was a captain by now—leader of the expedition. Chillingsworth got his old buddy Fife, and they set out for Cumberland Island."

"Probably," Culhane cautioned.

"Probably Cumberland. But wherever it was, they went back to the island, unearthed the demon skull after they found the cave and unearthed the rest of the map. It showed mountains and ridges, and some of the landmasses nearby were out of proportion, but the shapes were recognizable—one was Antarctica. And it showed some sort of entrance under the ice."

"What kind of entrance?" Partridge pressed.

"I don't know." She looked at Culhane. "Josh, did you get anything more specific out of it?"

"No, just that it was Antarctica, and there was some way to get under all the ice. And they took the demon skull with them, and they obscured the map—"

"That was the word Miles Chillingsworth used," Mulrooney interjected. " 'Obscured' the map."

"They could have destroyed it," Partridge said.

"Let's hope not—that Log isn't gonna tell anyone how to find whatever they found," Culhane told him. "I guess Chillingsworth was security conscious. But he drew a copy of the map by hand, and he destroyed it once they reached their destination."

"Once the *Madagascar* reached the Weddell Sea off Antarctica," Mulrooney went on, "it was late fall and almost impossible to navigate the area. Chillingsworth had taken ships around Cape Horn twice, so he was better acquainted with Antarctic navigation than most people. But it took them a lot longer to match the coordinates on the cave's map than they had figured, and it took three days of shooting the cannon at the ice to blow a hole in it and open up the entrance."

"The cave was coated with ice," Culhane said. "I guess it was on a hunch, but they drilled through or dug through into the ice and found a hard surface. They said it was a 'most peculiar iron.' They used axes and picks and sledgehammers to get handholds in the ice, then they climbed down through the cave."

"And then what?" Partridge asked excitedly.

Mulrooney shrugged her bare shoulders, losing the strap for her dress off her left shoulder and fixing it.

Culhane said, "After that, there's nothing specific about what they found. In fact, there's nothing at all, as if Miles Chillingsworth realized that what they'd found was so important he didn't dare write it down."

"I do remember one thing Miles Chillingsworth said, though," Mulrooney almost whispered. "He'd obviously read Dante's *Inferno*, because he called what they found 'the gilded gates of hell.' " Culhane watched her shoulders twitch as she said it.

"When do you folks want to leave for Cumberland Island?" Partridge asked.

"I'll have to get some things from my apartment," Mulrooney told him. "And I have to buy some camera equipment. I lost most of mine on the *Cherokee*."

"So what's the nearest town?" Partridge beamed. "We can meet there the day after tomorrow, and I can arrange transportation for you both."

Mulrooney laughed. "Ha! Talk about coincidence—or synchronicity. Remember the name of the Coast Guard vessel?"

Culhane nodded resignedly. "Same as the town—Brunswick, Georgia—where you get the boats."

"Where you get the boats." And Partridge raised his glass for a toast.

CULHANE MARVELED AT WHAT A WOMAN PACKED. Mulrooney had assumed they might go straight from Cumberland Island to Antarctica, and she had planned accordingly. She had everything from shorts, low-cut tops and sandals to thermal underwear, heavy woolen sweaters and insulated boots with removable fleece liners. And a purse that seemed even larger than her normal saddlebag-sized totes.

They had traveled by commercial jet to Atlanta, then by CIA-chartered helicopter from Atlanta to Athens. At the Athens airport they had picked up Mulrooney's car and gone to her place. She had purchased camera gear in Miami, and once her things were packed, they had loaded her Mustang and driven the fifty-odd miles to Culhane's A-frame on Lake Lanier.

There he packed *his* clothes—Levi's, thermal underwear, regular underwear, white socks, heavy boot socks, combat boots and faded, light green, military-style long-sleeved shirts—and his toilet items.

Mulrooney sat at the edge of the couch as Culhane went through his vault.

Just as Mulrooney's gun and a single speedloader were packed somewhere at the bottom of her purse,

Culhane, too, wanted something besides a gun he'd have to steal.

He took his Detonics Scoremaster stainless steel .45 with the adjustable Bo-Mar rear sights. For this he packed six spare 7-round magazines and two of the 8-round Detonics extralength magazines. The six spare magazines were stuck into the black leather Milt Sparks Six-Pack belt carrier; his character Sean Dodge used exactly the same gun and all the same accessories. Basically a much improved and slightly heavier version of the accurized Government Model .45s, it was state of the art and Culhane's favorite automatic, whether shooting at targets or shooting to stay alive. He was tempted to bring a .44 Magnum—either the four-inch Metalifed Model 29 or the six-inch customized Model 629, both Smith & Wesson—but he decided against these. Instead he took a second Detonics pistol, the smaller, original Combat Master .45 in stainless steel. He and Mulrooney would be travelling by chartered helicopter from Gainesville, near Culhane's lakeside home, to Savannah, then again by helicopter from Savannah to Brunswick. There would be no airport security searches, so he left both pistols loaded, the larger .45 in a Milt Sparks BN55 crossdraw.

Culhane closed the safe, noticing Mulrooney looking at him as he turned to face her. "Do you think two guns will be enough?" She was being sarcastic—or so he thought.

"Gonna have to do," he said straight-faced. He walked across the living room to his closet, took down his spare brown leather bomber jacket and slipped it on; the burned and stained one was still being cleaned. "I'll switch your luggage to my car, then get my stuff packed."

"Can I bring along your portable cassette player?" Mulrooney asked. "I forgot mine."

"Sure. You know where it is," he told her.

He'd been with her when she'd stopped at her post-office box and picked up her mail. Someone had sent her a cassette, by the look of the small package. He hadn't picked up his mail. He guessed there would probably be a letter from his publisher complaining about not having the end of Takers number seventeen, and probably a nastier one from his agent, Jerry, doing the same thing because the publisher had called Jerry when they couldn't reach him.

Culhane shrugged. There was a lot of luggage to move. Mulrooney didn't travel light.

THERE WAS A THREE-HOUR LAYOVER in Savannah while the helicopter was being refueled and serviced. Culhane and Mulrooney had gambled on getting in without reservations and had gone to The Pirate's House, a restaurant renowned for its desserts. They had spoken little during dinner, and now they walked along the riverfront, having taken a cab from the restaurant to the river and gotten out near the statue of The Waving Girl.

It was nearly dusk, and a half hour remained before they had to start back for the airport in order to rendezvous with the helicopter pilot. They sat, holding hands, on one of the little park benches near the statue.

"She was looking for her man. He went to sea and never returned," Mulrooney said abruptly.

"After Cumberland Island—if we find what we're looking for—I don't want you coming along the rest of the way. I know Steiglitz will find out about it, and he'll be there, either waiting for us or right on our trail."

"I'm not letting you go alone. This is my field—the occult, the unexplained. What if Thera really isn't Atlantis? What if there really was a supercivilization and the *Madagascar* really did stumble onto it somewhere down in the Antarctic? Maybe a hollow earth like they always say."

"Who always says?" Culhane asked, disgusted. "All this science-fiction crap.... I don't know what the *Madagascar* found—if they found anything. Maybe all they found was a cave under the ice. Maybe that's why Miles Chillingsworth didn't write more about it in the Log."

"What about the skull?"

"Have you seen the skull? Have I seen the skull?"

"What about the stuff in Henry Chillingsworth's diary?"

"All I know is that regardless of what we find, we've still got something very real, very concrete: that egomaniac Steiglitz and his crackpot daughter and their hired guns."

Mulrooney was silent for a moment. There was a barge moving along the river from a plant on the other side, and a coolness was coming with the night.

"I'm not like that girl—the girl in the statue there," she said, gesturing to it, her voice low, even. "I don't stand around and wave my apron or a scarf. I don't cry into a handkerchief. I guess all this time we spent together—all the things we've shared—that qualifies me as your woman. Well, professional reasons aside, I don't stay behind. I just don't."

There was a hardness in her eyes—not meanness, but the hardness of resolve. He leaned across to her and kissed her lips. The resolve in her eyes was still there.

"All right," he finally told her.

"All right," she whispered.

RATHER THAN THE FORTY-FIVE-MINUTE FERRY RIDE from the mainland to Cumberland Island, there had been still a third helicopter ride, but this helicopter bore the logo of one of the Atlanta network affiliate television stations and a film crew. Culhane had often appeared on local programs in Georgia, as had Mulrooney. And Partridge had explained that the network's helicopter had been the most logical choice.

"Maybe the station's doing a piece on the adventure awaiting people when they come on out to the island," Partridge had shouted over the whirring of the rotor blades, not bothering with the headset radio. "Anyway, two writers and a television crew are a lot easier to explain than a bunch of guys in three-piece suits. And minicams and sound equipment look a lot less peculiar than guns."

But Culhane had seen the guns: M-16s packed in carrying cases for sound and camera equipment. In the event Steiglitz was already on the island or had followed them, they'd be prepared.

Culhane had completed reading and rereading the Gladstone Log—the logbook of the H.M.S. *Madagascar*—as had Mary Frances Mulrooney. He knew the directions it contained to reach the cave, knew the directions as well, he thought, as Mr. Fife had known them when he had recounted them to Captain Miles Chillingsworth, as well as Chillingsworth knew them when he had written them down.

The helicopter had dropped them on the far side of the island, and it waited there as Culhane, Mulrooney, Partridge and the three penguins—the trio today wearing casual clothes and carrying camera and sound equipment—worked their way toward the higher ground. Culhane had insisted on waiting until late in the day so they'd attract less attention when they actually went to the cave. It was nearing sunset, and gray-white cumulus clouds seemed to glow incandescently as the sun lowered beyond the far side of the island. At a distance Culhane could see the white foam of the breakers lapping the shoreline and a campfire farther down the coast. It was unspoiled here, and seabirds pestered them throughout the day's work of pretend filming. Wild horses ran along the white sands unafraid.

As they walked now, Culhane retracing Fife's footsteps, he took Mulrooney's hand. "When this is all over, why don't you and I come back here, camp out maybe—"

Partridge walked up to them just then, breaking the moment, but Mulrooney's hand squeezed Culhane's in reply.

"How much longer have we got to go? All this fresh air's killing me."

Culhane stared ahead of them. "Up there, I think—in those rocks."

"I thought you knew it pretty well," Partridge panted, walking the incline beside Culhane and Mulrooney.

"I know Fife's directions by heart, but in a hundred years the topography can change, especially in an area subjected to winds and storms, like an island. Nothing matches perfectly."

"Aww, that's fuckin' wonderful," Partridge snapped, then looked past Culhane to Mulrooney. "Sorry, miss." Partridge dropped back, and Culhane and Mulrooney walked alone, side by side, Partridge and his three "television film technicians" perhaps fifteen yards behind them.

Already, long shadows from the rocks and foliage were making the ground dark beneath their feet. "I'm cold. I should've worn long pants," Mulrooney murmured.

"My jacket I can lend you. My pants—that's another story."

She laughed, saying, "I'll take you up on the jacket."

Culhane nodded. He let go of her hand, shrugged out of the brown leather bomber jacket and put it around her shoulders. It was cooling rapidly, and Culhane rolled down the sleeves of his pale green shirt.

In another ten minutes they would need his flashlight, which he'd shoved into his wide trouser belt on the right side. On his left side, his gun sat in the crossdraw holster. He kept walking.

"How much farther is it, do you think?" he heard Mulrooney ask.

"Just up ahead—or I don't know."

She didn't say anything.

Neither did he.

They kept walking.

Then Culhane stopped. He shone his flashlight on a flat slab of rock. Somehow, there was an odd texture to it. "What would you say about that slab of rock?" he asked Mulrooney.

"Didn't start out here. Looks like it's maybe from higher up."

"Yeah, my guess, too." He handed her the light. "Shine it here." He gestured toward the upper edge of the slab. "Partridge, gimme a hand." Culhane put his shoulder to the rock, but the rock didn't budge.

"Here, I got a shovel," one of the penguins said.

Culhane stepped away from the rock, and the light Mulrooney held showed the scrape marks on the stone as the penguin with the shovel set to work. The scraping sounds seemed very loud in the otherwise still dusk.

"Here, I'll try it," another penguin volunteered. The man threw his weight against the rock. In the light, Culhane saw the rock budge slightly. "Gimme some help," the man called out. Culhane put his shoulder against the rock, Partridge and the third penguin joining him, and the rock moved a little more.

"Get back a little, Fanny," Culhane rasped, groaning with the effort, his right shoulder still raw from the trip through the tunnel. Getting both hands on the rock, Culhane said, "We all give it a good heave on the count of three—"

"So this is the cave, huh—hid the entrance," Partridge observed.

"Maybe," Culhane told him soberly. "Maybe it's the cave, maybe not. One—two—*three*—" Culhane threw his body weight against it, painfully scraping the back of his left hand where he no longer had the bandage covering the burned skin. He kept pushing, hearing the straining sounds of the men around him, feeling the rock moving. Then suddenly the weight of it was gone and the rock fell away. "Get away, Fanny!" Culhane shouted.

The light shifted, dust filtering up in its beam as the rock tumbled aside.

"Gee whiz!" It was Mulrooney.

"You okay, Fanny?" Culhane called out.

"Yeah, yeah—just glad that sucker didn't land on my foot."

And then she was beside him, Culhane taking the flashlight from her and shining it where the rock had been.

A mass of spiderwebs, their filaments almost solidly interlaced, covered a shadowed opening.

"Yecch," Mulrooney offered.

Culhane smiled, but he wasn't wild about huge spiderwebs, either. They usually meant huge spiders. His smile broadened, and he turned to Partridge. "Why don't you send one of your guys in first? Just in case."

He could see Partridge's face as Partridge lit a battery-operated lantern. "You just don't like spiderwebs."

"You got it," Culhane said, laughing, "you got it." But then he started through the entrance of the cave, Mulrooney grabbing the flashlight from him and following him inside.

"I'm not gonna wait around until hell freezes over for— Ohh, geez—what a spider!"

And Culhane was beside her, pushing away the cobwebs sticking to his face and hands, taking the light from her. A spider the size of a half dollar was crawling across her white shorts. Culhane cracked her rear end with his hand, knocking off the spider.

"What the—"

"Had a spider on your butt." She pressed herself against him. "A big one." She pressed harder against him, then looked up.

"Or were you just looking for a—"

He felt himself grin. "That, too, but it was a big spider. Now stay behind me," said Culhane, holding the light in his left hand and using it to poke through some of the large webs. Together they started into the cave.

He could hear Partridge from outside. "Want us to come in?"

"Hang on a minute. If this isn't the right cave, no sense bothering." Culhane suddenly ducked his head. There was no time to warn Mulrooney verbally, so he just jerked down on her arm to make her do the same. As he rose to his full height again, he stopped, staring at the far wall at the end of the cave, at the drawing there. "This is the right cave," he murmured.

"Holy—" It was Mulrooney.

She wrenched the light from his hand, moving ahead, Culhane following her. "Holy—" She said it again.

"Holy what?" he asked her. "So it's a marking on a cave wall."

"Help me—gimme your knife," she whispered, dropping to her knees at the mound of dirt covering what appeared to be the bottom half of the cave wall markings.

"I'll do it," he told her, reaching to the leather pouch on his belt, getting the Bali-Song, one-handing it open and then digging with it. "This is the most expensive shovel you'll ever see," he told her.

But Mulrooney was already scooping away the loosened dirt with her hands, and in less than a minute both of them cleared at least half of what had been hidden.

The flashlight lay on the ground beside them, the markings on the wall visible only at the edge of shadow.

But then Mulrooney had the flashlight in her right hand again, brushing with her left hand at the wall itself, freeing the loose dirt clinging to it.

"Holy—"

"Holy what?" he asked her again.

"Holy shit. It's the Piri Reis aerial projection of Antarctica."

"The what?"

CHAPTER TWENTY-NINE

Except for one penguin guarding the cave entrance with an M-16, they all sat in a semicircle at the base of the wall. The entire map was exposed now, as was the peculiar but not wholly indecipherable writing beneath it.

Partridge spoke first. "Let me get this straight—this is a map made by a guy in a flying saucer?"

"She didn't really say that," Culhane answered for Mulrooney. "She said it was an aerial projection, but that it dates back to before there were airplanes or hot air balloons—"

"Well, there could have been balloons. Benjamin Franklin fooled with them, but even a balloon couldn't get hundreds of miles up," said Mulrooney.

"What 'hundreds of miles up'?" Partridge echoed.

Culhane watched as Mulrooney sighed audibly. "All right—from the top, huh, guys?" And she clasped her hands, resting her elbows on her thighs as she sat cross-legged on the ground. "In the early eighteenth century they discovered these maps—"

"Who discovered?" Partridge interrupted.

"I don't know who discovered!" she almost yelled. "Somebody did—in the Topkapi Palace in Istanbul—then Constantinople—they discovered these old maps that were the property of Admiral Piri Reis."

"Turkey has a navy?"

"I guess it did, Mr. Partridge—geez—" She lit a cigarette. Culhane saw that Mulrooney was losing her patience. "Some other maps of his were found in Germany, I think, but all the maps had one rather odd thing in common, aside from their phenomenal accuracy: they were aerial projections. And this was before they had airplanes or satellites or anything else. But yet these maps existed."

Partridge shook his head. "So what? So some guy traveled around the world before Columbus did."

"Magellan," Culhane pointed out.

"Yeah, I meant Magellan," Partridge said.

Mulrooney gestured behind her to the wall. "You're not paying attention. Look at the map, Mr. Partridge. Look at it closely."

Culhane had studied it, noticing the mountain ranges and other topographical details. "I think the whole point, Partridge, is that Antarctica has been covered with ice for about forty thousand years. The exact shape of the continent should be impossible to ascertain—"

"But it's still covered with ice!"

Culhane got up, left Partridge and the two penguins, and crouched beside the map, looking at the markings beneath it. From the left pocket of his shirt he took his little leather notebook and a pen and started to write.

Mulrooney looked back at Partridge and his CIA men flanking him. "The mountain ranges—show him the mountain ranges, Josh," she said to Culhane. He stopped writing and gestured to the mountain ranges on the wall carving. "You can go back to writing now." He did.

Mulrooney looked at Partridge. "See? Those mountain ranges were not even known to exist until the early fifties, just before the IGY—"

"IGA?"

"That's a supermarket chain. IGY was the International Geophysical Year. When was that, Josh?" she called over her shoulder without looking.

"The IGY—1957—maybe '56. But I think it was '57."

"Thanks." She continued gazing at Partridge. "The map Piri Reis had showed mountain ranges no one even knew existed until two hundred fifty years later. Maybe he guessed at the mountain ranges. Maybe somebody else did. But how come everything's so accurate? You see, the maps were checked, and the shapes of the continents did seem weird until you figured them as taken from an aerial photograph."

Culhane started to speak. "Imagine if Fanny's right. Say some guy in a UFO is mapping the earth—"

"What's this UFO crap?"

"Is mapping the earth," Culhane repeated, ignoring him. "Maybe he used infrared cameras, something like that. But he has the maps, or maybe the maps are real old and he got 'em from somebody else. Whoever made them—well, *somebody* made them."

"But that's impossible!" Partridge said.

Culhane said nothing for a moment. Mulrooney held her breath. Then Culhane started to speak and she exhaled. "Sure it's impossible—but then what the hell are we looking at on the wall of this cave here, huh? So let Fanny talk—she knows about this stuff. Listen to her," and he fell silent.

She cleared her throat. "The map shows an ice-free continent. It hasn't been ice-free since the last great period of continental drift—and don't ask me to explain continental drift—but when the last period came about, scientists conjecture that the tip of South America served to block warming currents that had kept Antarctica's climate moderate—at least compared to today. Like opening the door of the freezer and standing in front of it for forty thousand years. It turned to ice."

"So Perry Reis was in this cave?"

"It's not Perry like Perry Como—it's Piri."

"Piri what's-his-name—he was here?" Partridge asked again.

Mulrooney nodded. "He could have been, I suppose. But more likely it was the Phoenicians. Some people think they may have sailed this far."

"Maybe Vikings, too," Partridge added.

"Yeah, right, maybe Vikings, too," Mulrooney said impatiently. "But my guess is that somebody found this cave before Mr. Fife found it—found it and copied the map from the cave wall, and that's what Piri Reis had: a copy of this."

She heard a scraping sound and looked around. It was Culhane at the wall to her right, clearing away dirt with a shovel.

"What else did Piri Reis have maps of, Fanny?" Culhane asked her.

She pushed herself to her feet and half ran to get beside him, dropping to her bare knees in the dirt next to him. "South America, I think—and the coastline of North America, and I think the Mediter—"

Culhane leaned back from the wall. "Look like anything?"

She closed her eyes to focus better, but it was still there. Partially dirt-encrusted but recognizable was the southeastern coast of the United States. And there was a peculiar mark off the coast of Georgia.

"X marks the spot, huh?" Culhane said. "Cumberland Island."

"My God," she gasped. She hoped she'd brought enough film.

BY MIDNIGHT they had cleared away the mounds of dirt and debris all but covering the smooth walls of the cave. And on each side wall there were more of the aerial projection maps.

"I bet if we dig up the middle of the cave, we'll find the rest of the skeleton that belongs to the demon skull. And maybe the tools he used to carve the maps on the walls," Mulrooney said.

Culhane looked at her. "That's awfully chauvinistic—the tools *he* used? Could have been a woman."

"Sure," she agreed. "But a woman would have left the place neater."

Culhane wrapped his arm around her, staring at the maps in the light of the battery-powered lanterns Partridge and his three penguins had brought.

"You know what this means?" she whispered to him so Partridge wouldn't hear. "You know what it means, Josh? We're really not alone in the universe."

Culhane shrugged. "Maybe. . . ."

"Then what the hell else explains it?"

He felt his eye muscles tense, then relax. "I don't know, Fanny. I don't know."

"What the hell does this all mean, Miss Mulrooney?" It was Partridge's voice.

Culhane turned away from the map of North America. Where Cumberland Island would be, there was a tiny cross with a looped top: the ankh, the Egyptian symbol of enduring life. He felt Mulrooney turn around beside him.

"I don't know, but I can guess," he heard her say. She could always guess, he thought and smiled. "I think some extraterrestrial—maybe he was an explorer—died here. Maybe he got hurt—maybe his ship was disabled. But he left these maps as a record."

"Then what the hell did Captain Chillingsworth find in Antarctica that frightened the shit out of his men?"

Mulrooney started to answer, but Culhane spoke first. "For one of my books—I won't know which one it'll be in sequence until I get the research done—Sean Dodge—"

"Aww, crap," Mulrooney murmured beside him.

Culhane ignored her. "Dodge has to learn how to read Egyptian hieroglyphics to impersonate an archaeologist; I'm not sure why yet, but it seemed like a good idea. And I like languages, so the research was fun. And I just used it to translate parts of the writing on the wall under the map of Antarctica."

"You mean it's Egyptian hieroglyphics?" Mulrooney shrieked.

"No, it's like hieroglyphics but more simplified, cleaner. It's sort of like comparing Japanese and Chinese with the Japanese characters superimposed over the Chinese characters—the Chinese looks clearer."

"What the hell does it say?" Partridge asked, standing up.

"I copied the parts I could translate for later—and I'm no expert, but. . . ." He moved his arm away from Mulrooney and walked over to the wall, dropping into a crouch beside the writing beneath the map. "Now, some of these are just pictures, but I think this guy was maybe a scientist and used technical jargon for some other scientist to be able to read later. What I think—" he gestured toward the pictures "—is that they used the pictures to outline broad concepts, then used the hieroglyphics to amplify shades of meaning." He looked up at Partridge. Mulrooney crouched beside him. "Sort of like when you read something in an encyclopedia. The first couple of paragraphs give a broad outline of the material, and the later paragraphs amplify—like that. But I can't read the pictures. I mean I can tell what some of them are—"

"That's a flower," Mulrooney offered.

Culhane looked at her. "No shit? Of course it's a flower. It's a lotus."

"How do you know it's a lotus?" Partridge asked.

"You see them carved all over the temple of Karnak. It's a popular motif in Egyptian—"

"Then the dead guy with the funny head was an Egyptian?" offered one of the two penguins not guarding the cave entrance.

"I don't think so," Culhane said. "But I wish I did."

"So what does it say then?" Partridge said impatiently.

"Okay," Culhane sighed. "Here goes." He began pointing to symbols as he spoke. "This is some reference to a—well, here—let me explain it this way. The Egyptian system of writing was hieroglyphics, but just like a modern secretary would use shorthand or some other form of speedwriting—or better yet, why do you think we have handwriting instead of just printing?" He was sounding didactic and he knew it and hated it.

Mulrooney raised her hand and wiggled her fingers. "I know, teacher—because printing takes too long and when we connect all our letters together—"

"Shut up—but you're right. So that's exactly what the Egyptian scribes did. They rounded the symbols off and turned them into a form we call hieratic. Now the pure hieroglyphics, whether in original form or in hieratic, combined ideograms with phonograms. Ideograms were pictures, like I mentioned earlier—picture writing. The phonograms indicated sounds for how the words were to be spoken. Now this stuff seems to use separate ideograms that don't appear in Egyptian hieroglyphics, for the most part. Then there are hieroglyphs that combine ideograms and phonograms, but some of these look—well, most of them look vastly more simplified than the actual Egyptian ones. Sort of like a plain, neat handwriting as opposed to calligraphic script. You see this thing?''

"Which thing?'' Partridge said.

"All right—see this little tiny thing here that looks like an obelisk?''

"Like the Washington Monument, Mr. Partridge,'' Culhane heard Mulrooney translate.

"Gotcha,'' Partridge said.

"Right, a little obelisk with a small, almost rectangular object under it. And then this thing, like an upside-down eyebrow with a little stand under it and a left-sweeping arch coming up beneath the stand? See?'' Culhane pointed to the wall. "It forms a ship, sort of—right? And the ship—on the left side of it—has the details of the sail or the prow.''

"That a little bird riding on the boat?'' Partridge asked, pointing his light at the symbol.

"Right! Exactly! A little bird riding on the boat—kind of like a falcon. That's the word *djai*—and in straight Egyptian it would mean the god Re traveling across the sky in his sacred boat.''

"Picture yourself in ancient Egypt,'' Mulrooney began. Culhane looked away from the hieroglyphics and looked at her face, at her eyes, at the light in them. "Now you're a Fed working for the Pharaoh or something—like a secret policeman, right?''

"The CIA isn't the secret police,'' Partridge protested.

"Okay, fine, but you're there and along comes this strange-looking man, but he's not a man and he comes out of a flying saucer that just landed on the front lawn, right?''

"Okay, I'm following you. Go on.''

Culhane closed his eyes and turned his head away.

"So," Mulrooney continued, "you see this strange guy stepping out of this thing that flew out of the sky. The only thing you can relate the UFO to is a boat—like that. And who else would be in a boat that flew around the sky and landed on your front lawn but a—"

"You figure this meant *flying saucer* in the language of these aliens but for the Egyptians it meant a god?" Partridge responded.

"Right," Culhane said, "a god in a flying boat. And now this thing—looks like a combination of an oar and a boat's tiller—with this funny star-shaped object over that? I figure this is some sort of reference to the ship's navigational system. And now this word—" Culhane gestured to another rank of the hieroglyphics "—well, it means disaster in foul weather—or a storm—at least in regular Egyptian. The word is said *neshni*, we think. Nobody's alive who speaks the language of the ancient Egyptians."

"We think," Mulrooney cautioned.

Culhane just looked at her. He ignored what she said. "This squiggly line over a rectangle and then next to it another squiggly line over what looks like an animal with two tall ears and a forked tail—here." He pointed to it for Partridge. "This, I think, means that he crashed or had an accident."

"So," Partridge said, the words coming slowly as Culhane looked at him, "the guy was traveling in his flying saucer—"

"*Djai,*" Culhane supplied.

"And his navigational system got screwed up—"

"Except the word isn't quite right—something like his *hemi*—"

"Right—so his *hemi* got screwed up, making his *djai* crash—"

Mulrooney started saying it and Culhane shut his eyes tight, wishing he could shut his ears that way. "The *hemi* got screwed up on his *djai*, and he had a—"

"Neshni," Culhane almost whispered.

"Right," Partridge said, and Culhane stared at his grinning face. "He had a *neshni.*"

CHAPTER THIRTY

"That poor man—or whatever he was," Mulrooney whispered in the darkness. Culhane felt her roll over and put her head against his chest. "To die so alone like that—light years maybe from his friends, his family, his colleagues. And he must have known that if what he left behind was ever found by people from Earth, they wouldn't be able to tell his family—or anyone—anything."

"Poor bastard," Culhane murmured.

She sat up beside him in bed. "Why do men say things like that? 'Poor bastard'—that's not a nice thing to say."

"It's just a figure of speech," Culhane told her.

"But it isn't fair. He was a scientist, probably. You said that yourself. Maybe a very gentle man—or whatever. It wasn't his fault his flying saucer crashed and he was so injured he just crawled to that cave and then died."

Culhane sat up, finding his cigarettes and his lighter. "Want a cigarette?"

"Yeah," she said and pulled the sheet around her, off his legs and his crotch.

"You cold?"

"A little."

"You're wearing a nightgown, I'm naked, and you pull the sheet around you because it's cold?"

"You wanna borrow my other nightgown? I got a spare with me."

He lit two cigarettes, watching the orange glows as he inhaled hard on them. "No."

"Then don't change the subject. I feel sorry for him. We don't even know his name."

"I think it was that cartouchelike thing on the top of the writing."

"But what does it mean? How do you pronounce it?"

"I don't know, Fanny."

"Then we don't know his name," she insisted.

"You wanna call him Fred the Alien?"

"I'm being serious, Josh—to die like that. . . ."

"Maybe he had something like a laser pistol that he used to carve those maps and the writing. Maybe he killed himself with it afterward. I don't know. . . . Now you've got *me* doin' it." He watched the glow of her cigarette and his own in the dark, placed the ashtray between them on the bed, then looked past her to the light visible through the open balcony drapes, the Savannah night quiet. "Now I'm feeling sorry for him."

"All that way alone, though," he heard her whisper. "Just to find something that had disappeared more than thirty-five thousand years before—a legend maybe."

Culhane laughed. "You want a drink?"

"A little one."

He nodded, which he realized was useless since in the dark she couldn't see him anyway. He got up, finding the dresser by feel, then finding the bottle of Myers's rum. He wanted to avoid switching on the light in order to spare their eyes the necessary adjustment. He found the two glasses they'd used earlier, sticking his left index finger inside the lip of each as he poured so he wouldn't overpour. He walked back to the bed and sat on the edge. He found her hand and gave her a glass of rum.

"Here—eat one," Mulrooney said in the darkness. She felt for his hand, then placed the tiny, foil-wrapped disk of hotel chocolate in it.

Culhane shrugged and set his glass down between his feet on the floor so he could find it. He unwrapped the chocolate and put it in his mouth. "Good," he murmured, balling the foil, finding the ashtray from the glow of his cigarette and putting the foil in it. He picked up his cigarette, molding a tip out of the ashes.

Mulrooney was talking. "But an alien starbase under the Antarctic ice?"

"Maybe," Culhane cautioned, feeling like a wet blanket for her enthusiasm the moment he said it.

"That's what what's-his-name said. Fred the Alien sounds dumb, Josh."

"He was talking about a lost base. If it meant anything at all, it could have been a scientific outpost or something—like a lot of countries keep in Antarctica right now."

"It had to be a starbase."

"What's a starbase? Just something out of science fiction. We don't even know if there is such a thing."

"But that would account for what the *Madagascar* found."

"We don't know what the *Madagascar* found," Culhane reminded her.

"They found what he was looking for: that second ankh sign near the coast of Antarctica. That's where they went."

Culhane sighed loudly. "All right. But who knows what they really found? Maybe the ankh symbol is another 'X marks the spot' thing—and maybe it isn't."

"We'll know when we get there, won't we?" she whispered, Culhane watching the stray sparks of ash as she stubbed out her cigarette.

He stubbed out his own cigarette and took a first taste of the rum.

They had left Cumberland Island and flown directly to Savannah. Partridge had dropped them in the De

Soto Hilton's lobby at 4:00 A.M. They had gone immediately to bed after a drink. It was now five-thirty, and neither of them had slept.

Mulrooney had talked. Culhane had listened.

The next day was Sunday; it already was Sunday. They would meet Partridge for brunch in the restaurant downstairs at ten o'clock.

Culhane finished his drink and lay down beside her again.

She snuggled into the curve of his arm as he held her. He watched the ceiling. After a long while, he could feel her breathing become even. She was asleep.

He couldn't sleep, and he turned his head so he could see through the sliding glass doors of the balcony to the yellow-gold lights of the city beyond.

The demon skull. Josh Culhane wondered what kind of brain had been inside that skull. Had the "man" been some crackpot searching after a legend— much as they were?

THE HARPIST—A MAN IN A TUXEDO—was playing "Stardust." Culhane didn't drink the champagne, nor did Mulrooney. Partridge drank everyone's. "One more helicopter ride, boys and girls—to the U.S.S. *Churchill*—and then we go south, so far south it's almost north. Penguinland."

Culhane laughed at the part about the penguins. He closed his eyes for a moment and pictured tens of thousands of CIA agents in black or dark blue or gray three-piece suits, sunglasses and inconspicuous bulges. These, however, would be different penguins—but like the others, birds of a feather.

"Sounds like fun to me," Mulrooney effervesced.

The waitress came and talk ceased. Culhane ordered an omelet for Mulrooney and three Danish—provided they contained no coconut or nuts—for himself. Partridge took the buffet and left.

Mulrooney sipped her coffee, and Culhane stared into space. The restaurant was designed to resemble a garden, and was decorated in greens and whites and soft-to-the-eye outdoor colors. The harp music was lulling Culhane to sleep. He guessed he'd gotten three hours.

Mulrooney's voice brought him back. "I don't trust Partridge," she said and smiled across her coffee cup.

The waitress returned with large glasses of orange juice for both of them, then left.

"Welcome to the club. But it's probably our imaginations, Fanny." Culhane inhaled on his cigarette for the last time, then stubbed it out. He was antsy, nervous. "He doesn't need me; any bum on the street could be taught more hieroglyphics than I know. And a computer could do the work a hell of a lot faster. He doesn't need you—"

"But I'm one of the recognized authorities on UFOs, close encounters, unexplained—"

"Yeah, Fanny, but if all that crud you put in your books—no offense, kid—but if one percent of it is correct, the government already knows more about UFO sightings than you do or anybody else ever could." He turned his eyes from Fanny Mulrooney and watched Partridge fill his plate from the buffet.

"I wanna go anyway—and so do you. You always wanted a ride in a nuclear submarine. You told me that lots of times."

Culhane exhaled hard. "Yeah, I wanna go. Always wanted to see Antarctica, too, although it's the wrong season for it."

"What—higher rates?" she said, laughing.

"No, all the pools are closed at the hotels," he snapped.

"What's bothering you?" she asked gently.

"If I knew, it wouldn't bother me," he replied with a smile.

And then Partridge returned, his plate looking to Culhane as if it held half the buffet's offerings. "You gonna eat all that?"

"Yeah. Hey, listen, the food's great here."

"I know it is," Culhane said. He had stayed at the De Soto Hilton often. The three ate in silence for a while, then Partridge spoke.

"There's a reason for the submarine and that business about going out to meet it while it's under way. You see, Antarctica is neutral territory; no weapons of any kind are allowed. And I guess a nuke sub is counted as a weapon. But it's the only reliable way to get in under the watchful eyes of our neighbors in world harmony, though," Partridge said, then bit through half a hush puppy.

"You mean the Russians?" Mulrooney asked.

"Yep," Partridge nodded, wiping his mouth with his napkin. "I mean the good old Russians. If there is this starbase whatchamacallit down there, they probably got some pretty sophisticated shit." He paused. "Sorry, Miss Mulrooney, sophisticated *stuff*. We can't let the Russians get their greedy little hands on it."

"What about Steiglitz?" Culhane asked.

Partridge finished the hush puppy, saying through it, "Only five of us in the Company know anything about this: the deputy director, myself, and that's it—plus my three assistants. The submarine commander only knows he's picking up thirteen people and taking them on a little trip. We'll brief him once we're aboard."

"Thirteen people," Mulrooney said. "I like lucky numbers. How'd we get thirteen? You and your three men—that's four. Add in Josh and myself—that makes six."

"Support personnel—all hand-picked by the deputy director—and even they don't know where we're going. There are some linguistics experts, an archaeologist, people like that. And you won't be the only woman on board the submarine, Miss Mulrooney. There are three women on the team of experts.''

''What if one of the other seven is working for Steiglitz and his daughter?'' Culhane asked Partridge.

Partridge downed a forkful of sausage. ''No sweat,'' he said, and smacked his lips together. ''For openers, we can trust the crew 'cause those atomic submarine guys get security checks on top of security checks just to be on board. And the scientists and language experts don't know what they're getting tapped to do. And they all got security clearances, too. So relax. Just a nice little trip south to do some exploring.'' He punctuated his little speech with a bite of bacon.

Culhane wondered if Mulrooney was right about the number thirteen.

IT WAS AN OHIO CLASS SUBMARINE. Looking down from under the whirring blades of the Kaman SH-2F helicopter, Culhane hadn't realized the U.S.S. *Churchill* would be that immense a craft.

''That's a submarine? That's enormous.'' Mulrooney's voice came to him through the headset speaker, echoing his thoughts.

''Displaces sixteen thousand tons, if I remember right,'' he said into the small, teardrop-shaped microphone near his lips.

''Wow,'' he heard her say, her breathing so heavy it sounded like an obscene phone call.

He tapped Partridge on the shoulder, who turned to face him. ''I thought there were only a couple of Ohio class subs commissioned so far. And I never heard of the *Churchill* at all,'' Culhane said into his microphone.

''That's why it's named the *Churchill*; it's supposed to be in a class by itself. And once this is all over, you've never seen it—got me?''

Culhane licked his lips, nodding. "Yeah, I've got you. Any other surprises with the *Churchill*?"

"You said sixteen thousand tons. It's sixteen thousand six hundred surfaced, and underwater add another two thousand tons plus."

"That must be the biggest submarine in the world," Culhane heard Mulrooney's voice cut in.

Culhane started to answer, but Partridge beat him. "The Soviets have ones we call the typhoon class. They're about twenty-five thousand tons surfaced—big enough to almost swallow one of these."

"I'll rest easy tonight," Mulrooney commented.

The Navy pilot's voice came in. "We'll be landing on the missile deck in about three minutes, gentlemen, miss. Please make certain that your seat restraints are secure and that your life vests are properly secured as well. The *Churchill* will be under power at approximately five knots, and we'll be matching speed for the landing. It looks like rough seas down there, so it might be a little tricky getting this as smooth as a baby's ass." The pilot's voice cut off, and Culhane checked his seat belt and checked that his Mae West was secure.

Then he looked up and laughed as he watched Mulrooney check her life vest. "Just what I always wanted—a size fifty-two bustline." There was laughter over the headset, but Culhane wasn't sure if it was Partridge, the Navy pilot or one of the three penguins.

He could feel the helicopter's movement in his stomach as it dipped to port and started dropping, beginning what appeared to be a wide banking turn that made them skim the choppy ocean surface. Culhane watched the whitecaps cresting under them and saw the starboard hull of the *Churchill* looming up like a gray-black wall ahead. Culhane's stomach felt it again as the helicopter seemed almost to jump, skipping over the deck safety line supports, then settling quickly over what seemed to be a series of hatches.

"What are those?" Mulrooney's voice asked through the radio.

Culhane answered her. "Trident I SLBMs— Submarine Launched Ballistic Missiles."

"Cripes—are those things loaded?" Mulrooney asked.

The pilot's voice answered her. "Usually, miss— loaded but not armed. But they can be armed real quick."

"That's good," Mulrooney said uncertainly.

The helicopter was down, the swaying motion Culhane felt in his stomach that of the *Churchill* taking the rough seas at low speed. He undid his seat belt, then bent over to help Mulrooney with hers. "Keep the life preservers on, please," said the Navy pilot. "Rough seas out there—don't want any of you nice folks goin' for a swim."

Then Culhane heard a voice he hadn't heard before, and he turned toward the helicopter's portside passenger door. He saw a young-looking naval officer with a slightly florid face. "I'm Lieutenant Hardestey. Commander Macklin—the captain—sent me to welcome you aboard the U.S.S. *Winston Churchill*."

Culhane shot the man a wave, a "Hi," and continued helping Mulrooney. A seaman was already aboard taking their luggage as Culhane stepped down onto the *Churchill*'s missile deck, Mulrooney after him. She'd worn a dress; Culhane had told her it was a mistake. The skirt of her dress blew up in the wind from the helicopter's rotor blades and the air currents coming with the spraying waves over the hull. Mulrooney's face darkened in a blush as somebody on the deck made a low, loud whistle.

"Belay that!" Lieutenant Hardestey sang out. Then he turned to Mulrooney. "The other three ladies who came aboard at Charleston, Miss Mulrooney—well, they didn't get a whistle like that."

CULHANE AND MULROONEY followed Lieutenant Hardestey through the breach in the sail's bulwark. Culhane stopped for a moment, trying to mentally photograph it so he could someday use it in a book: the conning tower of an Ohio class nuclear submarine looking out to sea.

"Memorize it yet?" Mulrooney teased.

Culhane glowered at her. "Yeah, I memorized it." Then he started after Hardestey again. Culhane judged the sail to be some twenty or so feet above the level of the main hull and about a hundred feet, perhaps a little less, in length toward the prow. He recognized some of the hardware in evidence; the long, tubelike appendages extending upward were the snorkel inlet and snorkel exhaust. The electronic countermeasures package was up, and even higher than the sail itself were the extended radio antenna and radar dish. These were all retractable once the submarine was submerging.

Culhane followed Hardestey down from the flying bridge to the bridge below. "Please watch your step, and watch the low clearance," Hardestey cautioned.

Mulrooney, behind and above Culhane, was grousing. "You can tell whoever built these ladders wasn't thinking of high heels." Culhane looked up at Mulrooney. If he'd been a voyeur, it would have been a perfect spot.

"Communications is just over there—" Hardestey gestured forward as they started down the next ladder "—and now we're going to the control room. The captain is eager to meet all of you, especially you, Mr. Culhane. Commander Macklin's a great fan of your books."

"Thanks," Culhane told him, following him down, then helping Mulrooney to safe footing.

"We'll roll like this until we get below the surface," Hardestey said. "And now if you'd all follow me. . . ." Culhane walked through what seemed like a short corridor and stopped. To Culhane, the control room looked like the aftermath of an explosion in an electronics factory. Every square inch had some gadget on it. The instrument consoles were illuminated by overhead green lights, and everything seemed impossibly complex.

He felt better when he recognized something. A periscope dominated the center of the bridge onto which they now walked. Its steel casing gleamed, and brass looking handles were folded down from its sides. A short, wiry man, hatless, crouched beside it, shifting the periscope in a turn of forty-five degrees. He moved away from the periscope and smiled, white teeth shining as he picked up a cap dripping gold braid.

"I'm Commander Ed Macklin, captain of the U.S.S. *Winston Churchill*. Welcome aboard to all of you." He placed the cap on his head, then talked past them, saying, "Jimmy—"

"Yes, sir." It was Lieutenant Hardestey's voice.

"Get back up there, and let's start the ball rolling to get out of here and below."

"Yes, sir," Hardestey said, and he brushed past them, disappearing into the small corridor. Culhane could hear his footsteps on the ladder.

"Bein' the deck officer keeps you kind of busy," Macklin said.

Hardestey's voice crackled over a speaker system. "The helicopter's away, sir. The aft rail has been replaced—" footsteps were audible on the ladders beyond the little corridor "—and all personnel are below. Topside is clear. I repeat, topside is clear."

Macklin picked up a microphone, his voice firm, confident, seemingly filled with expectation. "Very well, Mr. Hardestey. Secure the bridge hatch."

"Secure the bridge hatch—aye, Captain," Hardestey's voice came back over the PA.

Macklin looked at Culhane. "I'll bet you're memorizing every word I say, aren't you, Mr. Culhane?"

"Just don't criticize the submarine lingo in any of my future books—I'll have gotten it from you," Culhane said with a grin.

"It's not that hard and fast a thing," Macklin said. "Every once in a while we still say standard submarine movie talk like 'prepare for negative buoyancy' and 'up periscope'—shticks like that."

Mulrooney, beside Culhane, laughed.

Then Macklin turned back to his hand mike. "Retract periscope."

A voice came from the bridge control room below: "Retract periscope."

Macklin grinned at Culhane. "Sometimes I say 'down periscope'—honest." Then he looked back to his mike. "This is the captain speaking. Since we're going under for a bit, thought it might be advisable to make sure we haven't sprung a leak, so hold your ears, guys. Maneuvering spaces—stand by to answer bells."

The PA system: "Maneuvering to bridge. Standing by to answer bells."

"Rudder amidships," Macklin said easily. "All ahead one-third."

Bells actually rang.

There were footsteps on the ladder behind them. Culhane turned around and saw Hardestey. The young lieutenant passed him, and Culhane followed the man with his eyes.

"Bridge hatch secured, sir!"

Macklin nodded. "Relay my commands," he said and handed the microphone to Hardestey.

Culhane could hear the sounds of the twin screw cranking through the water, as well as the sounds of water rushing around the hull. The throbbing was unexpectedly loud to him.

"Rig for dive," Macklin ordered, leaning over the rail of the bridge, staring below to the control room.

Hardestey's voice came back a moment later: "The ship's rigged for dive and compensated, sir."

"Very well—trim?"

"Pumped, sir!"

"Ballast control—let me hear from you."

Hardestey was wearing earphones with a headset microphone now as he stood near the periscope tubes at the bridge's center. "Ballast control ready to dive, Captain."

"Shut the induction, then bleed air—and remind 'em to hold their ears."

"Engine room, bleed high-pressure air. All personnel take note of high-pressure bleed!"

Culhane walked forward so he could better see Macklin at work. The captain was studying a barometer. The needle rose slightly, then stayed stationary. "Well, whaddaya know," Macklin said. "We don't leak after all" He turned to Hardestey. "I like the bleed."

"The ship is tight, sir," Hardestey responded.

"Open the vents."

Hardestey repeated that, then nodded almost imperceptibly. Macklin looked at Culhane and grinned as he said, "Dive! Dive!"

"Maneuvering bow planes," Hardestey announced. A bell rang, sounding like an out-of-tune burglar alarm.

"All ahead two-thirds once we reach periscope depth—and hold her there," Macklin said and reached out for the periscope handles. "Up periscope." He swung the periscope from side to side, stopping it, his hat cocked on the back of his head. "Tybee Island Lighthouse—mark on that."

"Mark," Hardestey repeated. Then, "Marked."

"Periscope retract. Take her down to 175 feet off the bottom and follow her out. Once we're another ten minutes away, Jimmy, keep her all ahead full on that southerly course we worked up to our next rendezvous. Notify navigation we'll have the final coordinates for them shortly, and not to get all nervous and upset and start hollerin'."

"Aye, sir," Hardestey answered.

Macklin turned to Culhane, Mulrooney standing beside Culhane now. Macklin said to her, "Haven't had a lady in here with a pretty red dress on since last Tuesday, Miss Mulrooney. How about I buy you folks a cup of coffee in my cabin and we settle a few things?" Then he looked right at Culhane. "And I'll get you the guided tour as soon as I'm able."

Macklin held out his arm for Mulrooney. She smiled and took it, and they started toward the small corridor.

CHAPTER THIRTY-ONE

Mary Frances Mulrooney had begged off for a few moments on the coffee, promising to join the captain after freshening up. She looked at her face in the mirror as she washed her hands. Her hair was a mess from being windblown on the deck of the submarine. She dried her hands and rolled down her sleeves—she'd promised the captain she wouldn't change out of the red dress—buttoning the cloth-covered buttons at the cuffs. She was searching through her purse for her hairbrush when her fingers found the cassette tape she'd gotten in the mail from Cletus Ball. She temporarily abandoned the search for the hairbrush, left the tiny bathroom and went into the six-by-six-foot cabin. Her luggage was already there, and she opened the maroon tote she normally used as carry-on luggage and found Josh Culhane's tape recorder. She opened the little Jiffy Bag and read the note Ball had folded around the tape.

Dear Miss Mulrooney: The tapes we made a few nights ago didn't come out too conclusively, but this one I just recorded did. It was made near a fresh grave of a person involved in a very violent death. Please listen and call me.

Gravely yours, Cletus Ball.

" 'Gravely yours,' " she muttered. "Smartass." She put the tape on the machine and pushed the Play button.

She went back into the bathroom and resumed the search through her bag for her hairbrush. She listened to Cletus Ball explain the time, the weather conditions and the type of tape recorder and tape he was using. She brushed her hair; it still had some curl in it, and she tried to make the most of it. Cletus Ball was still talking.

She put the brush back into her purse and found her lipstick. Ball was now explaining why the tapes the other night hadn't worked out: the rain had apparently been falling at just the right speed to set up a conflicting frequency with the voices. "Bullshit," she murmured, puckering her lips and putting away the lipstick. The bow at her neck was half undone; she retied it, then adjusted the spacing of the two gold chains around her neck.

She looked at herself, smoothed her dress, then turned away from the mirror. . . .

The graveside recording had begun. She felt cold and sick to her stomach. Her forehead and upper lip became beaded with perspiration. She leaned weakly against the frame of the bathroom door, listening, her fingers pressed to her lips. "Mother of God," she whispered over the voice from the dead.

CULHANE STOOD AND SO DID COMMANDER MACKLIN as Mulrooney was ushered into Macklin's office-cum-cabin by a young black lieutenant. "The captain's been telling me what a treat I had in store meeting you, Miss Mulrooney," he said and smiled.

Mulrooney, smiling back, thanked him and let him help her to a chair.

"Miss Mulrooney, you haven't been introduced to Lieutenant Ray Wilbur—my engineering officer and my exec on this trip," said Macklin.

The lieutenant smiled again.

Macklin stepped around from his desk. "May I offer you some coffee?"

"Thank you," Mulrooney said, and Macklin moved over to a low cabinet behind his desk that held a Mister Coffee. He poured some coffee into a white mug with blue stenciled letters that read "U.S.S. *Winston Churchill*." He came back around the desk and handed her the cup. "Thank you," she said again.

"You looked like the black coffee type," Macklin told her, and Mulrooney smiled.

Culhane took it all in. Fanny Mulrooney was turning on every man on the ship in a pleasant way. It wouldn't hurt.

Partridge stood up, stretched and took his cup back to Macklin's pot. "The captain wanted to know just what the heck we were doing. We told him you could tell him best, Miss Mulrooney."

The ball was in her court, and Culhane watched her play with it. "Well," she said, "did you have any kind of briefing, Captain—or should I say Commander?"

"Either will do—whatever feels better."

"Captain, then," she said. "Were you—"

"I was told that we were heading for Antarctica," he answered, his smile gone now. "Mr. Partridge told me that. That we're looking for a spot on a map you people copied off the wall of a cave. That the map was distorted quite a bit. But what does it all mean?"

"Did anyone mention the starbase to you, and the dead alien?"

Culhane laughed, Partridge choked on his coffee, and Macklin dropped the cigar he'd been starting to guillotine.

"I guess nobody mentioned it," Mulrooney said. "Well—" And she began recounting the findings on the cave walls, the story of Henry Chillingsworth, and the search for the Gladstone Log from the H.M.S. *Madagascar*.

After she had finished, Macklin said, "I'll want to see that logbook—or a copy of it. If I'm supposed to find this place, knowing what that Captain Chillingsworth went through should help."

"I have the original," Culhane said. "In my quarters."

"I think that would be best off in my safe. I have a safe around just for little odds and ends like that. And another matter before I forget. I've been told by the deputy chief of Naval Operations that I'm supposed to trust Mr. Partridge implicitly. And being a big fan of your books—" he looked at Culhane "—I'd like to trust you as well. And of course Miss Mulrooney. I haven't been told to trust the seven scientists and technicians—the three women are already aboard and the four men are coming aboard off Fort Lauderdale—so I won't." Then he looked at Partridge. "And since the possibility exists that this Steiglitz character might be up to no good and things like that—well, I think we'll all be safer if Mr. Wilbur receives any firearms any of you might have. Right now."

"I have authorization to carry a weapon—"

But Macklin interrupted Partridge. "Set a good example, otherwise I'll order searches. I wouldn't want to do that. Once you leave the *Churchill* to find your alien star-base or whatever—" he glanced at Mulrooney "—you can have your weapons back. I won't ask again."

Partridge walked over from the credenza behind Macklin's desk. He set down his mug of coffee, reached under his windbreaker and produced a revolver. He set the stainless Model 66 two-and-one-half-inch barreled .357 on Macklin's desk, then stepped away.

Macklin looked to Fanny Mulrooney. "Miss Mulrooney?"

Culhane saw her eyes search for his; he nodded.

She shrugged her shoulders, picked up her purse from the floor beside her chair and set it on her lap. "This'll take a minute."

"No rush at all," Macklin said, smiling.

Soon she had the Model 60 Smith in her right hand, holding it between her thumb and first finger at the grips.

Macklin reached for it. "It's loaded," Mulrooney cautioned.

Macklin nodded, then took the revolver and set it on the desk beside Partridge's gun.

"Mr. Culhane?"

Culhane inhaled on his cigarette, then reached under his brown corduroy sports jacket. He made the stainless steel Detonics Scoremaster appear, ejected the magazine, then worked the slide, catching the chambered round in the palm of his hand as it ejected through the port. He snapped the trigger to let the hammer fall and handed the gun to Macklin, then reloaded the loose round into the magazine and pocketed it.

"That it, Mr. Culhane?"

Culhane nodded.

"Just like Sean Dodge carries in your books—a real beaut." And Macklin looked to Lieutenant Wilbur. "Ray, empty these other two and take all three weapons down to the armory and have them locked away safely. Hunt up the three women passengers and the three co-workers of Mr. Partridge, and get their weapons as well. Then you'd better get back on duty. I'm going to run a full systems check before we pick up the other four—that should be at about 1400 hours."

"Aye, sir."

Macklin turned to Culhane. "If you would get me

that logbook of the *Madagascar*, I'd appreciate it, Mr. Culhane."

"Right away, Captain," Culhane answered.

"I suggest we meet in the officers' mess at about eight o'clock tonight, civilian time. I'm sure one of you folks brought a bottle or two. Maybe we can all share and talk over what's what and who's doing it."

Culhane stood. Mulrooney stood. Partridge was already standing. Lieutenant Wilbur was in the process of unloading Mulrooney's Model 60 Smith.

Then Macklin smiled. "Miss Mulrooney, I'd be honored if you and Mr. Culhane would join me and my officers for dinner tonight at about 1800 hours—at about six. I'm a great fan of your books as well as Mr. Culhane's. I thought you might be able to tell me all about the lost continent of Atlantis—since we may be going there."

MARGARET SPICER HAD BEEN IN THE BATHROOM for twenty minutes. Mulrooney wondered what the hell the archaeologist was doing in there. It was going to be interesting sharing that shoebox of a cabin with another woman. . . .

Mulrooney stood up, setting her notes on the Gladstone Log down on the bunk, and took off her robe. It was nearly six, nearly time for dinner, and she wanted to change before she fixed her hair. The four male scientists and technicians had come aboard at about ten minutes after four; Mulrooney had felt the swaying of the *Churchill* when it had surfaced to receive the men from the helicopter off the Florida coast. And Margaret Spicer, who had finished her tour of the *Churchill* only minutes before that, had been assigned to share a cabin with her. Culhane had been assigned to share a cabin with Lieutenant Hardestey. Since there were only four women and 171 men, four officers were relocated, and the women shared cabins. Mulrooney didn't like the arrangement at all.

She stepped into a gray tweed dirndl skirt, pulled the back zipper only halfway up, and found the black heels she'd worn earlier. She stepped into them, then went to the tiny closet she shared with Margaret Spicer and searched for her long-sleeved black blouse. Margaret Spicer did all right for an archaeologist, Mulrooney observed. If Spicer had brought a dress, she'd hidden it; only slacks and blouses hung in the closet, and their labels were ones Mulrooney recognized as expensive.

She found her blouse, pulled it on and had it buttoned halfway up the back, when she heard the bathroom door open. She turned around.

"Mary Frances, can I button the rest of that for you?" Margaret Spicer asked, smiling sweetly. She was a tall, black-haired woman with striking blue eyes. She looked almost too tall in the mid-thigh-length bathrobe she wore.

"Yeah, thanks," Mulrooney told her, turning her back to the woman.

She could feel the woman's hands working the buttons. "I like your blouse—it's beautiful."

"Thanks," Mulrooney said again, feeling the woman's hands now up near her neck, buttoning the three buttons set close together there. Mulrooney zipped up the skirt all the way and started buttoning her long cuffs, three buttons each. "I'll bet being an archaeologist is exciting."

"Sometimes," Margaret Spicer said. "There—all done."

"Thank you," Mulrooney said, turning around and facing her. Her cuffs buttoned, she stuffed the bottom of the blouse inside her skirt, then finished closing the zipper and waistband. She walked past Margaret to the small dresser where she had the top two drawers, opened the top one, found her gold chains and put them on.

"Do you know much about what's going on, Margaret?"

"My friends call me Meg."

"All right, Meg, do you know much about what's—"

"You mean why they pulled me off a two-year dig in Egypt and flew me to Charleston and gave me all the winter clothes I had packed away in my parents' house? No, not really."

Mulrooney thought about that. The clothes hadn't looked as if they had been packed away, but they were the sorts of things that never seemed to go out of style, either. She walked into the bathroom, leaving the door open, and started brushing her hair. "So they didn't tell you anything?"

"Just that I was heading someplace cold and to bring all my gear for deciphering hieroglyphics. Do you now anything, Mary Frances?"

"My friends call me M.F. Yes, I do, but I think all your questions will be answered at the briefing tonight."

"I can hardly wait."

"Me too," Mulrooney told Margaret, finishing arranging her hair. "What do the other two women do?"

"I only talked to them for a little while in Charleston. Janet Krull is some kind of biologist—a paleobiologist, I believe."

"Sounds interesting," Mulrooney said. "What does Angela Basque do?"

"She's an astronomer. She worked in Antarctica for six months once and now teaches at one of those fancy women's colleges back East."

"Which one? Do you remember?"

"You'll have to ask Angela—it sounded like she loved talking about herself."

Mulrooney finished in the bathroom, found her purse and began searching for a lipstick.

"My bet is we're heading somewhere in Central

America,'' Margaret Spicer said. "I worked a great deal on some of the excavations of the Mayan civilization. Maybe this cold weather gear is a cover-up—'' She laughed. "Get it? A cover-up?''

Mulrooney laughed politely. She put her lipstick away. Spicer was wearing a watch that looked as if it belonged on a man's wrist instead of a woman's. "What time have you got?''

"Five to six—at least that's the time if we're still in the Eastern Zone—and maybe we are.''

"Five to six—gotcha. Thanks, Margaret, uh, Meg.'' Mulrooney started for the door.

She stopped abruptly. She walked back to the bunk, picked up her notebook and put it into her purse. "I'm a writer. You never know when you might need to take some notes.'' And she started for the door again.

THE OFFICERS' MESS WAS A GOOD-SIZE ROOM, Culhane noted. He'd been memorizing everything he could to use the data in a book someday. Nuclear submarines and their workings were one of the most closely guarded secrets of any nation, and for an adventure writer, closely guarded secrets always represented problems. To write about helicopter chase scenes, it helps if you've flown in a helicopter and understand the basic workings. For detailed information on instrument panels—so the hero reaches to the left for something rather than to the right, for example—you might contact the helicopter manufacturer. Culhane had an extensive library of pamphlets, instruction manuals, photographs and technical diagrams. But none of this was available for submarines. To research them was a monumental effort, and this was a golden opportunity. He was more interested in the trip to the area between Wilkes Land and Victoria Land in Antarctica than what they'd find when they got there.

His right foot up on the edge of a chair, a cigarette

in his right hand, he glanced beside him. Fanny Mulrooney, looking pretty in her gray skirt and black blouse, had eyes that looked as if they were on fire. He knew why. She was on her way to an alien starbase under the antarctic ice pack—at least that was what she said it was. And for her, he realized, it was the opportunity of a lifetime, as well. On impulse, he reached out to her lap, holding her hands folded there. She looked at him, smiling, her green eyes like flashing emeralds.

Captain Macklin entered the officers' mess, and Wilbur shouted, "Ten-hut!"

"As you were, gentlemen, as you were," Macklin called out, cutting him off. Macklin sat at the head of the long table, as he had done at dinner. Culhane and Mulrooney sat at the opposite end. On Culhane's right were Partridge, the three CIA penguins and two women—Margaret Spicer and Angela Basque.

On Culhane's left, next to Mulrooney, was Janet Krull. Then came Lieutenant Wilbur, Lieutenant Hardestey and the four other scientists and technicians. Culhane had met them briefly when they'd come aboard, but he hadn't yet matched names with faces. He imagined there would be enough time for that.

Macklin was speaking. "Introductions may not be necessary, anyway. So let's get down to it." He paused for a moment. "Mr. Culhane, Miss Mulrooney, Mr. Partridge—tell these people all about the Gladstone Log, the alien starbase. Give 'em the whole nine yards."

Culhane felt Mulrooney's breath against his left ear. "You do it," she whispered.

"Thanks a lot," he muttered, standing up. He looked at the faces staring at him expectantly. "Well...."

HARDESTEY HAD GONE ON WATCH, Partridge's three men had left—either because Partridge had told them to do so earlier or because they really didn't care—and Meg Spicer looked bored. Lieutenant Wilbur was just smiling.

A short man with a goatee, an expert in human engineering, looked at Culhane. "Mr. Culhane, these so-called hieroglyphics indicating some creature from another planet crash-landed here—are they available for perusal or not?"

Culhane looked at Partridge, who said, "Couldn't much expect you to translate what we find unless you see this stuff first. I'll have packets of all the information in summary to all of you within the hour. My men are assembling the packets now. All of you will have the photographs of the cave drawings, the hieroglyphics—"

"If these are the Piri Reis maps," a tall, bald man cut in, "then I think we might all benefit from knowing the real side of the maps rather than what Mr. Culhane says Miss Mulrooney supplied." The man's name was Dr. Erwin Fell, and he was the linguistics expert.

"What the hell do you mean by that?" Mulrooney asked, getting up from her chair and stubbing out her cigarette.

"Relax," Culhane said to her through his teeth.

She sat back down.

"What I mean, Miss Mulrooney, is that you have presented only the sensationalist aspect of these so-called maps. There is another side. That Antarctica is represented at all is quite speculative indeed. Since not all of Admiral Piri Reis's maps have been found, it is impossible to understand the strange projection—"

Mulrooney cut in. "All I know is that Henry Chillingsworth, in his diary, spoke about starships, spoke about weird writing and pictures—"

"I should like the opportunity of perusing this document as well," said the goateed man.

"Fine," Culhane answered for her. "I don't think that Miss Mulrooney or myself wishes to have an adversary relationship. I'm not a believer in flying saucers or the occult or anything like that—and Miss Mulrooney knows it," he added, seeing her eyes boring into him. "But we found what we found, and the important thing is that this maniac Steiglitz seems to know something about it that we still don't. And whatever that is, it was important enough to kill Ethyl Chillingsworth for, to kill my brother, to try to kill Miss Mulrooney and me. And that's what I want to find out about. Whatever the hell the *Madagascar* found or didn't find, we've gotta know the answers."

CHAPTER THIRTY-TWO

Culhane looked at his notes.

The diving panel—metallic gray in color—depth gauges, gyrocompass repeater, speed indicator, annunciators—for use by bow and stern plainsmen. Much like airplane controls. These guys responsible for keeping uniform depths, etc. See if Macklin will let me sit in one of the red leatherette chairs and get the feel of it while on the surface next time.

He made a stab with his Bic pen to make the period and looked up from his notes.

As much as he liked submarines, other things were on his mind. The meeting in the officers' mess had confirmed something he'd suspected from the start. Though he didn't know who, someone aboard the *Churchill* had to work for Steiglitz. Partridge, perhaps. Partridge very likely. Perhaps one or more of the scientists—the linguistics expert who had known about the Piri Reis maps, perhaps the little guy with the goatee—was on Steiglitz's payroll.

Maybe one of the women. Perhaps one of them was Sonia Steiglitz herself.

He stood up.

Lieutenant Hardestey was still on watch. Culhane looked at his watch. It was just after midnight.

The suspect standing out in his mind, however, was Commander Macklin. They had been alone together for less than a minute. Culhane was using a head near the officers' mess, and Macklin came in. Both men were standing almost shoulder to shoulder while urinating. Macklin had said, "I really do read your books. If you've got that Detonics Scoremaster with you, I'd give even money to anybody you've got one of the little Detonics .45s with you, too. Just like Sean Dodge would. But you keep it—for you and Miss Mulrooney. Maybe you'll need it."

Culhane had zipped up, flushed and started to wash his hands. Macklin had done the same, but hadn't bothered washing his hands; he just left.

Macklin had been right. If Steiglitz had someone aboard, it was his move now.

AT AN AVERAGE SPEED OF THIRTY-FIVE KNOTS under the sea, traveling from approximately 25° north latitude and 80° west longitude, the distance to 65° south and 155° east spanned a hair's breadth over ten thousand nautical miles. These were Macklin's own figures, and on the morning of the second day, after their first night aboard the *Churchill*, the captain had announced at breakfast that the trip would last for slightly under twelve days. The "slightly under" part had already passed, meaning eleven days aboard ship. The *Churchill* was capable of speeds greater than thirty-five knots, but that speed was easier to maintain, and using that as an average would allow for the slower speeds necessary once they hit the polar ice pack.

"Eleven days?" Mulrooney had groaned. Then she had shrugged in apparent resignation.

Culhane asked Lieutenant Hardestey to see about borrowing a typewriter.

Over the first day and a half, Culhane had finished the last ten pages of Takers number seventeen. There was no way to mail them to his publisher, but at least they would be ready once they had returned. He'd only be a month or so late, he calculated. But to compensate for that, he began working on the outline for the next book so that with any luck he would be early on that one and make his publisher forget how late number seventeen had been.

Mulrooney, too, had borrowed a typewriter and worked up sheaves of material that she faithfully showed Culhane: pages on the Gladstone Log, on the voyage of the *Madagascar*, on the events at San Rafael Island, on the voyage to Antarctica itself. He'd told her she should write a novel about it, and she'd suggested they both do it. He'd told her he'd wait to find out the ending first.

Culhane had developed a schedule for himself. He typed while Hardestey was on watch and spent the other sixteen hours of the day equally divided between Mulrooney's company and sleeping, realizing that once they reached Antarctica, he had no idea what to expect. Sleeping was a preoccupation aboard the *Churchill*. There wasn't much else to do except for reading, playing wall-outlet-type personal video games and watching videotapes played on VCRs on the televisions in the crew's and officers' messes. It was the only way the televisions could be put to use, for even if the *Churchill* had been in range of a television broadcaster, picking up television and radio was impossible below the surface.

On the sixth day, Culhane had been asked to speak before a group of officers and enlisted men, all fans of his books. He enjoyed talking about his writing, and some of his listeners would occasionally ask good questions. But the key enlisted man aboard the *Churchill*, a chief torpedoman's mate, asked one he'd never encountered: "With all the women Sean Dodge goes to bed with in those books—I won't ask if that's all personal experience—how the hell does he avoid herpes?" Culhane, thinking fast, had replied, "Hell, fellas, all the girls Dodge makes love to have saved themselves for him to come along." There had been more laughter and more questions.

On the ninth day, making better time than Macklin had expected going through the Drake Passage between the tip of South America and the Antarctic Peninsula, Macklin had called Culhane, Mulrooney and some of the others to the bridge.

No one watched Macklin. Everyone was watching the color television monitor at the forwardmost portion of the bridge bulkhead. It showed ice.

"Good thing we made some time. We won't soon," Macklin announced. "Probably all of you have read about submarines going under the North Pole, and it sounds exciting. That's 'cause it is exciting. The South Pole is a little different. As far as we know, there is no way under it, no more than there would necessarily be a way under Pittsburgh. This is a landmass, not just floating ice. But we've got many of the same problems. Roughly seventy percent of the world's supply of fresh water is right here in icebergs and in the ice shelf coating the land—three miles thick in some places. Surface navigation is hazardous here. Small icebergs that people just started calling 'bergy bits' are more dangerous than the large ones. We all remember what happened to the *Titanic*; they saw a little bit of the iceberg above the water while the bigger part below the surface knifed through their hull. U.S. submarines use a single-pressure hull—we bump into the right iceberg at the wrong angle, and we're kissin' life goodbye. But we won't do that. We have passive sonar that is constantly monitoring the water around us, above us and below us. We also have active sonar, and with that we can sketch the shape on a graph and then estimate the thickness of the ice overhead should we actually wind up under an ice shelf.''

"How soon before we reach the target area, Commander?" Angela Basque, their closest thing to an Antarctic expert, asked abruptly.

Macklin looked at Culhane, then back to her. "I studied the *Madagascar*'s logbook backward and forward, and the photographs of the maps Miss Mulrooney and Mr. Culhane found in the cave on Cumberland Island. I've come to one conclusion: if the *Madagascar* found all the stuff Henry Chillingsworth talks about in his diary, Chillingsworth's uncle— Captain Miles Chillingsworth—was the luckiest navigator since Sinbad.''

There was laughter from the crew members nearby. "The Antarctic section of the map is the one we're chiefly concerned with, and it's very difficult to work from. But I figured from the *Madagascar*'s logbook more or less where she went. They searched several locations and just about used up all their cannonballs and gunpowder trying to bust holes in the ice. They were here in a different season than we are. Plus there's been one hundred years for the ice to change. I'm sure somebody could come up with some dandy statistics, but the cave the Gladstone Log mentions finding could be underwater by now, or it could be several miles back along the ice field.''

"What if it is? Either one, I mean," Mulrooney asked.

"Problems," Culhane remarked.

Macklin nodded. "If the cave entrance is under the water level, it depends on how deep. We've got some divers aboard, and we have insulated, cold-water diving gear. So maybe we can explore the cave mouth at least. But a detailed exploration with the gear we have available will be out of the question. I've got men with guts enough to try it, but I've got more brains than to let them."

"What about the other way?" Partridge asked.

"If it's across the ice pack, we can't fire a torpedo or a deck gun into the ice to blow it clear. We'd have to find it, then use conventional explosives. Which we don't have. But we have conventional explosives available from one of the torpedoes, and we can use that. So in essence, if we can safely plant a charge and safely detonate it, blowing a hole through some ice won't be that tricky. There is one big problem, however. We don't have a helicopter. We don't have a dog sled or an Arctic Cat. Even with all the cold-weather gear we've brought along, it'd be dangerous as hell going even a few miles out there on the ice. I can't order my men to do that, in good conscience. But Mr. Hardestey has already come up with a list of volunteers if that proves necessary, and the list is more than adequate."

"And we'd all have to go, wouldn't we?" Margaret Spicer asked quickly. "The scientific party, I mean."

"That's a matter for you to decide individually. It would be extremely hazardous. It's early spring for Antarctica now. Some ice is melting. Risk factors are high. There are crevasses—fall in one, and unless you get out double-quick, the crevasse'll close and crush you or bury you alive. Icebergs sometimes melt on the side facing the sun and then topple over like an axed-through tree—and we're talking tons and tons of ice. Those are only two—I don't even know all the dangers. We have only one person who's been to the antarctic before—and that's Dr. Basque. Maybe she can conduct some briefing sessions for the shore party in the event there is one."

"I'll be glad to," she responded.

"Good," Macklin said and nodded.

Culhane was still watching the television monitor. Something that looked like a gigantic tooth was dead ahead, stabbing down into the water.

"Sonar to bridge. Iceberg twenty-five yards to starboard, confirmed," Lieutenant Hardestey said into his headset mike.

"Get us away from it, Jimmy. Cut back to all stop," Macklin rasped.

"All stop," Hardestey repeated.

"We okay aft?"

"Affirmative on that, Captain," Hardestey said. "All clear at least five hundred yards aft."

"Very well. All back to one-third."

"Bridge to maneuvering. All back one-third."

"All stop."

Hardestey repeated the instructions.

"Twenty degrees left rudder, all ahead one-third. Steady as she goes and watch for ice above. If necessary, take her down another fifty feet and keep us running one hundred feet minimum over the floor."

"Aye, Captain."

Macklin turned back to face them. "It's going to continue to be like this—and sixty-five degrees south where we're heading is iceberg city—so when you fill your coffee cups, only fill 'em halfway. The ship's laundry always complains about coffee stains when we're maneuvering like this."

Mulrooney whispered to Culhane, "I should have listened to my mother and gone to modeling school."

IT HAD TAKEN TWENTY-EIGHT HOURS OF MANEUVERING at painfully slow speeds to satisfy Macklin that the ice pack had in fact expanded. The captain sat across from Culhane and Mulrooney in his office. "I did like Captain Chillingsworth must have done a century ago,'' he said and patted an elaborate brass sextant on his desk. "I went up and read the stars. They don't change that much in a hundred years. If the cave entrance he talks about, or tunnel or whatever it was is out there, I make it six miles inland and almost due south of our current position. There's a spring storm coming. We picked up the poop on that when we surfaced for me to take the sextant readings and compass bearings. We're talking maybe suicide here.''

Mulrooney leaned back in her chair. She was wearing blue jeans, running shoes and a gray-green crewneck sweater that was miles too big, which Culhane had lent her. "Why are you telling just us?" she asked.

"Good question," Culhane said.

"I look at this expedition as being—hell, it's the two of you. Your brother died trying to find what you both found, Mr. Culhane. And a blind man could read your face, Miss Mulrooney. Anytime I slip up and say Gladstone Log instead of the logbook of the *Madagascar*, it's in your face. You want to be there—where Miles Chillingsworth and Henry Chillingsworth and Mr. Fife went a century ago. You want to see the mysteries. You remind me of my daughter. She's a knockout looker, like you, and a hellion and a tomboy when she needs to be. If I were endangering the ship or the crew, I wouldn't even ask. But I have volunteers—sincerely interested volunteers—who don't even know what the hell we're going after. They just know that we're going. Mostly fans of your books—" he looked at Culhane "—and some of your books, too, Miss Mulrooney. Going out on an adventure with the real-life Sean Dodge and his lady sure sounds good to 'em. So I'm asking.''

"A hundred years ago," Culhane said, "the protective clothing wasn't as good, the gear in general wasn't as good, but they made it with a twelve-, maybe fourteen-year-old boy with them.''

"We've got four women—"

"Thanks a hell of a lot, Captain," Mulrooney interrupted.

"Facts are facts, Miss Mulrooney. Women tolerate extremes of cold better, but in a trek like this they tire more easily. Fact. And what you feel you can do may not be what the other three women can do. And at least three of the men are in their fifties and sixties. I'm fifty-one myself. Believe me—" his eyes lit with a laugh "—I know how that feels."

"They're your crew," Culhane said, "and I don't want to send innocent men to their deaths. But I'll tell you something—"

"I know what you're going to say," Macklin interrupted. "That Steiglitz has a plant on the ship. Well, from what I read about him in the newspapers in the sixties and seventies, you're probably right. He might own a couple of people on board. If we don't go, Steiglitz's man—or woman—will report everything— the position, the findings in the Log, the diary of Henry Chillingsworth, the ankh symbol on the Piri Reis map of Antarctica—all of it. They'll get there before we do."

"If it is a starbase," Mulrooney said, fishing in her purse for cigarettes and lighter, "I think you've gotta realize something." Culhane lit her cigarette for her, and she looked back at Macklin. "If it is a starbase, then it's probably more than forty thousand years old. There are answers to questions down there we haven't even thought of yet. Maybe our own origins, maybe things that we're better off not even knowing."

Mulrooney's words startled Culhane. She wasn't just the sensation-monger, the journalist before everything. She was still speaking. "Things that could change the way we even think about ourselves. The power Steiglitz spoke of—it was like he knew what was out there. If a man like Steiglitz—if he possessed a technology that brought intelligent beings here from the stars.... He's a killer, a psychopath—whatever you call him, if he controlled a superior technology—''

She stopped talking, her right hand shaking as she raised the cigarette to her lips.

Culhane took his eyes from her face, then he looked at Macklin.

"God help us all," Macklin breathed.

THE SURFACE OF THE WATER was such a dark blue it was almost black. The deck of the *Churchill*—a boat built for steadiness under the waves—rocked with the white-capped high seas, and chunks of ice the size of telephone books tossed with the waves around them. The wind was stiff and cold. Angela Basque mentioned that the air temperature was hovering at the zero mark, with a wind clocked at what Macklin had labeled a "balmy" forty-five miles per hour—a comparative dead calm. The windchill factor on exposed skin was minus fifty-five degrees Fahrenheit.

They stood huddled against the bulwark of the *Churchill*'s gray-black sail. A hundred yards to starboard off the flying bridge lay an iceberg, spires and pinnacles rising into the gray sky. The storm Macklin had predicted was coming. As Culhane watched it, the iceberg seemed to move almost imperceptibly.

"Uhh oh," Macklin said.

The iceberg—perhaps a quarter mile in height—was moving, swaying....

"A melt-out!" Angela Basque screamed.

Macklin yelled into the microphone to the bridge: "Hard left rudder all ahead full—securing bridge hatch, secure diving panel! Crash dive! Dive! *Dive!*"

Claxons sounded as the iceberg swayed, and Culhane shoved Mulrooney down through the bridge hatch ahead of all of them. He grabbed Angela Basque and pushed her down through the hatchway. "Move it!'' he shouted, then he looked behind him. The iceberg was upending, crashing downward in a direct line with the sail. "Jesus!"

Culhane slipped, his footing going, skidding, his gloved hands reaching out, grabbing at the hatch opening. He launched himself across the ice on the flying bridge deck by snapping his arms forward, crashing his body against the frame of the hatch, not bothering to stand, throwing himself down, grabbing at the ladder rungs, catching one with his right hand, stopping his fall, then loosening his grip, hammering down against the wet surface of the deck below.

Macklin was through the hatch. The claxons were still sounding, and the motion of the ship was tremendous. Culhane's body lurched with it as he tried to stand. Macklin wrenched at the hatch cover as icy water streamed down, caused by a wave from the toppled iceberg.

Culhane was finally up, but Angela Basque was blocking his way. "Move it, Angela!" Mulrooney shrieked, wrestling her away so Culhane could make it to the ladder. Macklin slipped from the rungs as a wave hammered through the open hatch over them.

Culhane hauled himself up, reaching out, trying to grab for the hatch. The water was like ice, numbing him as it flooded over him. He swung from the ladder's left vertical by his left hand and hung there as torrents of bone-chilling saltwater thundered around him.

He swung his weight back, forcing his body against the strength of the wave, his eyes blind from the water pressure, his right hand groping, finding what he hoped was the locking wheel of the hatch. He held it, throwing his weight away from the ladder, feeling his bones shudder as he fell, swaying from the locking wheel. Mulrooney was climbing the ladder. "How the hell do you close this?" she cried.

He couldn't answer her; he was choking from the water washing over him. As he hooked his left leg around the ladder, jerking his body weight down, he heard Mulrooney shriek, "It's closed! It's closed!"

Culhane grabbed the ladder with his right hand. His left hand and Mulrooney's right twisted the locking wheel. "No—this way," he shouted to her. They both worked at the locking wheel, and then the hatch was closed and sealed.

Culhane heaved his weight against Mulrooney. His teeth were chattering. Below them, on his knees in water, his left temple dripping blood, was Macklin. Angela Basque was beside him.

"I owe you one, Mr. Culhane—owe you a big one," Macklin rasped, then succumbed to a fit of coughing.

Mulrooney held Culhane's shaking body as he clung to the ladder. They could hear the roar of the turbines and the churn of the propellers and feel the sudden change in pressure.

There were men coming up the ladder from the bridge below, helping Macklin to his feet, as he barked orders.

Culhane, soaked to the skin with icy water, his teeth still chattering, said, "If the iceberg misses us, somebody'd better help me off the ladder. If it doesn't, don't sweat it—" He felt his eyes closing and his grip on the ladder loosening. Either the iceberg had hit and the sub's electrical system was going, or the blackness was because he was fainting.

MULROONEY HERSELF WAS COLD, but the water hadn't soaked through beyond her heavy parka. Culhane had been drenched, and she had argued until she finally screamed at the ship's doctor and Macklin intervened, ordering that Mulrooney have her way. And so Culhane, warm fluids inside him, his body still shaking, was in his bunk now, and Mulrooney, standing beside the bunk, was stripping away her clothes. It was the fastest way for one human being to warm another.

Macklin had been told by Hardestey that the iceberg's tip had missed the missile deck of the *Churchill* by an estimated ten feet, and only the high-speed dive had kept the impact of the iceberg against the water's surface from swamping the ship. Had the *Churchill* been surfaced, it would have been upended. And with the bridge hatch open, it would have been flooded and would have sunk to the bottom—if the pressure hadn't first collapsed the hull.

Mulrooney shivered at the thought, not to mention the coldness of Culhane's skin as she slipped in beside him in the bunk. He was barely awake. She wrapped her arms around him, bringing his head against her left breast, holding him, shivering as each new part of his body touched hers.

If he had died, she would never have forgiven herself. She had brought him what she'd thought was the Gladstone Log, the memoir of Henry Chillingsworth. She had virtually made him go after the real Log on San Rafael Island. And Macklin had said it—politely, but he'd said it anyway: it was her own obsession with finding what the *Madagascar* had found that was driving them on.

She wondered if it would bring their deaths.

It was an odd thought, holding the man she loved against her breast, warming his body with her own, feeling him hardening against her as her hands ran over the contours of his body. It was an odd thought to consider that they both might soon die.

Steiglitz. The ice pack. The horrors of what the H.M.S. *Madagascar* had found beneath the ice.

She shivered and couldn't stop.

CHAPTER THIRTY-THREE

There were more upended icebergs—toppled, strangely flat on one side, like fallen mountains—and smaller chunks of ice everywhere. Culhane, in fresh clothing and with a night's rest behind him, stood warm on the ice-slick deck of the flying bridge, Macklin and Hardestey flanking him.

"Because of continental drift," Culhane began, staring seaward at the massive blocks of ice, "Antarctica has been moving in a westerly direction. And because of some unsteadiness in the Pacific, the floor of the ocean has been moving east. Forty thousand years ago this was a paradise."

"They've found fossils here," Hardestey said, as if talking aloud to himself, "that may be two hundred million years old. Kind of awes you just to think about it."

"And kind of makes navigation difficult when you don't know the real age of your maps. I pity Captain Chillingsworth," Macklin added. Then he gestured over the flying bridge's starboard bulwark. "It was my fault we almost got creamed by that iceberg yesterday. An experienced Antarctic mariner would have known better, and my log will show that. Captain Chillingsworth lost one of his two other ships here, if I'm reading his logbook properly. It capsized when a glacier collapsed. Didn't pull any of the men out alive, although they searched for bodies for three days." He gestured again over the bulwark. "But along out there—see that kind of glow?" Culhane and Hardestey nodded.

"Well, Dr. Basque told me that's called an ice blink. It's the reflection of ice fields below the horizon against an overcast sky. That ice field is going to have to be crossed, and I've reassessed my calculations; it's seven, maybe seven and a half miles. The barometer's going wacko—mainly dropping. That storm's coming. We could wait it out nice and snug beneath the surface—"

"But that only means more ice to cover the cave entrance," Culhane protested.

"Well, more important, in the spring a lot more of this ice will be breaking off around here. That'll make it harder to get close to the ice shelf and makes it more likely you'll encounter tricks with the ice. You get stranded on an ice floe and you could be done for. A storm could last for days, maybe more than a week. I'm in no hurry."

"What's to say there won't be another storm right after that?"

"Agreed," Macklin said. "There should be that low sun the bulk of the twenty-four-hour period—it'll be like dawn all day. Dr. Basque was telling me the winds out there can reach 150 miles per hour. I've got some windchill charts, but at ten below—that's Fahrenheit—the charts don't even go beyond a forty-five-mile-per-hour wind. And the off-the-scale point is minus eighty degrees. Hypothermia—well, you know, Mr. Culhane."

Culhane nodded, wanting a cigarette but too wary of the cold to remove his gloves to light one. "I know," he sighed, nervous, feeling a churning in his stomach.

"I've had some of the guys who like to work with their hands rig a sledge out of some old metal tubing we had around, and harnesses can be rigged out of some of the rope," said Lieutenant Hardestey. "It'll give us a way to haul supplies without hauling them on our backs."

" 'Us'?" Culhane repeated, looking at the lieutenant. Macklin answered for him. "In waters like these, I can't leave the ship. This is a neutral zone, but Soviet and Chinese subs are around here a lot, I understand. This is a warship. I can't risk it. But Lieutenant Hardestey will accompany the men in charge of the shore party. Including the thirteen civilians and Mr. Hardestey, there'll be twenty-nine people. In the event of any problems, that leaves me Lieutenant Wilbur—he volunteered to come along, by the way—to lead a rescue effort, if feasible. I may not get the time to do this tomorrow...." Macklin extended his hand to Culhane. "Good luck, and don't die on us. A lot of Sean Dodge's fans would be awfully disappointed."

THE FIFTH OF THE SIX RUBBER BOATS used to bring the shore party and equipment onto the ice floe was in trouble on its return trip. Mulrooney started running toward the ice floe's edge, tripped on a pressure ridge, skidded and slid toward the water. Culhane threw himself after her, skidding along the ice, the pressure ridges hammering at his abdomen and rib cage. He reached out, grabbing for her ankles, and locked tight on them, holding her. He stopped her skid, heard her shouting at him through the toque that covered her face under the parka's hood, saw her eyes widening through the snow goggles. "They're gonna die!"

"And so will you if you go in after them!"

Holding her, jerking at her ankles to keep her from getting up, he looked past her. The fifth boat was swamped. He saw hands and arms waving in desperation, and the sixth boat was already back by the submarine, too far to help.

"Aww, shit," Culhane snarled, getting up, slipping, crashing to his knees, then getting up again. The fourth boat was unloaded and just about to cast off. Culhane ran across the ice and jumped for it, almost crashing into Hardestey and two seamen in the boat. "Cast off—now!"

"Do it!" Hardestey shouted, and the two seamen started paddling against the incoming flow of the ice-flecked water toward the two men of the swamped rubber boat. Culhane snatched one of the paddles from the seaman nearest him, took it in his gloved fists and dug the paddle into the waves with a vengeance. He could hear Hardestey on the radio: "Hardestey to bridge! Hardestey to bridge!"

A crackle, static, then a voice that sounded like Macklin's: "What is it?"

"Got a boat coming, Captain?"

"On the way—Wilbur's on deck and alerted me. Get 'em out of the water, for Christ's sake, and maybe we can save 'em!"

"Aye, sir." The radio clicked off. They still had a hundred yards to go to reach the two men in the water. Culhane could hear screaming from the men. From his experience the day before, he knew he could only begin to imagine what they were enduring in the freezing waters. Soon, before their limbs were inexorably, irreparably frozen, the cold that racked their bodies would keep them from breathing, and they would suffocate before they went below the water. They would never have the chance to drown.

"Get that line!" Culhane yelled to the seaman whose paddle he'd taken.

"Shit—this thing is frozen!"

"Here," Hardestey snapped. "Gimme that!" And Hardestey—Culhane snatched a glance back at him—was struggling with the rope, twisting it out of its ice-encrusted coils.

"Throw it in the water. If it's in the water, it can't quite freeze—the water's warmer than the air," Culhane gasped as he and the other seaman who paddled opposite him narrowed the distance to fifty yards.

He could hear the splash of the rock-hard rope as it hit the water. "It's working!" Hardestey shouted.

Twenty-five yards. One of the seamen was under.

Ten yards. The man hadn't bobbed up.

"We lost Travers!" Hardestey shouted.

"I'll get him!" It was the seaman whose paddle Culhane had taken. He threw off his parka, almost swamping the rubber boat as he stood. Culhane grabbed for him, Hardestey grabbed for him and shouted something, but the man was gone and into the water.

Five yards.

"Grab this line, Wiznewski! Grab it, man!"

There was incoherent babbling from the man whose gray face was still visible above the water.

The other seaman dropped his paddle, shouting, "Wiznewski, reach my hand!"

And the seaman's hands were in the water, the man screaming "Jesus!" over and over. Then, "I got him—Christ—I got Wiznewski!"

Culhane dropped his paddle, reaching for the seaman's shirt with one hand and grabbing for Wiznewski's sodden coat with the other.

Hardestey was shouting. "It's Saddler and Travers—Travers looks like he's alive!"

Culhane wrenched at Wiznewski, and with the other seaman he hauled him halfway into the rubber boat over the fabric of the gunwale, then, pulling one more time, got him to the floor. The seaman who'd grabbed for him was crying, his hands unmoving as he tried to cover Wiznewski with his body.

Culhane crawled past him. "Keep forward—we'll need the weight," he ordered.

Saddler—the black seaman who'd gone after Travers—was shouting from the water, "I got the son of a bitch—he's alive, Lieutenant!"

Culhane grabbed one of the paddles, digging it in, going with the current now, narrowing the distance to Saddler and Travers to five yards, then two. Hardestey was hauling in the rope from the water, slugging it out into the water again.

"My fingers—my fingers don't work, Lieutenant!" Saddler cried.

Then Hardestey jumped into the water, holding the rope and shouting, "Culhane—haul us all in!"

Hardestey was under for a second, then his head was up, and his arms were reaching through the waves that washed over him. The rope was looped around Travers and under Saddler's arms. Hardestey clung to it as well.

Culhane threw his weight back, hauling in the rope, pulling the boat closer to the men.

"Here—reach for me!" Culhane stabbed out his right hand, his left locked on the freezing line, Hardestey's gloved hand now in his. Culhane pulled again, getting Hardestey half up over the gunwale. Hardestey was inside now, on his knees, his hands numb, his face streaked with gray. The lieutenant twisted the rope around his wrists, tugging with his arms as Culhane reached out for Saddler's hand. Then Culhane had it at the wrist, his own fingers starting to stiffen as the water penetrated his glove. He had Saddler. He pulled.

Saddler was in the boat; Travers—blue-faced—was half in. Culhane grabbed Travers, wrenching the man onto his back. The eyes stared wide open.

Saddler was crying, the tears seeming to freeze on his cheeks. "The son of a bitch is dead! Travers—man—you can't be—" Saddler, on his knees, doubled forward across his friend's body and wept.

CULHANE'S HANDS HAD MADE IT. Though his right hand still hurt, there was no permanent damage, and he could move his fingers with effort. Both Saddler and the other seaman were suffering from hypothermia, but neither case was severe. Fingers and toes would be saved but would be useless for some time. With Hardestey, it was just his fingers and his little toe on his left foot. Wiznewski was suffering from shock but was expected to survive.

Lieutenant Wilbur had replaced Lieutenant Hardestey as commander of the shore party, and he walked at its head now. It had been agreed among them all that none of the four women, Mulrooney included, would draw duty in one of the six harnesses attached to the overloaded improvised sledge. Mulrooney had objected, but not too strenuously. Room had been left at the rear of the sledge for one, possibly two persons to stand in the event one of the older men of the scientific party proved unable to handle the walking.

It was Culhane's turn in harness to the sledge; with him were five of the seamen from the shore party. Radio contact was possible only every two hours, since the *Churchill*, a weapon of war, was prohibited from Antarctic waters by international law and would remain under the surface at all times except during the specified radio contact times.

Culhane felt something lurch against his chest and abdomen, and he stopped.

"Damn pressure ridge hung us up!" one of the seamen shouted, but already some of the women and two of the men from the scientific party were at the rear of the sledge pushing it up and over the ridge. There was nothing to do but stand still, and Culhane did, the hairs in his nostrils freezing as he breathed through his ice-encrusted silk toque.

Culhane watched Lieutenant Wilbur and the others more carefully now than he had watched them before the mishap with the rubber boat that had cost Seaman Travers his life. The rubber boat had been hauled in to the ice floe while the victims were being ferried back to the submarine. Culhane had inspected it. The filler valve inlet was torn; the boat had been leaking air. It was the boat Hardestey had been in on the way to the ice floe, but ice had apparently encrusted over the valve inlet sufficiently to keep air loss to a minimum. And Lieutenant Wilbur—the man who always smiled—was engineering officer. It had been his ultimate responsibility to check each of the rubber boats for seaworthiness.

"Carelessness," Culhane murmured to himself, watching his breath freeze in a cloud in front of his face. Or perhaps not.

"She's clear." It was one of the women's voices. Culhane looked at the five other men who shared the harness, and all of them nodded. He started forward, leaning into the harness to get the sledge moving; its runners were already frozen into the ice.

They marched on. . . .

Mountains of ice and rock dotted the distance now as they skirted the edge of the ice floe. A few penguins watched the procession from the leeward side of an iceberg striking up from the water perhaps two hundred yards out to sea. Culhane had done his half mile in harness, and now Partridge, one of the human penguins, the scientist with the goatee—his name, Culhane finally learned, was Dr. Felix Liebermann—and three of the *Churchill*'s shore party pulled the sledge.

Mulrooney beside him, Culhane walked in silence, watching the darkening horizon. The storm would be coming soon. He hoped it would be after they found the cave Miles Chillingsworth and his men had discovered. He noticed Mulrooney dragging as she moved. "Your feet okay?"

"Yeah—tired, but they're warm. How about you?"

Culhane nodded. "Almost beginning to wish I hadn't brought my gun. Then I wouldn't have to carry it." He laughed, watching his breath steam again. "Almost, anyway." And Mulrooney laughed, too.

"That was terrible about that poor sailor, Travers. His friend was so brave though."

"Yeah," Culhane agreed. Mulrooney was still walking strangely and sounded short of breath. "That pack making you sweat?"

"A little, but—"

"But nothing," Culhane said and reached out to her shoulders, stopping her. Then he started to unfasten the backpack's belt from around her waist.

"What are you doing?"

"You sweat in country like this and as soon as you stop sweating, the sweat freezes. It's the same thing that happens in the water. You freeze, you die. Gimme the pack."

"I don't want you—"

"Yeah, well, I wasn't exactly looking forward to it, either. I'll give it back in a few minutes." Culhane shouldered the pack across his left shoulder so it rode against his own, then started walking ahead, Mulrooney beside him again.

"Keep an eye out for people, especially once we hit the cave or the tunnel or whatever the hell it is."

"You're tired—you always swear when you're tired."

Culhane looked at her and laughed.

"You got any prime suspects, like they say in the detective novels?" Mulrooney asked.

"Yeah, Lieutenant Wilbur, the engineering officer. He would have checked all the rubber boats before they were launched. The boat that swamped, swamped because it had lost air—the valve had been sabotaged." He looked at Mulrooney. Her green eyes were wide through the snow goggles. "And I never did trust our friendly, neighborhood CIA man and his penguins."

"You and your penguins," Mulrooney said and laughed. Then she stopped laughing. "So maybe one or all of them are working for Steiglitz?"

"Or maybe for the Russians. If they got wind of what we're looking for, you can be damned sure—"

"You are tired."

He ignored her, saying, "You can bet the Russians would be out after this, too. Any way you cut it, we've got at least one murderer with us."

"See?" she said, touching his right arm, as they walked. "Doesn't that make you feel better about bringing the gun—even though it's heavy?"

"Oh, yeah—just what I want. A gunfight on an ice floe when I only know for sure I can trust one other person."

"How sweet of you to say that."

Culhane grinned, realizing she couldn't see it through the toque covering his face. "How'd you know I meant you? Hmm?"

Ahead were more penguins, similar to those on the iceberg. There were perhaps a hundred of them, and they were moving at high speed, running and sliding away from the edge of the ice floe. The sledge had stopped, and one of the women was running out toward the birds.

Wilbur was shouting after her, "Dr. Basque—what the hell are you doing?"

Culhane started to quicken his pace when he heard the woman shout, "They're Adélie penguins—I want photographs. There's a leopard seal out of the water chasing after some of them."

Culhane dropped Mulrooney's pack beside the sledge as he reached it, then shrugged off his own pack. "Damned fool broad! Look how close she's getting to that leopard seal...." She was between the seal and a small penguin and was snapping away.

There was a scream as Angela Basque fell on the ice.

Culhane started to run, pulling at the Velcro closures of his parka with his left hand, pulling the glove from his right hand with his teeth. He rammed the glove inside his coat to keep it from freezing inside, his hand already numbing in the silk glove liner as he reached under the parka for the Detonics Scoremaster. He'd never fired a gun in a windchill of minus seventy degrees and didn't know if his lubricant would gum and render the gun inoperable. Leopard seals were called leopard seals for two reasons: the silver-and-black-spotted body, and the fact that when hungry they would attack man.

The leopard seal was perhaps ten feet in length and was closing in. It was going for the fallen woman.

Culhane's right thumb had the Scoremaster's ambidextrous safety wiped down, his gloved fist was balled on the black rubber Pachmayr grips, and his left hand arced up to support his right. About twenty yards from the animal he fired, the crack in the cold air ear-splitting, the Detonics rocking slightly in his hands. He fired again, hitting the seal twice but not slowing it up. He fired again, then again and again until the seal was still.

Angela Basque got to her knees.

And from across the twenty yards or so of ice, she screamed, "You rotten butcher! You didn't have to kill it! Murderer!"

Culhane upped the safety on the Detonics Scoremaster and put the gun back into the crossdraw holster. It wasn't polite to do to a lady, especially a lady whose life you'd just saved, he thought. But he did it anyway.

Culhane gave Dr. Angela Basque the finger. Then he turned and walked back to the sledge.

IN HIS BACKPACK CULHANE HAD BROUGHT one spare box of fifty Federal 185-grain jacketed hollowpoints. Forty-five cartridges remained after he reloaded the partially shot-out Scoremaster. The Break-Free CLP lubricant hadn't gummed in the extremely low temperatures, and he made a mental note to drop the firm a line and mention it when he got back.

Culhane had reloaded his pistol while they had stopped for an hour's rest break. Because of the risk of sweating from overexertion—and the subsequent freezing—they rested every three miles. So far, because they had been unable to go a straight-line route to the coordinates Commander Macklin had worked out, they had traveled slightly more than six miles. Perhaps four remained. And then would come the task of finding the cave entrance. That, Culhane guessed, could consume days.

Wilbur was using the radio; it was a contact period. Angela Basque was sitting beside the lieutenant. Culhane imagined she was getting Wilbur to ask if he—Culhane—could be arrested or something for shooting the leopard seal that had tried to eat her.

"Liberals," he muttered.

Mulrooney, crouched beside him, asked, "What?"

"Nothing—almost there, Fanny."

"Oh, God—I feel like I've walked for twenty miles."

"Only about six," he said, folding his arm around her. They occupied a corner of a large lean-to pitched to cut the knife edge of the wind. The wind was increasing, and the sky was darkening.

He watched Lieutenant Wilbur come their way.

Wilbur ducked under the roof of the red lean-to and stopped, crouching. "The captain's spotted a Soviet submarine off active sonar, but he doesn't think it's spotted the *Churchill* yet."

"Ohh, that's peachy," Mulrooney said. With the toque removed from her face and the snow goggles dangling from her neck under her chin, she looked like a tired but happy skier.

"What kind of a submarine?" Culhane asked Wilbur.

"A thinking man's question, Mr. Culhane. It's a Typhoon class."

"Oh, Christ...."

"What's a Typhoon class?" Mulrooney asked, looking at Culhane.

"Lieutenant Wilbur could probably tell you better than I could," Culhane told Fanny Mulrooney.

"Half again the size of the *Churchill*—the largest undersea vessels ever built. The sub carries missiles that we suspect have better than a six-thousand-mile range. We don't know how fast one of the Russian ladies can go, but you'd better believe it's faster than the *Churchill*."

"So the radio schedule is off," Culhane interjected.

"The radio schedule is off. We set up a code series in case something like this happened. We'll use that now and keep to a different schedule in the event the *Churchill*'s able to surface and intercept us."

"So whether we find the tunnel or not, we may be stuck on the ice for a long time," Mulrooney said flatly.

"There's a research vessel on the coast off the Mertz Glacier tongue—an American ship. It'd be a long trek, and we'd have to get rid of the M-16s down a crevasse in case the Russians spotted us from the air, but I think we could make it. We'd have enough supplies. If push came to shove, we could build a solid shelter out of ice blocks and leave the women and the older men behind, and some of us could set off to the ship. They've got a helicopter, and once we're within their radio frequency range, we should be able to get the chopper out and then back to pick up the others."

Culhane let out a long sigh, stood and helped Mulrooney to her feet. He closed his coat, then said, "We've been here long enough. Just in case the Soviets have sent out a shore party, we'd better get crackin' before they wind up right on our tails. All this wind probably blew out our tracks, but they could have some other way of following us."

Culhane looked right at Wilbur, saying nothing else.

Wilbur, after a short silence, said, "You've got a good point, Mr. Culhane. Let's get going—another three or four miles and we should be at the coordinates."

Mulrooney was pulling her toque down over her face; she had rolled it up like a watch cap around her forehead. Her voice sounded muffled as she secured it in place. "I'm no Wilma the Weatherbunny, but that storm looks like it's closing in on us—fast."

The sky to the east—finding east at either of the poles wasn't easy, Culhane knew—was purple and black, and the sun, which moved more or less fifteen degrees an hour in this part of the world, was nearing the cloud mass. Soon the darkness would cause the already subzero temperatures to plunge.

"Let's move," Culhane announced, pulling on his toque.

CHAPTER THIRTY-FOUR

Culhane was on the sledge team again, and with the other five men he broke the path through the blowing ice and snow. He estimated the wind to be gusting at perhaps seventy-five miles per hour, and the entire front of his body was numb. A second toque covered the first one, and he'd wrapped a scarf over both. His snow goggles had frosted over to the point that he could barely see. And the wind seemed to be growing in intensity, exploding toward them to Culhane's right front as they pressed on. All the members of the party were lashed to one another with the climbing ropes, the lead for this tethered to the back of the sledge.

Visibility was perhaps a dozen yards, at times less.

Katabatic winds, they were called, Angela Basque had told them as the storm had closed in, sweeping from the Antarctic plateau with frenzied force. The turns on the sledge team had been reduced to fifteen minutes a man, and Wilbur had already insisted on stopping and erecting shelters. But Angela Basque, the only one of the party with Antarctic experience, had said it could mean their deaths. In two-man shelters, with the temperature dropping, if the winds kept up, they could all freeze to death.

An ice ax was lashed to Culhane's hand because his fingers were too numb to reliably keep closed. He hammered with the ax now to get footing, the ice floe beneath them as smooth as glass and dangerously slick in the near hurricane-force winds.

They had covered almost four miles without stopping, but there was no way to rest. After the last rest break, it had taken ten minutes of work with a blowtorch to free the sledge from where it had frozen into the ice. Culhane carried a G.I.-style lensatic compass in his clothing, but the compass would be useless so close to magnetic south. Wilbur controlled the bearings readings, and as Culhane's mind focused on this he suddenly felt a sick fear. What if Wilbur were working for Steiglitz, or perhaps in the employ of the Soviets? He could be so dedicated that he was willing to die; he could be leading them nowhere except deeper into the ice. . . .

Culhane hammered down again with the ice ax, losing his balance, swaying forward, shouting over the howl of the wind, "Crevasse!"

He was hanging, the ax swaying in his right hand like a pendulum. If the sledge went, he would be lost forever with the five other men. *"Crevasse!"*

The falling stopped, the harness around his midsection and chest binding tight against him. He felt himself being pulled up and saw two of the other men from the sledge team clinging to the sides of the crevasse.

Culhane hacked with the ice ax, steadying himself as he was dragged up along the smooth side, feeling hands reaching out to him.

A voice shouted through his parka near his left ear, "Josh—are you all right?"

"Fanny?" he screamed into the wind.

"Yes! Are—you—all—right—Josh?"

"Yes," he gasped, kneeling beside the sledge.

Someone else dropped beside him. Through the goggles he could see the black skin around the eyes. Lieutenant Wilbur. "Mr. Culhane, the crevasse seems to lead north by northeast. We'll have to work around it."

Culhane nodded, catching his breath. One of the shore party came up, helped to undo the harness, then put the harness around his own body. Culhane, with numbed fingers, undid the lashings for the ice ax. Then he staggered back and helped haul the sledge away from the lip of the crevasse.

Cutting to the left, following the course of the crevasse, they moved ahead.

The wind was behind them now, and Culhane's back and the backs of his thighs were numb as he and Mulrooney staggered along together, the wind almost propelling them. In that respect, the going was made marginally easier.

They were beyond exhaustion, but they couldn't stop. The old man with the goatee was riding the back of the sledge; he had fallen and was unable to continue on foot.

But the crevasse, which they followed at a respectable distance, was narrowing, and ahead—Culhane hoped—it would soon be closed.

They kept going.

After another fifteen minutes—Culhane had smudged away the coating of ice on the crystal of his Rolex—the crevasse was closed, and they had crossed to the other side.

And now they had to backtrack, and cut a diagonal to intersect their original path.

And the wind, which had previously aided them, now assaulted them.

They walked on, Culhane supporting Mulrooney with his arms around her, Mulrooney's steps dragging, her body heaving with exertion as he held her.

Culhane had another turn at the sledge. This time it was Culhane, Partridge, the three CIA penguins and Wilbur himself, the shore party commander taking his first turn. The elderly engineering consultant still clung to the sledge.

Wilbur had the lead, forging the route. Culhane, when he could see at all, watched him closely. Was Wilbur leading them to frozen death?

Culhane, barely able to lift his feet, kept walking.

It was time to change the sledge team, but Wilbur signaled not to. They kept on, Culhane counting the seconds to keep his sanity and to keep his legs moving. Two minutes, three—a full five. He had spent twenty minutes on the sledge team.

He wanted to scream at Wilbur.

But suddenly he was crashing into the man.

Wilbur was shouting, and Culhane turned his head so Wilbur could shout directly against his ear through the parka. It was the only way to clearly hear with the shrill keening of the wind.

"We're here!"

"Here" was the edge of an ice floe—no cave, no tunnel—there were not even rocks in the range of Culhane's limited visibility. One of the women was crying, and Mulrooney was rocking her in her arms.

"We've gotta fan out. Use the climbing ropes and leave the sledge as a base. If we can find the tunnel entrance, we can blast out part of it and use it for shelter. Otherwise—" Culhane let his shouted words hang.

Wilbur nodded, buttonholing one of the shore party, shouting beside the man's parka hood.

The man nodded and walked off, bending against the fierce wind.

They erected a shelter, a windbreak anchored as securely as possible with spikes driven into the ice and then lashed as well to the sledge. They used battery-operated lanterns now, for the darkness was intensifying.

With the lines tied to the sledge—five hundred feet for each line—parties of two lashed themselves to the ends of the lines and started walking. The plan was to walk the length of the climbing ropes, then, keeping the ropes at full extension, walk an arc of ninety degrees before turning back.

Culhane and Mulrooney—who insisted on being his partner—took the line that would be walked north. The wind hammered at Culhane, as he walked on Mulrooney's right to shield her body from the wind. Slowly they walked ahead, feeding out the rope, unable to talk or to see more than six feet ahead of them. He tried to judge the yardage. Counting his strides against the wind, he stopped at slightly more than 160 paces and pulled Mulrooney up short beside him.

He tugged on the rope; it was still loose. There was still play.

He leaned beside Mulrooney, shouting through her hood, "Hold the rope. When I tug at it, pull me back. Don't let go—in this visibility I could pass within two yards of you and never see you!"

"Why isn't the rope taut?"

"Maybe I miscounted, or my strides were off because of the wind pressure, but don't let go after I untie the line from your waist—don't!"

"All right. Be careful, Josh, please be—"

He nodded, untying the line from her waist.

He walked ahead ten paces—ten yards, he gauged.

The rope was still not taut. He walked ahead another ten yards. Still there was slack.

He had a sick feeling in the pit of his stomach. He tugged at the rope, then started back along its length, barely seeing Mulrooney before he bumped into her.

He could not see her face. It was completely covered by the toque, a scarf and the goggles. He knew she could not see his.

He took Fanny Mulrooney in his arms, his toque-covered mouth pressed against the side of her parka hood. "Either something went wrong back by the sledge and our rope came undone—or else somebody cut it." He felt her body tense in his arms. "We'll follow the rope back as carefully as we can, then try to pace it out. You'll count my steps with me. If I'm two steps off, it could mean—" He didn't finish it.

Unless the sky opened in a blaze of sunshine so they could see the camp at the sledge, with their line severed they would die of exposure.

No ifs, ands or buts—they would die.

He thought she knew it, but he didn't tell her, re-lashing the rope around her waist so they wouldn't be separated, then starting ahead.

IT WAS AN OLD CLICHE, he thought, huddled with Mulrooney in the Thermos sportsman's blanket, but at precisely ninety-three paces, they had reached the end of their rope. Even if following the remainder of the rope had gotten them nearer camp, they were still a minimum of forty-five yards from the sledge. And in which direction?

There was only one slim hope.

Culhane drew his Detonics Scoremaster, the trigger guard ample but a tight squeeze for his gloved right hand. He worked down the safety, then shouted in Mulrooney's ear, "We haven't got a flare pistol. If someone hears us before we freeze to death or I run out of ammo...well, hold your ears."

He held the pistol at an oblique angle and fired three shots in rapid succession. If anyone at the sledge were a deer hunter, or even a hiker, he or she would recognize the almost universal woodsman's signal of distress.

No answering shots came, no shouts. Perhaps the wind was against them. Mulrooney's body trembled on his left arm. Culhane again extended his right arm from the now ice-encrusted synthetic blanket, lowered the safety and fired three more shots.

No response. "Wrap the blanket just around you," he shouted to her. "I've gotta change magazines for my pistol—only one round left now. But don't worry—I've got plenty of spare magazines, and there's still some spare ammo in my pack."

"I'm freezing to death, Josh!"

He nodded, wanting to say, I know, but unable to say it. Instead, feeling stupid shouting it, his face against the hood of her parka, his left arm around her, he told her, "I love you, Fanny!"

It sounded stupid shouted like that, sounded—

Culhane looked up, ripping down his snow goggles. The wind had died.

Mulrooney looked up, pulling down her goggles, shouting through the toque, "Josh—Josh!"

She was pointing perhaps two hundred yards directly to their right.

Lieutenant Wilbur, Partridge, Angela Basque and Margaret Spicer were running toward them. "We heard your shots," Wilbur was shouting, "but we couldn't tell where they were coming from."

"Thank God you guys are alive," Partridge called out.

Then Margaret Spicer shouted, "Dr. Fell and I think we found the tunnel!"

THE EXPLOSIVES LIBERATED from one of the *Churchill*'s torpedoes worked. The tunnel or cave mouth—a hollow that was coated with ice—was visible as the snow, ice and debris settled after the blast.

Before they approached the tunnel, Wilbur called out for everyone's attention. "I'm setting out a homing beacon for the rescue party if we aren't in contact with the *Churchill* within the next fifteen hours. It sends a signal they can pick up twenty miles away so they can get it as soon as they surface."

"That's comforting," Dr. Fell said.

The goateed Dr. Liebermann nodded in agreement.

How the rope had become cut, no one knew—or admitted. But Culhane had reloaded the partially spent magazine of the Scoremaster, and despite the cold, his parka wasn't fully closed and the pistol was cocked and locked.

Except for Fanny Mulrooney, Culhane trusted no one now, despite the smiles, the tears of happiness and the hearty slaps on the back that they had remained alive. He had checked the end of the rope. It had been sawed through a strand at a time, to look as though it had frayed somehow and snapped. But Culhane had checked the rope himself before they had left the camp. There had been no fraying.

Someone had tried to murder them.

They approached the tunnel mouth and saw a cave in the ice. Behind the ice was a darkness suggesting the massive size of the cave. It looked to be as wide as the wingspan of a jet fighter and half as high.

Harry Rutgers, the physicist, announced, "My educated guess on first examination is that this cave was not naturally formed."

Culhane just looked at Rutgers, saying nothing.

The explosion had forced an opening approximately ten feet high and ten to twelve feet wide, the icy surface beneath their feet as they walked rough yet slippery.

"Are we *all* going inside? I mean, just in case..." Margaret Spicer asked.

"What would you suggest, Dr. Spicer?" Wilbur called back to her. He was standing by a wall of the cave, shining his battery-operated lantern against the ice.

"That we split into two parties, one keeping perhaps a hundred yards ahead of the other at all times. Then that way, if the advance party gets into trouble, the main party will be there to get them out—hopefully. You don't wander into a newly opened tomb with your eyes closed. It doesn't seem to be such a different situation here."

"Makes sense," Culhane agreed.

"All right. Volunteers for the advance party, raise your hands."

Mulrooney was raising her right hand and with her left pushing up Culhane's right arm. He looked at her, just shaking his head, but raised his arm. Margaret Spicer raised her hand, as did three of the seamen from the *Churchill* and Dr. Liebermann.

"Then you seven," Wilbur announced, "get yourselves roped together and take what gear you think you'll need. As soon as you do, we'll all shove off."

"Wait a minute, Lieutenant," Partridge called out, "make it eight. I should be there."

Culhane looked at Partridge, mentally calculating how long it would take Partridge to get his Smith & Wesson out from under his parka, if it came to that. Partridge was right-handed and carried his gun in a holster behind his right hipbone. It would mean shoving up the parka or opening the parka fully.

Culhane thought he could beat him.

Culhane hoped he wouldn't have to.

As they began sorting through the gear, Culhane mentioned to Mulrooney, "Remember Jules Verne's *A Journey to the Center of the Earth*?"

"Uh-huh." She nodded as she unlashed her purse from the side of her backpack.

"I feel like that now—like we're going down into something. I don't know. . . ." He lit a cigarette and looked toward the back of the cave through the hole the explosion had blown through the ice. He saw only darkness and the glittering of their lanterns as ice crystals caught and broke the light. It was strangely beautiful.

"I'll make a believer out of you yet, Josh," Mulrooney said, and smiled. She had taken off the toque and pulled down the hood of her parka. Her hair was covered with a blue-and-white bandanna knotted at the nape of her neck, under her hair.

"Just a funny cave, Fanny—that's all it is."

"You heard what's-his-name the physicist—not naturally formed."

"Fine. Maybe we're walking into a volcanic vent or something. Did you remember to load your gun when you got it back before we left the *Churchill*?"

"Yeah—why?"

"Whoever cut the rope is with us or behind us. Do me a favor—find the revolver and put it in the top of your purse or in an outside pocket or something so you can get to it in a hurry if you need to. Okay?"

"Okay—if you want me to. But I don't think whoever cut the rope will try anything with all of us around."

"Maybe and maybe not. But I don't wanna find out the hard way." Culhane stood up. Beside his pack on the ice of the cave floor were two battery-operated lanterns. Inside his pack was his own special flashlight. Battery life would be severely affected by the extreme cold, and it was good to know a light source—an extra light source—was there if they needed it. There was still the little Detonics pistol in the flat Safariland holster by his right kidney under his sweater. Only a careful reader of The Takers would suspect he carried it there, as Sean Dodge carried his. Commander Macklin had been a careful reader.

For once Culhane hoped someone didn't read his novels.

The killer who had cut the rope.

CHAPTER THIRTY-FIVE

Commander Macklin walked out of sick bay. He had just seen Hardestey and the other victims of the incident with the rubber boat when the shore party and the scientific party had been dropped off.

He checked his Rolex Submariner. The shore party had been out for more than nine hours. If no radio contact could be made by the time fifteen hours had passed he would send out a second shore party in a rescue effort. Each surfacing had brought no signal. Perhaps Wilbur's radio had been damaged. But there were the backup units.

He started making his way to the bridge....

On the bridge, a little less than an hour before the next radio-contact period, he called out, "Sonar— what's around us?"

"Sonar to bridge. Had a large fish, maybe a whale five minutes ago, sir. No traffic at all, sir."

"Keep listening, just in case we get some Russian friends or something."

The chief of ship was assisting on the bridge since Wilbur was off the *Churchill* and Hardestey was in sick bay. The chief was a good man—pushing sixty, married with grown children.

"Chief, come here for a second," Macklin called to him.

"Aye, sir," the chief answered, keeping his headset on, walking across to Macklin and leaning against the bridge rail.

"Bob, what do you think?"

"About what, sir?"

"Everything. I checked the rubber boat after it was brought back—the one that swamped. It looked like the inlet valve had been tampered with to make a slow leak."

"I looked at her, too, Captain. Looked like tampering to me, too."

"I think Mr. Culhane and Miss Mulrooney were right about this Steiglitz character. Somebody out there on the ice is a killer. I'm worried—Wilbur hasn't kept his radio contacts."

"Could be some electrical interference, sir, or maybe the lieutenant's radio is on the fritz."

"Yeah, it could be that, Bob, but then Wilbur isn't following orders. In the event contact was broken off, he was supposed to activate that homing beacon right away. Get us in there after him."

"Aye, sir."

"What do you think, Bob? Off the record, what do you think?"

The chief leaned closer to Macklin, covered his microphone with his left hand and whispered, "Ed, this whole thing—following a dead ship to some cave in the ice—gives me—and a lot of the crew—the creeps. The rumors—scuttlebutt—about what's supposed to be out there—it's crazy."

"Off the record, Bob, a hundred years ago that dead ship may have found something out there— maybe the lost continent of Atlantis—if it ever existed. Maybe some other civilization from the past, maybe even a UFO base—that's why we took 'em here. . . ."

"Lieutenant Wilbur's a good officer, Ed."

"Yeah, but you're thinking the same thing I am: that boat that was maybe sabotaged—"

"Aww, but Ed. . . ."

"I'm not saying I—"

There was a roar, an explosion, the sound earsplitting. The chief dropped to his knees against the bridge railing as the *Churchill* shuddered. Macklin barely kept his balance. Bells rang and sirens sounded.

"What the hell was that? Damage report!" the chief started repeating into the headset, but Macklin took it from him.

"No time, Bob!" Then, holding the headset, he said into its microphone, "Secure all watertight—"

"Maneuvering spaces to bridge! Loss of power on number-one reactor—"

"Engineering to bridge! We're flooding—hot water—hot—one of the reactors is—holy shit! The whole compartment—"

There was another explosion, and the ship rocked again. The air was filled with groaning and tearing sounds.

"Maneuvering spaces to bridge—" The crackle of the speaker died as the lights on the bridge and in the control room below its deck suddenly went out.

"Emergency power—now, dammit!" Macklin shouted.

"The panel," a voice called from the darkness below. "I'm getting water everywhere—holy—"

There was another roar, louder than the first explosion, louder than anything Macklin had ever heard. The portside pressure hull cracked, and instruments, equipment and bodies hurtled toward him.

"Mother of God—" Macklin made the sign of the Cross as the attack periscope housing wrenched free and came crashing toward him.

CHAPTER THIRTY-SIX

Mulrooney shone her light down into the ice and exclaimed, "This is it! This is it!"

Culhane and the others of the advance party stopped, turned around and looked back at her.

"Down there, Josh! Down there in the ice!"

Culhane dropped to a crouch. The ice all around them was largely translucent, and beneath Mulrooney's feet under perhaps a foot of ice was a wooden tool handle. It looked like an ax handle.

"This must be where the *Madagascar* stopped to examine the metal, the metal—"

"There's only rock and ice, Miss Mulrooney," Partridge said, squatting beside Culhane at Mulrooney's feet.

Culhane looked up at Mulrooney. "He's right, Fanny—I don't see any metal."

"Dig it out! Can we dig it out? Oh, please?"

"Better than that, ma'am," Maurice, a young black seaman volunteered, standing between Culhane and Partridge and Fanny Mulrooney. "We brought the propane torches." The seaman held up a small propane torch. "A little blast from this and that ice'll be gone to Sunday." Culhane searched his pockets and found the waterproof matchbox; he didn't trust a disposable lighter to ignite a blowtorch.

"I'm ready, sir," the seaman announced, and they could hear the hiss of the gas.

Culhane nodded and struck one of the matches on the side of the case, cupping his hands around it lest a stray current of air destroy the flame. He didn't know how vital matches might be as they progressed and had no desire to waste even a single one. Then they had it, and the seaman said, "Ma'am—and you two gentlemen—stand back a little, please."

"Don't hurt the ax handle, sailor."

"I won't, ma'am," he said, his voice loud over the roar of the flame as he applied it against the surface of the ice. It began melting immediately, steam rising in a tiny vapor cloud like the clouds of their breaths in the cavern with its ice-coated walls and ceiling and floor.

The seaman called out to one of the others from the *Churchill*: "Hey, Manny—"

A swarthy-faced man with thick eyebrows, who looked as if he was chilled to the bone, skidded on his heels on the ice and stopped beside them.

Maurice told him, "Get those waterproof gauntlets in my pack here while I work."

"You bet," Manny said, starting to open Maurice's backpack.

"In the right-side pouch I think—the top pouch."

"Right."

In a moment Manny produced the waterproof gauntlets, a rubbery-looking gray and past elbow length. The gauntlets were apparently made to be used without removing gloves already worn; the fingers seemed huge.

"I got 'em, Maurice."

"Here," Culhane told Manny, "I'll take those." He pulled on one of the waterproof gauntlets, and Mulrooney helped him with the second one.

The torch suddenly cut off. "Hurry up and get it out of there, sir. She's refreezin' already."

"Right," Culhane told the man. He dipped his gauntleted right arm into the puddle of water that was already freezing over on the surface. His fingers found the ax handle, and he wrenched it up. It seemed perfectly preserved.

"Look—look there near the bottom of the handle," Mulrooney gasped.

Culhane awkwardly turned the ax handle over in his huge rubber fingers, putting it into the light of Partridge's battery-operated lantern. Mulrooney, her voice hushed, read, "H.M.S. *Madagascar*."

"That the hundred-year-old English ship?"

"Yeah," Culhane said, nodding to Maurice.

"Damn—" It was Manny's voice. The seaman couldn't take his eyes from the burned-in letters.

"Partridge, get on the walkie-talkie and tell Wilbur to hold up the second party. We'll be here for a while."

"What for, Mr. Culhane?"

Culhane looked at him. "If they left an ax handle here, it's pretty likely they left the head, too. They were probably using it for something. The ax handle broke off—you can see that. Maybe this is where they hacked through the ice to find the weird metal or whatever they called it."

"They called it 'a most peculiar iron,' " Mulrooney said, her voice sounding impatient.

"Gotcha," Partridge confirmed. Culhane could hear the crackle of the walkie-talkie, then he started searching for the waterproof matches again as Maurice opened the propane torch's gas-outlet valve.

The torch was lit again, and less than an inch below where the ax handle had been, found the double-bit head. It hadn't even rusted. Culhane pulled it out.

"There's a manufacturer's name on it—see?" Culhane looked at Manny, to whom he'd handed the ax head. "Says—yeah—M.L. Woothridge Foundries."

"Hey, there's something shiny down there," Maurice said. The torch hissed, steam rose, and suddenly Culhane could see.

"Holy—it *is* metal," Mulrooney breathed.

Culhane stared down through the puddle of clear water and the cloud of steam above it. The metal was totally rust-free, brilliant, almost polished. "Melt away more of the ice. Get the torch on the metal itself and see what happens."

"Yes, sir," said Maurice, increasing the area covered by the torch. "Here goes." He focused the flame into a narrow blue-yellow tongue. "Don't look like anything's happenin'."

"See if you can make a more precise—"

"I hear ya, sir." Maurice adjusted the flame again, creating a pinpoint of yellow-tipped blue.

"Keep it up, keep it up," Mulrooney urged.

"Yes, ma'am—torch might be runnin' low."

Culhane rolled down the gauntlet, rolled back his sleeve's storm cuff, smudged moisture from the face of the Rolex Sea Dweller and watched the sweep second hand. One minute. Two minutes. Almost three, then a sputtering noise.

"The bottle's out," Maurice announced.

Culhane picked up a small chunk of ice and dropped it on the spot of metal. It didn't melt.

On impulse, he ripped the rubber gauntlet from his left hand, then his leather glove and the silk liner underneath.

"What are you doing?" Partridge murmured.

Culhane touched his little finger to the metal surface.

"It isn't even warm—not a bit—not at all."

"Man!" Maurice gasped.

"Not man at all," Mulrooney whispered hoarsely. "Not man at all."

THEY CONTINUED ALONG THE TUNNEL. It was definitely a tunnel, either man-made or made by someone or something other than man. The test they had given the metal was inconclusive, Culhane told himself. There could be and probably were numerous man-made substances that would be totally impervious to heat from a propane torch. He couldn't think of any offhand, but he was sure there were.

The tunnel was at a slight angle. Culhane hadn't realized it, nor apparently had any of them, until they had traveled its length for more than an hour. At a rest stop—they had signaled the rear party to rest, as well—Mulrooney had taken her lipstick from her purse, complaining her lips felt dry and chapped. She had set it for an instant on the slick ice, and the lipstick had just rolled away, deeper into the tunnel.

Culhane had gone after it, slipping, falling, but grabbing for it. The things a man does to impress a woman, he had thought, and it was then that he not only realized the tunnel was at a slight angle, but he also saw the button under the ice.

The translucent ice was less than two inches thick over the button, so he took his climbing ax from the utility belt at the waist of his parka and chipped away at the ice. Partridge had called out, asking what he was doing. Culhane had been evasive—and he hoped convincing. He still didn't quite know why. In a few seconds, the button was free.

He felt a queasiness in his stomach. It wasn't a button; he had seen it from the side only. He held the small object in his gloved right hand and stared at it.

Mulrooney's voice did not sound calm, but he could tell she was trying. "Hey—hey, guys! Hey—hey!"

Culhane stood up, pocketing the object he'd taken from the ice. "I've got your lipstick, Fanny!"

But she didn't look at him. She was staring at the far wall of the tunnel. The tunnel had gradually widened until now the ice seemed less thick, and in occasional spots the gleaming, strange metal could be seen through it.

But Mulrooney wasn't looking at the metal. Culhane could see that as he approached her.

Her battery-operated light made what was visible through the translucent ice seem even more horrible, he realized. He was proud of her that she hadn't screamed. He might have, he thought.

A human being wearing the clothes of a seaman of a century ago was encased in the ice. His eyes were wide open, and the body—except for a puckery quality in some areas of the face near the sunken eyes and the sunken cheeks—seemed perfectly preserved.

"One of the crew of the *Madagascar*," Mulrooney whispered.

Culhane put his right arm around her.

"God bless the man—to die here," Maurice said quietly.

Margaret Spicer said, "The cold mummified his body. Look there—the expression on his face. I've seen it on the faces of people who were buried alive. Maybe that—"

Mulrooney turned away and Culhane held her.

His left hand was in his coat pocket, and through his glove he could feel the outline of the object he had removed from the ice. A jawless skull of silver formed a school or fraternal ring. Two lightning bolts appeared on one side of the skull; on the other was the legend Mein Ehre, Treu—"My honor, my trust"—the original motto of Himmler's elite. It was an SS *Totenkopf* ring.

Perhaps that was why the body from a century ago, frozen into the ice wall of the tunnel, didn't shock him as much as it could have.

There had been Nazis here, in the tunnel. Perhaps Nazis had found whatever the *Madagascar* had found.

"We can't do anything for the poor guy now. Come on. Rest stop is over—time to move on." As he drew Mary Frances Mulrooney away from the frozen body in the wall, he moved his arm from her shoulder and brushed his hand against his jacket over the butt of his pistol. It was a good feeling.

CULHANE NOW KNEW HOW DANTE MUST HAVE FELT when led by Virgil into the underworld. Steam rose in seemingly impenetrable clouds, the cold of the ice that had been around them gone, replaced by warmth that in itself would not have been unpleasant, but the sudden contrast to the subzero surface temperatures made it seem almost stifling. Yet there were still patches of

ice here and there on the metal surface of the tunnel
floor, and with practically no visibility, moving along
the tunnel had become even more dangerous. The metal surface was as though polished and buffed. It
literally gleamed in the slightest light, and its slick surface compounded the hazards of walking on the
almost invisible icy spots. Each member of the advance party had slipped and fallen at least once.

The seaman named Manny slipped and broke his
ankle just as they passed the two-and-a-half-hour
mark in the ever more downward trek. The steepness
of the angle was such that as they walked—hugging the
sides of the tunnel—they had assumed almost a jogging pace, the toes of their boots at sharp angles to
their legs. When Manny skidded, fell and began to
slide, screaming with pain and fear, Mulrooney was
tugged after him. Culhane, tied behind her, skidded as
well.

"I've got ya—but only for a second here!" Partridge shouted.

Culhane splayed his gloved fingers, spread his legs
and arms and shouted to Fanny Mulrooney, "Spread
yourself out! Hurry!"

"All right!" she yelled up to him.

Manny was still screaming.

Culhane looked up. Partridge and Maurice held
them from above, and Felix Liebermann, Dr. Spicer
and the third seaman from the *Churchill*—Phipps—
held them from the wall side.

Culhane hunched his shoulders, sinking his head
down for an instant, and caught his breath. "Partridge,
warn the others behind us about how slippery it's gotten. Fanny, slide down a little and see if you can help
Manny. I'll boost you down." A cold sweat washing his
body, Culhane rolled onto his back, skidding only a little, and pulled up his knees. He braced himself with his
and Mulrooney's segment of the rope between his legs

just over his crotch. "Okay, try it, Fanny." He held the rope in his hands, feeling his rear end slide a little on the slick surface of the tunnel floor. As he watched Mulrooney edging down toward Manny, Culhane shouted to Partridge, "Partridge, have Wilbur send somebody back up the tunnel to where the ice is good and thick. Have him drive in some of those climbing pitons or something to anchor the ropes. If this gets any steeper, next time one of us slides we won't be able to stop, and we'd never make it out this way, never be able to climb up. It's too slick."

"There might not be enough rope," Partridge called back. "Maybe not enough to get to the bottom."

Culhane shook his head and watched Mulrooney. She was on her knees now beside Manny, gently touching his ankle. He could hear the sailor groan. "Broken—bad," she shouted up. "At least I think so."

Culhane called up to Partridge. "If we can't get down, we get back up to the surface and wait until we can signal the *Churchill* to get more rope. Get it flown in if we have to. In the mouth of the tunnel we can stay warm enough to hold out. But if we keep going much more without a guide rope, we'll be goners."

He looked at Partridge, and the CIA man nodded his head. "All right—agreed." Then Culhane heard the crackle of the walkie-talkie and Partridge talking into it.

Culhane, Mulrooney and the four others remaining in the advance party—Felix Liebermann, Margaret Spicer, Maurice and Partridge—now crawled by the side of the tunnel. The steepness had reached the point at which they could not walk. But with the rope secured above them, and each person securely tied to the next, they still made good progress. They had left Manny behind with Phipps to wait for the backup party. With twenty-one of them, there was sufficient manpower to handle the injured man. The mirror-smooth surface of the tunnel would make dragging him or letting him down a rope length at a time not too difficult.

Dr. Spicer and Maurice were in the lead now, Partridge and Dr. Liebermann were in the rear, and Culhane and Fanny Mulrooney were at the center of the security rope. Partridge was charged with letting out the line as they continued the descent. Twenty-five minutes had elapsed, according to Culhane's Rolex, since Manny's accident.

Suddenly Partridge shouted, "Watch out—hol—"

Culhane looked up and saw Partridge slammed against the tunnel wall as an object—a body—streaked past him.

Culhane reached for Manny, but he was going too fast. Culhane missed contact by inches. Manny's screams echoed in the tunnel, becoming fainter as he slid away from them. Perhaps five hundred yards down there appeared to be a bend in the tunnel. Culhane watched as Manny's body slammed against the wall and bounced off, gone from sight.

Margaret Spicer screamed. Fanny Mulrooney buried her head in Culhane's shoulder.

"Partridge—you okay?" Culhane called.

"Yeah," Partridge groaned back. "Winded me—"

Culhane heard the crackle of static: "Partridge to Wilbur. Come in. What the hell happened with Manny? Over!"

Culhane licked his lips.

"Partridge calling Wilbur. What happened? Over!"

"What's the matter?" Mulrooney murmured.

Culhane shook his head, motioning for her to be quiet.

Because the tunnel curved downward, and because it had been slower going with the injured Manny, the rear party was no longer visible above. Culhane estimated they were a quarter mile back.

"Could you be out of range?"

"Should be four miles, Dr. Spicer," Partridge answered. "Partridge to Lieutenant Wilbur. Do you read me? Over!"

There was no answer.

Culhane lit a cigarette. "Partridge," he called up. "Just for the hell of it, give a good tug to the guide rope, but brace yourself against the wall in case it gives."

"What are you—"

"Try it," Fanny Mulrooney urged.

Partridge looked down at them and nodded. Flat against the wall, Culhane watched Partridge as he tugged at the rope. It gave, snaking downward.

"Oh, my God—" Margaret Spicer wailed.

Dr. Liebermann intoned, "If above us they are in trouble somehow, we will never return to the surface."

Culhane felt the muscles in his neck tense. He swallowed hard. There was only one thing to do. "We keep going—down. There was rope dragging from Manny's armpits as he slipped past us. It would have been cut. There's a murderer above us. Maybe's there's another murderer with us. But we can't stay here. And I'm warning everyone now: if anyone touches Fanny or me, I start shooting. In this tunnel, bullets would ricochet from now until doomsday. No one would be safe—not even the murderer."

His parka was already open. The Detonics Scoremaster in the crossdraw holster would be visible to anyone. He wanted it that way.

"Keep yourselves tied to the safety line. If one of us goes, maybe the other five can keep him from slipping away." He turned and looked at Margaret Spicer and Maurice. "Let's go."

As they started, Culhane could hear Partridge trying the walkie-talkie one more time.

There was no answer.

THEY HAD CRAWLED THE FIVE HUNDRED YARDS to where Manny's body had disappeared. The tunnel had leveled off, and the body was about two hundred yards farther on. Culhane was the first to stand—his legs stiff, his back aching—and he inched like a worm over a metal surface slicker than the smoothest glass. His stomach churned and his palms sweated inside his gloves as he leaned against the tunnel wall for support. He felt as if he wanted to throw up.

He fought the nausea, then, after a moment, slowly bent to help Mulrooney to stand. He undid the rope at his waist, removed his pack and then his parka, then slung the coat onto the pack and secured it there. He pulled the toque from his head. It had been rolled up on the sides into a watch cap, but it was too warm now even for that.

He would have tugged off his sweater, but it would have shown the smaller Detonics concealed under it; the sweater was a heavy knit and hid the gun's outline well. He stood on one foot, Mulrooney helping to support him as he undid the lashings of the insulated boots he'd worn over his own boots. He pulled the right one off, unzipping the closure of his snow pants. He did the same with the left. He pushed the snow pants down to his knees, then sat on the metal floor of the tunnel, pulling them off.

In the Levi's, the sweater, the cotton flannel shirt and the thermal underwear, he was still warm.

Wordlessly, Mulrooney followed his example, and the others did the same, stripping off their cold-weather gear.

There was no need to run to Manny. From the angle of his head to his shoulders, it was obvious to anyone the seaman was dead.

Maurice finally broke the silence. "When I find out who cut that rope, I'm gonna kill the son of a bitch."

"Good for you," Culhane said, smiling. "But you

may have to take a number—I'm in line ahead of you."

Maurice looked at him and nodded, saying nothing else.

"What do we do now?" It was Margaret Spicer.

"We look at poor Manny," Mulrooney answered, "and we keep going on, I guess."

"I'm for staying here," Partridge announced. "My three men were up there. If some funny business went on and my guys didn't stop it, then they're dead. And I'm gonna get the bastards who did it."

Culhane lit a cigarette and rubbed his face. He could never remember being so tired. "All this is because of what lies down there. If Steiglitz was right about some fantastic power, then fine. We get down there, either sabotage it before he can use it, or learn to use it against him when he comes."

"The captain'll be sendin' out that rescue party in another nine hours if he doesn't hear from us," Maurice murmured.

Culhane looked at him. "I don't think so. And if he does, we're talking almost a day before they could reach us."

"What do you mean, you 'don't think so'?" Dr. Liebermann asked.

"If Wilbur is our man, or one of our men—and I'm using the masculine in the generic sense only—well, then that radio beacon he put out wasn't to the *Churchill*...."

"Bad shit, man," Maurice intoned.

"That sums it up pretty well," Mulrooney agreed.

Culhane sighed, leaning against the wall, then pushed himself away. He picked up his pack in his left fist and carried it like a suitcase by the straps, his outer clothing secured to it. "Let's go close Manny's eyes."

With Mulrooney beside him, he started walking toward the dead seaman two hundred yards farther down the tunnel's length.

They closed Manny's eyes, then wrapped him in a blanket. The rope end had been cut.

There was a light, brighter than the lights of their battery-operated lanterns, and Culhane, walking in the lead now, tired, worn, Mulrooney beside him, shut off his light and stared at it. He started to laugh, his laughter ringing in the tunnel.

"What's. . ." Mulrooney began.

"Trite phrase for the day: 'There's a light at the end of the tunnel'—there! Look!"

Culhane started walking toward the light. He guessed it was perhaps a hundred yards. He only realized he was walking rapidly when he heard the faster tattoo of Mulrooney's boots on the almost luminescent metal of the tunnel floor beneath their feet.

At the end of the tunnel he stopped. He rejected seeing what filled the area before him. Around him were other tunnel mouths—seven more, he counted—radiating like the spokes of a wheel, not in a circle but in a semicircle. Directly opposite where he stood in the center tunnel, he could see a wall of stone with a triangular opening leading into what seemed to be another tunnel. But even from where he stood, there was light visible at the far end of this new tunnel with the triangular entrance.

Mulrooney was holding his hand, and he closed his eyes, seeing what lay between the seven spokelike tunnels and the triangle cut in the rock at the far side through her words, through her eyes.

"Josh—oh, my God, Josh.... They really exist—all these years, all the people who saw them—and they're right here in front of our eyes."

He opened his eyes as he felt her drag at his hand, drawing him forward from the tunnel mouth.

He heard Partridge behind them. "Flying saucers—God Almighty!"

PART FOUR
THE STARBASE

CHAPTER THIRTY-SEVEN

He walked beside her, looking into her eyes as she looked up into his. After more than three decades of existence, Culhane finally understood the meaning of the expression "Like a kid in a candy store." That kid was Fanny Mulrooney.

"I'd like to say go and play, but—"

"I know...." And she stood beside him. He watched her fists balling closed, opening, then balling closed again.

"It's a hangar bay! Wow!"

Culhane looked around at Maurice. As if explaining himself, the *Churchill*'s crew member said, "When I first joined up three years ago, I was put on an aircraft carrier—the *Enterprise*. I guess I felt like a dried-out pea in a barrel. She's big, man! Then I got into submarines, but this is like that, like the big carriers—it's a hangar bay."

"Those are launching tunnels. We walked through one," Mulrooney murmured.

"They aren't saucer-shaped at all, are they?" Margaret Spicer remarked.

Culhane looked at her, then back at the ships. He counted twenty-one of them, arranged in three clusters of seven. The ships were apparently constructed of the same luminescent metal as the tunnels, or at least a similar alloy, Culhane theorized.

"They're airfoils," Mulrooney said, her voice hushed as if she were in a cathedral.

"From above or below they'd be triangular-looking," Partridge announced.

Culhane looked at him, then at Mulrooney. Only the older man with the goatee had remained silent. Culhane looked at him. "Well, what do you think?"

"I presume that since no one—or nothing—has molested us, the owners of these craft are not, at the moment at least, present. I doubt these persons have been here since the *Madagascar*'s crew explored the tunnel through which we passed. Were a ship of this type to pass through the tunnel, I would surmise air resistance would generate a great heat. Your experiments with the tunnel surface when this gentleman—" he patted Maurice on the shoulder "—melted through the ice were most interesting, if inconclusive. But such great heat resistance would imply a rational reason behind its implementation. If great heat were generated, then the block of ice in the wall where the body of the seaman from the *Madagascar* had been found would have been melted and the body incinerated. No, I should say these ships have been unused for some time."

"Just what the hell do you do, anyway? I never got that straight," Culhane asked the man. "And it's Liebermann?"

"Felix Liebermann, yes," the little man said, walking ahead.

"The Egyptologist, right?" Mulrooney asked.

"Wrong. That's Cornblume. He's the professor of Egyptology."

"Then you're the astrophysicist," Culhane said.

"No, that's Harry Rutgers—a good friend of mine, Harry. No, I'm a professor of human engineering at that little western university no one can ever remember; we don't have a football team. I'm a special consultant to the Central Intelligence Agency." He looked over his shoulder as he took a pair of wire-rimmed glasses from under his parka and perched them on his nose. He looked at Partridge. "You knew, the deputy director knew—and the deputy director decided I should know, too." The little man smiled.

He turned and looked at Culhane. "I suggest we inspect the ships without touching anything. It appears their hatches are open to us, almost inviting us. If I'm not mistaken, I'd be the logical person to tell you something about the people or creatures who once flew them. Come." He started ahead toward the nearest seven-ship squadron, Culhane following him, Mulrooney beside Culhane.

The little man stopped. Without turning around, standing less than a half-dozen yards from the entrance to the nearest of the triangular airfoils, he said, "One can ascertain much from the construction of the entry system to the ship. The aliens were apparently taller than man and of tremendous girth, if the demon skull that was spoken of in the memoir of Henry Chillingsworth and in the logbook of the *Madagascar* itself was typical. The width of these entryways would accommodate a tall creature with bovine horns. Shall we enter? But touch nothing, hmm?"

Culhane watched as Liebermann started to circle the ship.

Culhane dropped his pack to the hangar floor, opened it and plowed inside.

"What are you looking for?"

"What I might need most." He removed the extra magazines for his pistol and the two spare 8-round extension magazines as well. There was a musette-style shoulder bag folded into his pack. He removed it, opened it and placed the spare magazines inside, then the partially emptied box of ammunition. He found his flashlight and placed that and the three extra D-size Duracell batteries for it into the bag. Six packs of Pall Mall reds went into the musette bag. A pair of leather gloves, thin for shooting. He stuffed these under his left armpit for the moment. He started going through the pockets of his parka and found the box of waterproof matches, which he added to the musette bag. The ring.

"What's that?" Mulrooney asked, stooped over beside him.

He looked up into her eyes. "A secret—tell you later." Then he stood, pocketing the ring. His pack closed, he slid it across the floor toward the tunnel through which they'd come. "Only way I'll be needing that coat is if we make it back through that tunnel." He looked at Mulrooney. "Get rid of what you don't need."

She seemed to think about it a moment, then went into her pack and removed a large black canvas purse with double handles. She pitched the backpack and parka next to Culhane's and put the purse under her left arm. "I'm ready."

He smiled at her and shouldered the musette bag. It was heavier than he would have liked, but everything except the cigarettes was vital—and those were vital to his sanity. He looked at Maurice. "Go through the packs and get all the food, water and medical gear into one pack. We can take turns hauling it."

"Yes, sir," said Maurice, starting away. Then he stopped. "Can I—"

"Yeah," Culhane said and laughed. "Look inside the ship first. Go ahead." Maurice trotted after Dr. Liebermann.

But Dr. Liebermann stepped away from the entry hatch. "We are ready then. I will go—"

Culhane cut him off. "Dr. Liebermann, no offense, but I've been thinking. Without Fanny—Miss Mulrooney—without her, we wouldn't be here. If there's going to be a person who's the first person from this expedition to enter an unidentified flying object, it's gonna be her. There's the danger factor—I know that. But I think she's got the right more than any of us." Culhane looked at her, his voice lowering so only she—he hoped—could hear it. "I won't say that if we get out of here alive I'll never make cracks again about

the books you write. But I'll try to understand what
you do a whole hell of a lot better. I promise.''

She got up on tiptoes and kissed him hard on the
lips, then ran toward the nearest ship.

MARY FRANCES MULROONEY, author of fifteen
books—including those soon to be published—on the
occult, the supernatural and unexplained phenomena,
touched the toe of her left foot very gingerly to the
threshold of the doorway into the aircraft. For some
reason—she didn't understand her own feelings—she
wanted to cry. And she wanted to laugh.

Nothing happened when her foot touched the alien
craft. She set her other foot onto the threshold. No
tingling sensation, no closing of the hatch, no shrieking of alien sirens, no clapping of bells.

Nothing.

She inspected the doorway—the hatch seemed to
close from above and below—then she looked inside
the ship.

''Josh. Josh.'' She cooed the word until she felt him
beside her.

''Fanny.''

She swallowed hard to get rid of the lump in her
throat. ''It's. . .Jesus, it's beautiful. . . .''

To her left were instrument panels—or at least she
assumed they were instrument panels. Diodes of some
sort were embedded in a darker metal, and the metal
seemed somehow thinner to her. It was only logical
that instrument panels would be of a different material
than the hull, she rationalized. But the diodes were not
lit.

To her right, approximately at the center of the
boomerang-shaped airfoil when measured from side to
side, were three steps. The treads were very broad and
the height of the steps very low. With Culhane holding
her hand, she started ahead toward the steps, looking

upward. There was a railed deck of some sort overhead, and she ducked her head instinctively as she started up the steps and under it.

"They would have walked slightly bent forward and, considering the apparent size of their skulls, were most likely bowlegged as well," she heard Dr. Liebermann saying. "I used the skull size earlier to estimate their height, and I'd say close to seven feet. And the fascinating part of it is that the airfoil from side to side is roughly forty-nine feet—or seven times the height of the occupant. The depth of the craft from the apparent nose behind us to the rearmost portion amidships— some sort of drive unit, propulsion system, what-have-you—is approximately twenty-one feet, and the ship is roughly fourteen feet high. It rests on three points that form a triangle. . . ."

"Threes and sevens," Culhane mused. "Curious."

"The number seven has been significant to numerous cultures," Mulrooney said, reaching the top of the steps. A dome made of some transparent substance like glass was above her. The dome, which had three sides and resembled a rounded pyramid, rose to an apex. She stood beneath it at its exact center, facing the steps she had climbed, looking toward the forward section of the ship. She stood between two chairs of massive size.

Dr. Liebermann was talking again, and mechanically Mulrooney found herself listening. "A crew of three. I had expected that—the ship is too small for seven." Mulrooney looked at Liebermann, then at the chair to her right. That chair was at the center of a cluster of what appeared to be more of the instrument panels.

"What a bridge," Maurice whispered. "That's what this is, folks—it's the bridge of a goddamned flying saucer! Hallelujah!"

Culhane looked at his Rolex. It was apparently still

working, and he was mildly surprised the spacecraft didn't exude some sort of energy force that would have stopped it. About ten minutes had elapsed since they had entered the hangar bay.

"Maurice, I hate to break this up," Culhane said, "but it's time to work on the gear. Then I want you to get out there and guard the tunnel mouth, and signal if somebody comes."

"You mean the lieutenant?"

"You got a gun, Maurice?"

Maurice slung back his parka. Under it was a GI shoulder holster, the butt of a .45 visible in it against his chest.

"Go stand guard," Culhane told the man.

"Right—yes, sir," Maurice said and, glancing back longingly it seemed at the bridge of the aircraft, he started down the three steps and disappeared through the hatch.

"They'll try for us, won't they?" Mulrooney asked.

"If some of them up there are working for Steiglitz," Culhane answered, "they probably have things in mind even Sean Dodge couldn't imagine."

"Look here," Liebermann called.

Culhane walked over to one of the two large chairs at the center of the bridge. Liebermann was using a steel tape measure and was measuring the pillowlike section on the elevated seat back. "Miss Mulrooney—sit in the chair, please—here."

She turned to Liebermann, wondering what would happen if she sat in the chair. "Why?"

"An experiment—but a perfectly harmless one. Please, Miss Mulrooney, sit."

She licked her lips. Her mouth was dry. She walked to the front of the chair, her knees going together as she sat down. She folded her hands in her lap, a little afraid to touch the armrests of the seats. It was strange material, similar to leather but not quite. It was the most comfortable chair she could ever remember sitting in. "What's the point of the experiment?" she asked Dr. Liebermann.

"In just a moment...please, Miss Mulrooney, would you stand up and would Mr. Culhane sit down?"

Mulrooney stood quickly and gave her seat to Culhane. As she walked across the bridge she could hear Culhane asking, "What does this prove?"

There was a panel of something dark that looked like glass. Mulrooney could see herself in it. Still listening to Mulrooney and Liebermann, she took the blue-and-white bandanna from her hair. She set her purse on an instrument-free part of one of the control consoles, plowing through the purse to find her brush.

"It proves something rather interesting, something I had already surmised and mentioned to you both before we entered the ship. The creatures do indeed all have the demon skulls, as we call them. Miss Mulrooney?"

She kept brushing her hair, not looking at him. "What is it, Dr. Liebermann?"

"How tall are you?"

"Five-seven. Why?"

"And Mr. Culhane—your height?"

"A little over six."

"From the headrest position, these creatures, beings—call them what you will—were approximately seven feet tall. They actually had the horns like the skull so much talked about in the Gladstone Log. These headrests were constructed to accommodate the width."

Mulrooney was finished with her hair, then refolding the bandanna and tying it over her head, under her hair at the nape of her neck. "Then everything they constructed was in multiples of their height?"

"A sensible arrangement, perhaps," said Liebermann. He was smiling.

"How about how the ship works?" Mulrooney asked.

"Hmm—a good question, good indeed. There seem to be no actual manual controls as such, unless these devices that appear to be similar to light-emitting diodes have a true mechanical function. I think not. I understand there have been some experiments in laboratories in the Soviet Union with the electrical impulses emitted by brainwaves...."

Mulrooney felt herself jump. It was Maurice shouting from outside. "They're comin'—but some of them ain't there!"

"LET'S GET OUTTA HERE—down that next tunnel under the triangle!" yelled Culhane's voice. "Fanny, Dr. Liebermann!"

Partridge ran from the tunnel under the triangle.

"Where the hell were you guys?"

"In one of the ships," Culhane called back. "We got company. Where were you?"

"Margaret and I were inside over there. It's like something out of a dream—you won't believe it."

"Any places to hide?"

"Yeah—plenty!"

"Get going and wait for us at the end of the tunnel. Wilbur and the others are coming, but some of them are missing—like one of your guys."

"If they—"

"Get goin'!" Culhane rasped, reaching the entrance to the ship. "Fanny, goddammit!"

"Coming," he heard her call.

"Hey!" It was Maurice at the entrance to the tunnel to the surface. "I'm with you guys."

"Get the gear I asked you to collect—the food and stuff—and move it down that tunnel under the triangle. Wait at the end."

Maurice said nothing, but as Culhane watched, he picked up a bursting pack and started to run.

Mulrooney was in the hatch of the ship. "What's wrong?"

"Maybe everything. Come on! Bring Liebermann—and hurry!"

Instead of running toward the triangular entranceway into the tunnel on the far side of the hangar bay, Culhane ran toward the tunnel through which they had entered, the Scoremaster .45 in his right fist.

He threw himself against the side wall just outside the tunnel mouth.

He shouted along the tunnel's length as he shot a glance around the edge. "Wilbur!"

"Mr. Culhane—yes!"

"Wilbur, don't come down the tunnel—not just yet."

"Why not, Mr. Culhane?"

"Some questions need some answers. . . ."

"Is that a threat, Mr. Culhane?"

"A threat, Lieutenant. What happened to Manny?"

"He died, I presume."

The voice didn't sound any closer.

"Why? What harm could a man with a broken ankle have—"

Wilbur's voice cut him off. "You should know the answer, Mr. Culhane. I never read one of your books; I don't read that sort of stuff. But I understand people get killed right and left in your novels. Why do you think I had to kill him?"

Culhane felt his right palm sweating on the butt of the .45. "I give up. I write adventure stories, not mysteries."

"He was what you'd call a good guy, Mr. Culhane, loyal to his country and to his ship. I'm sure he watched every John Wayne movie ever made."

"Aww, shit," Culhane said. "You working for Steiglitz?"

"Yes, he *is* working for me."

The voice was that of the linguist, Dr. Erwin Fell.

CHAPTER THIRTY-EIGHT

There had been labeling of some sort on the instrument panels in the huge airfoil. Culhane had glanced at it, and given the right books, perhaps access to a computer, and time—time most of all—he felt he could have deciphered it.

Steiglitz, on the other hand, was a genius with languages.

If there had been explosives available and a way to detonate them, Culhane would have blown up the airfoils. Instead he fired three rounds high into the tunnel and started to run. He had fired high in the event that some of those in Wilbur's and Steiglitz's party were innocent hostages, and there had been no time for accuracy.

Culhane had gotten off three rounds, and now, with gunfire echoing from the tunnel mouth as he ran, he moved as if the Devil himself were chasing him. And perhaps Steiglitz was just that.

A devil come down to an alien hell.

Mulrooney was waiting under the apex of the triangle, her little revolver in her right hand. "Come on!"

"Run, dammit! I could always outdistance you! I'll catch up!"

And he could see her start to run.

He was halfway across the hangar bay, when there was more gunfire, louder this time.

He threw himself down behind one of the ships. There were two men in the tunnel mouth: one of them from the *Churchill*, the other a CIA penguin. Culhane fired two shots from the Scoremaster.

Gunfire rained heavily against the hull of the ship. He heard Steiglitz shout, "Don't damage any of the ships! Be careful!"

The lighter crackle of submachine-gun fire erupted from the 9mm P Uzi the CIA penguin was carrying. Culhane rode out the burst, then poked his head from behind the ship. The seaman with the M-16 raised his weapon to fire. The distance was fifty yards.

Culhane pumped the Scoremaster's trigger twice using a two-hand hold, the hull of the aircraft steadying him. The crew member from the *Churchill* doubled over and fell forward, his M-16 burst firing into the hangar bay floor, the bullets ricocheting everywhere.

Culhane was up, his right thumb working the extended magazine release, his left hand catching the empty magazine. All his spares except one were in the musette bag hanging from his shoulder. He reached for that one spare in his shirt pocket. When he had it, he jammed it into the Scoremaster's butt, his thumb working down the slide stop as he ran for the triangle in the far wall.

While running, he upped the safety, then saw the tunnel's far end perhaps a hundred yards from the triangular entryway. His breath was coming in short gasps. "Too much writing, not enough running, Culhane," he thought. He threw himself into a flat-out sprint.

"The light at the end of the tunnel." The phrase ran through his mind again and again as he ran, his shins screaming. Sweat was pouring down his back and under his armpits and streaming from his face. He was very hot in the sweater, the flannel shirt and the thermal underwear.

He kept running.

At the end of the tunnel he skidded to a halt.

Margaret Spicer had a knife in her right hand. It was braced across Fanny Mulrooney's throat just below the jaw line. Fanny's head was cocked back, and the woman's left hand was twisted in Mulrooney's hair.

"Drop the gun or I'll cut her dead, Culhane!"

Culhane looked at Mary Frances Mulrooney, then at the knife and at the woman who held it.

"Sonia Steiglitz, right? Ever listen to Hopalong Cassidy on the radio?"

The woman said nothing.

"Guess not. Anyway, Bill Boyd was always one of my favorites when I was a kid. Hoppy was the first really adult Western character, ya know."

"I'll kill her—drop that gun!"

"That's what made me think of Hoppy. I had this plate I used to love to eat off. It said 'Best wishes, Hoppy' on it. But getting back to the radio, a guy once told Hoppy to drop his guns. He had pearl-handled six-shooters, and he said something like, 'I won't drop these—I'll set 'em down.' "

Culhane stooped over slowly, setting the cocked and locked Detonics Scoremaster on the floor. As he looked up, he was inside the largest pyramid he could ever imagine.

"You and Hopalong Cassidy!" Mulrooney snapped.

"Wait'll you hear me get goin' on Windy and Lucky. That reminds me—next Christmas, get me a set of spurs, okay?"

"Quiet!"

Culhane looked at Sonia Steiglitz. Then he looked at Dr. Liebermann. The little man with the goatee stood on his right and held no weapon. Culhane wasn't sure. He looked back to Fanny Mulrooney. "Now when you get me those spurs, I want the good ones. Not the little dinky spikelike things that they use in English riding—"

"Quiet!" Sonia Steiglitz jerked back on Mulrooney's hair, brandishing the knife toward Culhane.

"But the kind with the big hard rowel at the back of your heel, Fanny, with the rowel at the back of your—"

Mulrooney did it, her left foot flashing out and snaking back, fast, into Sonia Steiglitz's left shin. Culhane's left hand shot out. He could see it, could see

Sean Dodge doing it, Sean Dodge who used the martial arts like a veritable Chuck Norris, Sean Dodge with his lightning reflexes, Sean Dodge. . . . Culhane's left connected hard with the interior of Sonia Steiglitz's right wrist, and she loosed her hold on Mulrooney's hair. Mulrooney's elbow hammered Sonia Steiglitz in the abdomen, causing the woman to roll back, but her hand still held the knife. Culhane wheeled to his right, the toe of his boot jabbing up and out as Sonia's knees buckled. He got her on the side of the head.

Culhane bounced on his foot as Sonia Steiglitz's head snapped to one side. His leg still extended, he back-kicked her in the side of the jaw, punching her body back and down, the knife skittering across the floor.

Her head started to rise. Culhane finished the turn, on both feet now, and began to move for her, but then her head dropped back.

"Josh!"

Culhane looked at Mulrooney, then followed her eyes. Dr. Liebermann was holding the Scoremaster.

Culhane wheeled toward him, his eyes on the .45's gaping muzzle.

"What do I do with this? I am only a consultant to the CIA—they never showed me how to use a gun."

"Give it to me." Culhane smiled. "Keep your finger off the trigger." Culhane reached for the gun, taking it gently. The safety was still on. He exhaled hard. Steiglitz and the others would be through the tunnel any minute. "Where the hell is Partridge?"

"I don't know," Mulrooney said, holding Sonia's knife in her right hand and picking up her own revolver from the floor with her left.

"When we rushed in here, Dr. Spicer came from that vault over there," Liebermann volunteered.

"She's Sonia Steiglitz. There probably is a Margaret Spicer someplace—probably in a shallow grave."

"I haven't seen Maurice, either," Mulrooney said.

"Wonderful," Culhane muttered. He looked up. The pyramid was vastly larger than the Pyramid of Cheops in Egypt, the glowing walls made from a strangely luminescent metal similar to that used in the tunnels. Along the lengths of the walls as far as he could see were the peculiar hieroglyphics and more of the ideograms, the picture writing. He looked all the way up to the apex of the pyramid. A cloud of vapor partially obscured the very top. Culhane guessed it was over seven hundred feet high. He could hear shouts from the tunnel.

"Come on—down toward that vault where Sonia came from!" he said.

"What about her?" Mulrooney insisted.

Sonia Steiglitz was unconscious or faking it; Culhane didn't know which, and there wasn't time to worry. "Keep her knife—she's declawed—and let's leave her. Now run for it!"

Pushing Liebermann ahead of him, Culhane glanced back toward the tunnel. Two of the CIA men with their Uzi submachine guns were just coming out. They aimed their weapons at Culhane and Mulrooney. Culhane fired two rounds from the Scoremaster toward them, then broke into a long-strided, loping run.

Submachine-gun fire hammered into the walls of the pyramid, ricocheting and whining around him like mosquitoes on a humid summer night. The vastness of the pyramid was confirmed as he ran across it. At its center, dominating the enormous space where nothing else at all was evident, stood a statue. More accurately, it was a group of statues forming one sculpture: an infant, a male child—human, lifelike—the child marching forward to a hulking, larger than human-sized male. The male stooped as if in worship. There were no horns on the infant, the boy or the bowing male. The adult male bowed before a huge figure of a human or humanlike female that was perhaps one hundred feet tall. Her face was upraised, her arms outstretched, and in her hands she held horns as if the horns were to be bestowed on the male bowed at her feet. And above her face and hair, above her head about one hundred more feet up toward the cloud of mist obscuring the pyramid's apex, was a crown in the shape of a halo, seven starbursts evident on it. And it stayed there in midair without wires or cords or supports. It was suspended. It defied gravity.

Culhane kept running.

Ahead of him, Mulrooney and Dr. Liebermann disappeared inside a triangular opening in the wall. Culhane finally reached the triangular entranceway, throwing himself through and rolling onto his knees as assault-rifle fire—distinguishable by its sharper crack—rained down near the chamber entrance.

Mulrooney was on her knees as well. In her lap she cradled Maurice's head. "It must've been Sonia. There's a knife wound in his back." Culhane was up, firing two shots toward the triangular doorway, then he ran to Mulrooney and the seaman. Culhane looked at Maurice's face, then bent over the man. Inches from Mulrooney's knee was a pool of blood. Culhane touched his left hand to Maurice's cheek. He closed the eyelids, saying, "He's dead, sweetheart—a good man."

Culhane looked at Mulrooney's eyes. Tears filled them as she bowed her head and looked away. Culhane touched his hand to her shoulder, then ran back through the chamber to the triangular entrance to the pyramid.

"They're coming!" Liebermann shouted.

"Terrific," Culhane rasped.

He looked around the chamber. The walls were covered with pictures of men with the heads of bulls. He peeked into the pyramid and watched as Wilbur, Steig-

litz and the others advanced. Indeed, there were innocent hostages; he could make out Angela Basque, Dr.
Rutgers, Dr. Cornblume and Janet Krull with one of
the CIA men across the pyramid near the tunnel from
the hangar bay.

Culhane fired three shots toward the far right wall
of the pyramid, toward Steiglitz and the CIA man, but
the distance was more than a hundred yards and he
missed. Steiglitz and the CIA man pulled back.

Culhane felt his own sweat. He could smell it.

He searched the musette bag and found the two
spare extension magazines for the Scoremaster. He
loaded one in the .45 and put the other in the pocket of
his Levi's. "Where the hell is Partridge?" he snapped,
working the .45's slide stop and the slide running forward, chambering a round. He upped the safety.

"He wasn't here. I don't know," Mulrooney called
back, resting Maurice's head on the floor. She took
the bandanna from her hair, unfolded it and covered
the dead man's face.

"Perhaps Mr. Partridge got away," Liebermann
suggested, crouched beside Culhane at the entranceway.

"Or maybe he's with them," Culhane answered.

"Keep an eye on the outside and let me know when
they're coming up again," he told Liebermann. "I can
try to hold 'em back."

Culhane stood up and studied the chamber. Whoever the aliens were or had been, they liked space, he
decided. Not outer space, but living space. There was
no clutter; the floor space was vast. He thought for a
moment that if he were seven feet tall or so, and horns
spread from both sides of his skull, he'd be tired of
bumping into things, too.

"I'm no archaeologist," said Mulrooney, who'd
walked up to Culhane and had taken his hand, "and
I'm no Egyptologist, but I'd be damned surprised if

these guys didn't have a lot to do with ancient Egypt. And that statue out there—the crown of stars just *is* there, like there's no gravity!''

Culhane nodded, biting his lip. The chamber they were in was apparently an entrance hall; there were more of the triangle-shaped doorways at its far end. ''Maybe those rooms there were quarters or laboratories or—hell, maybe storage rooms. Maybe they had laser guns like you see in the movies, and we could use those against Steiglitz,'' he told her. ''Hey, Dr. Liebermann—''

Liebermann turned from the entranceway, looking toward him. ''They are not coming. Perhaps they are holding back because of your expert marksmanship, or—''

''Yeah, it's *gotta* be somethin' else,'' Mulrooney teased.

Culhane just looked at her. She really knew how to hurt a guy.

Then he said to Liebermann, ''This way—let's check out those rooms back there. Come on!''

''Coming!'' said Liebermann, and he started jogging from the doorway.

''How does a guy his age do that? He was bushed on the way down....''

''I guess he got his second wind. Who knows?'' Mulrooney started walking toward the seven triangular entrances at the far end of the chamber.

Culhane started to run, passing her, and he heard Mulrooney start to run, too. He stopped at the nearest of the seven entrances. He heard a voice, faint but distinct: Partridge. ''Dr. Spicer, come in here and look at this!''

It came from one of the entranceways farther down. Mulrooney ran past him. ''Watch it, Fanny!'' Culhane rasped.

Partridge's voice came again, a little clearer now. ''What the hell was that shooting?''

The voice came from the third entrance. Culhane outdistanced Mulrooney, running through the entranceway into another tunnel. He kept running, the Scoremaster in his right fist.

"Dr. Spicer," Partridge called again.

Culhane skidded on his boot heels at the end of the tunnel and stopped. It was a vast laboratory, perhaps five thousand square feet. The walls formed a pyramid, rising high, but not nearly as high as the main pyramid. Culhane saw what looked like laboratory tables on which were containers. Partridge stood at the far end of the pyramid, beside one of the tables. He turned around. There was a gun in his right hand.

"You were doing all the shooting, huh?" he asked.

Culhane shouted back across the pyramid. "Only some of it. Dr. Fell is Jeremiah Steiglitz. I saw two of your guys working with him. Lieutenant Wilbur is working with him. And Margaret Spicer is Sonia Steiglitz. She's out cold with a sore jaw. Mulrooney's got her knife."

"Sonia Steiglitz—no shit. You should have killed her when you had the chance."

"And should I kill you?" Culhane called out. He heard Mulrooney's boot heels stop beside him, but he never took his eyes off Partridge.

"Kill me? Depends on who you're working for, I guess. Whoever these people were—or aliens—they were working on something and then just abandoned it. There's something like a burial vault down in the next room. Maybe that's why we don't see any demon skulls lying around. But somebody had to run it, to put the last body inside it—"

"You don't read much."

"I read your books, Mr. Culhane. I know you've got a little Detonics in a holster under your sweater behind your right hipbone—just like Sean Dodge."

Culhane looked at the gun in his hand. "And a big one in my fist—more than twice the barrel length of that little 66 snubby you've got. I can nail you from here.''

"I'll bet you can.''

"The translation," Culhane called. "The translation of the message the dead alien left under the map on Cumberland Island—''

" You read it to me." Partridge's voice created no echo. There should have been one, Culhane thought. But there was no echo from his own voice, either. The pyramid walls—what were they made of, that they could absorb sound?

"Whose side are you on, Partridge?''

Partridge, his gun still in his hand, was walking slowly toward him. "Whose side do you think I'm on? Steiglitz's? Just because I'm CIA? Because two of my men are working with him?''

Culhane's thumb worked down the .45's safety. "I always did." He raised the pistol to eye level, setting the sights on Partridge's chest. "I can't miss.''

"You think I set up your brother, right?''

"Yeah." Culhane felt his right fist tightening on his pistol. "I think you kept Steiglitz one jump ahead of him all the way, I think you—''

Mulrooney screamed. Culhane wheeled. There was a shot, then another, and Culhane fell back against the nearest lab table. One of the glasslike containers crashed to the floor but didn't shatter.

The little man with the goatee, Sonia's knife held in his right hand like a dagger, looked vaguely surprised as red stains blossomed on his chest and abdomen.

He fell facedown to the floor, the shattering of the lenses from his wire-rimmed glasses the only sound in the stillness.

Culhane looked at Mulrooney. Her eyes were wide open in terror. In her right hand the little stainless steel .38 was at gut level.

"There's your man from the CIA who worked for

Steiglitz," Partridge said. Culhane looked at the dead man at his feet. Partridge was still talking. "So let's get the hell out of here."

CHAPTER THIRTY-NINE

They had run to the farthest of the seven triangular entryways and raced down through the tunnel to its end.

Partridge, out of breath, panted, "I haven't been a field agent for a long time. Makes you wish you never got into overeating and sleeping late...." He sagged against the tunnel wall.

"I don't understand this," Mulrooney declared, still holding her gun.

"All right," Partridge said. "Only two guys in the Company knew what Mr. Culhane's brother was working on—me and the deputy director. I knew about Liebermann right after we got on board the submarine. You see, the deputy director had a heart attack the day before, and he died. It was his fourth heart attack. When I spotted Liebermann, well, I figured the deputy director had tagged him to come along. We knew each other in the days when he used to be a planner for Steiglitz. Anyway, Liebermann told me the deputy director had contacted him less than twenty-four hours before. That was impossible, because the deputy director was in a coma for more than thirty-six hours before his death. He couldn't have contacted Liebermann. One of the last things he did was contact the Navy and arrange for the *Churchill* to ferry us down here."

"Why the hell didn't you—"

"Kill nice old Dr. Liebermann? Well, for openers, in books—like you write—us CIA guys waste people right and left. But if I killed Liebermann, who was still on CIA payroll, my ass would have—" He flicked his eyes toward Fanny Mulrooney. "Sorry, miss."

Mulrooney didn't smile.

"Let's leave it that I would have been in hot water. I pegged him as doing something for Steiglitz, but I didn't know what. I also figured he wasn't alone in it. Since *I* wasn't feeding stuff to Steiglitz and *I* knew that, it had to be the deputy director. He was like this with Steiglitz in the old days." He raised the first and second fingers of his left hand, bringing them together tight.

Partridge looked behind them down the tunnel. "I'd say if we're gonna do anything, we'd better do it fast. We can talk while we try figuring our options, okay?"

Culhane nodded, starting into still another pyramid-shaped room. It was similar to the laboratory and about the same size. Massive tables and exotic machinery were everywhere.

"Fanny, you take the far side. I'll take the middle. Partridge—"

"Gotcha. Anything special we're looking for?"

"Weapons, maybe," Mulrooney sang out.

Culhane walked backward, looking down the tunnel, at any moment expecting Steiglitz and Partridge's rogue CIA penguins.

"Anyway," said Partridge, talking louder now, "since the deputy director—God rest his soul—had arranged for the *Churchill*, I figured maybe somebody on board the *Churchill* was with Steiglitz."

"Wilbur," Mulrooney called out.

"Yeah—Wilbur. So I hadda let 'em play out their string. I didn't have anything concrete on Liebermann, and I wanted to nail Steiglitz." Culhane's eyes met Partridge's. "Your brother—he was a good guy, an honest Fed. I wanted to nail Steiglitz, see, for getting Jeff, and nail it so tight even Steiglitz couldn't pry himself out."

Culhane nodded, still dividing his attention between the tunnel and the bizarre machinery. He could hear Mulrooney: "If I saw a laser gun or something, I don't know if I'd recognize it. This is weird stuff!"

"Hey," Partridge called out. "This is some kind of a gear, but the teeth are in the shapes of little dinky pyramids."

"Keep looking for something we can use against Steiglitz," Culhane advised.

And then Culhane heard Fanny Mulrooney scream.

He ran toward the nearest aisle between the tables, threading his way through them like a rat in a maze.

She was staring down at the floor, and Culhane stopped when he saw what she was staring at. Partridge hadn't told them everything. And, almost bitterly, Culhane thought, neither had his brother.

Culhane fingered the ring in his pocket—the death's-head—in German *Totenkopf*—ring.

On the floor at Mulrooney's feet were two bodies. One of the bodies wore the resplendent black uniform of an Obersturmbannführer of the SS death squads.

The flesh had not rotted. It was loose on the bones, but the bodies had been strangely preserved by the environment. The second body, beside the SS lieutenant colonel, was that of an enlisted man. Culhane did not know *Kriegsmarine* rank.

"Well, I'll be damned. They really did make it down here!"

Culhane crouched beside the dead SS man and looked up at Partridge. He took the ring from his pocket and held it up for Partridge to see. "I found this in the ice on the way down."

"What the hell is going on?" Mulrooney asked. "Nazis? In a forty-thousand-year-old starbase? Look at their faces."

Culhane studied the two men. Their faces showed shock and terror, the glazed-over eyes pinpoints of fear. They hadn't been trapped and starved; they hadn't died over a long period of time. The SS officer's uniform tunic was fully buttoned, the knot in his tie perfect. There was not even the usual five o'clock shadow found on the most clean-shaven of dead men. Culhane had researched that once for a book. After death, the beard keeps growing for a time. But here the beard growth had stopped.

"Something croaked these guys real fast and real good—whatever it was."

He heard Mulrooney repeat, "Whatever it was."

"There should be more of them, then," Culhane said. "And there aren't any other weapons in here. Let's try one of the other rooms." Both of the dead Nazis had pistols.

"What about Steiglitz and his people?" Partridge asked. "Are they still out there with Uzis and assault rifles?"

Culhane looked at Partridge again. "If Steiglitz had wanted to close in, he would have by now. He's waiting for something. Let's move." Culhane pulled Mulrooney and looked back at Partridge. The CIA man was starting to take the Iron Cross from the neck of the dead SS officer.

"What the hell are you doing?"

"D'ya know how much one of these'll bring in a World War II souvenir shop? I'll be right with ya."

Culhane grabbed Mulrooney's hand and started to run.

THE PYRAMID WAS NOT NEARLY AS LARGE as the main pyramid beyond the hangar bay, but it was about twice as big as the laboratory and the machine shop. He guessed it was the quarters for the base personnel. It looked to Culhane almost like a scout encampment. And the walls of this pyramid were adorned differently.

There were drawings of constellations. But they were unrecognizable, at least to Culhane.

But Mulrooney, her hands almost caressing one of the drawings on the lower surface of the wall beside her, whispered, "I think this is the Big Dipper."

"That's not the Big Dipper," Partridge declared. "My oldest boy's into astronomy, and it doesn't—"

"But I saw some computer-generated graphics once of what the Big Dipper would look like viewed from a distant star," Mulrooney insisted. "These are their pictures of home, Partridge. They were homesick." The last word was almost lost as she said it. Her voice cracked a little.

Partridge was walking toward some of the tablelike structures near the right-hand wall. Culhane started after him. Suddenly Partridge called out, "Two more navy guys, and one SS—the SS guy's a Scharführer—like a sergeant." Culhane reached Partridge, and they both looked down at the dead men. As with the other corpses preserved by this strange place, their eyes seemed to show something. Partridge dropped to a crouch and began removing the Iron Cross from the sergeant's neck. Culhane shrugged. If the sergeant had been Wehrmacht, just a soldier doing his duty, Culhane would have objected to the violation. But SS had always been scum, and death didn't change any of that. Like the others, these men had carried only pistols.

"Over here," Mulrooney shouted. Culhane took off toward her at a dead run. She was beside the far wall of the pyramid. He stopped a dozen yards from her. What she stared at, what he stared at, were more complete versions of the maps found on the cave walls at Cumberland Island.

He walked over to stand beside Mulrooney, still keeping an eye on the tunnel entrance. She began to speak. "These must have been long-distance aerial projections made before Antarctica shifted its position and became covered with ice."

"The base probably dates from before then—before the ice, I mean."

She turned to face him, and he looked down into her eyes. "But what happened to them all?"

Culhane had holstered his gun, and he put both hands on her shoulders. "I think except for that statue out there, 'The Three Ages of Alien'—" he smiled, but Mulrooney didn't "—except for that and these constellations.... Maybe they aren't pictures from home. Maybe all of this is a history. They used their knowledge, even as they acquired it, like an art form. Why hang pictures when you can hang ideas? Follow me?"

"But what happened to them?"

Maybe some disease, maybe...." He thought about the look in the eyes of the dead Nazis. "Maybe something else."

"Mr. Culhane!"

Culhane looked around. Partridge was beside the tunnel entrance. Culhane grabbed Mulrooney's hand and started to run with her.

He stopped beside Partridge at the tunnel entrance. There was no use hiding at the mouth of the tunnel.

There were too many of them.

Steiglitz, Sonia, the two CIA men and a dozen other men with M-16s were approaching. Lieutenant Wilbur stood at the head of the armed men. And he was smiling.

CHAPTER FORTY

Steiglitz shouted from the far end of the tunnel: "I can make no long-term promises, Mr. Culhane, but if you lay down your weapon—my daughter tells me you don't care to drop it—" there was a long pause "—if you do this and surrender, there will be no immediate harm to yourself, Miss Mulrooney, or even Mr. Partridge. Mr. Partridge and I were once friends."

Culhane could hear Partridge whisper, "Do what he says. Maybe he won't find your other piece. I got a few surprises, too."

"Why didn't you recognize him?" Mulrooney asked Partridge.

"Last time I saw him was five years ago. A full head of hair, mostly gray. The eye color was wrong with Fell, and he even changed his voice. So I blew it."

Culhane didn't look at him. "I'd say that."

"I have the answers you and Miss Mulrooney seek," Steiglitz shouted. "If you do not surrender, Lieutenant Wilbur will simply order my men ahead, and your meager weapons will be no match for assault rifles and submachine guns. If you do surrender, at least when death comes it will be quick and you will know the answers to your many questions."

"Don't do it," Mulrooney whispered.

"Do it—it's our only chance," Partridge urged.

Culhane raised his .45 above his head, then very slowly crouched, setting it on the tunnel floor. "If he starts his men shooting, run for it—back behind those tables where the three Nazis were."

He stood. The armed men did not advance. Steiglitz called out, "I am pleased. You have pleased me. And you shall know your answers."

Mulrooney set her gun down and so did Partridge.

"Oh, boy. . ." Culhane said under his breath.

CULHANE WAS THE FIRST TO BE TIED UP. By the time Partridge—the last one—was seated on the floor and Wilbur's men began tying Partridge's ankles, Culhane's wrists were already stiff. Culhane, Mulrooney, Partridge, Janet Krull and Harry Rutgers sat at the base of the towering statue in the giant pyramid just beyond the hangar bay.

Cornblume and Angela Basque held handguns. They were with Steiglitz.

Steiglitz stood before them, hands on his hips. "You need to shave your head again, Jeremiah," Partridge said with a laugh. "Your stubble's starting to show."

Steiglitz smiled. "You know, Calvin, I worried over that. I thought of dying my hair, but shaving it off seems to alter the face so much more." He bent forward, his left hand holding open his eye around the socket, his right hand cupped beneath the eye. He raised his head, then lowered it again, working on the left eye. "But these things—these contact lenses—I hate them. They served to alter my eye color, so, like shaving my head, changing my voice and affecting a slight limp, it was worth the discomfort to deceive you. And it all worked so well." Steiglitz laughed, a good- natured laugh, Culhane grudgingly admitted to himself.

"So!" Steiglitz began again. "I promised answers. And answers you shall have."

"What happened to the people here?"

"They were not people, Miss Mulrooney. They were humanoid creatures from a star system very far away. I'm afraid that without the detailed analysis of their wall writings and drawings, I cannot be more specific than that. And where did they go? That I can answer very handily. The answer, in fact, is the root cause of my being here after forty years of searching."

Steiglitz dropped to the floor in a cross-legged position, smiling as he spoke. "During World War II, I was a double agent for a time—with the full knowledge of the OSS, of course. It was really quite curiously coincidental how I came upon my discovery. Hitler was insane, as we all know, and he was also superstitious. There has been much recent conjecture as to how superstitious, how obsessed with the occult he actually was. Suffice it to say he felt there were mysteries in arcane studies that when brought to light would yield power. As his armies swept across Europe, he came into possession of a variety of interesting things, among these a very small museum in Poland and its treasures. In the basement was a papyrus scroll and a skull that seemed half human, half bovine. By sheer chance, during my stint as a double agent, I was forced to kill an SS officer who, like myself, was interested in such matters and a student of antique languages, and I came into possession of the scroll. The skull had been inadvertently destroyed. But the scroll, written in conventional Egyptian hieroglyphics, spoke of the god who had come from the cold lands of the south in a boat that soared out of the sun. It fascinated me, but I thought little more about it until the hapless Miss Chillingsworth brought me those first few pages of what I thought was the Gladstone Log and what you—'' he gestured broadly to Fanny Mulrooney, tied up beside Culhane ''—proved to be only the diary of her uncle. After the war, in my position with the OSS, I made it my concern to acquire records of Hitler's sorties after this arcane knowledge. He had sent men everywhere, poor devils. He had even sent men to Antarctica. Two expeditions. The first returned with reports of finding mysterious man-made caves of metal beneath the ice. They had no equipment and no instructions to explore them. Sheer chance had brought them to the source of the half-human, half-bovine skull. Or some other document that has since been lost. I'll never know. The second expedition never returned. They are the dead men you see here. Unfortunately, the coordinates of the tunnels were lost. To calculate the odds of two accidental findings of these tunnels would have been staggering. And the wealth necessary to mount such an expedition was beyond the reach of anything but a government.

''Whether or not there had been some document leading to the first expedition's discovery, as I indicated, I am uncertain. But from records I secured, I learned the names of eighteen survivors of that first expedition who had survived the war. I personally tortured each man before I murdered him, but no significant details were forthcoming except for the fact that after returning from that first expedition, the same officer led the second, taking twenty-one new men. The men who returned from the first expedition had suffered so greatly from exposure-related illnesses that they could not be sent back. Even the SS had a heart.'' Steiglitz laughed.

Culhane's stomach churned.

''Why didn't the first expedition go down into the tunnels?'' Mulrooney asked. ''If they found the tunnels, not exploring them was stupid.''

''A good question and one that annoyed me greatly. But it appears that they were looking for the lost continent of Atlantis. Now doesn't *that* sound stupid? Nobody had told them to look for tunnels leading under the ice—especially metal ones. And the one virtue of the true Nazi was following orders to the very letter. That was in 1937, and the papyrus scroll and the demon skull weren't discovered in Poland until 1939. The second expedition left shortly after that. I presume they never found Atlantis. In any event, alien spaceships and advanced technology interested me more greatly than Plato's ruminations.''

Steiglitz chuckled. ''The Nazi expedition employed the latest in high-frequency sound equipment, using it to search for irregularities under the ice that might have indicated some passageways beneath it. That's how they found the tunnels. History has repeated itself, so to speak. Apparently all the other tunnel mouths are so heavily covered with ice, finding their outlets was impossible. But this one, thanks to the perseverance of our friends aboard the *Madagascar*, well....''

Culhane eyed Steiglitz's daughter. She was looking at him, rubbing the bruise marks on both sides of her jaw. Her eyes read "hate," Culhane thought. Steiglitz and Sonia had found his second pistol after he had surrendered. They had found a second gun on Partridge also, a little Beretta Jetfire .25 in a crotch holster on a garter clip.

"Now to the specifics of where the aliens went, hmm?" Steiglitz looked directly at Mulrooney. Culhane watched her face; she looked afraid. Then he looked back at Steiglitz, who was smiling. "Since the skull found in the museum in Poland was originally from near Luxor in Egypt, we can assume, I think, that a number of things transpired. The maps on the wall of the Georgia cave, which you so fortuitously discovered with Mr. Culhane, show a world before the last great epoch of continental drift had ended. It was a time near the end, however. We can see why the continents are positioned where they are today; one can see how they separated. And it was approximately forty thousand years ago that Antarctica's climate changed. It didn't happen overnight, of course; it was a slow and gradual shift. So they—whatever they were—established a scientific research station here, or perhaps a military base. But the craft we see out there—" he gestured back toward the hangar bay area "—are not what it would seem likely they used to cross great interstellar distances. Sending three-man ships in a fleet would be senseless. Either the mother ship left them and later crashed or for some other reason failed to return, or they used some dimensional portal and for some reason couldn't go back through it. I think the former is more likely. You've seen the scientific laboratory in one of the seven chambers, and the machine shop. They were evidently trying to make something and couldn't."

"If there was a mother ship," Culhane noted, "and it crashed somewhere far from here...."

"Yes, go on—I've kept you alive because I respect your mind, sir!"

Culhane sucked in his breath, then continued. "If it crashed, that would account for a lot of things. Let's say they used something like radio to communicate, and it was useless at the protracted distances in space. So the mother ship set down this colony or base or research station—whatever it was. Most likely the maps were taken from a still-earlier craft—a fly-by, or maybe even an unmanned craft. Say the mother ship crashed into a chunk of rock in the asteroid belt or ran out of gas—"

Steiglitz laughed.

"Or something like that. All record of where the research station had finally been planted was lost."

"I think perhaps a war, or some other natural or alien-made catastrophe prevented other interstellar ships from searching for our former hosts, and they were stranded. And then the most interesting parts emerge...."

"The statue," Mulrooney murmured.

Culhane looked at her. She was looking up at the very human figure of the woman.

"Holy Jesus," Mulrooney whispered.

"Exactly. Or at least 'My God'—quite literally."

Mulrooney sounded strange when she spoke, Culhane thought. She was talking as if mentally writing, the words somehow flowing differently. "Faced with the possibility of total extinction, even given a vastly longer life-span than mankind perhaps, the space travelers sought at once to preserve and continue their race. Two steps were taken: the mummification of the body to preserve cell structure for some future date when the body could be revivified, and the mating with early human females."

"Very good, Miss Mulrooney, very good. But a step further. I believe that somewhere here are contained tapes—electromagnetic depositories of the minds of these creatures—so that when the bodies were revivified, the minds would be intact."

"Aww, come on," Culhane growled. "That's right outta Flash Gordon or something."

"I may be proved wrong, but I think not," Steiglitz said. "Their people traveled here, and some of them never returned home, perhaps because of the breakdown of equipment too long without replacement parts or, more likely, the ego-satisfying idea of being treated as gods. A hardcore group stayed here, and they died. I venture to say that the burial vault in the second chamber there—" he gestured to the far side of the pyramid "—contains one or two bodies that are not mummified, not preserved. The processes of mummification, as practiced by the Egyptians, were handed down over the millenia—and botched up, I might add, so they preserved the heart and destroyed the brain. Mummies—"

"You're crazy!" Culhane cut in. "What the hell are you talking about? We haven't found any mummies of these guys—"

"Hardly crazy, Mr. Culhane—and your hyperbole is getting a bit wearisome. But the mummies of those who ventured forth from here, if mummification were indeed possible under their individual circumstances, have simply not yet been unearthed. Perhaps they're in the snow-covered Himalayas, or in an untrekked jungle near some forgotten Mayan temple. Perhaps beneath the Great Pyramid in Egypt. Some of those locations may well become evident after we decipher the secrets here."

"The *Churchill*'s rescue party—it'll come for us, find the tunnel...." Partridge began.

Steiglitz laughed. "Lieutenant Wilbur was engineering officer of the *Churchill*. Does that suggest something to any of you, to any of you at all?"

Culhane verbalized what he had suspected. "Wilbur sabotaged the *Churchill*."

"Blew so many holes in her hull, nobody'll ever find the pieces," Wilbur said and smiled.

Dr. Janet Krull, tied up on the other side of Partridge, began to sob.

Dr. Rutgers said something that however sincere, sounded terribly trite to Culhane; it was a line right out of an old B movie. "You'll never get away with this, Fell—or Steiglitz or whoever you are."

Sonia Steiglitz walked over to Rutgers, stopped in front of him and spat in his face. "My father *has* gotten away with this, Dr. Rutgers," she snarled.

"Sonia, please—you have such a vile temper," Steiglitz remarked. "All hope is lost to you—to you all. Your lives are dependent on my whim and my whim alone. I can shoot you now, can turn you over to Sonia who has this obsession with hurting things, causing pain—"

"I want her."

Culhane looked at Sonia. She was staring at Mulrooney. And then her eyes shifted.

"And I want him." Her knife flashed into her right hand, the point of it suddenly against Culhane's throat. "I'm going to hang him up from something and skin him alive and tie her under him so she drowns in his blood!"

"Why don't you just beat him to death with your bag of quarters, you two-bit slut!" Mulrooney raged.

The pressure of the knife blade was gone, and Culhane saw Sonia arc the knife toward Mulrooney's face. "Damn you—no!" Culhane shouted.

Steiglitz's voice was very quiet, very calm. "Not now, Sonia. I have a research project in mind that involves Mr. Culhane and Miss Mulrooney. Death or disfigurement would ruin my plans to get Mr. Culhane's assistance by using Miss Mulrooney as a wedge."

Sonia held the knife less than an inch from Fanny Mulrooney's right eye. Fanny had fallen back to the floor of the pyramid. Sonia didn't move her hand, and

Mulrooney didn't scream or cry. Culhane knew she'd said what she'd said to save him.

"Your father's right," Culhane said to Sonia, and then he looked up at Steiglitz. "She touches her with that knife or anything else, and you can just go ahead and kill me right now. I wouldn't give you the time of day."

"Sonia," Steiglitz repeated, "obey me—now!"

Sonia moved the knife, leaving Mulrooney lying on the floor.

"What do you want from me?" Culhane asked Steiglitz.

Steiglitz puffed again on his pipe. The tobacco smelled good, Culhane thought. "I spoke of ultimate power, and I have it within my grasp. But I must also keep it. You've no doubt surmised, Mr. Culhane, Miss Mulrooney—and perhaps you as well, Calvin—" he looked at Partridge, then back to Culhane "—that the research vessel so nearby that Lieutenant Wilbur spoke of is my ship. These additional personnel are my men from that ship. When it is learned that the *Churchill* is down, the possibility exists that military power may be dispatched to Antarctica to investigate. The possibility also exists that some connection between my ship and the demise of the *Churchill* might be suspected. I don't need the ship. All the supplies we'll need to sustain ourselves here have been flown in by helicopter already or will be soon. The hull of my research vessel is fitted with explosives and will soon detonate. No traces will be left behind; no one in the world above will be left alive to share my secret. I have a crew of men working at the face of the tunnel, winching down the supplies. And those men will soon join us. Yet the possibility of needing to defend this establishment before I have full mastery of the knowledge contained here does exist. Therefore, I intend to utilize the fleet of alien aircraft to do my bidding. They would be superior to any weapon anyone could hurtle against me, and this pyramid would doubtless survive even a nuclear explosion. We are invulnerable here, and the spaceships shall be our defense.''

"No offense meant," Culhane began, "but you're nuts. How the hell are you going to fly one of those things?''

"No offense taken—luckily for you, Mr. Culhane. While you and Miss Mulrooney and Mr. Partridge were wandering around in those chambers, finding dead Nazis and picking up Iron Crosses as souvenirs—" he smiled, looking at Partridge "—I was more productively employed. In preparation for this day, I have developed over the years the most intimate of familiarities with Egyptian writing. After you so kindly provided the photographs of the writing beneath the wall maps in the Cumberland Island caves, I studied them. Using the computer on board the *Churchill*, plus my own prior knowledge, I developed what I would label as an adequate reading skill in the language of our dead alien friends. Such can be done, I assure you, when one has sufficient intellectual gifts and the right tools with which to work. Fortunately, I possessed both. I discovered, admittedly with some difficulty, that I could read the control panels on the ships. And, amazingly, there are no physical controls—rudder pedals, throttles and the like.''

"Like Dr. Liebermann intimated," Mulrooney said. Culhane just looked at her.

"Did he mention that?" Steiglitz asked. "A brilliant man, Liebermann. I shall mourn his loss." Then his smile died. "However, with the help of Dr. Basque, an accomplished engineer as well as an astronomer, and Dr. Cornblume who is nearly as skilled in the reading of hieroglyphics as am I, I anticipate having one of the ships operational. Hopefully quite soon.''

"What about fuel for the damned things?" Partridge asked.

"It's a different type of power source," Angela Basque supplied. "I imagine that the ships were kept refueled and ready in the event they were needed. The significant likelihood exists that the ships can still be flown."

"Bullshit," Mulrooney snapped.

"Hardly," Steiglitz answered.

"What do you need me for?" Culhane said, almost afraid to ask.

"Your penchant for realism in your books. I've never bothered reading them, but I had them read while I was researching you. You're quite an accomplished pilot, Mr. Culhane: fixed wing, helicopter, even jet qualified. I can see why you write so many books. You must spend a fortune doing all these things before your rather stupidly heroic Sean Dodge does them in your books."

"It's a living," Culhane said.

"I have helicopter pilots available, and I myself am qualified on jets, but why risk my own life or the life of one of my men? And think of the thrill of being the first man to fly an alien spacecraft."

Culhane swallowed hard. The light in Steiglitz's eyes was insanity, not brilliance. "And what's to stop me from flying the thing out of here, assuming I can fly it? Or using it against you?"

Steiglitz smiled. "Sonia, very neatly cut off Miss Mulrooney's right ear at the count of three. One. . . ."

"HE PROBABLY WON'T BE ABLE to get the old crates started anyway," Culhane whispered.

"If he does, and you can fly the things, well, forget about me—just get out of here," Fanny Mulrooney said.

Culhane looked at her right ear—it was still there. He had agreed to fly the spacecraft or die trying before Steiglitz had counted to the number three. He remembered the look in Sonia's eyes—disappointment. He swallowed hard, trying to make the vision of the wild beast look in Sonia's eyes leave him. It wouldn't.

They were still bound at the foot of the massive statue, guarded at some distance by three men with M-16s, men Culhane presumed to be from the research vessel. Wilbur's homing beacon had obviously been left to guide them in rather than alert the submarine rescue party.

He thought about the men aboard the *Churchill*: Macklin, Hardestey, all the men who read his books, such as Bob, the chief of ship. A lot of fans were dead. Sean Dodge owed them something, and so did he.

"Maybe what killed those Nazis will get Steiglitz." It was Partridge speaking, interrupting Culhane's reverie.

"I can't understand why he wasn't more worried about that," Mulrooney mused.

"What did those Nazis everyone's been mentioning look like? What killed them, I mean?" Janet Krull asked.

Culhane shrugged. Maybe she would understand it. "Just dead—instantly—as if whatever happened, happened so fast there was no time to react. And one funny thing we noticed—unless it has to do with the pyramid here—is that there was no beard growth after death like there normally would be."

Dr. Rutgers asked, "Were there any marks on their bodies—maybe some burn marks—as if they'd touched something that had been running a power charge or something?"

"Not a mark on 'em," Partridge said definitively.

"He's right," Mulrooney said. "And it doesn't make any sense."

"Heart failure—maybe a stroke," Janet Krull said, sounding to Culhane as if she was merely thinking out loud.

"It's like the curse of King Tut's tomb," Mulrooney

whispered. "When Lord Carnarvon died in Egypt, his dog, which was thousands of miles away in England, howled and fell over dead at the same instant. Like something reaching out to strike down the intruders who defiled the—"

"Intruders," Culhane cut in. "Intruders...."

"I've read enough Takers books to know whenever Sean Dodge talks like that, he's onto something for sure," Partridge said.

Culhane licked his lips. He looked at Partridge, then at Krull and Rutgers, then at Mary Frances Mulrooney. "You just told me what happened. It's the only explanation. It has to be—"

"What?" he heard Partridge ask.

But Culhane still looked at Mulrooney. "Remember you kept telling me that I was trying to memorize the submarine? Well, I was. I asked Macklin and Hardestey every question I could think of. It was Macklin who told me. If something happened, and the *Churchill* were boarded or taken over—like what happened to the U505, the German submarine our guys captured during World War II—they had an intruder-defense mechanism. Macklin could throw one switch from several different spots throughout the ship, and the only way to counteract the system was for Macklin, Wilbur and the chief of ship to put together nine numbers in the right sequence. Each had memorized six. And the numbers worked like a combination to shut off the system. That's what this is."

"You lost me," Rutgers said.

Culhane looked at him. "Okay. Suppose everything we've been conjecturing about these alien guys is pretty much true: only a small group stayed behind here, and eventually they were all dead. The last couple of guys would have activated an intruder-defense system. Just think about it. The reason they'd want themselves mummified was so they could be revivified maybe—

and perhaps even what Steiglitz said about somehow recording their minds is true. Who knows? If they could fly here from another star system more than forty thousand years ago, maybe they could do that, too. But they valued the idea of being revivified. So they wouldn't want anybody messing with their bodies and destroying the pyramid—and if somebody did, *whammo!*''

"You mean—" said Mulrooney.

He twisted around to see her better. "Macklin told me that what happened with the *Churchill*'s system was a two-pronged defense. Once he activated the system, all compartments would be flooded with a gas. He couldn't tell me what kind, but it would even penetrate clothing, so a gas mask wouldn't do an intruder any good. But Macklin, Wilbur and the chief of ship all had a pill they could pop, which would counteract the effects of the gas, and they'd wake up a couple of hours before everyone else. But in the meantime, after the gas was expended, say somebody got aboard with the right protective clothing, or he beat the combination for deactivating the system out of all three men, but one of the numbers was given wrong, if he tried to deactivate the system or touched the maneuvering gear the reactors would blow up and destroy the ship.''

"There's something like that here?" Partridge whispered.

Culhane looked at him. "The Nazis were killed by the aliens' intruder-defense system. The system was probably set for some kind of delay to allow whoever found an intruder— like more aliens, like the guy who died on Cumberland Island—enough time to find the spot in the pyramid where the system could be deactivated. If after some time elapsed—who knows how long, maybe a few hours—and the system still hadn't been deactivated, then *whammo!* The intruder couldn't be one of the aliens and would be killed.''

"Then you think the Nazis were gassed?" Janet Krull asked.

"Maybe—or it was something like a gas."

"If the system was activated once we got inside the hangar bay..." Partridge started.

Culhane couldn't see his wrist to read the Rolex. "I make it we've been in here for about three hours or so."

"The earth always rotated at the same speed—nearly a perfect twenty-four hours in one day—so if they divided the day into twenty-four hours like we do..." mused Mulrooney.

"But they could have divided the same period of time a dozen different ways," Culhane told Mulrooney.

"There's an element of truth in what Miss Mulrooney suggests," said Rutgers. "Of course, a segment of time could be constructed containing 180 of our minutes, and then, of course, there would be eight 'hours' in a day. But the apparent origin of the twelve hours of day and twelve hours of night dates to ancient Egypt before the building of the Great Pyramid. So the twenty-four-hour day goes back at least forty-six hundred years—perhaps longer. And the hour being divided into sixty minutes is from the Babylonians using a number base of sixty. So perhaps there was interaction between the two groups—"

Culhane interrupted him. "But when this starbase was built, there were no Egyptians or Babylonians or any kind of civilization. These guys were functioning on a time system of their own. What if...."

"What if what?" Mulrooney asked impatiently.

"These guys seemed obsessed with the number seven. The measurements of the spaceship were based on their height—seven feet more or less, right? Seven tunnels out of the hangar bay, seven chambers beyond the main pyramid here. What if they broke up the time it takes for the earth to complete one rotation into seven subdivisions? Then in our minutes, each one would be—" He looked at Mulrooney, who raised her eyebrows and shrugged her shoulders. Another English major was just what he needed at the moment.

"Each seventh of the twenty-four-hour solar day would be roughly 205.7 minutes. I can figure it more exactly for you," said Rutgers.

"How many times does sixty..." Mulrooney started.

"Three hours and twenty-five minutes—but again, that's an approximation," Rutgers answered.

"Let me see your watch," Mulrooney said suddenly, bending over, losing her balance and bumping against Culhane. "Let me see your watch."

Culhane twisted on the floor, losing his own balance and slumping forward.

"I—I can see it. Holy—"

"What is it?" Culhane asked her.

"We've been in here almost three and a half hours."

Punctuating her words was a thunderous noise. Culhane had never heard the sound of a UFO's engines firing up before, but somehow he knew it when he heard it. And touching the aircraft would be like touching the sub's maneuvering gear; it would activate the second and final part of the intruder-defense system. Very final, Culhane thought.

CHAPTER FORTY-ONE

"For the last fifteen minutes, I've been working on my hands. Almost got the ropes cut from my wrists," Partridge announced.

The engine noise had died after what Culhane guessed to be five minutes' duration.

"You think he actually made it fly?" Mulrooney gasped.

Culhane nodded. He'd been working on his hands as well, but he couldn't budge the knots. "You got stuff then, Partridge? They didn't clean you?"

"Had an A.G. Russell Sliver sewn into my shirt sleeve on the seam alongside the open part. It took me ten minutes to get the damn thing out so I could use it. And there's one of those Freedom Arms .22 mag boot pistols taped against the inside of my left thigh—if I can get to it."

Culhane looked up, still slumped on the floor. Steiglitz, Sonia, Wilbur and some of the others were coming across the base of the pyramid, coming toward them. "He's going to want you to fly that thing," Mulrooney said.

Culhane licked his dry lips. "Partridge, don't try anything now. Wait until they get me by the passageway into the hangar bay, then I'll create a disturbance. Your hands almost free?"

"In another minute, maybe."

"You get to that gun, and get Fanny and Dr. Krull someplace fast. You and Dr. Rutgers—"

"No!" Mulrooney almost screamed it.

"Do as I say, Fanny. Maybe Partridge can find a way to—"

"No! I'll blow the whistle on the whole thing, I swear to God I will!"

Culhane twisted his head to see her. "He's gonna kill all of us. Maybe this way some of us have a little chance. He'll keep me alive to fly his damned spaceship. Maybe we can parlay it into something. We gotta try!"

"He'll kill you!"

Before Culhane could say anything, Partridge—his voice a hoarse whisper—said, "All I gotta do is give a good hard tug and I got my hands free—I think. I didn't graduate from CIA spy school for nothing. What about this doomsday device or whatever it is?"

"The intruder-defense system," Mulrooney supplied lifelessly.

"Yeah, the intruder-defense system," Partridge repeated. "And how come Jeremiah Steiglitz isn't worried about it?"

"If we're right and Dr. Rutgers figured his minutes right, it should start anytime now. And Steiglitz is too preoccupied with playing master of the world to worry about it. He's nuts."

Steiglitz was walking briskly beside his daughter at the head of the group. He was almost within earshot now, Culhane guessed. "Remember, Fanny—do what I say!"

He looked at her once more. She closed her eyes and touched her lips to his arm.

CULHANE REMEMBERED THE LOOK in Mulrooney's eyes after his hands and feet had been untied and he'd been taken away. It was as if she thought she'd never see him again. And now, walking ever nearer to the tunnel leading to the hangar bay, waiting to make a move and create a diversion, he would have taken bets Mulrooney was right.

"If you intend some noble sacrifice, Mr. Culhane... well, I wouldn't. If you crash the ship into the hangar bay, it will only succeed in killing yourself and not me. And I will most assuredly turn Miss Mulrooney over to my daughter's tender care for disposition. If you crash the ship outside the tunnel—on the ice or in the sea—I will do the same. If, however, you execute your assigned task faithfully, you have my personal assurances that my daughter, Sonia, will not be indulged, that you and Miss Mulrooney and all of the others will be given swift and merciful deaths. That is my word as a gentleman. Hopefully, you'll accept it in the spirit in which it is given."

Culhane looked at Steiglitz. Steiglitz had both of Culhane's pistols in his belt.

Culhane wheeled, his foot snaking out into a double kick against Steiglitz's crotch. He finished the turn, the knife edge of his hand swiping against the side of Steiglitz's face but missing the neck and the chance to kill him.

The nearest guard with the M-16 started to swing up the muzzle. Culhane wheeled again, kicking against the M-16's front handguard, deflecting the rifle. A long burst started, Culhane feeling the sound more than hearing it, feeling the hot brass as he swung back, slapping the weapon to keep the muzzle away. He reached up and out, getting to the gunman's Adam's apple, his fingers closing tight as he crushed the larynx. Sonia Steiglitz screamed and ran toward him with Wilbur and the others.

He wouldn't make it, he realized.

There was a shot from the statue: Partridge and his little gun. Culhane knew that Partridge couldn't hit anything at the range, but Sonia turned, shouting orders to Wilbur and the men with her.

Culhane jumped toward Steiglitz, who wrenched the Scoremaster from his belt. Culhane's body crashed against him, his right hand hammering up into Steiglitz's face, his left hand finding Steiglitz's throat. Suddenly he felt a nauseating wash of pain. He doubled up, rolling, his hands covering his testicles.

Steiglitz was up, both pistols gone from his belt, and Culhane heard gunfire as he wriggled across the floor toward the dead guard's body. Culhane grabbed for the M-16—

All gunfire stopped. All motion ceased. There was a scream, a scream more hideous than any Culhane had ever heard, more horrible than he could ever imagine originating from a human throat. Something in the voice made him remember Angela Basque's scream when she had been attacked by the leopard seal on the ice. It was Angela Basque who screamed, but it was a different scream.

And then the scream stopped.

Dr. Cornblume came running from the triangular tunnel entryway leading to the seven chambers. He was shouting at the top of his lungs: "It killed all of them—it killed—it killed—"

"It?" Culhane whispered. He picked up the M-16. His own two pistols were on the floor where Steiglitz had dropped them. The two Detonics .45s in his left hand, Culhane fired a burst from the M-16 with his right, locking the buttstock against his hip. Sean Dodge was a better shot, he reflected bitterly. The burst missed, Sonia Steiglitz shouting more orders rather than falling down dead.

And Jeremiah Steiglitz now had an M-16 in his hands. Culhane rammed both pistols into his belt, firing as Steiglitz fired. But Culhane's M-16 was empty. Culhane threw down the rifle and threw himself to the floor, the wall where his head had been taking the long burst of .223s. Culhane pushed himself to his feet and ran into the tunnel.

There were three men running toward him from the hangar bay at the other end of the tunnel. Both Detonics pistols in his hands, Culhane raised the Scoremaster in his right, firing. One man went down. Assault-rifle fire spewed from the other two men. Culhane threw himself to the tunnel floor, firing both pistols simultaneously, and another of the men went down.

The third and last man fired, the burst exploding on Culhane's left. Culhane rolled right, firing both pistols, emptying the Scoremaster and the little Detonics Combat Master almost simultaneously.

The man went down.

Culhane pushed himself to his feet. "Watch Sean

Dodge try and do that," he gasped. Then he started to run. Both his pistols were empty, and his musette bag had been taken; he was out of ammo. As he ran, he holstered both pistols, after working the slide stops to close the actions.

He skidded to a halt at the nearest of the three dead men and picked up an M-16. There were two spare 30-round magazines in a pouch on the guy's belt. Suddenly a face appeared at the pyramid side of the tunnel. Culhane opened fire, and the face pulled back. The M-16 was empty. Culhane rammed one of the fresh magazines up the well, then ran toward the hangar bay. If there were more men out there, they'd be up his back in a minute, he thought.

He snatched up another M-16 and two more magazines, stuffing those in his belt and holding the other spare in his left hand. He passed up the last M-16, but he took the magazine from the weapon, snapped off the last round in the chamber, then picked up the two spares.

With five spares, one partially loaded spare, a full magazine in one rifle and a partially spent one in the other, Culhane reached the hangar bay end of the tunnel.

Steiglitz's men were coming from the launch tunnel leading up to the surface. One carried an armload of boxes; the other carried two rifles and a box. Culhane shot the man with the rifles first, then the other one.

He knew that more men might come down the launch tunnel at any moment.

Culhane started back up the tunnel, racing toward the pyramid with one rifle slung across his back, the other in his hands.

When he reached the end of the tunnel, he looked at the statue at the center of the massive pyramid. He could see Partridge—somehow he'd gotten an M-16— cut down two men as Sonia prodded them out from the triangular entryway to the seven chambers.

"Partridge! I'll cover you! Send 'em out toward the tunnel here—one at a time!" Culhane shouted.

Mulrooney called back. "I found my purse! And your purse, too!"

"Shit," he rasped to himself. He didn't have a purse—it was a musette bag.

Partridge yelled. "Here we go!" Mulrooney ran first, her pistol in her right hand. Culhane didn't know what she was shooting at, but she was shooting, anyway.

"Hurry up!" Culhane screamed at her, firing the M-16 in his hands toward the far side of the pyramid and the entryway to the seven chambers. The range was ridiculous; it was hundreds of yards. He knew he couldn't hit them, but they couldn't hit him, either. Mulrooney was halfway to him, and Culhane felt what he always made Sean Dodge feel: the hairs on his neck suddenly coming erect.

He wheeled around. Two men were coming up behind him through the tunnel from the hangar bay and behind them were a dozen more.

"Dammit!" he shouted, firing the M-16's magazine into them, dumping the empty as he started to run, ramming a fresh one in as he shouted to Mulrooney. "Go back! We're cut off! Go back!"

Running forward but looking behind him, he fired the M-16 toward the hangar bay tunnel. Assault-rifle fire was coming at him from the tunnel mouth.

He looked ahead of him. Mulrooney had dropped into a stylized combat crouch and was firing her two-inch snub-nosed .38. Hitting anything with it at that range was a sheer impossibility, especially the way she handled a gun. "Run, Fanny, dammit! Run!"

Men were running from the triangular entrance to the seven chambers, and Culhane fired a burst from his M-16 toward them. Mulrooney ran back toward the statue as Culhane ran after her.

Partridge was firing the M-16, firing toward the entrance to the seven chambers. Culhane looked behind him and saw faces of Steiglitz's men peering out from the hangar bay tunnel, weapons pointing toward him. He fired a burst, and there was answering fire as he ran on.

Mulrooney was safe at the statue—he could see her.

Gunfire came from behind him. He threw himself into a run, his mouth open, gulping air. Gunfire slammed into the pyramid wall far to his right and the pyramid floor beneath his feet. As he ran, he saw Partridge standing up and shooting.

Culhane could see it almost in freeze frame: Partridge taking the hit, stumbling back, the assault-rifle burst firing toward the magically suspended crown.

The crown was rising. It seemed perhaps a hundred feet higher than it had been.

Partridge fell back, and Mulrooney fired her revolver again.

Culhane skidded across the floor like a base runner sliding into home, slamming into the base of the statue.

Rutgers had a pistol and was crouched behind the portion of the statue with the adult male bowing before the woman about to bestow the horns. He fired the pistol—a .45—three times.

"Save your ammo!" Culhane shouted. He rolled onto his back, firing between his legs with the M-16. Men were advancing from the hangar bay tunnel, but they fell back when Culhane dropped one. The M-16 was empty, and Culhane rammed a fresh magazine up the well, unshouldering the other weapon. Mulrooney dragged Partridge back by his feet to the shelter of the statue. Partridge was moving, but his chest was soaked with blood. "Mr. Culhane—we're trapped here," he groaned.

Culhane shouldered his M-16, firing toward the entryway. "No shit? Just 'cause you got shot, don't think you can state the obvious and get away with it!" And then Culhane looked at Mulrooney. "How is he?"

"How should I know? I'm no nurse," she cried.

"I know," Partridge said weakly and coughed, some blood dripping from the corner of his mouth. "It's called a sucking chest wound. Pretty soon—if I don't bleed to death first—I'll go into shock. I think my left lung is collapsed."

Culhane skidded on his knees to be beside Partridge.

He looked at the wound. Culhane had seen men die before, and Partridge looked just like them. The man's skin was gray. "Listen, that dame Angela Basque—I haven't seen her since there was that scream. And Dr. Cornblume—Sonia Steiglitz cold-cocked him to shut him up. I think the thing started—the intruder-defense system." Partridge labored for breath.

Culhane nodded. "The crown with the seven star-bursts above the statue is up about maybe another hundred feet. I don't know why."

"Maybe it's part of the system," Rutgers called out.

"Maybe," Culhane said. He didn't see Janet Krull. He looked at Mulrooney. "Where's Dr. Krull?"

"When the guards came and Mr. Partridge shot one of them and got his rifle—" she gestured to three bodies perhaps twenty yards from the statue "—she ran off toward that other passageway under that little triangle. I shouted after her that some of Steiglitz's men were down that way, but I didn't hear anything after she left—no gunfire—nothing."

Culhane nodded. At the third side of the pyramid was a triangular entryway, but this one was smaller, only about three feet high. Culhane had seen it earlier and dismissed it.

Partridge was coughing again. Culhane looked down at him, then said to Mulrooney, "Remember that time I took you shooting—the time we took the rifles?''

"Yeah...."

"Take that other assault rifle. On the left side of the receiver there's a lever. Move that lever into the spot for Semi and fire at those guys back by the hangar bay tunnel, then fire at the other guys over near the seven chambers.''

"Gotcha," she answered. He moved his hands to Partridge's face and thumbed the eyelids closed. He'd liked Calvin Partridge.

Culhane searched the floor near the statue and spotted his musette bag. He crawled over to it, hearing gunfire hitting the statue. Shots came from both the opening to the seven chambers and the hangar bay tunnel.

He reloaded both his pistols as he talked to Mulrooney and Dr. Rutgers. "If Janet Krull never came out of there—that little entrance—either she's dead or maybe she found a way out.

"They can't rush us without a lot of them getting killed if you both use the assault rifles. Just fire single shots, a little at a time—no full-auto at all. We're not made of ammo." There were five loaded spares on the floor beside the base of the statue. Partridge had probably taken them from the dead men. Those plus the spares Culhane now pulled from his belt still didn't change the odds that much. He handed the spares to Mulrooney. "Think you can reload one of these rifles? The magazine catch is over here," he said, showing her.

"Yeah, I can do it."

"Whack the base of the magazine good and hard when you put the new one in. Otherwise the thing won't feed right. I'm going over to see what's beyond that smaller triangle. Don't worry about covering me. I should be pretty much out of range for those guys, anyway. Just keep 'em back.''

"What if . . ." Mulrooney started to ask.

"Don't worry, we'll figure out something," Culhane said. "I'll be back in five minutes or so, whether I find something or not. Ready?"

Mulrooney nodded, then leaned toward him, kissing him full on the lips. "Be reckless, huh?"

Culhane felt himself grinning at her. "You bet." Then he was up, running toward the smaller triangle, the one through which Janet Krull had disappeared.

He could hear Mulrooney and Dr. Rutgers firing behind him. He kept running, hearing gunfire from the tunnel and the entrance to the seven chambers, but he was out of range.

He reached the smaller triangle, breathless, the big Detonics Scoremaster in his right fist, the safety down, the hammer up. He started through into the tunnel behind the triangular doorway, his shoulders hunched, his knees bent as he half crawled, half walked forward. He could imagine the difficulties one of the horned aliens would have had.

He could see Janet Krull at the end of the tunnel. There was a chamber there that seemed to be some sort of powerhouse. He could hear the faint hum of something, hear the crackle of static. She was on her knees.

Culhane called to her, "Dr. Krull—Janet!"

Her hands covered her face. She turned to him and slowly lowered her arms. Her hands were blood-covered as she moved them, her face ripped and torn, as was her neck and chest. Her blouse was torn open and drenched with blood. He kept moving toward her. "What happened?"

"They're dead! Steiglitz's men—Nazis—men with the horns of bulls—all dead!" She screamed the words, and he knew what happened. She had gouged her nails into her own flesh, ripping at it, screaming. There was a flash of light from beyond the end of the tunnel, and Culhane shielded his eyes from it. He heard Janet Krull scream. He glanced back, then crawled closer to her through the tunnel. He looked at her face, past the self-inflicted gouge marks, to her eyes. They were fixed, dead—like the eyes of the Nazis. Beyond her—dead men and two dead aliens. The final guardians of the pyramid? And from behind him, in the main hall of the pyramid, he heard another scream. Only this time it was Mary Frances Mulrooney.

Culhane half crawled, half ran back out of the tunnel. If it was the intruder-defense system he'd seen what it could do. He'd seen the wide-eyed faces of sudden death.

He reached the end of the tunnel. Rutgers was firing his M-16 and actually hit one of the men running wildly from the triangle that formed the entrance to the seven chambers. There were flashes of light throughout the great vault of the pyramid, and as the flashes came, men screamed and died. Where the light didn't flash, the men ran.

Culhane looked up to the starburst crown above the statue. It was nearly to the apex of the pyramid now, partially obscured by the gray-white cloud of mist that hung there.

He jumped from out of the tunnel exit, running back toward Mulrooney and the base of the statue. "Let's get out of here! Make for the hangar bay tunnel!" The flashes were popping everywhere now. When Culhane was beside the statue, he grabbed Mulrooney, who had her purse over her left shoulder and an M-16 in her right hand.

He could see Steiglitz, Sonia and a dozen of their men. There was a flash of light, and three figures some distance behind Steiglitz and the others died instantly and sank to the pyramid's floor.

"What the hell is this?" Mulrooney cried.

"I don't know, Fanny. Just run for it!" Culhane holstered his pistol, then wrenched the M-16 from her

right hand and shouted to Rutgers, "Take another rifle and the spare magazines! Come on!" Holding Mulrooney's hand in his left hand, and the M-16 in his
right, Culhane started to run again. Flashes of light
from nowhere were accompanied by screams of mortal
agony.

Culhane could see Steiglitz reaching the hangar bay
tunnel. He, Sonia and Wilbur disappeared inside, five
men running after them. A flash of the brilliant light
exploded, and the men went down, at least one of
them screaming.

Suddenly Culhane felt a trembling in the floor
beneath him, a rumbling shudder in the very fabric of
the pyramid itself. He looked back to the statue and to
the crown, which had passed through the cloud and
seemed almost to touch the apex of the pyramid. The
trembling and shaking increased, a groaning sound
coming from the luminescent metal walls themselves.

They were nearly to the hangar bay tunnel when
Culhane looked back once more. The statue was beginning to shake, to shift on its base. The figure of the
woman holding the horns began to tremble.

"Rutgers! Hurry, man!" Rutgers, running, holding
an M-16, stopped in his tracks. Culhane watched as
the man dropped his rifle and stood stock-still, then
turned to face the statue that was shaking violently.

A noise like a loud, low whistling but somehow, too,
like thousands of whispered voices heard indistinctly,
emanated from the walls of the pyramid as the trembling increased.

The statue of the woman began to fall.

"Rutgers!" Culhane screamed the name, his throat
raw from the shout.

The statue was coming down, but Rutgers just stood
there, waiting to die.

Mulrooney screamed. Culhane dropped the M-16
and wrapped her in his arms.

He looked back once. Rutger's head and left arm protruded from beneath the beautiful, upturned face of the statue.

The shaking of the pyramid was more violent now, the walls visibly moving, the noises coming from the walls louder, becoming maddening as their intensity seemed to grow.

Grabbing Mulrooney's hand, Culhane started running again toward the hangar-bay tunnel entrance.

Three men were in the entrance to the tunnel, M-16s blazing. Culhane snatched the Detonics Scoremaster, firing toward them and shouting, "Give it up and run for your lives!"

There was more of the rumbling, the cacophony coming from the walls and the groaning and tearing sounds of metal twisting against metal mixing with the noise of the senseless gunfire. Two of the men ran, the third continuing to fire, but his assault rifle ran out of ammunition as Culhane narrowed the distance between them. It was Lieutenant Wilbur. Culhane's pistol was empty, and there wasn't time to reload, wasn't time to grab at the second gun he carried.

Culhane threw himself at the man, crashing the pistol down toward his skull. Wilbur fell back, blood dripping from his forehead. But in his right hand flashed a knife—Culhane's Bali-Song.

Culhane's foot snapped out against Wilbur's forearm, the knife sailing out of the man's grip and down the tunnel.

Culhane edged back and rammed his empty pistol into his holster. "Give it up!" Culhane shouted to Wilbur, who was now on his feet. "Run for it, man!"

But Wilbur threw himself toward Culhane. Culhane dodged right and hammered his fist into the traitor's midsection, doubling him over.

Culhane started to run after Mulrooney down the tunnel. He heard Wilbur's footsteps behind him and felt him grab at his sweater. Culhane could feel his balance going. He fell, catching himself on his hands, then sprawling.

Lieutenant Wilbur, his forehead bleeding more than before and an insane grin on his lips, was on his feet.

Culhane got up and stepped back. Wilbur's hands were moving now as he settled into a classic martial-arts fighting stance.

"Give it up!" Culhane shouted over the sounds of the pyramid falling around them, over the inhuman noises emanating from the walls.

Wilbur shouted something—Culhane thought it was a martial arts yell—then started into a flying kick.

Culhane drew the little Detonics from the holster on his right hip and shot Lieutenant Wilbur dead with six rounds in the chest.

Culhane turned on his heels and ran after Mulrooney, who was almost at the end of the tunnel. Chunks of the rock surface of the outside entrance to the hangar bay tunnel were falling now. Culhane shouted to her, "Be careful, Fanny!"

"Hurry, Josh!" Mulrooney screamed to him.

Culhane felt the rhythm of the vibration beneath his feet increasing. The tunnel seemed to be twisting around him, fissures appearing in the metal surface now, Culhane having to jump one that opened up suddenly before him.

He was at the end of the tunnel.

"Steiglitz and Sonia—I saw them get into one of the UFOs! I don't know—"

If she was still talking, Culhane couldn't hear her. The wailing from the pyramid walls at the other end of the tunnel, the ripping and tearing sounds of the metal, all of this was obliterated by a roar like the one Culhane had heard earlier when Steiglitz had tested the ship and activated the second part of the intruder-defense system. Except this roar was almost unbearably loud because it was so near.

The ship seemed to move slightly, then suddenly it was up, hovering, airborne, turning away from the tunnel entrance in which Culhane and Mulrooney stood, starting slowly, almost hesitantly across the hangar bay as chunks of rocks and debris pelted against it and around it.

The entrance to the tunnel through which they had come from the surface, the center one of the seven tunnels, suddenly collapsed, rocks and metal crashing down.

The airfoil hovered there near it, then shifted to Culhane's and its right toward the next tunnel. There was a roar louder than the first, and the ship shot through the tunnel.

"I picked up your knife," Mulrooney said, handing it into his right palm.

"Very thoughtful!" He looked into her face.

The entire underground complex was being destroyed, the hangar bay falling down around them. The tunnels were closing; another was collapsing. The tunnel behind them leading into the main pyramid seemed to explode as Culhane pulled Mulrooney away and into his arms.

There was only one way out.

Culhane said nothing, but holding Mulrooney's hand, he ran toward the nearest of the aircraft. They reached the hatch, rocks from the cavelike vault of the hangar bay tumbling around them, the metal floor of the hangar bay fissuring, giant cracks running the length of the floor surface opening all around them. One of the ships plunged down as a crack opened, and it vanished from sight.

Culhane started inside, ducking his head as he took the three low steps to the bridge in one stride. "You're the UFO expert, kid—help me fly this sucker!"

He slumped into the right of the two seats at the center of the bridge. It faced the more complex diode console.

He could barely understand one out of every two dozen symbols of the bizarre hieroglyphics before him.

The noise from outside the ship was even greater now, and through the open hatchway and the dome above him, he could see the hangar bay ceiling collapsing, chunks of gray rock raining down.

Culhane sat rigidly in the pilot's seat. He hoped it was that, anyway.

He closed his eyes and willed the hull door to close.

Mulrooney screamed, "The door closed—you closed the hatch!"

Culhane opened his eyes.

He tried conceptualizing it to be like the submarine. He decided to speak aloud to the machine. Above them, through the glasslike material of the dome, he could see the fissuring of the cavern ceiling. The hangar bay was about to be completely destroyed.

"Maneuvering engines—activate!" he called out. Nothing happened.

"Maybe you can't do it by talking out loud," Mulrooney suggested.

"Maybe," he said to her. He felt stupid talking to a flying saucer. And *thinking* to a flying saucer under millions of tons of rock and ice in the middle of Antarctica seemed even sillier.

He closed his eyes, then opened them. Maneuvering engines—on, he thought.

There was a low rumble.

You have to see it, to feel it in your mind, Culhane thought. Full maneuvering power, he thought, visualizing the ship as ready, almost eager to move out. The hum increased. He visualized the ship floating on air, thinking, Hover! Looking through the dome, he could see that the craft was rising. He could feel it in his stomach. Approach the tunnel to the far right—to far starboard, he envisioned, he thought, he commanded. The ship responded. He could feel the movement, could see it through the dome.

He looked straight up. The central section of the cavern ceiling was collapsing toward them. Engines to full power, into the tunnel at full takeoff acceleration speed! All monitoring systems ready to respond!

The diode panel before him illuminated, and Mulrooney was hurtled into the seat beside him as the ship trembled once. Through the transparent dome they saw a blur of gray as the ceiling collapsed, then the sheen of the luminescent metal of the tunnel.

But it, too, was blurred. Culhane could feel the speed.

He twisted in his pilot's seat. Behind them, the tunnel seemed to be collapsing, the ragged lines of fissures blurs around them. "Hold on tight, Fanny!"

Maximum cruise—flank speed—get us out of the tunnel!

He visualized it and it happened.

The hum of the engines or whatever they were was loud now, and Culhane could feel something like an invisible hand hammering him back into the seat. The arm to the left of his seat rose and dropped in place across his abdomen like a seat belt. He glanced over at Mulrooney; she too was held in her seat now.

"What's happening?"

"The hell if I know," Culhane shouted. As he looked at her, he could see she was fumbling with her purse. "What the—"

It was a camera, ridiculously small, and she was working it inside the ship and through the dome. "You'll never get those exteriors—your film couldn't be fast enough!"

"I'm gonna try. What's—"

Culhane looked ahead of them at a solid wall of ice.

"We're going to crash!"

Culhane put her voice out of his mind, thinking, Weapons system—activate—destroy the ice!

The tunnel walls instantly glowed, but it looked to Culhane like rays of reflected light. Through the dome, he watched the light pulse rhythmically, and chunks of ice before them exploded a split second before there would have been impact. There was more ice ahead. Again came the golden rays of light. More of the ice exploded around them, the ice covering the tunnel walls now. There was more ice and more light. Steam filled the tunnel from the melting ice. Behind them the tunnel was crumbling, huge chunks of it flying and crashing down in their wake. And the collapse of the tunnel was getting too close.

Culhane thought to the ship, Maximum obtainable speed under these conditions.

He could feel his head being pressed against the seat back, could hear the whining hum of the power source increase. They were going faster and faster. The weapons system still functioned, but the ship seemed to be outrunning the ice, burning through it, blasting it apart into boulder-sized chunks split seconds before the ship would have smashed against it.

"How fast are we going?" Mulrooney screamed.

"Maybe not fast enough," he told her, looking behind them again. The tunnel's collapse followed them like a wave, advancing on them, massive chunks of the tunnel ceiling heaving downward, the floor of the tunnel bursting upward, the walls falling inward against their own weight, closing forever.

"I know why Steiglitz wanted these. With one of these ships—just one of them—you could rule the world!" As he said it, his eyes met Mulrooney's for an instant.

But the instant was broken, chunks of debris pelting the ship from behind, crashing against the dome itself. Maximum obtainable speed. Weapons system—maximum obtainable firing rate, he commanded the craft.

The pulse of the light weapon flickered before them

against the mass of ice, flickering like the jerky action of a silent movie, and suddenly, as Culhane looked up, there was nothing visible but a tunnel—not of metal and ice, but of light.

Culhane stared straight ahead. Blocks of ice split and crumbled, but he could see around their edges as if somehow he was standing both ahead of and behind himself at once. He peered through the dome and saw things ahead of and around and behind him. Everything was blue, a brilliant blue that at the edges of his perception seemed to fade to red.

Culhane looked down at his watch. The second hand had stopped. He felt a chill work up his spine, the feeling some people label as knowing when someone is stepping on the ground that will someday be your grave. He stared ahead, then back to his watch. The second hand still hadn't moved.

The blur had changed now. What he saw were no longer pieces of ice and chunks of the tunnel, but in the blue focal point of light he saw a different blueness, lighter shades and darker: the sea.

"We're over the ocean!" Mulrooney shouted.

Culhane was riveted to what he saw, to the incredible beauty. He knew the phenomenon: time dilation. They had traveled near the speed of light—but for how long? He looked at his watch. The second hand was still stationary.

"Josh! Slow us down! Josh!"

She was screaming at him. Mulrooney was screaming at him. Why was she screaming at him?

"Josh! It's hypnotized you! Slow us down, Josh!"

He felt himself smile. It was silly of her to talk that way. He was only staring. Staring....

He felt something against his forearm. Mulrooney's nails. They were digging into his skin and hurting him. He looked away from the light show and at Mulrooney. "Fanny—"

He felt the nails gouge him and heard Mulrooney scream, "Come out of it, Josh! For God's sake!"

He looked down at his arm. There was blood, and his shirt, and sweater sleeves were rolled back. Blood. Pain. "Dammit, Fanny!"

And he looked back through the dome at the darkness, but it was now blue tinged with points of. . . .

"Shit!" He thought, Engines decelerate to minimum safe cruise. He could feel it. He stared at his watch; the second hand ticked once and was still again. The weapons system had shut itself off when no longer needed. Darkness and gray blueness was beneath them. "Holy—" Then he thought to the ship, Return to first coordinates beyond the tunnel mouth at minimum cruise speed. The ship was turning, moving, a reddish glow around them. Then, as if they broke through something, there was the sudden blueness again, then whiteness. As the ship angled downward, he could see whitecaps, could see the ice field in the distance like a white line of horizon. It grew and grew, then the craft stopped, hovering.

He looked at Fanny Mulrooney, at her wide green eyes. He looked at his arm. It was streaked with blood from her nails gouging him. He looked at the Rolex. The sweep second hand moved normally. "Did we just do what I think we just did?" he asked Mulrooney.

"I think so. . . ." Her camera was in her lap, her hands clutching it. She looked away from him. "You're right. If Steiglitz has one of these. . . ."

"And if he got out of the tunnel, he'll have to kill us."

Culhane closed his eyes. He looked up through the dome as he opened them. There was the blink of a pinpoint of light hard to port. He thought, Maximum acceleration! The ship lurched around him, the sky above him a blur. Culhane thought, Slow to half maximum, bank to port.

The ship slowed and banked, and beneath them was the ocean. In the distance appeared the outline of the ice field, and to starboard was the open sea. "What was that?"

"I think Steiglitz is after us," said Culhane, watching through the dome. Then he thought to the ship, Three quarters maximum—bank hard starboard, and he felt the wrenching in his body. The blur of clouds and sea around them through the dome was nauseating as he watched it, and a pulse of light filled the airspace they had just left.

And then he heard a voice, a voice that filled the ship as if it emanated from the consoles around them. The voice of Steiglitz. "One merely must think of the other ship—in my case, of your ship—or at least if I read the instrument panels correctly, it appears that is all that is necessary. If you can hear me, respond, Mr. Culhane."

Culhane thought, I can hear you, asshole.

He heard Mulrooney's voice. "What are you doing? What's happening?"

"Didn't you hear Steiglitz?"

"No...."

"You had to! I could hear him all through the ship!" He was shouting at her, screaming the words.

Again he heard the voice filling his brain: "I heard you, Mr. Culhane. Apparently the ship itself serves as the transmitter, it's analogous to how the controls function."

Drop dead, Culhane thought.

He heard Steiglitz, but he saw from her face that Mulrooney didn't. "You have by now realized that this ship, or rather these ships, are the most powerful weapons mankind has ever possessed."

Culhane thought the ship to go just above the waves and hover. He felt the ship move.

Steiglitz's voice persisted, and he realized it was in his head. "Whoever controls such a ship will be the master of humankind. I control one such ship and I wish to be the master. If you maintain control of the other ship, soon you, too, will lust for the power it can give. I can feel it, somehow. Trust me on this. Land your ship on the ice near the tunnel mouth. My helicopter from the research ship is still there. You can take it and fly to one of the permanent scientific stations nearby. You and Miss Mulrooney will live. My pledge. Otherwise, I will destroy your ship, and you and Miss Mulrooney with it. I understand the ship's capabilities because I can read the control panels. You cannot, and so you do not. And there will be no time for you to translate the symbols on the panels. Your cause is hopeless. I can hear you when you think to me, but not when you think to the ship. But I can think to your ship."

Culhane looked at Mulrooney. She was staring at him. Then he heard Steiglitz's voice again: "Maximum acceleration!" The ship lurched, and Culhane slammed back into the seat, Mulrooney screaming. Culhane forced his mind, forced himself to envision the ship slowing, and it slowed. He thought for it to hover. It hovered. "See what I can do?" Steiglitz's voice echoed in his brain.

Culhane closed his eyes, thinking to Steiglitz's ship, Dive into the ocean. His own ship jerked but did not move.

Then Steiglitz's voice: "Absolutely no effect. I assume you ordered my ship to do something. But I blocked you. Now surrender, and you and Miss Mulrooney will live."

Through the dome, Culhane could see Steiglitz's ship hovering perhaps one hundred feet over the ocean.

Culhane pictured it in his mind, then thought to Steiglitz, Take your goddamned flying saucer and shove it up your—

There was a flash of light, and Culhane thought, Dive under the waves, hard to port, full cruise!

The ship moved, and Culhane heard Mulrooney scream, "We're underwater!"

Then Culhane heard Steiglitz's voice in his head: "Ship—dead stop."

The ship started to slow. Culhane visualized, then thought, Follow my command—full cruise! He could still hear Steiglitz in his head, hear him giving conflicting commands to the ship. The water above them as they sped beneath the surface was erupting in explosions that rocked the ship. "He's using his weapons system and tracking us," Culhane told Mulrooney.

"Are you and Steiglitz talking with your minds?"

"Yeah, I guess we are—don't ask me how. It's like the ship is a telephone for his mind and mine."

"Why can't I hear it?"

"Because he's only talking to me and to the ship—or thinking to it—trying to confuse things so he can shoot us down. He offered a deal if we gave him the ship."

"Nobody should have this ship—and especially not Steiglitz," Mulrooney muttered through clenched teeth.

Culhane watched through the dome, ordering the ship hard starboard at half cruise, then to climb. When they broke the surface of the water, Culhane saw Steiglitz's craft. He thought, Weapons system activate—fire! He envisioned the light beam destroying, vaporizing Steiglitz's ship. He could see the light beam, then saw it suddenly diffuse as if bouncing off the aircraft. Steiglitz's ship was untouched. The pulse of light was reflected toward them; there was no time to outmaneuver it.

In that instant he thought, I hope science fiction writers know what they're talking about—shields up!

The ship rocked, Culhane averting his eyes as the

beam of light pulsed against them and diffused, but
the ship was out of control. Culhane willed it to dive
under the surface again, then willed half speed. To
starboard, dogging them laterally, he could see Steiglitz's ship. A pulse of light glowed through the water.

Shields stay up, he thought, and the ship rocked
again, but the light diffused.

A school of fish fanned before the ship like a wave,
parting, rocks below them punching up suddenly.
Maneuver around those rocks, Culhane thought. The
ship lurched right, then left, then up, then leveled and
sped ahead. Behind them, Culhane watched their
wake, and riding above the wake was Steiglitz's ship.
Another light pulse flashed, and Culhane thought,
Evasive action—shields up! The ship cut hard to port
and climbed, Culhane glancing below them as the ship
moved angularly through the water, the field of rocks
through which they had been passing exploding under
them. He thought the ship hard to starboard, ordering, Weapons system—fire! He envisioned a direct hit
on the dome of Steiglitz's craft, but that ship was
gone, moving to starboard, diving. Culhane ordered
his own ship to dive, then to go on maximum cruise.
The Antarctic waters around them were vaporizing,
and Culhane saw Steiglitz ahead. Weapons system, repeat firing, duplicate enemy ship's evasive actions, he
commanded. The light beam fired, and Steiglitz's ship
evaded it, banking hard to starboard and climbing.
Culhane's ship was doing the same, still firing, rock
formations beneath the sea disintegrating in bursts of
light. Steiglitz's craft broke the surface ahead of them,
Culhane's ship following in a billowing cloud of vapor
surrounding the ship as it, too, broke the waves. Steiglitz's ship was moving hard starboard and skimming
the water. Culhane willed his ship to follow.

The ice pack was ahead of them. Steiglitz's ship was
less than five hundred yards distant now, and chunks

of the ice's surface buckled, sucked after it. Culhane ordered his ship to avoid the ice and pursue.

In the distance, across the field of near blinding whiteness, Culhane could see mountains. Steiglitz's ship was flipping on edge like a boomerang-shaped coin, passing between the peaks, losing elevation, Culhane pursuing.

Then the enemy ship stopped and turned, the mountain peaks framing it, caressing it as silver or gold would hug a diamond. Culhane heard Steiglitz in his head: "Shields down!"

Culhane saw the beam of light and ordered his ship, Evasive action! The ship rocked, starting downward, the forward portside quarter of the dome blackened, the ship bouncing, rocking, falling. Shields up! Culhane directed. Steiglitz's craft was in pursuit now, Culhane thinking his own ship to climb, ordering the weapons system to Fire—fire—fire! as he banked the ship back toward Steiglitz, climbing. Three light pulses bounced off Steiglitz's airfoil.

He could hear Steiglitz's voice in his head again: "I almost had you. Soon you and Miss Mulrooney will be dead, as your brother is dead. How fitting." There was a light pulse, and Culhane heard the voice, "Shields down." Culhane thought the shields up, then thought for hard starboard and climb. The ship took the pulse, shuddering, but he guessed it was undamaged.

Culhane estimated their altitude to be about a half mile above the jagged, toothlike shapes of the ice-encrusted granite mountains.

Hover, he thought.

Steiglitz's ship was about five hundred yards off, hovering at the same altitude.

"Taking a breather?" he heard Mulrooney ask.

He looked at her, then back to Steiglitz's ship. "When that light beam hit us a minute ago, he'd ordered my shields down. I couldn't stop him because he caught me by surprise. If I could distract his attention so I could override his shields, I could get him.''

"Get him to talk to me. I can distract anybody....''

"He won't do that. He's too smart to divide his attention. He knows it'd put him in his grave.'' And he looked at Mulrooney; there was something in her eyes then, something in her face.... She was clutching her purse against her on her side, then she started to open it. "Lipstick at a time like this?''

"No, your little tape player. I know what will distract him. When you hear Steiglitz's voice, is it really like his voice? I mean—''

"Yeah, just like it.''

"Do you think you could relay something to him?''

"Like the ship itself does?''

"Yeah. Could you?''

"I don't know.''

"Try this,'' Mulrooney said. "Listen to what I say and just concentrate on Steiglitz's hearing it.''

Culhane nodded, concentrating. His head ached and his eyes hurt. He heard Mulrooney's words; it was like listening but not listening, trying to make Steiglitz hear them. "Peter Piper picked a peck of pickled peppers, a peck of pickled peppers—''

And Culhane heard Steiglitz's voice: "Miss Mulrooney is reciting nursery rhymes? Has the strain unhinged her?''

Culhane looked at Fanny Mulrooney. "He heard you—I don't know how—but he heard you and he knew it was you.''

And then Culhane saw his little tape player and watched as Mulrooney took a tape from a plastic case. "I hope the batteries still work.''

Culhane looked away from her. Steiglitz's craft was beginning to move again, and Culhane started after it, the other ship accelerating, Culhane matching its speed. The ship was out of the mountains, skimming the ice, ripping up huge chunks in its wake as Culhane followed. Over the ocean's surface, columns of water plumed up on both sides, rising perhaps a hundred feet in the air and washing over the dome of Culhane's ship as he forced his craft to pursue.

Then Steiglitz's craft plunged under the water, Culhane in pursuit. He could hear Mulrooney talking, her voice calm but somehow strange.

Steiglitz's craft was accelerating, and Culhane ordered his own ship to speed up. The distance between them was about two hundred yards, he reckoned, and this would be the last encounter. Either he would get Steiglitz, or Steiglitz would get them.

Weapons system fire, he thought, and the pulse flashed, but Steiglitz's ship seemed unaffected. Steiglitz's aircraft was rising now, and Culhane's was right behind it, a column of water on both sides as they skimmed the ocean just beneath them. Then Steiglitz's ship accelerated even more and Culhane ordered his craft to do the same; Steiglitz's ship climbed, and Culhane followed. For some reason Fanny was babbling about the man who'd made the graveside recordings for her. Culhane felt sweat, cold sweat. Steiglitz had leveled off. There was a landmass ahead of them with mountains. Steiglitz's ship was climbing, descending, flipping on edge and skimming through the mountains, Culhane right on his tail.

"Your brother...he didn't know it was your brother. He didn't! I wouldn't have let him...."

"My brother...?"

"Mr. Ball made a recording. He wanted someone who had died a violent death, and he wanted a fresh burial so the clarity of the graveside recording would be intelligible and understandable—"

"My brother and some damn recording from the grave...? That's nuts! That's—"

"It's your brother's voice—from the dead!" she screamed. "I heard it! I played it when we were on the *Churchill*, when I was all alone...it made me sick. It's your brother, Josh. Do like you did when I said the nursery rhyme—just listen and concentrate on Steiglitz hearing it. When you see him react, shoot him down and be done with this, Josh! Be done with this!"

Culhane looked at her for an instant, then back to Steiglitz's craft a hundred or so yards ahead of them. The mountains capped with snow had turned to jungle lowlands. They skimmed the treetops, the trees bending in Steiglitz's wake, collapsing as they broke. Culhane had no idea of their speed, but fire tipped the edges of the ship's boomerang shape, and as he looked to port and starboard of his own ship through the dome, the air around them seemed to be on fire.

And then he heard it. His brother's voice. Recognizable but horrible, horrible in the strangeness of the sound. It was Jeff Culhane, and Josh Culhane thought the words to Steiglitz: "Josh...get Steiglitz. He murdered me. Josh...get Steiglitz so I can rest—The pain swallowed me, Josh. Get Steiglitz so I can—"

His vision blurred with tears. But he could see that Steiglitz's craft had changed course and was moving erratically. Culhane shut out his brother's voice as the words were repeated over and over and over: "Get Steiglitz so I can rest!" He thought, Shields down on Steiglitz's craft! Shields down! Then, Weapons system, fire—fire—fire—fire—fire—fire—fire—fire—fire—

The ship barely one hundred yards ahead of his rocked, light beams engulfing it, then dispersing, then engulfing it again. The ship was spinning now, crashing downward, and a mountaintop loomed ahead. Culhane followed the aircraft, repeating in his mind, Fire—fire—fire—fire— Each pulse of the light struck, each pulse rocking Steiglitz's craft. Then the alien

spacecraft impacted against the mountaintop in a burst
of light, and it was gone.

Culhane heard Mulrooney screaming at him to climb.

Climb, Culhane thought.

The mountaintop was directly in front of them, and
then Culhane's stomach felt the lurch. He looked up;
the blueness above them was blinding through the
dome. They were climbing, going up. He could no
longer hear his brother's voice. . . .

"Josh! Josh!"

It was Fanny Mulrooney again.

Culhane closed his eyes for an instant, then opened
them. He looked through the dome—a blue-black
darkness was growing above them—and he ordered
the ship, Level off—slow cruise speed.

The ship obeyed.

Culhane looked at Fanny Mulrooney, at the small
tape recorder in her hands, at her eyes.

"What do we do now?" she asked, her voice soft,
girlish.

He didn't answer her, but he began trying to envision the Atlantic coastline of South America as he ordered the ship into a gentle dive.

CHAPTER FORTY-TWO

They had sat beside the ruins of the monastery for
some time, talking. The UFO, parked on the granite of
the natural runwaylike surface leading along the crest
of the mountaintop to the monastery itself, dominated
Culhane's horizon. He stared at it.

Overflying the island before landing the craft, Culhane had spotted what looked like the mast of a radio
tower on the far side of the island beyond the swamps.
There had been huts there and a few crude buildings.

He was willing to gamble that they would be able to find a radio and signal for help to get them off the island. He could make up a story; being a writer, making up stories was his business.

The UFO was a hundred yards away—he estimated that was enough for now—so he could see it in full perspective.

"Are you sure about this?" Mulrooney asked. She held tightly to his arm as she sat beside him at the entrance to the ruined monastery.

He looked at her. She had stripped away her heavy shirt but still wore the long-sleeved thermal underwear top. The sleeves were rolled up, and perspiration streamed down her face. He had discarded his heavy sweater and heavy shirt. He wore his reading glasses, and his eyes burned and his head throbbed, the voice still haunting him.

"Would you trust anybody with this—even me?" he asked.

He watched her green eyes. They flickered to the boomerang-shaped spacecraft and then back to him. "Even me—I don't know if I'd trust *me* with it," she whispered.

And she shook her head.

Culhane stood up, taking off his glasses and handing them to her. He walked back toward the ship. On the pilot's seat—he could see it in his mind—was the Xerox copy of the diary of Henry Chillingsworth and the graveside tape of his brother. It was his brother, he realized, who had finally defeated Jeremiah Steiglitz and Sonia. And with these was the last copy—all other copies had either been buried beneath the ice in the destroyed alien starbase, lost with the *Churchill* or incinerated with Steiglitz—of the Gladstone Log.

He stopped twenty yards from the ship.

He envisioned the engines to start. They were loud, earsplittingly loud when heard from the outside. A flock of birds soared out of the jungle below, and Culhane watched them for an instant until they disappeared from sight.

Culhane envisioned the hatch closing. And the hatchway in the starboard blade of the boomerang-shaped airfoil closed, its seam with the hull invisible.

And then Culhane thought, Mark this command— follow this time sequence. Mark—ten, nine, eight, seven, six, five, four, three, two, one. At commencement of sequence, all systems gear to maximum acceleration, evasive action to avoid collision with any objects in path. Continue maximum acceleration until impacting with the bright yellow star visible overhead. Culhane squinted against the sun.

Sequence begins: ten, nine, eight, seven, he thought. He felt Mulrooney's hand hold his. Six, five.... The roar of the engines grew steadily louder. Four, three, two.... He felt her hand move, saw her raise her hands to cover her ears. He did the same, thinking, One.

The craft streaked skyward. The earth shook with the thunderclap of the sound barrier broken.

Culhane hugged Mulrooney to him. But he looked up, and just off and away from the sun, he could see the dot of it, then it vanished.

Gone.

Mulrooney was talking, she always talked, and his ears rang so that he could barely hear her. "But I know if I did, my readers would never believe it—even *my* readers—and—"

Culhane leaned his head against her forehead, touching his right index finger to her lips. "Shh," he whispered. Mulrooney fell silent. There was a light breeze and he could feel her hair as it caught the wind and blew around them, feel it as it touched lightly at his cheeks, his mouth.

He brushed the hair away from his mouth, from her mouth, with the back of his right hand.

"I need you, Fanny—I need you very much," Culhane whispered. Her fingertips touched at his face, softly, with a gentleness that Culhane realized he could never set to words in one of his books.

Fanny Mulrooney's lips parted and Josh Culhane kissed her, feeling her body mold itself against his body.

"Eat your heart out, Sean Dodge," he thought.

JERRY AHERN AND S.A. AHERN

Jerry and Sharon Ahern's writing partnership is an extension of a life partnership that dates back to their early teens in Chicago, where they were high-school sweethearts.

Their habit of working together is firmly entrenched. Sharon has provided all the photographs for Jerry's more than six hundred magazine articles. And from the early years, when Jerry first began his successful career as a novelist, Sharon has researched, edited, rewritten and proofread all of his work.

Like their two heroes in *The Takers*, the Aherns make their home in Georgia and frequently travel from coast to coast and border to border to do research for their books.

Together, Jerry and Sharon Ahern have investigated devil worshippers and been involved in a situation that led to their having to check under the hood of their car each morning for explosives before taking their two children to school. They have fended off a gang of muggers in a foreign city, and a near-fatal automobile crash in the middle of an ice storm almost led to a gunfight with a pair of hoods.

Evidently Josh Culhane and Mary Mulrooney don't have a corner on the action market!

GOLD EAGLE